The Sunshine Man

Also by Emma Stonex

The Lamplighters

The Sunshine Man

Emma Stonex

PICADOR

First published 2025 by Picador
an imprint of Pan Macmillan
The Smithson, 6 Briset Street, London EC1M 5NR
EU representative: Macmillan Publishers Ireland Ltd, 1st Floor,
The Liffey Trust Centre, 117–126 Sheriff Street Upper,
Dublin 1, D01 YC43
Associated companies throughout the world
www.panmacmillan.com

ISBN 978-1-5290-4736-3 HB
ISBN 978-1-5290-4737-0 TPB

Copyright © Emma Stonex Ltd 2025

The right of Emma Stonex to be identified as the
author of this work has been asserted her in accordance
with the Copyright, Designs and Patents Act 1988.

[permissions to come]

All rights reserved. No part of this publication may be reproduced,
stored in a retrieval system, or transmitted, in any form, or by any means
(electronic, mechanical, photocopying, recording or otherwise)
without the prior written permission of the publisher.

Pan Macmillan does not have any control over, or any responsibility for,
any author or third-party websites referred to in or on this book.

1 3 5 7 9 8 6 4 2

A CIP catalogue record for this book is available from the British Library.

Typeset in Fournier MT Std by Palimpsest Book Production Ltd, Falkirk, Stirlingshire
Printed and bound by CPI Group (UK) Ltd, Croydon, CR0 4YY

This book is sold subject to the condition that it shall not, by way of
trade or otherwise, be lent, hired out, or otherwise circulated without
the publisher's prior consent in any form of binding or cover other than
that in which it is published and without a similar condition including
this condition being imposed on the subsequent purchaser.

Visit www.picador.com to read more about all our books
and to buy them. You will also find features, author interviews and
news of any author events, and you can sign up for e-newsletters
so that you're always first to hear about our new releases.

For CERO and EKRO,
with love

*Why does this light force me back
to my childhood? I wore a yellow
summer dress, and the skirt
made a perfect circle.*

Jane Kenyon, 'Evening Sun'

It must be wonderful to be free.

from Brendan Behan, *Borstal Boy*

I

1

The week I shot a man clean through the head began like any other. I woke at the normal time, quarter past six, and it was dark outside. I heard the sound of the heating coming on, a rattling chuckle in the pipes. Tom was still asleep, his bare shoulder pale in the moonlight; I put my nose in his neck to check he smelt the same, which he did, of gently scorched wood and the inside of the biscuit tin.

I dressed in the dark and went downstairs. It was unnaturally quiet. I opened the curtains and saw there'd been snow in the night, unexpectedly; it hadn't been forecast. The fall was piled inches deep on the garden bench and the birdbath was rounded off like a wedding cake. It never snowed in our Wiltshire village. Every other part of the country got it but we never did; the children's sledges hung unused in the shed like bats. I switched on the radio. It was a DJ I didn't like, sitting in for someone else, playing twangy songs from Broadway musicals. I made a cup of tea. The milk was past its best-before; I poured it down the sink then buttered two slices of toast and sat at the table in my slippers. The toast had the consistency of cardboard; I heard my jaw click as I chewed.

The show tunes stopped and the news began. The aftermath of air disasters, falling unemployment. The telephone rang. I reached for it.

'It's today,' she said. 'Sorry for the short notice, the arrangements have changed.' It would be midday, she anticipated, these things usually happened before lunch.

I thought there must be a response from my immediate surroundings. The stove catching fire, a chair tipping over. But nothing changed. The tea had an oily film across its surface, which quivered as a grit lorry rolled by. Here it was. He was getting out.

∾

Tom came down in an ironed shirt and I remembered he had a big meeting today. He'd be away overnight, in Bath. 'Who was that?' he asked. I told him a wrong number.

'You were talking to them,' he said.

'Yes. I was telling them they had the wrong number.'

He looked inside the bread bin. 'How about the snow? That's a turn-up for the books.'

'I know.'

He kissed me. 'The kids'll be beside themselves.'

I turned away to the sink to rinse a glass that was already clean. I thought that in another, ordinary life, I would be wrapping our children in jumpers and mittens, unhooking the sledges, lighting a fire so it would be good and warm when we got home.

'Are the schools open?' said Tom, spading coffee into a Chippenham FC mug.

'They'd better be,' I said. 'I've got things to do today.'

'Like what?'

I twisted the tap off. 'An errand.'

'Ah. Say no more.' My husband's tone changed from concern to conspiracy; I realized he thought it was about his birthday, next month. The notion was so far removed from my intentions, it felt almost like the worst lie of all.

'I thought I'd ask your mother, if school's closed,' I said.

'Good idea.' He filled a pan with boiling water and lowered an egg into it, considerately, like someone releasing a fish. 'Do you want one?' He glanced up. 'Bridget?'

'I'm not hungry.'

He saw the half-eaten toast. 'Are you all right? You seem a million miles away.'

'I'm fine.' I opened the fridge. 'Here. I made you some sandwiches.'

'You're a wonder,' he said, taking them. 'I'd better check the trains are running.'

'They are. Travel's just been on.'

'Well, thank God for that. It'd have to pick today, wouldn't it? The weather.'

My hand shook as I closed the door. 'What do you mean?'

'Greg and this ruddy presentation,' said Tom, not noticing. 'There'll be hell to pay if it gets put back again, I'll never hear the end of it.' He scratched a stain on the nose of his tie. The top of his head was almost totally grey now. We were grown. I hadn't grown.

'I'll ring the school,' I said, as the egg timer went off.

The line in the hall was engaged. On my second attempt the office answered and told me they were open as usual. I felt relief. The next hour arranged itself into slots of twenty minutes. Twenty minutes to give the children their breakfast. Twenty minutes to stick them in front of the television while I packed a bag that had been waiting eighteen years to be packed, made arrangements with Wilma for collecting them, got their satchels and Philippa's lunch money. Twenty minutes to drive them there. When I had thought of this day in the past, I had imagined myself in a panic. Now it was here, I felt quite calm.

I went upstairs and found Philippa wrestling her tights on under the covers.

'I'm cold!' she complained, when I told her she should get up, it'd be easier.

'It's snowed,' I said, drawing back the curtains. 'Look.'

Her face lit up. 'Do we get the day off?'

'Sorry.'

She climbed out of bed and went to the window, her tights puddled around her ankles, her hair at the back a nest of spun sugar. I loved her so much.

'It's like Narnia,' she said. 'Can we go outside?'

I thought of wet uniforms, hairdryers. 'Later. Nanny's picking you up.'

She turned on me. 'Why?'

'Dad's away tonight. And I have to visit a friend.'

'What friend?' Philippa was a child who was suspicious until reassured.

'Someone old from school,' I said.

'How old?'

'As old as me.'

'You're not old.'

I helped her into her vest, daring a kiss on her shoulder. 'I'm older than you.'

'What's her name?'

'Peggy.' It was a character in a book I was reading.

'Where does she live?'

I zipped up her dress and touched my forehead to hers. Her eyes close up were flecked with gold. I had always wanted eyes like that. Nothing like my own.

'So many questions,' I said.

'You're always telling me to ask questions.'

'She's in hospital,' I said, drawing back to fold her nightdress.

'Is she dying?'

'Maybe.'

The cat slunk in. Philippa turned her attentions to him as I slid her nightie under her pillow and patted it gently. Joe wouldn't be as challenging, I knew. He was still asleep next door, his cheeks flushed, his eyelashes a line of commas. He was heavy and affectionate, drawn into our morning hug, his arms round my neck, a sweaty rabbit pressed in the warmth between us. I looked at the clock on the wall.

'Come on, sweetheart, let's get you dressed.' I took off his Danger Mouse pyjamas; the top had a smear of Marmite on the sleeve, which worried me disproportionately – that Tom would not notice or know later to put it in the washing machine, and how many days, therefore, it would remain, the same as the number of days it took me to come back.

Joe trailed me downstairs, screaming with delight when he saw the snow. He opened the back door to the kitchen and put his Rabba in the drift to show him how cold it was: 'See? Like the North Pole.' The cat had moved into the garden now, perched disdainfully on a snowy fence post, looking in at me with sharp green eyes. The cat and I had never got on. Somewhere, a dog barked. The cat dropped out of sight.

'Can I have Coco Pops?' asked Philippa, swinging her legs at the table, starting on some colouring. I thought that I would not have time after to clear it up.

'You can,' said Tom. 'But *may* you?'

'May I?'

'No,' he said. 'They'll rot your teeth. Anyway, there's no milk.' He turned to me, buttoning his coat. 'Could you pick some up later?'

I nodded. 'Sure.'

'Peanut butter!' exclaimed Joe, climbing onto his cushion and reaching for the jar. I heard the jingle of the news returning. I turned the radio down.

'Wait – I want that,' said Tom.

'Why?'

'The headlines.'

He turned up the volume. Various items rolled on but there was nothing about him. I shouldn't have imagined there would be. He was the sun around which all my planets revolved; to anyone else, a name eclipsed by time and other tragedies.

The toast popped up, startling. Tom took his briefcase off the counter.

'See you tomorrow,' he said, hugging me then hugging the children.

'You forgot these,' I said, giving him his sandwiches. I was keen to get him out before Philippa said anything about Peggy. 'Bye.' I paused. 'Good luck today.'

'You too,' he said, smiling at me. 'Whatever secret mission you're on.'

∽

While the children were brushing their teeth, I wrote a note to my husband. Though I had contemplated every other detail, I had never settled on what I'd say to him. I wrote:

I'll be gone a few days. I hope you understand.

Which was asking a lot, but it was better to be brief.

'We're ready,' said Philippa, lingering at the door. She'd plaited her hair into two mooring ropes. I folded the note and put it behind my back. 'D'you think Lucy will be in?'

'She might,' I said.

'I'll have no one to partner with in PE. I hate PE.'

'Ten minutes, darling,' I said. 'Put on a video.'

'I don't want to.' That suspicion again.

'I have to get your things together for Nanny.'

She twisted the end of her plait, eyeing me before going downstairs.

I pulled Gamma's carrycase out of the wardrobe. I hadn't meant to take this one but now it was happening it seemed right. Maybe what she'd have wanted. So often in my life I had sought to emulate my grandmother's principles, but on this I had none: it was bigger, more serious, than either of us. The bag was tan leather with tarnished metal buckles. Its leather was lightly cracked like the icing on the cakes she used to bake on Sundays after church. The best bit about church had been thinking about those cakes, while the vicar talked on about abstinence and Jesus looked down at me from the cross with his lamenting eyes and the wounds in his feet, and I hadn't heard a word he'd said.

I didn't know how many changes of clothes I would need. I folded in a few and plenty of knickers, as those seemed to me the most important things. Then I opened the chest of drawers and fumbled in the top towards the back until I felt it. I'd told Tom the box contained my sister's music and a few of the long, colourful letters she'd written me from school, which naturally he'd accepted, and he'd accepted too that I would never want to open it and take the contents out. I set the box down, waiting for a revelation, but none came. The lid shone. I saw my reflection in it, as clear as if I were meeting it in a perfectly still pond. My palms were dry. My heart ran steadily, like a faithful car engine.

I reached for my engagement-ring case. The small silver key was stitched into the cushion. I'd been aware when I'd done that of some unsettling irony, difficult to pinpoint, and was pleased to remove it now: I picked the thread and put the key in the lock, which opened smoothly, in agreement. I lifted its lid. A smell rose to meet me, deep and oaky.

The gun was a Beretta Cheetah. I had been told the model but wasn't concerned. Would it kill a man? Yes. Was it compact enough to conceal? Yes. I felt no need to hold it in a display of reunion or exchange of trust. It had waited for me for a decade, patiently.

I secreted the gun in Gamma's bag with a pair of

disposable gloves, and zipped it shut. The obvious place for Tom's note was on the bookcase – he'd see it straight away when he got home – leaning against the spines of some Dorothy L. Sayers. Then I decided that could look rather contrived so I moved it onto his bedside table. I collected the bag and left the room.

∞

The snow was heaped up in banks on either side of the road. Salt grit made red slush of the tarmac. The car door was frozen shut but gave with enough of a yank, snow sliding off the driver's window like a dropped blind. I fished about in the glovebox for a scraper, locating it behind a bag of stuck-together mint humbugs and a Joy Division cassette. It took a long time to clear the windscreen. This I did methodically, from top to bottom and left to right, with the fans on full blast. Philippa sat in front picking silver polish off her fingernails. Joe dropped his packed lunch in the footwell and cried. Finally, we departed.

There weren't many parents at the school gates. Philippa saw a friend and was keen to get away. My fingers brushed the sleeve of her blazer as she carelessly exited the car; it was like trying to catch a scarf as it flew off the deck of a ferry. 'Bye then,' I said.

'Bye, Mum. See you.'

'See you.'

I watched her link arms with the friend. They skidded,

laughing, on the pavement, pretending to skate. I thought about going after her, but there wouldn't be a reason.

Joe and I made slow progress towards his classroom, where a teacher I didn't recognize welcomed us: the usual one couldn't start her car. I gave Joe his lunch bag.

'My mother-in-law will be collecting him this afternoon,' I told the teacher. 'I'll let the office know on the way out.'

'Lucky you,' she exclaimed to Joe, as if I hadn't spoken. 'Grandma picking you up? What a treat. All that fun you'll have with Granny.' Clearly she had never met Wilma.

Joe was clinging to my knees.

'Come on then,' said the woman. 'We've got the paints out.'

I crouched to hug Joe. His hair smelt of almonds and clean towels. I breathed him in, every last bit of him, the lovely heft of him in my arms, his soft cheek on mine, the groove at the back of his neck where his Cash's nametape poked out of his collar.

'Have a good day,' I whispered.

I felt better when I got back in the car. The snow made it necessary to think of little else but navigation of the route. I joined the main road, trying not to catch sight of Joe's vacated booster seat in the rear-view mirror and the thumb-sized purple dinosaur he'd dug out of a cereal box and brought along for the journey. My tyres churned wetly. The landscape looked fresh and eerie. I had known these fields a long time but now the ice made strangers of them, washed-out, indistinguishable from one another, lacking any detectable notes of scale. Dark straws pierced the banks, wet bark and the stalks of rotten vegetation. A shape crossed the road in front of me, small and quick, low to the ground, so quick in fact it could have been a ripple of paint or light, or the onset of a migraine.

Wilma's house was in the heel of a cul-de-sac. When I pressed the bell I heard a contracted version of the *William Tell* Overture ringing into the air-freshened hallway.

'This is awfully short notice,' she said when she came to the door, checking to see if the neighbours were watching. 'You're lucky I'm available.'

'I know. Thank you. Tom will get them tomorrow.'

'And when will you be back?'

I gave her the children's suitcase, which she took, and parted the handles and looked inside as if she'd been expecting a present. 'I'm not sure,' I said.

'All right then. Well.'

'Philippa's likely to have homework,' I said. 'If it's maths she'll need help.'

'Fine.' She sighed. 'But there'll be no snowball fights. No tramping it all through the house. I've just had the carpets done.' She stood back to let me see.

'Very nice,' I said.

'Are you sickening for something, Bridget? You look awfully peaky.'

'Just a headache,' I said. 'It's not too bad.'

'You should get those seen to. Who knows what might be going on? Jill's nephew had a brain tumour; he went completely blind in one eye. He wears a patch now.'

'Well, you know. Life gets in the way.'

'Until it doesn't.'

She looked at her watch. I looked at mine.

'Thanks again.' I returned to the car and started the engine. She waited in the doorway until I drove off and turned out of sight. I waved to a postman getting out of his van, which seemed a weird thing to do, very far from where I was in my mind, but I thought it might be the last time I did something ordinary. Besides, I knew him. Wilma had tried to get him taken off the round once, on a claim he'd stolen money, the envelope split and her friend's ten pounds for a bistro lunch gone from inside. Wilma didn't trust people. She didn't trust me, which made her a wily bird, I supposed. She'd been frank about it from the start, at least. She hadn't tried to keep the pinch from her face when Tom and I had announced our engagement. When we'd first brought Philippa to visit, she hadn't greeted the girl in a grandmotherly way, just stared hard at me over the rim of her Silver Jubilee teacup. Tom would have been better off with someone else, she thought. Someone easier, less problematic, without that baggage dragging along after her. More of a woman, for surely in her mind – and often in mine – these things were related.

Still, she put her best foot forward with the children, which was as much as I could ask for, and Tom said not to expect too much. I didn't think she felt a great deal for Philippa. Maybe it was to do with girls and women and having a son of her own (she'd said to me once, '*A daughter's a daughter for life, Bridget; a son's a son until he finds a wife*') – but she was fond of Joe. She found it easier to love him because she'd known him from a baby. Babies, I thought, as I came to the coach station, were so easy to love.

I wiped my eyes and unclicked my seat belt. The snow

stopped. People huddled at the entrance checking tickets and smoking cigarettes, bundled in scarves and coats.

A sister is a sister for life.

I opened the car door. It was too late to go back. I took my bags and went inside.

2

I was born on the bathroom floor of a terraced house in Devon in July 1948. My mother hadn't known she was pregnant, or had, and pretended it wasn't happening until it was. She'd gripped the side of the bath and screamed once and once only, so long and loud it stopped the children playing in the street and a car passing with its window open thought the air-raid sirens were back. I was early, too small ('thin as a comb,' said Gamma), and there was a hospital stay, kept in an incubator and fed by syringe. There's no way I can remember it, but I do remember it. Stuccoed ceiling like cottage cheese. Nurses' hands, rough and capable, the rubber teats of faded milk bottles. White rabbits dangling on a mobile above the cot, blue tails, pink tails, cardboard spinning circles in the sun.

From the start my mother was out of the picture. She was a teenager and had got herself in trouble. The father wasn't interested. I think he might have been married, though I have no proof of this. *My* father, I should say, but who is he to me but a stranger and I'm past caring besides; he's irrelevant to me. She gave me to Gamma, said she couldn't cope with the responsibility, and Gamma said fine, six months then you're back to it, Mary, all right? You've got yourself into this, you can get yourself out. And Mary said yes but then she ran off to Westward

Ho! and never came back again apart from as a visiting relative like Great Uncle Clarence or Cousin Norma, a few times for the sake of it, with gifts and pats on the head, and knobbly knees in tights I was made to sit on clutching my garibaldi, which Gamma always called a squashed-fly biscuit. There's a picture of me sitting on Mary's lap when I was three years old; she's got a patterned dress on like a field of a thousand flowers, open at the neck, and a gold chain I've wound around my fist. I kept that photo and looked at it all through my childhood, searching her expression for clues as to why she didn't want me, but I never found one.

Gamma believed in God. Both her parents had died when she was small and she'd been sent to live with maiden aunts in London who'd been into heaven and hell and the hereafter, and they held seances to summon the dead. Once they'd summoned Gamma's father Benjamin who'd been a miner in the coal pits. He'd appeared to them with his sooted face and loving eyes and complained about how windy it was being caught at the entrance to the tunnel, but they had never ascertained whether this referred to the adit or a channel of the afterlife. Gamma said these days she disapproved of mysticism, but that her aunts' fervour had shown her the importance of believing in *something*. She gave no credence to spiritualism, but to witness their faith had instilled in her a sense of wonder, of openness to whatever the world had to reveal, for it was ignorant to imagine that there was nothing more to unveil than what our earthbound lives were capable of experiencing.

She took me to church every Sunday. We dressed as smartly as we could. Gamma took pride in what little we had, she mended and washed endlessly, so even if I wore the same thing every day I might have been wearing it new. The mothers on the road gave us clothes and some of them were for boys but Gamma told me beggars couldn't be choosers so off we went, me in my long shorts and chestnut shoes, my hair tucked under a smooth felt cap because if we were in for a penny we might as well be in for a pound. The congregation spoke to Gamma outside church, their murmurs travelling like biplanes far off over my head. I knew they were talking about Mary. Every child needs its mother, they said. What a shame it was, what a pity, a young thing left behind like that with no more ceremony than a sackful of sugar, and I guessed that thing they were talking about was me. Then they went back to their houses to discuss it some more, what an awful business it was, what a scandal, who was to blame? Was it that cad Ronan O'Brien, he'd always been trouble; or Sam from the butcher's or Reg from the post office; or that boy of Robert Ackland's who'd never been the same after the war? Mary must have run off to be married and would come back for me after, surely she would, but time was passing and long-suffering Violet – my dear Gamma, who had taken me in and cared for me and made me feel safe and loved – was too old for this, she deserved a medal, she did, that poor woman. I thought I sounded like a burden she'd been left with, but when I asked her if I was, she said, 'You're a gift, my little bird, and I wouldn't change you for anything.'

Our house on Marlborough Avenue had new people in it every day. The women came by for Gamma's apple tart. Sometimes they'd talk, sew or listen to the wireless, sometimes they sat in silence, just for the company. A procession of toddlers stumbled across the carpet wiping snot on the sofa and wetting themselves. Though I wasn't much older myself, I observed these clumsy beasts as if they were another species, seeing the rusks they dropped on Gamma's carpet and their reckless destruction of the wooden-block towers I built to sustain their attention. When they left there was crayon on the walls.

I couldn't understand why these creatures, who were not so well behaved as I, had doting parents. I wished to have a mother and father, to be an ordinary child, no longer to be the odd one out. Had I wronged Mary at a time before I could remember? Had I cried too much, kept her awake, caused her pain by being born? These were the reasons I could think of. I asked Gamma if next time Mary visited I should say sorry. 'Whatever for?' said Gamma, crossly. She knelt in front of me and took my hands. 'You've nothing to say sorry for,' she said, soft now, tucking my hair behind my ear. 'Ours is a happy home. We're happy, aren't we?'

'Yes,' I said, and we were.

'Then don't mind what people say.'

Occasionally we had men visitors. Gamma tidied up beforehand. She dusted under the shepherdess ornaments on the mantelpiece and got out the best china to serve the tea in, brushing cobwebs out of the cups. There were chips in the rims of the cups but Gamma said it was the thought that counted, and it was important these men saw she had thoughts in her head because they were men of God and could give us things we needed.

There were three that came mainly, on rotation. Two were

interchangeable in my mind. Both were very fat. They each had to take chairs without arms because arms could not contain them, and when I saw them from the back (as I often did, spying on them from my hiding place), their shirts stretched over their bulk like cloth wrapped round meat at the butcher's, I marvelled that they did not fall through the wood altogether. Sometimes Gamma told me to go off and play, sometimes she brought me in, where I met the men's piggy stares and rough, veined noses. They patted their laps as if enticing a puppy. 'This is my little bird,' Gamma said, while I stood shyly behind her legs, nervous of being seen; 'aren't you going to say hello, Bridget?' But I never wanted to. The men seemed to fill the room and block out the light; the more I looked at them the larger they grew, until all I could see was an enormous shadow in front of the window and all I could hear was the sound of their chuckled remark: 'Cat got your tongue, littl'un?' I wondered if my father had been like this, big and looming with a sideways smile – would I even know him if I saw him in the street? The men lured and repelled me. I wanted to run to them and run away from them and I couldn't understand why I felt like that. Upstairs, I put my ear to the floor and listened to the vibration of their voices, their low laughter, the clink of teaspoons on saucers like the sound the rain made when it fell on the tin shed at night. Later, when they went, I didn't even have to wait for the click of the door; I could tell by the way the house lifted, regained its brightness, and the daylight streamed back in through the glass.

The third man lodged most firmly in my consciousness. Once or twice I rose from a dream and he had been in it. In the dream he was chasing me through yellow woods. The trees were yellow and the soil was yellow and the sky between the branches was yellow. I never met him in the dream but I knew he was there, following, and that he was stronger and faster than me. When I woke I saw his face grinning at me in the dark, a grin full of teeth, and I called for Gamma but I couldn't explain what I had seen, or why.

He was younger than the others. He said he'd found Jesus in El Alamein, to which I asked had Jesus been hurt, what did Jesus say, did you help him, and the man and Gamma smiled at each other. He had small sharp teeth, very white, and his top lip was bigger than his lower one. The suit (he always wore a suit) must have been too small because his long legs made the fabric ruck up, and between where his trousers ended and his shoes began were his socks, bright yellow, true yellow, like lemons in sun. His hair was missing in clumps and he had a scar across his cheek that looked silky to the touch, almost pearlescent. Occasionally he had a bag of sugared almonds, pastel pink and primrose, which he offered when the tea was served. I was happier to be with him than the fat ones. 'Why does he look like that?' I asked Gamma when he left.

'Because he fought for us,' she said.

'Why?' I said.

'For our freedom,' she replied. I said why would he want to do that if he was going to end up being hurt? She put the ginger cake back in the tin. 'Because that was the honourable thing,' she said. 'That's what it took to be a man.'

Gamma liked to pray. We prayed together at bedtime, kneeling on the floor, our hands clasped, eyes closed, then Gamma got into her bed and I got into mine and I'd ask her to tell me stories until I fell asleep. She told me how she believed that God had a plan for all of us, whoever we were; she told me good things could always be found if I was willing to look for them; and she told me about Benjamin down the coalmines, and her mother, Joyce, who'd been a wonderful dancer apparently, and how sometimes, right before Gamma went to sleep, in that funny time when your mind's nodding off but your body's holding on, she had the sense that Joyce was carrying her up and away in her arms, across the dance floor, spinning her round, their skirts trailing about them like windmills.

∽

One evening, the week before I turned five, I prayed out loud for Mummy to come back. Normally I did that in my head so Gamma wouldn't hear, but I wanted to see how the word 'Mummy' sounded and how it felt in my mouth. It felt the same as the clothes from the boys down the street, several sizes too big. Gamma looked sad when I said it, then put her arm round me and pulled me close and said, with a squeeze of my shoulder, 'The Lord doesn't always give us what we want. That's because He's planning to bring us something else.'

But the Lord did give me what I wanted because a few days later, my mother showed up on the road. I was playing jacks on the porch when I heard my name called and looked around. There was a woman standing on the corner. She wore a neat skirt and jacket, and white gloves that clutched the handles of a small, square bag. I thought at first she was someone from church but then I recognized the curl in her hair, the same as mine.

'Hullo,' she said. 'Would you like to come with me?'

I hardly remembered meeting her those times she'd come before, the flowery dress and gold chain as vague in my mind as not to have happened. She opened the latch on the gate. I went to her and took her hand. The glove felt soft. There was a smell coming off her, once floral, now marshy, like the rotted stalks of daffodils Gamma kept for too long in the window.

'Do you like the park?' she said. I nodded. We went there. The ducks on the pond moved serenely. Mary took a breadcrust from her bag and started picking it apart, rolling the crumbs inside her flattened palms until they made tiny balls which she passed to me. We didn't speak; she just kept on rolling the bread and I kept throwing it. More ducks came, dipping their oily necks, flapping their wings, scooting across the water. There was one at the back who never made it in time. I felt sorry for him. I threw the bread as close to him as I could but he was never quick enough to reach it. He seemed content to let the others get on with it. After a while, I felt angry and upset. Come on, I thought, I can't help you any more, you've got to help yourself. I felt relieved when the bread ran out.

Mary touched my shoulder. 'Are you hungry?' she said. 'It's lunchtime.'

We sat on a bench. The sun came out, twinkling on the water. Everything turned blue and green. 'You like eggs, don't you?' said Mary, and gave me a sheet of brown paper with a hard-boiled egg inside, halved, the orange yolk fringed with grey. She watched me avidly. How had I not noticed her eyes before? They were very sad and very wild at the same time. 'What else do you like?' she asked me. 'Do you like pets? Celia has a rabbit.'

'Who's Celia?'

'She's the person I live with.'

'What's the rabbit called?'

'The rabbit doesn't have a name.'

I finished the egg. The texture was furry on my tongue and the inside of my cheeks. I longed for a drink to take the taste away, but Mary's bag stayed closed, her gloves back on, perched on the clasp. Her knees were tightly drawn together and there was a ragged hole in her stockings through which her skin could be seen. She took the brown paper off me, greasy with the lost heat of the egg, and creased it in half then creased it again, neatly scoring each fold with a fingernail. A man walked past with his dog and lifted his cap. All that could be heard was the crisp hard scoring of the paper.

'You should know he came in through the window,' she said. 'Celia says why did you open the window? But it was hot that night, so I did. Your Gamma thinks she knows everything that goes on in her house but she didn't know that.' The paper was a nub now, too small to fold again. Mary rubbed it between her fingers. 'I could see his eyes shining in the dark,' she said. 'They were filled with the pupil, like a cat's. He told me he'd come a long way. Walking, I mean. He'd travelled through a forest. A bear tried to eat him. In the end there'd been no choice but to get good at climbing trees, which was why he was able to climb up to my window. Do you see now? He asked to be with me, and I said yes.'

I wanted Gamma. I worried that the duck had died of hunger.

'I knew about you,' said Mary, turning her body slightly so she was able to peer down at me. 'Before we met. I knew you were in there. I felt I had a nest of dry sticks in my stomach. I thought if I lay out in the sunshine I would catch fire. I had a picture of you in my mind. Sleeping under the stars. You had eyes like his. Like a cat's. Only your eyes aren't like that – are they? They're like mine.' Her look became gentle again. 'That's all I wanted to tell you. Looking at you now, I don't know whether to feel disappointed.'

She took my hand then placed it in my lap, as if it was something I had dropped and she'd picked up and returned to me. She said, 'I have to go. Celia's waiting.'

I followed her up to the road but her mind wasn't on me then. She waved to a car parked by the green and at last she turned round. 'Aren't you going to go home?' she said.

∽

Gamma didn't know whether to be angry or relieved when I got back. She covered me in kisses and gave my bottom a smack. I told her what Mary had said. 'It's the drink,' she said, hugging me. 'Heaven knows she's enough demons without adding that to the mix.'

That night in my bed, I couldn't stop thinking about Mary.

She'd sown a seed in me, bright and worrying, a stink of rotted daffodils. As I drifted to sleep I saw an open window on a hot night, curtains blooming. A man's hand on the ledge, his crooked arm, his head, the whole of that man climbing in, the yellow sky rushing in behind him.

3

I had never shot a gun before. Fired a gun, whatever it is you say. I didn't like violence, for obvious reasons. I couldn't watch horror films or TV hospital shows and the sight of blood made me faint. I wasn't an executioner, I was a mother. The gun would be quick.

I hadn't always felt this way. For years I had wanted him to suffer. I had thought of it every day, fantasized about it, the possibility of it coming to pass by my hand, but as time went on I became less interested in his suffering. Simply, I wanted him gone. It wasn't enough for him to have been detained, where he'd been able to walk and sleep, be interested, be aroused, be hungry, be fed. I wanted him deleted. He didn't deserve to live.

Snow turned to rain. Droplets ran in rivulets down the outside of the glass, which was fogged by body heat. The coach was half full. I sat in an aisle seat with Gamma's bag safe by the window, my coat laid across it. The driver had tried to get the bag off me for stowing in the luggage compartment; I'd had the rash idea he'd known about the gun: surely everyone here could sense it, as I could, a small fire burning, its smoke beginning to curl from the centimetre split between the end of the zip and the ear of the leather.

Every so often there came a thump from beneath as another case was heaved in. Out on the tarmac, a couple was arguing. The man had a backpack hanging off one shoulder and she was crying, gesturing with her arms. A minute later she stalked off. *Thunk*, went the backpack. He came up the steps and sat on the seat in front of mine. I heard his Walkman click then the subdued notes of a Morrissey song.

We joined the motorway. Everything was brownish grey. The fields had thawed or else it just hadn't snowed out here, our village the only one touched. We passed billboards for the limestone caves and purchasable ones with ADVERTISE HERE! scrawled across them in paint. Barns, houses, bridges. Cows grazed at a distance in such orderly formation they could have been farmyard toys. The backpacker couldn't stop shifting about. He rearranged himself constantly to get comfortable, changing the tape in his player, getting bored of it, opening a book whose title I tried to glimpse through the gap between the seats but couldn't.

There was a traffic jam joining the M25. We sat in it for a while. Heads popped up near the front to see what was going on; someone groaned. I looked at my watch. From the terminus it would be forty minutes across town: two tube lines then a short distance to the prison. I'd allowed extra time. I felt relaxed. Peaceful, even. I felt that it wasn't possible to fail. Even if our transport broke down, even if the wheels caught alight, even if a comet came hurtling towards Earth and the clouds turned to icy flames, Providence would carry me to him and I would have my opportunity. Superstition, Gamma would have called it: wishful thinking at best. I didn't mind that. I was used to wishing. I hadn't believed in much since the summer my sister had died, but I did believe in that.

The clog loosened. We moved on. City buildings stacked and we arrived at the coach station. Everyone stood before the driver had opened the door. I found myself wedged against the backpacker's arm, Gamma's bag to my chest, the smoking gun inside.

'Do you want me to help you with that?' he asked.

I shook my head. I clutched the bag tighter. I was making things worse.

'No, thank you,' I said. My mouth was dry and the voice that came out of it wasn't mine. He gave me an odd look then walked down the steps and was lost in the crowd.

∽

It was a while since I had been on the Underground. The last time had been supper with Tom's colleagues in an expensive hotel in the West End. The food had been Japanese. I'd ordered soft-shell crab without properly reading the menu and the entire crustacean had arrived on my plate, filled with an unidentifiable black liquid. Mostly I associated the tube with journeys to or from seeing Mary, and the peculiar mix of sadness, dread and relief those journeys entailed, depending on which direction I was travelling in.

I bought a ticket and joined the escalators. Commuters glided past, bleached and burned out. I considered how I must appear, an unremarkable lady of middle height and middle age in a fawn ankle-length coat, her handbag over her shoulder and a battered case by her feet. I was out of place, in from the sticks for the day, queuing bewildered at the turnstiles, standing on the left until shunted out of the way. I heard the train come in and hurried down to the platform. The doors sealed shut behind me, the carriage packed, infused with a smell of newsprint and damp coats. A sign read DON'T PUT YOUR FEET ON THE SEATS. I stood between the frills of knees with Gamma's bag under my arm, my thumb stroking the handles. Everyone ignored each other, their attention buried in the papers: books were being burned in Bradford; Reagan was on his way out. Next to me, a Boy George lookalike ate a roll sheathed in clingfilm; when he bit into it a trail of sauce shot out of the end. I changed at Stockwell and joined the Northern line. We got stuck in the tunnel at Balham and I tried not think about how many tons of earth there were between my head and the sky.

Although I knew where I was going almost to the step, when I emerged onto Trinity Road I took out my *A–Z* and moved to the marked page. I had circled my destination, a bus ride and a short walk from here. I liked that the map made me look like a tourist. A girl walked past me, around the age Providence had been, and smiled at me so suddenly and happily that for an alarming moment I thought we knew each other, but when I turned I saw she was greeting a friend, and hadn't, in fact, noticed me at all.

∽

Wandsworth was infamous. One of the 'big hell-holes', as the papers dubbed them, among the great prison families of

Dartmoor and Strangeways, Wakefield and Leeds. I'd started paying Catriona two years in, once I'd realized my agony wasn't going anywhere. People said it would; the hurt would pass, or if not that then its edges would blunt and it would become easier to live with. It hadn't. As my private investigator, Catriona had fed me word about his sentence and care (care!), where he was serving time, likely transferrals, bad behaviour, good, when his legal team were priming for leniency. Then in '76 he'd made it to a newfangled therapeutic lock-up in the Buckinghamshire countryside which was meant to help people like him, but it sounded lax to me, a bucolic holiday, interested in his recovery and rehabilitation which was all well and good but she would never have rehabilitation and recovery, would she, and where was the fairness in that? I'd told Tom that the more I knew, the more in control I felt. That was a lie. The more I knew, the more arbitrary and unwieldy this idea of justice became, and only by plotting my own means to an end could I bear it. If they'd got him for murder, he'd have had life. As it was, manslaughter on the grounds of diminished responsibility. Quite what that diminished responsibility was continued to evade me and no one to date had explained it in a way that made me see it as anything more than an excuse well-articulated by his defence. As far as I was concerned, he deserved to be banged up till the end of his days, and the sooner they came, the better.

He'd missed capital punishment by a few years. But then he'd been nineteen with an 'abnormality of mind' (didn't all murderers have abnormality of mind?), so I doubted they'd have strung him up anyway. Instead they had stated and speculated over his reasons; they had made an exhibit of him, given him time and breath and consideration when she had had none of that. He was one of those whose urges had overtaken him; 'he couldn't control himself', the lawyer declared. And if that were the difference between man and beast, between civilization and savagery, the ability to tell oneself one could not do what one pleased for there were consequences to those actions, then he was an animal.

But this I knew. Whether he'd been hanged or not, this I knew. Reintegrate them into society, the wisdom went. Jail for a spell then out, bettered, ready to demonstrate what they had learnt, how they had learnt never to do it again; well bully for them then, good on them, what did they want for their restraint, a trophy, a welcome rally, did they want a prize? Prize enough that they could still be useful, still put something positive into the world. He could do anything now. He could move away and change his name: no one would know who he was or what he'd done. He could start a job and have a family and walk on the beach with a soft-furred pup given to him by a friend. He would know the sensation of a cool glass of water on a hot day, of hearing thunder from a warm bed, of putting his cheek to the fresh side of the pillow. Providence would have none of these things because they had been taken away from her by him, as permanently as the stool kicked from under the scaffold. An eye for an eye wouldn't bring her back, but it would make me feel better.

I stood opposite the main gate with Gamma's case between my feet. Rain pitted my shoes. A Black Maria parked beyond the wall next to a convoy of police vans and a metal trailer.

People rushed past under the black shells of umbrellas. I put up my own and waited. The entrance was a portcullis, a large wooden square beneath a latticed iron grille. It seemed impossible that he would shortly be appearing in it. If I did it here, would there be sympathy for me after? Would they see I'd had my reasons? Of course I had my reasons. But years had passed and a grudge was unbecoming in a woman; she should have got over it, they'd say; he'd done his time, he'd paid his price, this was the law whether she liked it or not, this sad person who couldn't move on with her life.

I had tried to move on. I'd left our Devon village, settled in another county; I'd got married, had Philippa, had Joe, thinking if I had them I could be pure in spirit as mothers should be. But he had come with me; he had never lessened his grip. Over time, I had trained myself to confront him just once a day. My doctor had advised an hour at first. During that hour I would sit alone and go through every part of what had happened to my sister, sift it through my fingers until it was a fine powder: what he'd done to her, every bit of it real and imagined, her rising panic, her pain, at what point precisely it had settled on her that she would die – had she called for me? When I'd finished, I washed the powder from my hair and hands and got on with things that needed to be got on with and I didn't think of him again until next day, when the hour resumed and the lumps would have to be milled through once more. Soon, that hour lessened to half an hour, twenty minutes, ten, my thoughts no fewer but compressed into this new timeframe, easily granulated, recognizable to me now, no longer with the power to strike me at my middle.

I was done with being tied to this man. Locked up with him. He had had too much of my life, and I of his. There could be no universe in which the two of us existed.

I fixed on the gate. I was afraid that if I glanced away from it for even a second he would appear and I would miss it. It felt significant to see the point of his freedom, the exact moment he moved from being imprisoned to liberated. Several people came and went but none of them was him. A lorry pulled up, obscuring my view. Briefly I fretted, considering a relocation to the other side of the road, then someone got out and the lorry moved on. The gate stayed closed. I began to question if there had been a mistake, if Catriona had got it wrong. I imagined getting home later and listening to her phone messages. I felt suddenly exhausted at the prospect of Philippa's questions about the fictional Peggy. My family, so precious, in their snow globe, a hundred miles away. It wasn't too late to go back. I still could. Perhaps all I'd needed was to be here, on this day, on the brink of attainment, to realize I didn't have to go through with it. I pressed the possibility like a burn, testing its edges, how much it hurt, and it hurt too much to be true.

These were the thoughts in my head when at last he appeared. He came from nowhere, surfacing from his background like a float in water. My throat tightened; a metallic tang crossed my tongue like the aftertaste of a nosebleed. Otherwise, nothing changed. I carried on breathing. I carried on standing. People walked past, none of them tripping over the invisible string that surely bound us. It seemed incredible that he should not turn and see me, that he would not feel the force of my presence and my intentions towards him. But he did not. Several officers gathered round him. He shook their hands. Someone gave him a bundle that might have been clothes. Another patted him on the back, like an American sportsman. Carrying his bag, he stepped out onto the road.

And just like that, James Maguire was free.

The rain was a fine, freezing mizzle. It did not seem to bother him. He was wearing a white T-shirt, the sleeves rolled high above his elbows, and pale-blue denim jeans with a slash across each thigh like a reclining crescent moon. His hair was thick and slicked back. His complexion was bloodless, his skin chalkier than I remembered, and he was taller, more rounded in the shoulders, as if he had spent a lot of time looking at the ground. But he moved just the same, a lazy sort of uninterested slope, which had played against him in court, coming in like that looking as if he hadn't a care in the world, as if he were turning up for no more than a film at the cinema he didn't particularly want to see. That and the hard, heavy-lidded blue eyes. I waited for those eyes to train on me.

What would he do if he saw me? I had changed in two decades, deliberately: new hair, new build, glasses I hadn't any real need for — and I wouldn't have put it past him anyway to have blocked me from his mind. While I had memorized every line on his face, every pore of his skin, not once during the trial had he looked at me and let me know he admitted to and was sorry for what he had done. Instead he had sat in the dock staring straight ahead, the long fingers of one hand stroking the crazed knuckles of the other, answering yes ma'am and no ma'am and showing no emotion when presented with the horrors of his crime. *His* crime, no one else's. Try as he might to blame another man, it was he who had done that monstrous thing, and he hadn't the courage, the *courtesy*, to own his wrong and proclaim it. The jury decreed he lacked remorse. That, at least, was right. His defence said this was part of it, he didn't understand what he had done. I didn't believe that. I thought he understood perfectly, he always had, and it made no difference.

I closed the umbrella. Cold mist landed in my hair. I watched Maguire put a jacket on, greasy green material with a logo I couldn't decrypt on the front breast. He lit a cigarette, cupping his hands round the lighter, his brow quirked. When he got it going he took a long inhale, blew out smoke in a thin, high jet then lifted his face to the sky and shut his eyes, the cigarette smouldering by his side. It troubled me that he should derive pleasure from this cigarette. It occurred to me that he would go on to derive pleasure from many things. Let him have his cigarette, I thought, observing his upturned neck with its Adam's apple I could have hung a shirt on. Let him take what he could from the hours he had left.

He stayed like that for a minute, then opened his eyes and turned away down the road. I hurried to keep up with him. A blister rubbed on my heel. He moved faster than I had predicted, the jacket flitting ahead of me. I'd imagined the years spent in prison might have slowed him down some, those crawling, empty days, suns rising and suns setting through a brick-sized hatch cross-sectioned by bars. Either that or he'd feel unworthy, now outside, of keeping pace with ordinary people, counted among them as if he were one of them, a man on his way to work or to make an appointment. He was not that man. Or was he? To my surprise he stopped outside a Menzies and began talking to a woman there. She was young, no more than eighteen. She had on a red-and-black-checked lumberjack shirt. A dark braid ran down her back. I thought she must be flogging a street paper, but then she took the parcel of clothes from him and there followed a brief dispute wherein it appeared he didn't want her to take it, before they started off together towards the buses. They walked a foot apart, he in front. I wondered if she was one of those women who wrote to killers in prison: *There was something about him, he only wanted a friend. God told me to be there for him.* But the way they were with each other wasn't right for that. She was nervy, eager to please. He seemed to want rid of her.

We waited for a bus. I made sure there were bodies separating us but I was close enough still to see the spots of rain on his jacket and a zit on the side of his jaw.

The bus came, spraying water. A man with a burgundy briefcase pushed in front of me. I saw them move down inside, behind the steamy windows. My hands trembled as I took out my fare and paid the driver. I made my way along the aisle, turning my face away but they were both looking out onto the pavement. The girl was picking her nails.

I sat behind them. He was near enough to touch. I almost did touch him, resting my wrist on the rail in front, his shoulder an inch away. Instead, I held Gamma's bag close. Where were we going? I trusted that Providence was by my side and would come with me there and show me how. And that when James

Maguire's and my time came, it would be us, just him and me, as it was always meant to be – not this girl, not anyone else, just us – and then he would recognize me. He would see me and know who I was.

Right before I did it, he'd know.

4

I wonder if I've spent my whole life following people in one way or another. There's this longing I have that whoever's in front of me will turn round and say, *I felt you there, right from the start; why don't you show yourself?* We used to play 'What's the Time, Mr Wolf?' in my friend Jenny's garden at number 14. Everyone ran squealing when her father in his too-tight braces rounded on the pigs with a growled, 'Time for my supper!' – except for me. I always stayed still. 'Why won't you run, little miss?' he would ask, a puzzled wolf disabled by his stationary prey. And I'd say, 'That's OK. You can catch me if you want.'

It was 1953 and the day of the Queen's Coronation. Excitement was high, everyone wanted to celebrate. Elizabeth II had been chosen by God, said Gamma, it would be like a wedding; this afternoon she married the country and the Commonwealth. Gamma had woken me early and together we'd watched the sun come up, wrapped in blankets on the porch, mugs of cocoa warming our hands; the sun had set fire to the woods, lighting the treeline like an edge of singed paper. Later, I helped Bill Mackey string bunting from the bricks, steadying the stepladder for him as he wobbled around in his hobnail boots. Mrs Lovell and the big boys put tables end to end up the length of the road, decorated with Union Jack flags, balloons and crackers, bottles of ginger beer and fizzy cherry Corona. I'd felt part of something, a family bigger than just the two of us. It started raining a bit. Gamma was worried about that. She glanced up at the clouds and pronounced it a bad omen. The tablecloths flipped up in the breeze; Bill pinned them down with clothes pegs.

Mrs Lovell had a television which the grown-ups gathered round in her sitting room. I spied the grainy box in the slits between their waists, a parade of hats and horses, carriages and crowns, so many people bunched outside Buckingham Palace that it took me a second to realize they were people at all and not some moving quilt of different textures being rolled down the Mall. The Queen looked young, I thought. She reminded me of one of Gamma's shepherdesses, her pale arm emerging from her snowy furs, holding her sceptre, and her benevolent, enduring smile. The ceremony went on for a long time. I rested my chin on the back of a chair, thinking about lunch, intermittently picking a thread on Gamma's skirt and watching an assortment of babies crawl between the adults' ankles.

Soon I got bored and went outside. The tables were piled high with bowls of curried chicken and potatoes, ham salad and roly-poly pudding. Cucumber sandwiches, cut into triangles, lined the long trays like the little roofs of houses. Some older boys were knocking a football about. The ball dribbled into an alley and they ran after it, their shouts jumping off the bricks. The food looked like a scene in a fairy tale about a banquet being laid then everyone who was meant to eat it falling asleep for a hundred years. The boys' shouts faded. Everything went quiet. A napkin blew onto the ground. I went after it but the napkin kept flicking away from me; I tried to stamp on it but it was like stamping on my shadow. Then the breeze lifted it into the air and I was able to take it from right there in front of me, straight out of the air, and put it in my pocket.

Gradually I became aware of a low whistling sound, a continuous muted note like the kettle rising to boil. It was coming from the other end of the street. I wandered past the houses, past the alley where the boys had disappeared. The whistling grew louder. I thought it might be coming from inside my head. Just as I convinced myself of this I saw a man in the distance, walking away from me. I took my hands off my ears. The whistling stopped. I followed him to the corner and across the park and over the bridge that separated the fields. He walked close enough in front of me that I could see his yellow socks in the gap between his shoes and his suit trousers. We started down Nail's Lane whose verges burst with grass and bluebells and the white wisps of dandelion clocks. A magpie swooped into a tree. Midges hovered in sticky clouds. I longed to touch the back of his head which made me sad for some reason, those mossy clumps of hair and the way he never wore a hat to hide it, and I thought that was to do with his having found Jesus and that Jesus had told him it didn't matter about that, what he looked like.

Soon he was going too fast for me to keep up with and I couldn't see him any more. There was a stile going onto the Brewsters' field, but when I looked past it the land was a sea of startling yellow rapeseed, a giant wooden scarecrow rising from its waves. I didn't like that scarecrow. He was so big he touched the sky and his grin was painted red and his eyes were black and watching. Gamma had brought me once for the harvest fair: while the other children danced round him I'd kept away, afraid that if I moved, he would too.

I climbed over, thinking this must be where the suited man had gone. The crop was as tall as my neck. The earth was uneven where a tractor's wheels had churned it up, slick and muddy in some places and dry soil in others. I found a path but the path petered out into weeds and ruts, one of which contained the skull of a small animal. Dark clouds clotted. Rain spat and got harder. I felt the wooden scarecrow hovering over me, behind me, everywhere – where? I pushed through the rapeseed but all I could see, all that surrounded me, was yellow, oily and dense, and a sour smell like sweat and leaves. The more I walked, the further I travelled from the afternoon I was meant to have been part of. I felt in my pocket for the napkin and it moistened in my palm. My skin prickled with goosebumps. I was thirsty and cold. I thought of paper straws poking out of sweet cherry drinks, huddled with Gamma under an umbrella, holding her cardigan. A woman's voice was calling. I thought it was my mother. 'Hello?' it said. 'Are you there? Who's there?'

I ran towards the voice, my knees weak. Mary had come. I'd known she would. She kept on calling, 'Is somebody there? Are you lost? Here I am, come, here I am,' and a hand appeared as if from the sky with a wedding ring on its finger so I knew straight away it was not hers, and I looked up into a stranger's face and she said she'd take me home.

The summer I turned eight, Gamma decided I was old enough to come to work with her now, it was time I put myself to some good. She suggested it on our way to church. It was the first Sunday of the holidays.

'Does that mean I can go to the Fairfaxes' house?' I said.

She licked her thumb and wiped a blot on my cheek. 'It means you can *clean* the Fairfaxes' house. Heavens above, Birdie, how do you get dirt on you just from *walking*?'

Communion was busier than normal because of the heatwave, which had already lasted a week. Sunlight baked the brick and the air was thick and still. Everything moved slowly. Plants perished, exhausted, in pots. The pavements burned to touch; on the last day of term we'd tried to fry an egg on Jenny's doorstep but it had turned milky at the edges then later a dog licked it up. Gamma wore the same smock dress every day, her hair stuck to the back of her neck in shilling-sized rings as she went about opening windows and fanning herself with a rolled-up *Mercury*, saying, 'Lord have mercy, we'll cook in our skins!' At night, as I lay in my bed with damp sheets tangled round my feet, I pictured what this looked like, my body dried like the rind of a jacket potato, the crackle the knife made as it slit through the crust and steam came out.

Church was the only place that kept cool. The vicar was happy about it: Sunday service had never been so full. Gamma said God's House would always provide, but after we'd filed back out into the heat I heard Mr Dillard saying it was only the stone.

Talk turned to the stained-glass window. Someone had thrown a rock through it on St Swithin's Day, shattering

Bartholomew's head at the Last Supper. They hadn't taken anybody to the police station yet. I thought the police were too hot to bother. The adults exchanged opinions about it outside the vestibule, limply gathered there like a bunch of wilted stems in a vase, knowing that gossip was unchristian but unable to help themselves. The Reverend had asked us to pray for this person, who had allegedly also done the break-in at the greengrocer's and robbed the cash register at the hardware store.

'I can't think who would do such a thing,' said Betty Mackey.

'I've a fair idea,' said Bill, darkly. 'The Maguires. They're trouble, the lot of them.'

Betty took a fan from her bag and started wafting herself with it. 'Which one?'

'Does it matter?' said Bill. 'They're all the same.'

'The great unwashed,' put in Frida, whose second name I couldn't think of.

'It's one thing going for the money,' said Betty. 'But the church? What did that poor apostle ever do to them?'

'Those lot don't need a reason,' said Bill. 'Smash and grab's the rule they live by.'

'Then it's the only one,' said Frida, in her tidy white shoes and stockings with seams running up the back like piped icing. 'It's the mother's fault, letting them run riot.'

Gamma dabbed her brow with her hankie. 'Whoever did it has to be a desperate lamb. You heard what the Very Reverend said in there, we're to keep him in our prayers.'

'She can't stop having them,' said Frida. 'Her youngest's only two. John, is it?'

Someone said, 'James.'

'Poor mite,' said Frida. 'And that hoodlum of a father's never around.'

'Frank Maguire's a nasty piece of work if ever I met one,' said Bill. 'Getting drunk, starting fights in the Wagon. I'm telling you, that family's a blight on this village. If it's not one it's another – barely back from prison a week before they're off stealing again.'

'Or vandalizing our religious buildings,' said Betty.

'It might not have been the same person,' said Gamma. 'We've no proof it was.'

'Five pounds says it was,' muttered Bill, to which Gamma tsked because betting was unchristian too. We walked down the path to the gate, Gamma's hand on my shoulder, as if to say, *You know what's kind, don't listen to them.* The leaves on the trees were unmoving. Shade was scarce, the ground too luminous to look at, the road beyond the wall slipping like a melting ice lolly. A girl from my class rode past on a bicycle but the bicycle made no sound. All I could hear were Bill's boots shuffling along the tar.

'Admit it, Vi,' he said, wedging his flat cap on his head to stop his bald patch burning. 'We'd no problems before the Maguires came along. It's no coincidence.'

'Now you're talking nonsense,' she said, clicking the latch open.

'Forget your lambs, they're a pack of wolves.'

'And they've been terrors at the school, by all accounts,' said Frida. 'That is, when they deign to attend. Brawling. Cursing. Throwing their bully beef at the dinner ladies.'

'We don't have bully beef at school,' I said, but only Gamma was listening. It struck me then, in a marvellous, shining bolt, how very lucky I was that she was mine. She could have said no to Mary, all those years ago. Seen out the six months then given me away. To whom? I could have been sent anywhere, to anyone, one of these people, and it reached me properly, for the first time, outside church in the unholy heat with Gamma's hand held in mine, how different my life would have been if I hadn't had her.

'What's the one with the shaved head?' said Betty. 'Maurice Fairfax's been scared horribly by him. They're saying so on the Institute. What hope has this James got?'

Gamma closed the gate behind us, as if God wouldn't be able to hear us any more as long as we weren't in his back garden. 'If it's anything,' she said, 'it's a cry for help.'

'Society's gone soft in my view,' said Bill. 'Acting like the felons are the victims.'

'Born irresponsibly,' agreed Frida, 'they live irresponsibly.'

Next to me, Gamma stiffened. 'As long as there's someone around to love them it doesn't matter how they're born,' she said. 'So long as they're protected and cared for and given a little bit of direction. Has it occurred to you that might be what's missing? Well, how I see it is that's all the more reason to show those qualities ourselves. I intend to, even if you don't.' And we stalked off together, leaving their small group simmering behind us.

On Tuesday we went up the hill to the Fairfaxes', Gamma carrying her mop and bucket and me puffing alongside on my Hercules, whose basket was laden with soaps and scrubbers.

I thought Dr and Mrs Fairfax's was the most beautiful house I had ever seen. It was brick, like ours, but instead of brown it glowed in the late-day sun like embers in the grate. Climbing plants crept round the windows, which were arched and filled with green bevelled glass. We came up each year for the spring fete, when the lawns were scattered with hoopla games and stalls selling chocolate cake. I always liked to pretend that the house was mine. It was right about now, as we approached the clipped grass and I climbed off my bike and wheeled it the rest of the way, I imagined that the Fairfaxes were my parents and I was their girl, and we would go inside to take tea together at a polished dining table – Gamma too, wearing a glamorous robe and a smart hat with fruits on, not needing to lift a finger for once – with jugs of lemon and a plate of fondant fancies served beneath a cloche I could see my face in, which was always prettier than in real life. Instead of boys' clothes, I wore a delicate outfit with a ruched lace neck, not belonging to this time but another, lost era, known to me despite the fact that I had never seen any such garment on a living person. It was only years after, as I was sorting through boxes in Gamma's attic, that I found its replica on my childhood doll Celeste, Mary's plaything once upon a time, a lilac satin gown on a body made of stuffing but for the head and hands and feet, which were formed of smooth porcelain and finely painted, the lips as tiny and vivid as a pinprick of blood.

Mrs Fairfax was everything I thought a mother should be.

Her hair was swept into a curl of vanilla buttercream, her cheeks flushed pink like Fry's Turkish Delight. She had the most wonderful clothes made of silk and velvet. I wondered if Mary ever wore such nice things as Mrs Fairfax did. I remembered the holes in her tights when we'd sat together in the park and wished I knew what I could give her that would make her happy.

I had never been inside the house before. There was so much to look at. Portraits of stern-faced men with hounds by their heels; cloudy misshapen bowls the colour of forget-me-nots, prompting Gamma to gasp when I went near them with a duster ('Go *round* them, Birdie, don't touch *anything*!'); ornate clocks of molten gold. The pelt of a large white animal (a polar bear? I couldn't believe it) coated the flagstones like a bucket of milk. Mrs Fairfax apologized for the mess, but there wasn't any. Fresh flowers adorned the hall, whose floor was clear and hard like an ice rink; her heels ticked as she walked across it. I thought of our cramped, cosy, higgledy-piggledy home, the overloaded laundry basket, the furniture pitted with woodworm, the bedroom I shared with Gamma on account of whichever waif or stray was residing in Mary's old room, and felt guilty for comparing them. That was my real home – a haven for misfits and lost souls, of which I was one.

That first evening, I was waiting outside on the steps for Gamma to finish, lifting the plant pots to free the woodlice, when I heard a tapping sound coming from above. I looked up to see a single dormer window in the roof, its frame painted yellow, and a face hovering there behind the glass. It was so unexpected that I nearly dropped the pot. The face was so still, I thought it was in fact a vase or some other ornament. It observed me with great intent, like a cat on the lip of a goldfish bowl.

Gamma came out. I collected my bike and we made our way down the lawn. When I glanced behind me, the pane was empty.

'What's on the third floor?' I asked.

'Where?'

'At the top of the house. Someone's up there. They saw me.'

Gamma sighed. 'As God is my witness, Birdie, I swear you go *looking* for trouble.'

'No, I don't.'

The air vibrated with insects. Against the gloaming sky, the silhouettes of trees were blacker than black. A bat flickered like a dying wick, ahead of us then gone.

'It'll be Maurice,' she said. The name rang a bell. 'Their son.'

'They have a son?'

'You knew that.'

I supposed I had, but I preferred not to know it. I envied Maurice before I had even spoken to him. 'She's keeping him at home over the summer,' said Gamma. 'He's been having some trouble with the local children.'

'With those boys you were talking about?'

She hesitated. 'At church?' I reminded her. 'That family of wolves.'

'Never you mind, little bird.'

'Was it the one with the shaved head, like Betty said?' I tried to think if I had ever seen him at school. Maybe once or twice. Tidy Frida had said he hardly went.

'That's Mrs Mackey to you.'

'What did he do to him?'

Gamma said that was enough now, we were best off staying out of it. Were the Maguires evil? I wanted to know. 'Nobody's evil,' she said.

'What, no one? Ever? Not even thieves and murderers?'

She said, 'It's more complicated than that, you'll understand when you're older. Sometimes' – and she said this last part tiredly, as if it wasn't what she meant to say at all but something was needed to put me off – 'boys will be boys.'

The phrase stayed in my mind, past the church and through the terraces, past the houses with the bicycles thrown upside down in the yards, past the unlit windows of the Maguire place: *Boys will be boys*. I didn't have any friends who were boys. I thought about the yellow dormer, the fear that had seemed to come from behind it, within it, and what could be so bad about these Maguires that made everyone take against them. I decided to pity them, and took pride in that pity. Gamma and I found the best in people. We didn't have much but we did have that, and it made us richer. It was a good, warm feeling.

∾

The next time we were at the house, I waited until I was alone then ventured up to the attic. There I found an empty passage, silent but for a fly pestering a cobweb in the light-shade, and at the end of it a shut door. The door worried me slightly, in a pleasurable way.

I went to it and knocked. A voice replied, 'Mother?' I said, 'No, it's me,' as if we knew each other, or that the meeting had been expected, and accordingly he said, a touch impatiently, 'Come on in, then.' The door opened easily. Inside, the room was dim. There was a bloodlike glow because the curtains were red. It was odd seeing the window from this side, a bent, impossible perspective, like looking out from the interior of a dolls' house. I made out chunks of furniture, an imposing wardrobe, a rug, shelves with various objects on them (a steam train, a stack of funnies), and on the bed the outline of a boy.

'What's your name?' asked the boy.

'Bridget,' I said into the red. 'But my friends call me Birdie.'

'Oh,' he said. 'Where's your mother?'

I thought he meant Gamma. 'She's not my mother. She's my grandmother.'

'But where is she?' he said again. 'Your mother, I mean.'

I wasn't sure how to answer the question. 'She doesn't live with us,' I said.

'Doesn't she want to?'

'I suppose not.' There was nothing more to say.

'Would you close the door, please?' he asked. I did, but with a strange domino effect it triggered in me an urge to open the window. 'Don't,' he said, when I went to.

'Why? It's dark.' I parted the curtains and undid the catch. A shaft of sunlight struck the rug, which I saw was decorated with many small monkeys, each hanging off the tail of the one above. I recognized Maurice from Friday assemblies, one of Miss Tilly's class, a couple of years older than me, but meek-looking. His hair was as neat as a conker and his shirt and trousers were pressed. But he had a punched eye that was fading to green and his hands shook when he spoke.

'I told Mother I fell over,' he explained, crossing his arms. 'I always tell her that. She doesn't believe me, of course. Always runs straight to Mr Fortescue. She knows I've been getting it but she can't prove who from and I'm not about to tell her. If I do, they'll only come at me harder. "*Nothing worse than a grass, Maurice Minor.*" Now I'm stuck here every day, she won't let me out of her sight.'

'What happened?' I said.

His shoulders were as round as a spoon. I remembered the duck on the lake that never got to the bread in time. 'He's got a knife. A proper one. With a leather hilt.'

'Who has?'

I heard him swallow. It was a damp, mechanical sound. 'Ron Maguire,' he said. 'He's been going at me for months now. Waits for me after school by the rec then follows me through the woods so he can rough me up. He's never used it – the knife. Just threatens me with it. Says if I rat on him, he'll cut me.'

'You should go to the police.'

Maurice snorted. 'What are they going to do about it?'

'They'll help.'

'No, they won't,' he said. 'Not fast enough anyway. He'll get me first. Worse.'

'Not if you're here.'

'D'you want to bet?'

Neither of us spoke. Then I said, 'So what will you do?'

He pouted, as if the query were pointless. 'Keep quiet. What else can I do? Maybe they'll forget me by September. Get to picking on someone else.' He eyed me. 'You should stay away from them too.'

'That's OK,' I said. 'I've never had anything to do with them.'

He glanced at the monkeys. 'You will,' he said quietly. 'They're wicked.'

'Gamma says no one's completely wicked.'

His solemn face turned to mine. 'They are,' he said. 'You wait and see.'

∞

Maurice and I made friends. Gamma let me off cleaning early so we could play, and at weekends I visited alone, spending long, happy Saturdays exploring the garden, hanging upside down from the dark, smooth branches of the copper beech tree and making dens of moss in a hollow in its trunk. We set up snakes and ladders on the lawn while clouds made shapes in the sky above us, drifting slowly, changing forms as they went, from horses to cowboys to ocean liners. We took tea with the Fairfaxes, as I had in my dreams, dishes I had never tried like salmon and tinned asparagus, served not under a cloche but on plates with tiny blue dragons chasing round the rims. Maurice picked flowers and gave them to me with a kiss.

'I've never had a friend like you, Birdie,' he said. 'A best friend. Promise me we'll always be each other's?'

We linked our little fingers. 'I promise,' I said.

Summer came to an end. The sun dimmed his light; leaves

dried and changed colour on the trees. Gamma and I were walking home one night after work when she said to me, 'I'm sorry she's not like that.'

It took me a second to realize whom she was talking about.

'I ask myself,' said Gamma, 'was it something I did? Or didn't do. I don't know.'

I felt embarrassed. Gamma never talked about Mary.

'It's all right,' I said. I was riding my bike so slowly I could hardly keep balance; the yarn mop skewed across my lap as I weaved from one side of the road to the other.

'You'd rather stay there,' she said, 'with them. I couldn't blame you if you did.'

'No, I wouldn't.' And in saying it aloud, I knew it to be true. For all I admired the Fairfaxes' world, I would never have swapped it for our own. There were many things I could have said to Gamma in that moment but I was too self-conscious to say them. I thought how frail she looked. How she struggled in lifting the pail, how her back ached, how she wheezed when she got out of a chair. I loved her. I didn't want her to be old.

Mary had a way of doing this. Her presence – her absence – wheeled back on us every once in a while, and each time Gamma sensed it coming. She'd walk into a room and stop abruptly, reminded of something she must have forgotten, a vague look taking her over, of sadness and remembering, then the next day Mary came knocking for money or food or whatever else we didn't have enough of. Or Gamma would merely talk about her, not even by name, like now, and we both knew that somehow we had summoned her.

Still, neither of us could have expected what was waiting for us by the gate when we got back. 'What's this?' said Gamma, when the gate got stuck. 'Birdie? Can you see?'

It was a wicker basket shrouded in cloth. I thought at first it was apples under a tea towel. But then it moved, a sudden, sharp stroke like a swimmer on his back.

Gamma lifted the basket and took it inside. The electricity wasn't working so I lit a candle while Gamma set the basket on the table. It was mewling now. I thought it was not apples but kittens and felt excited but also quite sick. She peeled the coverings back.

A tiny human face gazed up at us. The head was no bigger than one of the stolen oranges from the greengrocer's shop. She had shining eyes, a tiny nose, a rosebud mouth.

'It's a baby,' said Gamma.

We both stared at the baby. The baby stared at us.

There was a postcard stuck on the blankets, messily written. Gamma read it to me:

It's just a while I promise. I'll come back I promise. I can't now. Sorry. Your Mary.

Gamma put down the note and picked up the baby. Its screwed-up face frowned at her. The blankets smelt terrible.

'Poor love,' said Gamma, and held her cheek to cheek.

'Is she my sister?' I said. But I knew that she was.

Gamma passed her to me. Her hair was gold. She felt like a warm loaf of bread. In the corner of one of the blankets was a label, on which letters were stitched: GOD'S PROVIDENCE.

'That's what we'll call her,' said Gamma.

5

The bus chuffed along, shushing and spitting each time it came to a stop, pulling people on and coughing them out. I never took my eyes off James Maguire. I drank in every detail of the way he moved, the pale horseshoe of his lower face tilted to the window, the swamp-green jacket which was rucked up against the seat, the back of his hair cut straight and neat to the neck and the trio of small moles under the ear, arranged like Orion's Belt.

He was restless and fidgety. He dug around in his jeans pocket. The girl spoke quietly to him then he came up empty from his pockets and took a stick of chewing gum off her, which he unwrapped with slender fingers. I saw the muscle in his cheek as he masticated the gum, grinding, grinding, and thought of shoving his skull into the kerb.

'... plain stupid,' the dark-haired girl was saying. 'If she wanted to do that she'd have gone off ... Seven to one, I told her it was ... the wake-up had nothing to do with it ...' Then something about strawberries and the cost of wallpaper, but that couldn't be right.

He kept saying, 'huh,' and 'yeh,' and 'mebbe,' but never turning to her. I thought about how that thin, mean voice with its pecked-out syllables had been the last that Providence had heard. There had been no music, no chatter of birds, no rhythm of water flowing – just his clipped, cold intonation, and I'd never know for sure what he'd said.

Anyone could see that the dark-haired girl wanted his attention. I worried for her. What was she doing with him? Didn't she know what he'd done? Didn't she know that he attacked young women; he'd done it once and he'd do it again? But he seemed oddly uninterested in her, and the girl anyway more fluent and in control than he. I thought that even if the youngest Maguire planned to harm this person, he'd never manage it, because I would harm him first.

The bus filled up. Teenagers pushed past on their way to the back. A baby started crying, strapped into a pushchair, its face wrinkled and puce. The mother offered it a Farley's Rusk, which it grabbed off her and threw between the wheels. The mother got the baby out and held it struggling over one arm while she collapsed the pushchair with difficulty. She looked bewildered, as though she didn't understand what she was doing or how on earth she had got here, or what else she could do that could improve the situation for either of them. I saw myself with Joe in the supermarket soon after we'd brought him home, belting him into a trolley while he howled into a new hour about a trouble I could not cure. I'd looked at him and thought, *who are you? I really have no idea who you are.*

The dark-haired girl was talking. I tried to tune in to what she was saying but it was hard. She'd given up facing him now, and was turning the clothes bundle in her lap, looking down at it, so her words kept getting lost in her chest. I heard the name Victoria; she said it a few times and he'd nod when she did, in recognition or approval. I thought Victoria must be a friend of his, or theirs, someone they were on their way to see.

I was deciding in what way this mattered to me – how hard Victoria and the dark-haired girl would be to get away from – when a woman took the aisle seat next to mine. I regretted my position by the window. Should I ask her to change? I didn't want to draw attention to myself. Equally, I had to be able to move. And as that notion entered my mind, so my fear played out in reality. The dark-haired girl pushed the bell to get off.

'Excuse me,' I muttered to the woman, who was lifting a bundle of peach-coloured knitting from her bag, messy as a jellyfish with a pair of needles sticking out of it. 'Excuse me – I have to get out.' The woman huffed and repositioned herself, making to stand but the wool was in the way and she'd only just sat down, it was inconvenient; she had to put her bag on the floor but then she couldn't get to her feet so she set it in the passage, then one of the teenagers tripped over it and fell against the mother with the baby. The dark-haired girl was getting up and Maguire going after her, that louche, couldn't-care gait as they overtook the melee and the doors hissed open and they were out, they were gone.

'Please, excuse me—'

I almost trampled the woman; I would have trampled them all. I shoved past, not minding the curses that were uttered in my wake, and made it through the doors as they were closing, but as I stepped out I was pulled back. The straps of Gamma's case were in my hands but the rest, I realized with horror, was stuck, the driver waving his fists and shouting at me, and a young man on the other side of the door inexplicably yanking the case towards him while another socked the glass to get my attention. I gripped the bag so fiercely I thought the skin would be stripped off my palms. The bus's engine rumbled. I caught the eye of the woman with the knitting and she looked back at me, blank-faced.

Suddenly I was ejected onto the road, into the hard, heavy rain, the bag a punch to my stomach. Horns blared. A cyclist beat past – 'Watch where you're going, stupid cow!'

My heart was up in my ears. I searched right and left for that green jacket, tried to see beyond the crowd, through it. There were people everywhere: they'd swallowed him.

A new string of buses pulled up. All I saw was red. Headlamps bled in the rain. I stood helpless, my hair plastered to my head, and realized I had left behind my umbrella.

∞

I found a phone box and called Catriona. She answered on the second ring.

'What is it? Where are you calling from?'

I told her. Then I asked where they had sent him.

'You know I can't tell you that.'

'Please.' I was shaking. 'It doesn't matter how much, I have to—'

'Bridget, what's going on?'

I said I'd come to her office. She gave me the address of a cafe on the Common.

'Half an hour,' she said. Then added: 'Bloody hell.'

I found the coffee shop, Checkers Café, which was more of

a greasy spoon. It was muggy inside, the tables covered in rubbery black-and-white cloths; the waitress indicated I take one by the door. I put Gamma's bag in first and clutched it like a lifeline.

The waitress came over. She wore heavy earrings that pulled at the lobes.

'What can I get for you?'

'I'm waiting for someone.'

'That mean you can't have nothing?'

'Tea,' I said, but I felt too sick even for that.

'You want to dry out in the back, lovey? We've a hand-dryer in the ladies.'

'I'm fine.'

She shrugged. 'Suit yourself.'

I took off my coat. My hair was leaking down my collar and my reflection in the window was foggy and indistinct, the eyes smudged, the mouth an expectation of where a mouth should be. I covered Gamma's case with the coat. I longed to rest my head on it and sleep until Catriona arrived so I wouldn't be conscious of the minutes it took for her to reach me, the same minutes as were simultaneously carrying him away. Images tormented me of his vanishing beyond recovery, across oceans, across deserts, through dripping jungles and sweeping steppes in his race to elude me, all of it accelerated until I saw him halfway up a mountain thousands of miles from here, in a location with an unpronounceable name, and when he reached the top he turned back briefly to look at me, smiling thinly on one side of his mouth, waved to me once and then dropped down the other side never to be seen again. I knew this was impossible. Maguire had no passport; he couldn't cross these borders. And yet it seemed even more impossible that I would ever find him now.

A TV above the counter played a soundless daytime soap. A boy with glasses was being pushed around in a park. One of the bullies chewed gum on a swing. *You'll never be one of us, Jason!* the subtitles read. Jason replied, *Wait till I tell Alison Brooks about this!*

'There you are.' Catriona sat down opposite me. She pulled off her jacket and scarf and hung them on the back of the chair. 'I took a cab in the end, tube's a nightmare.'

The waitress delivered a plate of eggs to a table by the counter. Its recipient had a copy of *Time Out* with WHY LONDON IS CRACKING UP stamped on the cover but I couldn't tell if it meant lunacy or humour.

'Coffee, please,' Catriona said to her when she brought over my tea, milky grey with the spoon still in. 'And a bacon roll. Bacon well done. Do you want anything?'

I said no. I could still smell the egg yolks.

'Best bacon butty this side of the Thames,' she said, when the waitress had gone. 'Come on, Bridget, you look awful. Eat. I'm buying. Do you mind if I smoke?'

I leant forward. 'Where's the welfare house?' I asked.

She drew a cigarette from a packet and lit it. 'What welfare house?'

'Supported accommodation. Special lodgings. Whatever they call it.'

She blew out smoke, narrowing her eyes. 'What are you doing?'

'What do you think I'm doing?'

'Something very stupid.'

The man had finished his eggs and was pretending to read *Time Out*, but he kept glancing over at us. I lowered my voice. 'I'm going to tell him I forgive him,' I said.

Catriona laughed.

'That's the only way I can draw a line under it,' I said. 'I've realized that now.'

'That's been the point of all this, has it?'

'Of what?'

'Of me.'

'Not originally,' I said. 'I've come to see it over time. It's taken time.'

She smoked for a few seconds, not saying anything. 'So you . . . ?'

'I followed him. I thought once I caught up with him I could speak to him. Only he's with someone – it put me off. They got off the bus ahead of me. I lost them.'

Catriona glanced at Gamma's bag. I kept my grip on it.

'This is all very proper of you,' she said.

'Not really. It's how I move on with my life.'

'*Have* you forgiven him?'

'Yes.'

'Despite the fact he's never confessed?'

I put my tongue into the groove behind my top front teeth, prodded the gums there and nodded. The coffee came. Catriona took time putting milk in and stirring, then slitting a sachet of sugar and tapping it in. She did all this with the cigarette hanging from her bottom lip like a knocked car exhaust. 'I'm having trouble believing that,' she said.

'Believe what you like. Just tell me where they've sent him.'

She reached for an ashtray. Jason on the TV was getting shouted at by his mother: *What more do I have to do with you?* I wondered where Alison Brooks fitted into all this.

'Can I expect a call from Tom?' asked Catriona. 'I assume you've concealed this expedition from him. Which is strange since you make it sound so innocent.' She put out the cigarette. 'You've got a lovely family there, Bridget. It's not worth sacrificing.'

'I'm not sacrificing anything. I'll be back home before they know it.'

'I should imagine Tom already knows it.' She checked her watch. 'Or he will soon. I take it you didn't drive to town. What was it then – train, coach? You'll have parked at the station, I expect. He'll easily join the dots once he discovers Maguire's been freed.'

'Tom's always supported me.'

'Only so far. He's supported you in your grief. But he wouldn't support this – whatever this is. You've got children together. Children you worked hard for—'

'That's got nothing to do with it.'

'I'd have thought that had everything to do with it. They're relying on you.'

'I could get this over with today if you told me where he is.'

The waitress returned with the bacon roll. Catriona took the top off and squirted brown sauce on it from a bottle. She took a bite and offered it to me. I shook my head.

'And then what?' she said, chewing.

I didn't answer her.

'After you've told Maguire this is all water under the bridge,' she said. 'Because that's all you're doing, isn't it? You're going to buy them a Paddington Bear and a clicky pen and go home as if nothing's happened? I'm telling you, it's not worth it.'

'You must know where he's going.' A lump dogged my throat. 'You have to.'

'What makes you think I do?'

'For God's sake, don't you owe me this?' My whisper broke. 'This is my decision, not yours. I'll pay you more money, whatever you want—'

She put the sandwich down and dabbed the corner of her mouth with a napkin.

'It's not the money.'

'But—'

'You're right,' she said, 'I do owe you. I owe you sensible advice.'

'He's gone for ever if you don't help me. It's over.'

'Then write to him.'

'Where?'

'Care of my office.' She pushed her chair back. 'I'll make sure it's forwarded.'

She put on her coat. The roll remained on the plate, a chunk taken out of it. 'I care about you, Bridget,' she said. 'I cared about you from the moment we met and you told me your story. I wanted so much to help you. And I was glad to help you, as a client. As a friend. I don't make friends in this business but I have with you and I'm glad of that. I want the best for you. Everything that's happened, you can get past it now. It won't take away the significance of it, it'll just stop it taking any more of your life. I understand, I sympathize, I do. But I said to you on the first day what I'm saying to you on the last: it's eyes on the inside, not the outside. Once they're out, they're out. I'm nothing more to do with it then. It wouldn't be safe otherwise – for him *or* you. Forget about Maguire. Spend the money on your children instead. They'll be waiting for you.'

Catriona put a note on the table and the salt shaker on top of it. 'I'll call you soon. OK?' She picked up her things and left, the door swinging shut after her.

'Everything all right, lovey?' The waitress cleared the plate and mugs and folded the money into her apron. I blinked stupidly at the vacated seat, as if the longer I looked at it the greater the likelihood she would reappear in front of me. 'Anything else for you?'

I shook my head. I groped for Gamma's bag and took it with me towards the back. A clock on the wall said 2 p.m. I'd be home before Tom. Before Wilma had a chance to give the children their tea. Something and nothing, that was life all over, today and that day and every year in between, all my design, all my yearning, all my hope and determination, what did it matter, what did fifteenth May 1970 matter, what did any of it count for when time passed and wounds scabbed and the world told you you should just get over it?

On the wall by the cubicles was a pay phone. A pile of theatre fliers sat beneath it, next to a *Yellow Pages* directory. I opened it, leafing to V. 'Victoria' was all I had. I didn't expect to find anything; it was desperation, a last-ditch attempt, going off an eavesdropped conversation and the name of a stranger.

Immediately, I saw the advert:

VIBRATO PIANO LESSONS. Learn from the best, £5/hr, nursery rhymes to 'Nocturne'!

And below that, the address of a hostel: *Queen Victoria Welfare Hostel SE1*.

I tore out the page. Outside, it stopped raining.

II

6

He'd grown accustomed to seeing the change in the weather from an up-high window in his flowery dell, a postage-stamp square of cloud and sun and pale white light, deep purple at night, but to be in it and feel it and smell it were things he'd forgot, not forgot exactly for the detail was still there, still in him, buried beneath the thickets of the years, delayed but not lost, rising notes he recognized from when he'd been a boy and the rain had smelt the same then, of a ha'penny kept too long in his pocket, but Donna said it wasn't ha'pennies any more, it was pounds and fivers, and he wasn't a boy now, he was a man.

It was true what they said, that you didn't know up from down, left from right, spin him around and tell him which way and he wouldn't know still, not a fegging clue, would likely go stumbling out into the road and that would be curtains, day one and then done, and sure they'd say after it was destined that way, he'd had a dent in him right from the start, stupid too, gone in the head, evil and dumb (what it was to be both), as evil and dumb as they come. But he'd been banged up an eight-stretch in a cell it took five seconds to circuit, five point five to be precise, two steps down one side, three down the other, back to the door where the voices came in – '*Open up, Walsh! Open up, Parker! Open up, Maguire!*' – then slop out in the troughs and back to his bunk for a diet can of porridge, an ounce of sugar if he was lucky, trapped in the walls and the hours and the fug of his brain, in the haze of weed and the waste of his life, slow and slack and forever stopped still, yet here it was everything everywhere, all in a hurry in a place too busy, too many, lights changing and rain chucking and the world tremendous and too much.

The bus had been OK but the Underground station wasn't. Donna put him by the big mouth of the stairs while she went to buy tickets. He stood in the middle of bodies rushing past. There were a lot of faces. Some were old and some were young. None of them looked at him. He had got used to being looked at, every move he made measured and monitored, and it had always sat uneasy with him that they should want to watch so closely the thing they claimed to despise. An hour ago, he'd been let out. There must be part of the screws that thought of it like that, how close it ran to unchaining a beast and letting it rampage through the city streets with no way of knowing if it would rip out a man's throat or if it would put on a suit and go to work. He had a longing for the glimpse of daylight he'd had to stand on a small table to meet, run through with bars but no less a promise for that – a promise of what? The outside. Well, here he was with the fruits of that promise and they hung bloated and strange. He felt the floor ride away from him. Someone crashed into him. He said sorry to a stranger who couldn't care less, and searched the throng for Floyd but of course he was not there.

He couldn't see Donna. Had she told him to wait by the stairs, or meet by the machines? He couldn't think which. Signs pointed to exits and tunnels. A map of tangled coloured lines hurt his eyes. He got shunted along in the tide of people then there was another stairway – the same, or different? – and flapping plastic barriers that opened and closed by themselves and someone was cursing him – 'Bloody move it, mate, are you coming or going?' He didn't know. His tooth ached. It had ached since Friday. Smiley said it was gate fever, the apprehension of going out. That was when the body came at you with all its complaints, which was a shock because you'd been in a state of limbo in there, a numb sort of limbo, where it wasn't in your interests to feel very much at all.

He thought he saw Donna's red shirt but it turned out to be someone else. '*Git orn with it, yew idle bastard, git a move orn!*' Blood pounded in his head. '*Lick sharp, yew waste of space, yew lazy swine, I'll have my boot in your arse 'less yew hurry yewself along!*' He was scared of the clipping open-and-shut gateways and pushed his way through the horde, carried towards a shaft of light that poured from the sky, and the crowds were hurrying up and down stairs, over the litter of fag-ends and stomped-in chewing gum, heels clattering, bags thumping. He got a grip on the rail and dragged himself up.

Maybe Donna had left without him. It was impossible to tell. He'd never be able to tell. If it was bad down there then it was worse on the street, no order to it, mayhem, bodies crossing over so fast he couldn't keep up, he didn't see how they did not fall into each other. '*Smarten your tie, iron your shirt, do as I say, yew shower of sods! It's bastards like yew'll turn a good officer bad—*' He saw the faces of the landing screws on passers-by, saw his Principal Officer with his little clipped moustache that curled up at the edges and his hair sticking up straight like a stiff yard brush. Nothing seemed real. Nothing was solid. He put a hand on a bollard and his hand went through it. Drumsticks had said it'd be like this. You thought you'd got away with the long, drab years, thought you'd kept your wits intact reminding yourself of the good things outside, bonfires and horses and autumn leaves, but it turned out you hadn't, you were just toppling along with everyone else on the high wire between sanity and madness, all of you the same from high to low, from the nonces to the FP merchants to the petty thieves with their walk-on parts – and to him, the worst of the lot – doing your bird just the same whatever you were in for. Outside was meant to be sanity and inside was meant to be madness but it was the other way round.

He had a feeling like pins and needles. His legs threatened to give way. Donna had his things, all he had, without them he was invisible. He felt cold, craving the blanket on his bunk and the mumbling fat pigeons on the window ledge, the bare calm walls, the easy predictable voices on the radio that Drumsticks had left behind when he went, the guarantee of the best dog-end in his stash for after meals, the sureness of the allocated hours, the heavy turn of a key in a lock and whump of doors and men coming to life and the cry that heralded the start of the day: '*Rise and shine, Maguire!*' He did not know how to find his way back. That place anyway would never have him now.

∾

Dad, came the word, came the name, not a word he'd spoken or ever thought anything of, but it arrived in that moment for him, from a person's mouth he hardly knew. 'Dad, over here! – Dad!

Where did you go?' She took his hand. Hers was sweaty but cool. They sat in a shop doorway. The windows were filled with expensive leather bags and slithery belts coiled up like liquorice. 'What happened? Are you OK?' She looked upset, like she thought he'd been trying to run away from her. His mouth was parched and he couldn't speak. He wanted his fags but he couldn't remember where he'd put them.

'Here,' she said, lighting one and passing it to him. Porter had given him a pack on the way out. It was a long time since he'd had a proper one. He'd got used to his rake-ups, his collection of butts that he'd twist the remnants out of to roll a new one. Smoking was the best part of the day. The expressions on certain evenings of the men around him, when the light was just right, the planes of their faces lit by a steady burn.

He smoked for a bit and felt better. He felt better with his civvies on his lap, the clothes he'd come in with all those years ago, the only bits left of the boy he'd been. He felt silly in the jeans Donna had sent him. She'd said in her note they were 'rad'; she'd wanted something new for him to wear on his way out, but he didn't know why they had cuts and tears in them. He thought maybe the screws had hacked them as a joke.

'Sorry,' he said.

'It's all right,' she said. She had chunky rings on her fingers. The one on her thumb was half an inch long and came up to the knuckle. 'I didn't know where you were. Don't go off like that again, Dad.' She said that word too much. 'Stay with me.'

'I couldn't find you.'

'Just don't wander off. Stay where you are. Then I can find you.'

There was a bloke on the kerb outside Woolworths holding a placard that read: JESUS IS COMING. REPENT YOUR SINS! JUDGEMENT IS NIGH!

Donna said, 'We can walk there instead if that's better.' He felt her eyes on him as he sucked the last of the fag and posted it through the grills of a drain by his feet.

'If you like,' he said.

He felt like a child and she his mother. They'd tried to teach him how to be with her. Workshops instructing him how to play with her favourite toys when she was small, slot train tracks together, brush a dolly's hair, do a game of Connect 4 so when she visited he wouldn't just be sitting there not knowing what to say.

'*Poor girl growing up without her daddy, yew make me sick to my stummick, yew do.*'

He'd written her letters. Started doing it when he'd talked to the psychs. They'd said it would help. '*Take your time and think what to say.*' He'd had so much time he didn't know what to do with it. He'd had so much to say he didn't know where to start. There'd been scores, maybe hundreds of letters, some sent, some not. He'd no idea if she had read them, or if Rita had torn them up. She must have read them, if she was here.

'Let me carry that,' she said.

'No.'

'It's heavy.'

'Nah it's not.'

'You shouldn't have to carry it.'

'I want to.'

'Why?' She tried to take the package off him.

'I said I —ing want to, all right?' he said, sharp enough for her to back off and put her hands in her lap. He felt straightaway guilty.

'I didn't mean that,' he said. 'Just.'

Just what? Just he was the man she'd been told over and over he was. Frequently he believed he wasn't that man. Other times he was that man and there was no escaping that fact when he was stuck in his cage on his own with all the hours in the world and every regret and bitterness this life had to offer, stuck in the Before and After, thinking he could get closer to God but God knew what he'd done and wherever he went in his mind God followed him. Too many days to think and feel, or not feel, because it wasn't in him to do that, and he started to wonder if there might be a bit missing, the psychs had known it and so had he, a vital bit everyone else had but not him, he was lacking the piece that could've made him good but no matter how he searched for it, it wasn't there to find.

They crossed the street, past the man with his poster, who shouted after him but he didn't hear what. 'Do you know the way?' he asked her, contrite now. She said yes but didn't turn round, and he had to move swiftly to keep up with her for she had long legs like her mother and her stride was substantial. He marvelled at her height and elegance, the definiteness of her movements and the luxury of her hair, which was drawn into a plait as thick as a rolling pin with a waxy sheen on its surface, iridescent almost. It put him in mind of certain birds' wings. Water birds. Blues and purples, the underside of the wing. He couldn't recall their names. The image got mixed in with summers spent in the canal among the narrowboats – he remembered what those were called, all right: *Contessa*, *Shore Thing*, *Forget-Me-Knot* – and Floyd swimming by him, his bare back shining at dusk.

Donna didn't talk to him the whole walk there. When finally they reached the address she seemed to have wiped her features clear. She opened her purse and took out a chit and looked up at the building, squinting. 'Here we are then. Shall we go in?'

He'd heard about the doss-houses with the landladies cramming twelve men in a room, taking their last pennies off them for the pleasure of living like swine. '*They're all the bleedin' same*,' Drumsticks had warned. He could see his friend now, sitting on the wall in the exercise yard, elbows on his knees, chewing a Capstan, the old grey shiv mark sliced through his eyebrow. '*Opportunists, every —ing one of 'em. Think you deserve dignity, Jimbob? Think you deserve respect? Course you —ing don't. Let 'em say what they want but they're no bleedin' better. Here or there we're the odd men out. Society don't want us. They'll make the right noises. Get you your voucher, write you your letter, send you onto the Welfare. Tell you you're getting on, going straight. But you'll see. Someone's always waiting for you to trip up and if you don't they'll rig a rope to make sure you do. They're always waiting to bring you back.*'

'Dad?'

But he was looking behind him, down the street, past the shopfronts. A wiry dog was sniffing a drainpipe. Pigeons scattered. The rain resumed its thin, relentless fall.

He'd felt it on the bus and he felt it again now. Everyone knew the coppers trailed you for a bit when you got out. They thought the second you passed the gates you'd be back in the game, seeing through the job you'd cooked for a decade, plotting it in the yard or over grub or falling in for showers, where better to fix up and learn your contacts than in prison with the best of them? He'd never had one of those minds though. Kip had got enough for both of them, for all of them, and it wasn't a grace, it was a curse.

What was it, then, this sense of being followed?

In his memory, he turned down the shady path that ran behind Providence's house. Sunshine made green pools beneath the leaves. She and her sister waved to him.

'Dad,' said Donna, again. 'What is it?'

He returned to her. 'I got lost in my head. That's all. I got lost in my head.'

She took his arm. It sent a shiver through him.

'You're hungry,' she said, as he pulled away. 'You haven't eaten. Let's go.'

He looked up at the entrance to the building. The facade was stained with rivulets of damp that trickled bleakly down the stone. Queen Victoria was carved in profile, cut out of a large half-circle above the door. Bird shit covered her crown. They went inside.

7

HM Prison Grendon, Buckinghamshire
Group therapy meeting, 1977

15 August
James but people call me Jimmy. In for killing a girl. I dunno, they said I'd get something out of it. Freedoms I'd not get elsewhere. Grendon's not like other places, they said. The system's —ed but Grendon ain't, it's new ideas, even the screws are all right, they'll treat you like humans not animals, they won't slam you up like they do in the regular nicks. You've got to talk about your problems, they said. Come to terms with your offence so it ain't on your brain. What's that s'posed to mean? I'm to sit round here talking with you lot but what good's —ing talking gunna do me? It *weren't my —ing offence*, do you hear? It were someone else's and he's free as a bird. Course you bleedin' don't. You believe what you want, mate, I don't care about that. I'm past caring. I've told this story till I choke on it and everyone I tell it to's the same, you all think you know better. But you dunno my life. You dunno who I am.

I should tell you then. A bunch of —ing rapists and psychopaths and —ing pervert nonces, what use's your opinion? Then there's the mind-tapper over there writing it down like that's gunna solve my problems. You call this place revolutionary but it ain't no —ing revolution, you're the same as the rest of them only it makes you sleep better at night thinking you're helping us sods not just sliding the bolts. Go on then, tick your —ing boxes, put me in your —ing classifications then feel like you've done me right. All this about trying to help me's a waste of time, none of you's tried to help me. You just want to reassure yourselves I fit the mould so there won't be nothing about me that frights you no more. I know the deal. All this starts in childhood, don't it? Show me a crook with a happy youth and I'll show you a pig with wings. I dunno if that made me who I am, you be the judge, you're good at that. Who —ing minds anyway? I'm done talking. Talking don't change a thing.

28 August

I ain't guilty of what they say I did. But I were there. I watched it happen, I didn't stop it. I've got to live with that fact and that's how it should be, it's the price I've got to pay, there's no going back and doing things differently. I told them so in my letter here, I admitted my part in it. Said I were with him and I let him do it. They called me an *exceptional case*. What were it now? *We won't straighten you. You'll do that for yourself.*

The night I got sent down for killing her, I cried like a baby. I cried for six months —ing straight. There were nothing that made me feel no better but that it were up to me when I ended it. Only the screws didn't want that for me. Not for pity, no – just it's a cop-out, ain't it, an early exit. They knew I had it in me so they took away my braces and blades but still the —ing turnkey at Bedford said each night he banged me up, 'If you don't do it yourself, Maguire, I'll come down 'ere and do it for you.' Stick that in your paperwork, son. What it's like to expect you'll get your throat slit if not by the smackhead sharing your cell but the bloke that's meant to be guarding it.

Here they'll call me in the doctor's office; they'll say, 'Sit down, James, tell me how you're —ing feeling' – course they don't swear, they don't —ing smoke neither, they probably don't take a shit 'less it's on the Queen's lavatory – and they're all, 'Are you depressed? Why d'you think that is?' Call themselves medical people, it's a —ing joke, why'd they —ing reckon? They give me sleeping draughts which is just as well with the racket in the dormitory, it's like borstal all over again, snoring and wanking and some Scouse —ing psycho pounding the walls till morning 'cause he's stuck in his thick fat murdering skull and he can't get out. I want my own room but they say I can't have one 'cause I'm an *active suicide risk*, they think the second I'm alone I'll top and maybe I will, I haven't decided. I don't see how it makes a difference one way or the other. Having it in my pocket, though, that's what gets me through. Thinking no matter how bad things get I've always got a way out, you know. I can always —ing finish it.

Exeter for a year then Bedford for six. Exeter were grim but Bedford were worse. Proper frightening Victorian bang-up. Bare walls, bare floor, cold slate, the smell of piss and soap. An English jail. The minute the sweat-box dropped me there I thought I can't —ing do it, I can't —ing stick it, but stick it I did and every one of those two thousand one hundred and eleven days were a living —ing nightmare.

To society it's what I deserve. No more or less than the

consequence I cut out for myself. Ain't that right? There'll be a girl in your family. Sister? Daughter? Niece? Same age Providence was. You'll picture her with me. All you do that, the screws do it too no matter what they tell you 'bout how here it's gunna be different, it —ing ain't, they're thinking the same, about that girl of theirs getting done, that's why they want me dead. Only they don't want me to —ing do it: they want to do it themselves.

I let her be killed. But I weren't the one that killed her.

It were *him*.

Floyd had it in for her all along. *He* did. I'll find him when I get out, swear to God it'll be the first —ing thing I do. Then they'll see the mistake they all made – the screws, the courts, the —ing judiciary. I've played out in my mind how it goes seeing him again. So many times, I have. It starts with him saying sorry. Then thank you. Sorry and thank you, Jim, for this thing I carried for him. Years I carried it while he was off living his life and no one —ing believed me. Then I worry he won't say these things, or he's gone away or I can't find him, then I'll never know what it is he meant to tell me, and this seems to me the worst outcome. But how could all of you understand a dream like that?

9 September

Mother never around, father bashed me up. That's about the height of it. Neglect, addiction, drug-taking, crime. I can go on if you want. I can go on all —ing day.

I hardly knew the old Mum. She had various jobs back then. Rag factory, shoe shop, charlady. Some days ended and she never came back. The Mister were off driving lorries or in the pub geeing up coppers. I were one of four brothers. Kip were the biggest then Alf then Ron then me. Kip were the one who cared about me. He looked after me 'cause I were the littlest. He used to disappear when I were a kid, off then back, off then back, half the time I didn't know where. Borstals, remand homes, detention centres, all that. Sometimes to the foster families when Mother Maeve were in a state. Kip said, 'Don't worry, Jimmo, I'm fixed for a job, we'll have a bit o' brass after.' But I didn't want a bit of brass, I only wanted him. His heart were in a good place. All Kip were doing was trying to get life going for us. There were no other way open to him of doing it than that.

When she were at home she were mostly in her bed. Pissed or dosed or crying. She passed out with her clothes still on from the shoe shop and the badge she had on when she worked there – it said, *Maeve, Here to Help*, and I thought how —ing funny it were that it said that. She always left her lace-ups lined up real neat in a row on the floor, the shoes were the smartest things she owned. She brought them back from the shop in fancy —ing boxes with tissue paper in. Her boss were a bloke called Houlihan. Kip called him Shoulihan. I asked Kip how she paid for the shoes and he said I knew where she went at night, didn't I? I were eight, I didn't know —ing nothing but what he told me. He said, 'She's doing nice things for Shoulihan, Jim, don't you get it? She puts the tongues in the greaser boots for him.' He were sitting on the stairs reading a *News of the World* and puffing his rake-ups and the walls were dark as water 'cause the leccy were off. I can see it now, how the smoke went up to the ceiling in a funnel over the pages.

Kip were twenty then. Maybe twenty-one. Not long back from his first spell in prison, an adult one, a proper hard-men's jail. It were for shop-breaking. That's what did it, that's round the time when it started – this feeling I had that I weren't real no more. Not that – I dunno – I can't explain, this feeling I had like I were fading away. Like no one could see me no more so I didn't —ing matter, nothing —ing mattered. I always thought when I turned into a man I'd have life sorted, it'd get better, but that didn't come true for Kip so I guessed it weren't coming true for me neither. I guessed getting nicked weren't something that happened to boys before they grew up but men before they grew up and it'd happen to us for the rest of our —ing lives.

What Kip said about the greaser boots, that were a puzzle in a young boy's mind. I got this idea in my head I couldn't shake off. Some — in school called me a bastard and it got me thinking, like it were right —ing screwing with my head – how I didn't look nothing like the Mister. I didn't look nothing like Kip or my brothers. They were all dead spits of each other with sticky-out ears and hair like creosote – 'cept for Ron; he had a shaved head – which the older ones slicked back with margarine. People said to Mother Maeve, that one's an ugly duckling, ain't he? Kip said they just meant I looked different. I looked up bastard in Alf's dictionary and there it were in black and white, what I'd known all along. *Born of parents not married to each other, illegitimate.* I'd seen my name written down on letters from the social – *James I. Maguire.* I always thought illegitimate was what the 'I' stood for. Kip said, 'It's Isaac, idiot.' Then he said it could also be Idiot.

My brothers didn't have middle names. I came to imagining

Isaac were a code. A secret message, like. Mother Maeve's way of telling me my real dad's name. I made it up how Isaac'd been a hero in the Great War. An American airman, —ing Dan Dare or some —ing nonsense. It made everything make sense. How Mother Maeve didn't like me. How the Mister were a thug to us all but he were worst by far to me, and I reckoned each time he walloped me he were actually thinking about walloping that shithouse Yankee wife-thief who'd surely been decent and good 'cause that was what I intended to be and what I thought I had inside me. I weren't a thrasher like the Mister. I weren't a drunk. I weren't a bully or a raper. I didn't smash up a man in an alley 'cause he looked at me wrong. I'd never flogged a boy till his eye burst open then told him it were his own —ing fault 'cause he should've been —ing well looking where he were —ing well going and if that weren't how I remembered it then there were ways to remind me. Isaac were it: he were my real father and one day he'd come back. I saw the old Mum weep and booze and fall on her arse and all I could think were, why'd you have to drive him away?

She let things slip. She said I were just like him and both of us knew she didn't mean the Mister. 'Hot-headed' were the word she used. It were the only word I had of him. I didn't see hot-headed as bad. Only after Providence did they tell me it were my problem. That same fever I get in my brain when I've let events run away from me. When I've lost control of what I know is the right thing to do. I do know the difference.

∽

Dear Donna. I hope you dont mind me writing to you. Today you came to see me. You had a red dress on and red shoes. Your shoes put me in mind of apples at the grocers all shiny in their boxes. Do you like apples? I dont know this about you. There are lots of things I want to ask you when I see you but I cant seem to say them when your infront of me. Like how I imagined you before we met. I did. You were a secret I had that no one else knew about and when I thought of you I felt happy. I hope you can read my writing.

༄

22 September
Old as time, ain't it? Daddy never loved him. First —ing plea in the book. 'S where all the great tragedies start. Thing about tragedies though is they repeat themselves. The cycle keeps going, don't it, you can't break it and before you know it you've got the same —ing problem in front of you that you were in. That's why whatever my daughter thinks about me, she can't be in doubt about that. That's one thing she has to know whether she wants to or not. She's six now. I ain't been around for a single —ing week of it. I started writing her letters. I dunno if she's getting them. Depends how her mother feels about it, I s'pose. It don't matter if she gets them or not, they don't say much important.

28 September
Funny how you all want to talk about Floyd. Years I've been saying it and no one's turned their —ing heads then all of a

sudden he's a person of interest. Some screw chats me up yesterday, all matey-like, comes in and sits on my bunk like we're best —ing pals, he says, 'How goes it, Jimmy, you must be flipping your lid over that feller that got you here.' So I say yeh, what of it, I've been flipping eight years but no one's been fussed, if you're so —ing bothered now why'n't you go out there and find him yourself?

They're always prodding me about him. How's it gunna do me any —ing good dragging him out when all I want's to have him gone? But it's Floyd this and Floyd that, tell us, Jim, go on – I know they're taking the piss like you are now. It's a damn sight less of a piss-take when you're banged up for a crime that weren't yours, knowing the person that did it never saw so much as the inside of a —ing Law car.

I met him round the time Kip got done for that shop-break. He were there one day kicking a ball down the road. That —s with my head, you know. Always thinking that's the bit I went wrong, that's the bit I could go back to and find that small me and shake him and say, *See him, that fair-haired one? Stay —ing off him, whatever you do, just stay —ing off him*, but it's pointless thinking that. Like that screw said yesterday, what's done is done. I were nine when Floyd turned up. I were walking to school one morning when he came up next to me, like he were saying, I'm here now, we're friends, that's how it'll be. He had light hair, not like my brothers, like me. His bag were on a long strap, banging against his knees. Strange what sticks in the mind. First thing he said were, 'Stuff me, your shirt's gone red,' and I were narked 'cause I knew the cuts'd bust open and the teachers'd see and it were easier then if I didn't go. The Mister'd given me a lashing in the night. Not the first time nor the last. He did it when he were oiled, clomp upstairs mad as a hornets' nest and what I remember is the sound his belt made when it came out of its loops, it were like boat sails flapping in a wind. Alf told us he'd been —ed over by an associate, that's why he'd the hump. At breakfast Ron found a cut-off ear wrapped in tin foil in the freezer. The ear looked like a conch. The Mister fried it up in a frying pan and made us watch him eat it. He said, 'You be my witness, Jim, now I'll hear everything that traitor says about me.' Mother Maeve sat in her dressing gown and a pair of shoes off that Shoulihan bloke, smoking her —ing Players, doing —ing nothing. She saw my blood and she didn't do nothing.

Nah, I didn't think Floyd were messed up from the off. Why would I? He were a normal kid as far as I could see and I knew enough mess-ups to tell them apart. He were the first person since Kip that gave a — about me. That were worth getting to know, weren't it? That screw said hindsight's a valuable thing. It don't make me feel valuable.

∾

4 October
Providence. I never came across that name before or since. I thought it were the dumbest name I ever heard. All my people had short hard — you names and hers were up and down and rolling like a song. I were ten when our paths crossed. Just back from a Foster place in the Midlands. I did it on purpose, all that. Made myself bad so they'd send me home. I wanted to be with

Kip, wherever he were, free or banged up, if I were with him I'd be all right. But most times he weren't back there anyway, he were off behind bars. I thought if I made trouble they'd put me behind bars too, with him. I kept hoping. Dunno why. After a while I weren't trying to be bad no more, it were just what I was.

Once I said to her, what's that mean then? Your name. She said it were to do with God. How God's guidance pours out the heavens and shows you what you're s'posed to be doing and where you're s'posed to be and if you've gone wrong it'll right you. Only righting I've had's been —ing Misters and screws and Governors and —ing pigs with —ing truncheons locking me in —ing body belts. I trusted Providence though so I'm waiting for it. I'm waiting but it never comes. I don't want to speak about her now.

10 November
They said I had to participate or I can sling my hook back to Bedford. What do they want me to say then? What d'you want me to say? Wind the clock back, take a good hard look, get to the nuts and bolts of it, well what the — else've I been doing all these years but winding the clock and taking a look and getting to the —ing bolts and all it does is make it worse. Talking about it makes me sad. Makes me depressed. It gets in here then I can't get it out again, stuck in me like a —ing bug, eating me up. One day it's this, next day it's that, forget the —ing schizos, it's this place that can't make up its mind. Screws saying one minute move on, time to get ahead now, get you better for when you're out, then saying nah, actually, you

can't —ing do that till you've dug it up again. I don't see how it's anyone's business here what happened to her but my own.

14 November

It were summer. Always summer in my mind. There must've been times that weren't summer but I can't remember them now. When I think of Providence it starts off warm and light, like it were back then, and it's nice but I know the heat's going and the cold's coming. I want to pull the sun right back from where he's sinking and make him stay.

Kip were home that time so everything were bright. Him and Ron and Floyd and me'd gone out the village to get money off some bloke. We were walking back on the road when Kip and Ron had a fall-out. It were always the same fight. Kip saying with the payment he'd go straight from now on, get out of this place and take me with him, and even though I'd heard it before I still liked hearing it. But Ron said he'd never, he were being a traitor by saying that, when'd he realize this were us, it were our blood, our —ing brotherhood, we were chips off the old block. That were the Mister all over, a —ing block, a —ing rock I couldn't get past.

Ron got the needle. Floyd said chase him. Kip said leave him. Soon we couldn't see him no more. Kip said did I believe him, about us getting out? I believed he wanted it but not that it'd happen. Maybe that were enough, him wanting it, maybe that were all he were asking. Floyd gave me a shove and I thought he weren't buying it neither, but he didn't mean that, he meant the girls. There were two of them ahead of us in the lane. One were tall and dressed like a boy. The other were a kid. The kid had skin like glass, it were so pale I could see right through it. Ron were further up, sitting on the field stile. The older girl were talking to him. Then the see-through girl looked our way and said, 'They're coming' – like she'd known all along we would, and her voice weren't usual, it were a long way away, a weird sort of echoing voice like she were calling me from way off down a tunnel.

Some nights I still hear her calling me. Half there and half not. I see her on the back porch of her house, calling me and I want to follow her. When I tune into it, it scares off.

Ron were down off the stile with this great big knife in his hand. I said, 'Where the — did you get that?' But I knew all right where he got it. None of us moved a muscle, Ron and Kip and me and Floyd and the girls, the one like a boy and the see-through one, and there were someone else too, there in my memory, in the field behind Ron – a scarecrow made out of wood. We used to call him the Sunshine Man. He were a cut-out board, life-size with a scrappy hat and his trousers too short so you could see his socks above his boots. He were an ad for this oil they got off the land: *Yellowfields Seed Oil. A Taste of Sunshine.* The crop shone him up like a torch. Floyd said let's go but Ron were on one, vexed from the fall-out, said he'd stick the tall girl if she didn't stop yakking, if the little one didn't stop crying. Then he grabbed the older one and started pushing her about. The see-through girl were a baby, seven at most. I told Ron stop it, you're hurting them; he said shag off or he'd chin me. Kip got in the fray. He shoved Ron off and they bundled on the road. Floyd were excited, telling me to get in there. Ron got a knee in but Kip nailed him down, said he couldn't take his eyes off Ron for a minute, could he? The lousy stinking bastard, the useless —ing waste of space. Kip were mad about the cutter; he said, 'What were you gunna do with it, you stupid —ing —? Think you're a hard man, do you?' Then the older girl said, 'Come on, Providence,' and that's the first time I heard it, her name, and I thought what a dumb name it were, not a proper name at all.

The girls ran off. Ron were spitting blood. Said he were only reminding them who was boss; that's what the Mister'd told him to do so he did it. Kip called him a poxy — then Floyd yelled the nick and the others jumped to it. It weren't uncommon, 'specially when we were together. Folk clapping eyes on us then ringing Old Bill when we weren't even doing nothing, just hanging about. Kip got shot of the knife as the wagon pulled up. Two constables got out, two right prim —s. One said, 'Would any of you ne'er-do-wells care to explain to the good hofficer and I what's going on?' They all talked like that, Hofficer this and Sir that like they'd rods up their arses. Ron said calm down, it were only a lark. The constables found this funny for some reason. They got laughing and we had to laugh too or they'd nick us for disrespecting their authority. The other — said, 'Well that's all right then, those girls we passed by must've been mistaken, talking about these boys having a flick knife – who'd you believe, then, Hofficer, them or these Maguires?'

They got off on it. Every —ing minute. Same as the Exeter screws, same as Bedford, getting pleasure from the domineering and we're s'posed to be the vicious ones, ain't we? Soon as those —s got that call they all wanted a go – the Maguires again, always the —ing Maguires – they probably drew —ing straws, they couldn't wait to do us in.

Here it ain't like that, I'm told. Well it's always —ing like that. Grendon's just another way of doing it. Make us think they give a —, they're listening, what we say —ing matters but it don't matter, it's never —ing mattered, it's one giant —ing con as far as I'm concerned. They reckon here if they make me talk enough, I'll admit it by mistake. I won't. I'll never confess to her murder 'cause it were Floyd's —ing doing, not mine.

So they're enjoying themselves, these prim —s, and the first goes up to Kip and says, 'We know it's you, Christopher Maguire. You want your licence revoked, boyo? Bird-happy, are you?' Kip said we never had no knife but if we frit those girls we'll say sorry, but the copper said no you bleedin' won't, none of you's ever to go near that Doyle family again. He said it were plain as day to him that Kip were the ringleader, and if it weren't for the fact of his knowing Kip'd be back before a Judge before the week were out, he'd haul him in now to save them all some trouble. Kip just stood there and took it.

There ain't nothing worse than a grass. Kip drummed that into me from day one – Ron too, and the Mister. Whatever you do, keep your mouth shut, Jimmo, whatever you get done for, even if it ain't nothing to do with you, keep —ing quiet and carry the can 'cause if you're a nark that time then a nark you'll forever be. I'd have hid anything for Kip. I'd have hid anything for Floyd. I told myself I weren't a grass, no matter the cost. But when the time came, I dunno . . . When I stood in the dock and they told me what I did to Providence, every —ing bit of it, that see-through girl with a funny voice I met that day on a sun-beat road, how I made friends with her after just so I could swindle her, how I never cared for her, never loved her, never felt nothing for her 'cause that ain't possible in me, that ain't who I am, how I thrashed her and strangled her and left her for dead – I couldn't. I couldn't say it were me. I ain't a man who would do a thing like that.

∾

Dear Donna. Theres a librey here. Today I read a story about a time machine. I pictured it like a globe of the world with gold doors and wires sticking out of it and a line round the middle where the ecuator would be. If I had one Id use it for you. Like when you come see me and the jurney takes you ages Id make it so your here in the click of a finger. Id make the hour your with me last a day or however long you wanted it to. Id go back in time to when your life was just starting. Id do it all again.

8

It wasn't a doss-house but a charity set up by ex-prisoners. An old sweat in a crinkled jacket with ink up his neck met him at the desk and took his chit and offered him a Bible. 'Welcome,' he said, 'to the start of the rest of your life.' His eyes were milky and his hands were soft. Above his head hung a polished cross, set wonkily off the nail. A panel announced: IF WE CONFESS OUR SINS HE IS FAITHFUL TO FORGIVE.

They gave him a room on the first floor. The stairwell was concrete with smears up the walls and stank of smoke and disinfectant. A bunch of grey sheets was piled up in a corner. When they got to his digs, Donna said, 'Could be worse,' and went in and sat on the bed, a sagging mattress on an iron frame. He put down his bag. The room was bigger than his cell by half but the bed was the wrong way round, it should have been up against the wall, and there were no curtains so people could see in and he could see out, and the door was made of flimsy wood so anyone could come past and kick it in if they felt like it.

He went to the window. People rushed to and fro on the street. A dog like Ginny was tied up outside a tobacco shop. 'What do you want to do?' said Donna.

He was all mixed up. What time was it? Four. He'd be on the wing now sewing mailbags ahead of a suet-pudding supper.

Then book and bang-up at eight, the slam of doors, echoing voices, men's shouts bouncing like tennis balls off the metal, game for the same tomorrow. Where were those people going? How did they know what they were meant to do next?

'I don't want to stay here,' he said.

'It's not that bad.'

He turned away from the window. 'I don't like it.'

Donna was reclining with her head against the wall. Her posture reminded him of Drumsticks lounging on his bunk in his oversized prison garb, looking like a Boy Scout but for the cauliflower ear he'd acquired in a canteen riot. She was twisting a narrow leather hoop between her fingers. 'It's got to be better than . . .'

'I dunno what's better than that,' he said. 'I dunno nothing, do I?'

She slipped the hoop over her wrist and sat up. The mattress made a creaking sound like an animal getting its tail stepped on. Maybe she was right. Maybe it was better than the lock-up bunks with their inch-thin straw paillasses and splotched deposits from the geezer before, the reek of the brimming buckets of forty other blokes, the walls of his peter mottled due to the many cups of tea that had been hurled at it in fury or frustration.

'Then I'll tell you,' she said, optimistically. 'I'll fill in the blanks. Go on, Dad. Ask me something.'

He didn't. She said, 'I know. Today's Monday, sixteenth of January. The year's 1989.'

'I know what —ing day it is. You think I'd forget the date of my —ing release?'

'Sorry.'

'No. I am.'

'You heard about Lockerbie?'

'I've got a radio.'

'The plane got bombed. Before Christmas. Over Scotland. Lots of people died.'

'Why?'

'The plane blew up.'

'I mean why'd it get bombed?'

'I don't know.' She saw he was worried. 'What else? Margaret Thatcher's prime minister.'

He watched her, stonily.

'I can tell you the last film I saw,' she hurried on. 'It's called *Three Men and a Baby*. I saw it at the cinema in Greenlakes. There's a big cinema there now. And a bowling alley. And a spaghetti place but Mum says that's a rip-off. It's about these guys in New York who get a baby left on their doorstep and one of them's the father only they don't know who.' She went pink under her eyes.

'That sounds dumb.'

'It is a bit.'

'What happens at the end?'

'They all end up wanting to be the father. None of them wants to at the start but by the end they all kind of want to.' She bit her nails. 'Anyway, it is sort of dumb.'

He picked up the Bible the man downstairs had given him. It didn't look to ever have been opened. The pages were whisker-thin, almost transparent. He saw Drumsticks grinding his dog-ends, gathering the tobacco with his sturdy fingers in a small, carefully moulded pile: '*Bible pages make the best rolling papers, Jim. Smashing fine, they are . . .*'

'Prince is my favourite singer,' said Donna, lying back again.

He put the Bible down, face down. 'Who?'

'Prince. Not a real prince. That's his name.'

'His real name?'

'Yeah. I think so. I like Guns N' Roses too. Maybe you'd like them.'

'Is that a band?'

'Mum always said you liked T. Rex. Do you remember when we came to see you and she told you Marc Bolan died?'

'Yeh.'

'I never liked those visiting rooms. They always smelt gross. And the men looked squeaky clean, kind of greasy. With their hair combed back and their shiny skin.'

'Did I look like that?'

She shrugged. 'I tried not to look at you.'

He glanced out of the window again. The rain had stopped and the dog had gone.

'Does your mother know you're here?' he asked.

'No.'

'You didn't tell her?'

'She'll guess. Anyway, we had an argument.'

'About what?'

'What do you think?'

He scuffed his boots on the carpet. There was a brown stain in the middle of it, the shape of the Isle of Wight. He was dying for a fag. A sticker said no smoking. It was a joke setting a place up for blokes just out and telling them they couldn't have a burn. The one downstairs, he'd seen the likes of him before. Coming into prison to tell the Great Story of how he'd rehabilitated, turned his back on booze and drugs, turned to God, he was probably the one who'd stuck up the sign, all smug with himself as he did so.

'You shouldn't have come,' he said. 'I didn't want you to.'

'Who else have you got, Dad?' she said. She wasn't going to cry, was she? He didn't know what he'd do if she cried. He'd never rubbed her knee when she'd fallen over or looked after her when she'd woken from a bad dream. He'd never heard about friends turned to foes or some boy who broke her heart. Rita had done the decent thing visiting – but for what? Once a month, a hundred miles cross-country, a long day with a child – all to see her murderer one-time lover, the father of her girl, who'd sat in a plastic chair saying sorry and this is good of you over and over again like a broken fegging record. Who else *did* he have? There'd been no one else meeting him. He had no friends out here. The PO's reedy voice still snaked in his ears from the week after Drumsticks had gone out: '*It pains me to break it to you, Maguire, oh it sorely does, but your china's only gone and got himself croaked. Topped himself with a gas fire first night in the flop-house.*' Smiley said it weren't true, you couldn't trust a word the old pig said. Still, he'd laid in his bunk that night and the feeling had gone hard inside him. All that was soft before prison, all that could be changed and touched, retreated and solidified and died.

His reflection appeared to him in the mirror above the bed. Rust bled through the cracks in its edges. He looked like he had never known nineteen.

'I need to get down south,' he said.

She came up straight, her hands in her lap. 'What for?'

'Things I need to do.' He turned away from the glass. 'People I need to see.'

'Who?'

'Ron, for a start.'

For the first time Donna looked fearful. He'd thought she would have looked fearful the second she'd laid eyes on him, but she hadn't. 'Why?' she said.

'We've got business.'

'What business?'

'That's between us.'

'I really don't think—'

'I —ing do. I've done nothing else but —ing think. All that thinking, no —ing doing. Kip and Alf, too. I want to face things. Put the past right – as right as I can get it.'

'You don't have to.'

'Yeh, I do.' He sat next to her on the bed, steepling his hands. He said, so quietly she almost didn't hear, 'I've got to see that place again.'

She let his statement hang. 'You mean . . .'

'Yeh.'

'Dad, don't. Not after how far you've come.'

'Three —ing miles across London?'

'You know what I'm saying.' She kept swallowing her spit; her throat bobbed up and down like a pumpjack. 'What about this place? Your probation officer? Your licence? You can't just be upping and going, you'll break your conditions, they'll send you back—'

'It's already done. I've got permission.'

'How?'

'This screw inside, he sorted it for me.'

'Why are you punishing yourself? What about the future? Your opportunities—'

He laughed. 'What —ing opportunities? What am I good at? What can I *put back in*, as they like to say? I've spent the best part of twenty years sitting on it, I don't know nothing else. I ain't ready for another life – least not till I've mended this one. I ain't got cured of whatever they said back then's the matter with me. It's just got worse, brooding on it and getting bitter, all that bird-lime on top of what's already the problem. Making me the invisible man then all of a sudden I'm out and they can see me now all right.'

'What do you mean?'

'Watching every —ing move I make. I feel it. Their eyes on me.'

'You can't rake all that up again, Dad.'

Rake up a fag, rake up a problem – they were right, there was something wrong in his wiring, all these meanings, things that meant double, words that got warped the more you thought on them and you thought they meant one thing but they actually meant another. To rake up Floyd depended on Floyd having at some point been buried. Only he hadn't been buried, he'd lived with him in that miserable peter every hour of every day.

'I couldn't do nothing banged up,' he said. 'Now I can. I'm going.'

Donna was staring at him. He didn't like how she was staring at him. If he was out then why did he have to get stared at and have all these questions muddling his head?

'There ain't no other way,' he said. 'I've got to meet it again. Just me.'

He opened his bag and counted the notes in the pocket. There were three tens and a five and some coins. 'I didn't want you here anyway,' he said coldly. 'It were a mistake you came. Leave me alone and go back home.'

∞

She returned in the night with a car from a rental place round the corner. She'd recently got her licence, she said, it was easier to drive. He argued he didn't want the car, he wanted the bus and anyway to do it alone, but they both knew he wasn't capable of it.

He couldn't see the car well in the dark. Just that it was small and red. She parked it on the street. 'We've got to be gone by nine or the officer comes round.'

'Officer?'

'Traffic. They stick penalties on the windscreen if you park in the wrong place.'

After a while she fell asleep. He drew a blanket over her and sat on the floor. She looked like Rita had at the same age. Was there anything of him in her? Maybe he saw Mother Maeve in the gap between her nose and mouth, an upper lip like a gull wing.

He smoked out of the window till the pack ran out, then closed it. An ambulance siren went past. The room looked strange, a thin L of moonshine cast across the ceiling like a hangman's gallows. He put on the television. A late-night horror flick was showing, a cream-haired girl in a nightdress staring at static on a TV screen. He kept the sound low so he didn't wake Donna, and found himself drifting, the room sliding sideways and he tipping with it like sand down a chute; the film crossed over into his dreams, which were half-formed and shivering; he was back in borstal on the fruit farm by the sea, numb fingers scraping the soil in early morning, the earth split and barren, the screws yelling to *'git orn with it, yew feckless bleedin' bastards, put your bleedin' backs into it!'* then someplace warmer, in a field scored by lines of trees, the sky bruised as an apple kicked in grass, where grapes and peaches fell from drooping boughs and the Governor's voice called from above, the voice of power, the voice of God: *'Those are mine, you thief!'*

A tap at the door roused him. The film was still going. The pale-haired girl reminded him of Providence, as many things did – a particular shade of blue, the same as her eyes, same as the sea in an atlas, promising great distances; Jane Fonda in a postcard Drumsticks had pinned up in his cell, a smile that knew parts of them they themselves didn't know; 'Knock Turn' played lovely late at night, Providence sitting at the piano on the porch as the sun gave up on the day, the tune whistling through him like wind between rocks, and he'd felt happy, truly happy. Then all was replaced by that last, unspeakable tableau: her clean skin radiant with blood, her body felled lifeless on the ground, and he had watched this terror unfold and been unable to stop it.

The tap came again. He went to answer it and because he was unused to opening doors from the inside, stopped before he did and asked, 'Is anybody there?'

He pictured a visitor. Breathing, listening, waiting, as he was, a mirror of him, only some improved version. *Is it you?* But nobody answered. He was alone. Somewhere down the landing, another door opened and closed. He heard voices. He turned the TV off and sat in darkness with his hand on Donna's ankle, and stayed awake until morning.

∽

There were more things on wheels in the city than he had seen in his life, the roads fast and snaking, a series of funnels that converged then came apart at alarming, changeable speeds, before finally they passed beneath a gigantic sign to The West and were out.

'You never learnt to drive,' Donna said matter-of-factly.

He was busy pushing buttons on the radio. 'No point. I weren't going nowhere.' He stopped on 'Wichita Lineman' and sat back and shut his eyes. 'Kip had a motor. Used to do them up to earn a quid.' He looked across at her. 'Don't s'pose you ever met him.'

'Mum didn't think it was a good idea.'

'Nah. Guess not.'

The motorway opened ahead of them. Donna got in the fast lane despite there being no other cars on the road. Trees replaced high-rises; buildings gave way to fields.

A couple of times he turned in his seat to look behind him.

'What're you doing?' she asked.

'Nothing,' he said.

'There's no police cars there.'

'I know.'

'Then what?'

He glanced in the wing mirror. 'Nothing,' he said again.

He fell asleep and dreamed of Floyd in the wheatfields at home. Wading through the whiskery crop, gold up to their waists. The sun was high in the sky but the sky was scarlet. Floyd caught a mouse by its tail and held it aloft. He told him, '*Let it go.*' Floyd dangled the mouse upside down; its tiny claws scrabbled against his chin. '*Let it go.*' Floyd opened his mouth and the mouse got closer to it, twisting, vanished. He woke up.

There were signs for Exeter. The name stirred in him a second-hand horror, as if it had been someone else's before his. Donna turned off. 'I need the loo,' she said.

The service station was a strange place full of brassy food-shop signs and a bitter smell of chips. He smoked while Donna went inside. 'Get yourself something to eat,' she said, handing him two pound coins. He found a shop selling thin refrigerated sandwiches and stood in front of them for a while, trying to remember how many shillings fit into 55p, before taking one to the counter. The cashier returned some small silver pieces, one of which he used to buy a *Sun* newspaper. RIDDLE OF QUARRY BODY ran the cover headline, and there was an advert for a cruise on the Mediterranean.

He went back out. He couldn't see the car. The thought crossed his mind that Donna had left him. He was considering what to do next when he spotted a booth with a phone in. He took a small, rumpled booklet from his coat pocket and leafed through the pages to find Alf's number. He went to the phone box and closed the door behind him and put a coin in the slot. After a few seconds, the line rang.

'Hello?' said a woman's voice.

'Hullo,' he said.

'Who is this?'

'Are you Alf's missus?'

There was a short pause. Then the voice came back harsher: 'Who is this, I said?'

'Is Alf there, please?'

There was a shunting crackle, the sound of the phone being passed over.

'Who am I talking to?' said a man. He sounded like Alf only plummy, like he had a boiled sweet stuck in his cheek. They'd used to do voices like that when they were impersonating Mr Fortescue the headmaster.

'It's your brother,' he said. 'Jimmy.'

He thought Alf had hung up. He pictured the good wife touching his arm with a floral oven glove. Then Alf said in his teacher's voice, only lower, 'What do you want?'

'I thought I could come up and see you. I'm out now. You know I just got out.'

'How did you get my phone number?'

'Kip gave it me. Ages back. I didn't know if you'd still have it. I wouldn't stay — I wouldn't even stay the night if you didn't— if she didn't . . . Just a cup of tea. I've got this idea for what to do now I'm out. Get myself on the right track, make a fist of it. Thing is, I need a leg-up. Just a little bit of money to get me started, I'd pay it back—'

'Not a chance, Jimmy.'

'You haven't heard what it is.'

'I don't need to hear.' The voice was brisk now. He remembered Alf telling them off for digging holes in the yard and filling them with Mother Maeve's jewellery. How it was Alf who'd packed his, Jimmy's, lunch for school, sharpened his pencils, polished his boots. How when Alf had left for Manchester for good, wearing his fedora hat and carrying his suitcase, he hadn't looked back. He'd never come to the trial. 'There's a reason I haven't seen you,' said Alf now. 'I haven't wanted to, Jim. I didn't then and I don't now, I'm finished with you. I've got a new family to think about. That's all there is to say.'

A tarnished sun strained through the glass. In its reflection he saw the sleeve of his green jacket, holding the phone. His slightly separated lips, stumped for what to say.

'I'm sorry, Jim. Goodbye.' There followed a click and a droning electronic tone.

He put the phone back in its cradle and the book back in his coat, fingering the soft edges of its pages. He opened the door. Donna was waving to him across the car park.

∽

'Who did you ring?' she asked, fastening her belt. 'Oh,' she said when he told her. 'Sorry.'

He understood what Alf was saying, about his reasons. Alf

didn't think he did but he did. They drove off. Through the window he saw a tall, motionless figure, standing by the building, looking at him. The figure was far away so the impression he had of its gaze on him was not so much from any detail in its face as from the way it held itself, expectant, fixed on him, as if it might at any second come running, fast, towards him.

They rejoined the road. He stared out of the window and tried to forget about it. '*You'll see 'em all places,*' Drumsticks had said. '*People from before. People you did wrong.*'

Donna asked what sandwich he got. He picked it apart and grey stuff fell out.

'Tuna,' she said, glancing over.

'I thought it were ham. It said ham on the shelf.'

'They must've got them mixed up.'

The car filled with a rancid smell. He didn't want the fish. He didn't want the wheels. He didn't want Donna sitting by him, knowing what he knew. It struck him that he didn't want to be anywhere; even if he made it down south, what then, what did he do next? There was nowhere on this earth that wanted him, and with it came a horrid, sudden sensation, like the seat going out from under him. He felt it inside him, this wind-up thing, a marble turning circles, shaking his hand so hard he made a fist just to keep it shut out, this rage, this fury, coming up on him, rising like a tide; it was how Donna was sitting so close to him, close enough to hurt (why did she sit so close?), it was Alf, it was the fegging sandwich, and something else too, something else but he couldn't touch what.

He unwound the window and chucked the bread out. A car blared its horn.

'It did get mixed up,' he said into the wind and the horn.

'What?'

He put up the window. 'At Grendon. It weren't what I thought.'

'I know.'

'No, you don't. Everything's back to front. *I'm* back to front. The whole —ing picture. I could get my head round it banged up. I can't get my head round it out here.'

'We'll work it out. You always said we would.'

He turned away so she couldn't see his face. 'That were before.'

'So?'

'Don't you care what they jailed me for? Don't that never cross your mind?'

She kept her eyes on the road, her knuckles held tight to the wheel.

'Yes. I care.'

'She weren't much younger than you are.'

'Dad—'

'I'm not your dad. You don't —ing know me. You shouldn't be here, you're stupid to be here, you should've listened to your mother, it's your own damn fault.'

Neither of them spoke.

'We don't have to go back there,' she said. 'We can turn round.'

'And go where?'

'Anywhere but there.'

'You don't have to,' he said. 'I do.'

'Then leave Ron out of it.'

'I can't. There ain't much I can make good now, but I can do that.'

He heard her swallow. 'Maybe he's changed,' she said. 'Haven't you changed?'

'No,' he said. 'I'm the same —ing psychopath I were when they turned the key, don't you know. That's what it says on my record so I s'pose that's right what I am.'

'I don't think that's what you are.'

They drove on. Rain freckled the windscreen.

9

HM Prison Grendon
Group therapy meeting, 1978

21 April
You want to talk about getting —ed? I can talk about getting —ed. Not once, not twice, many —ing times, and lately I've got to thinking, well, — me, what if that hadn't gone on, what if they'd not done that to me, all those chances there were not to kick me in the —ing grit yet here I am, here we all are. Those people ain't around to reckon with no more. All we've got to reckon with is ourselves. If they could look in on this room right now with all the crying and rueing, they'd think how'd you bleeding-hearts do what you're in for in the first place? Half you lot wouldn't say boo to a goose.

Keep saying that, go on, I dare you. Say it again and I'll —ing flatten you. I'm no coward. Floyd's a coward. This is his seat here, not mine. I dunno what he'd do if he were in it. Not much, I don't think. Just sit and watch. Stay nice and quiet then he'd —ing ruin you; you'd forgot he were there but turned out he'd been listening to every —ing word you said then he'd come at you. But he ain't here, is he? He's out there, living the life of Riley.

Woe-is-me, banged up for a felony I didn't commit, squire – if every man said that was telling the truth we'd have a prison full of —ing innocents now, wouldn't we?

Only I am telling the —ing truth. Grendon's built on that, so they say. And if it don't get it then that means we're not cooperating and we can get shunted back out to a normal nick.

I'm still here, so what's that showing you?

23 April

Next time I saw her, it were on the street where she lived. She'd come off her bike, sitting next to it with the wheels spinning round. She were on her own. I didn't know what to do really, I were only a kid myself, but she were crying and her knee were bleeding and I didn't have nothing on me to wipe it with so I used my sleeve, first on her face then her knee. I said, 'Where d'you live?' and she told me in that whispery voice of hers, but she didn't say nothing else after that. I took her back to her house and once I knew she were all right I left her there, I didn't want no one to see me. Then a few days later I were walking in the road minding my business when up she comes running out the park, with her sister calling way out behind her. Her knee were all purple and crusty from the scab. She had two lollipops, one in each hand. maybe one were for the sister but the sister never got it 'cause she gave it to me, and smiled sort of shy and we stood there for a bit sucking these lollies. I'd never had one before; it was sweet and sickly and I didn't like it much but that didn't seem polite to say. I knew right then we'd be friends.

Providence called me her golden boy. It were 'cause of my

hair. Fair, like hers. She said when she'd seen me on the lane that day with Ron and the knife, she said she'd known I were good. *Golden good*'s how she put it. Said my brothers were bad but she could tell right off that I weren't, even then she could tell. There ain't many happy memories I can look back on – not feeling sorry for myself, just saying how it is – and I think you need a happy memory, one'll do fine, to tell you life might be all right for you on the outside, 'cause it ain't all dark and lost, it could be bright some other day like it were that one time. If you're capable of feeling it once then you might be able to again.

She's my happy memory. Summers get mixed in my mind but there's always that impression. Blue skies. Pink sunsets. Days that went on for ever. Floyd weren't with us, it were just her and me. When we were young I taught her rummy and she taught me kick the can. When we were grown I told her stories and she wrote me songs – she were musical – just the words, then she put them to her piano next time we were at hers.

It were the same field we went to. That one, the only one. We stayed so long into evening, the sun ran away from us. Wherever we were sitting, we had to move to keep up with him. We chased him piece by piece across the earth till he disappeared in the trees.

Providence said I had the sun in me. No one else saw it but her. She said I were always chasing the sun, trying to stay in the warm and the light. It were a long time ago.

3 May

The dog did me in. Me and Providence found her one day I were meant to be at the vicar's. He used to have me round there on weekends, s'pose he felt sorry for me, thought the youngest might still have something worth saving in him. Floyd never came with me; the vicar didn't want him, he said, 'Just you, Jimmy, remember? I only want to see you.' I wish he had come that day though 'cause then he'd have spent the same time with Providence that I did and maybe he'd have liked her then. But you can spend your life on what-ifs. I've unpicked it a hundred —ing times and none of it —ing gets me nowhere.

We were down in the stream by his house, Providence and me, building a dam. After a while she went off. I could tell she were bored with the dam, it'd been my idea, then I heard her calling in her down-a-tunnel voice, she were saying, 'Steady, it's all right, steady now.' She had a dog with her. Black and scruffy with its paw caught up in some wire. She were trying to get it out. I were good with my hands and we got it out quickly. I said, 'Whose is he?' and she said it ain't a he, it's a she.

I thought the dog'd run off the second it got free but it didn't, it just stayed there licking my face. Providence were happy. I can see her standing there with her skirt bunched in her knickers, laughing her happy laugh, and her skin flickery with the sun coming in through the leaves like how things look on old films. She said she's got to like you then – the dog, that was. We thought someone'd be missing her so we got out dripping wet with our shoes squelching from the water still in them and set off down the Wagon, thought we'd put a notice in there. The dog's paw were bleeding. When we got there the landlord said he'd seen that mutt before; someone must've dumped her. He said he'd ask the punters later but the way he were —ing eyeballing me, knowing the Mister's reputation and Ron's by that time, I didn't reckon he'd put much grease into it.

You know what they ask me here? 'Look, Jimmy, let's take this *hypothetical situation*: what do you think's the *right thing to do*?' Well — me, the right thing's to — off so you can't ask me these —ing numbskull questions no more. I dunno anyhow. I dunno right from wrong and that's what the Judge said and that's what it is. Knowing that's either in you or it ain't. You can't learn it, you can't pretend it, you know it or you don't.

Providence did the right thing. The Judge said I took advantage of that. Said I knew full well she'd never say no and that's why she came with me that last night.

But that ain't it. Floyd made her come. *He* took her there.

She did the right thing with the dog. Said we can't just leave her; I'd have to take her home with me. I said, 'Why can't you take her home with you?' but she said her gran wouldn't let her. Mrs D'd seemed fair when I'd met her – I'd met her a few times by then – a kind lady, and the gangly sister too that looked like a boy, they'd both been nice to me. Providence said the dog'd taken a shine to me. She must've felt bad 'cause she offered to help me clean her up if I liked. I took them back to my house. I'd never done that before. I'd never had no one else over there but Floyd. I were spooked he'd be there waiting for me like usual but that day he weren't, he were gone. I were spooked by him a lot. He crept up on me when I were least expecting it, silent like, and I never knew what mood he'd be in.

I hoped when we got there it'd be spick and span 'cause the

old Mum'd got up and sobered up and it were a normal —ing house like normal people live in but it weren't. Filthy mouldy walls. Smell like kippers and ale. The Mister's bet cards across the table and a bottle of Greenall's gin which the dog got to sniffing. I said, 'Let's call her Ginny,' and Providence said it were a good name. It were hard to see in the dark but I knew she were looking right at me and I weren't used to being looked right at. Mother Maeve never. The Mister never. Now I come to think of it, Floyd hardly ever. It were only when I got nicked that I got looked at properly, but not like Providence did in the kitchen that time.

We got saltwater in a bowl. I held on to Ginny. Providence soaked a towel in the water and wrapped it round the paw. The room filled with sounds. The squeeze of the towel being wrung and the panting of the dog that were part pain and part relief. Providence frowned while she concentrated. It felt good to make something feel better.

∽

Dear Donna. You were sick today so you couldnt come. Your mum told the officers and they told me. They said I should spend the hour we wouldve been together writing to you so your still in my head that hole time youd be here but youd be in my mind anyway so that dont work. They reckon I should write letters for me aswell as you but I think that ought to be a oneway street as far as thats conserned. Theres a man on my wing from Ireland. His names not Paddy but we call him Paddy. Hes always telling poems. I wrote one for you. It goes THERE WAS A YOUNG GIRL CALLED DONNA. HER DADDY WAS

NEARLY A GONER. BUT THEN HE HAD HER, AND HAD TO INFER, FROM THAT DAY ON HED BE STRONGER. The guvner helped me with infer it means guess. The poem dont add up really. The 5th lines meant to ryme but it dont properly. I like the poems though. There funny, the ones Paddy tells anyway. I hope you get well soon.

∽

11 May

Floyd wrote me letters. When he couldn't find me he left them at the house. After I met Providence I had more of those letters than before 'cause I weren't spending as much time with him then. That were one of the reasons he hated her. The main reason though was that he reckoned she were up herself. You know, posh. She spoke proper and dressed neat and they went to church on Sundays, her and the gran and the sister. No mum or dad, but since when were that a bad thing? I thought she were —ing lucky for not having them.

Floyd said Providence would wreck us someday and he were right. He were always drip-feeding me bad thoughts about her. There were one time on the rail tracks, it were a hot day, the rails looked sort of greasy in the sun. I'd gone there with Ginny; any chance I got I took her out the house so Mother Maeve wouldn't find her. I'd been hiding her three weeks by then and her paw'd got worse. Me and Providence'd gone round the village cadging for coins, thought we'd pay for a veterinarian to see her if we got enough of them. I'd said no —ing way folk round there'd hand me no money, but Providence said they would if she were with me and d'you know what? They did.

So I were listening for trains when Floyd came up quiet and surprised me. It were 'cause he never wore shoes, he just went round barefoot no matter what he were walking on. He said, 'How'd they let you keep that cur?' I said, '— off, she's a good dog,' and anyway Ma weren't the wiser 'cause I'd been holing her up in Kip's room. Which had used to be Alf's room too but he were never about no more, always off with his judy. Kip couldn't do his nut anyhow 'cause he'd been nicked again, got himself stuck in a pattern, hadn't he, getting into worse kinds of grief than before, home-breaking and drug-dealing, crimes of the serious sort. Some of what the Old Bill ferried him off for were stuff he did and some were stuff he didn't – half the problem were Kip were never a Judas. He'd take the blame when he'd nothing to do with it. I knew he'd never be a Judas to me neither and when he got home he'd help me keep the dog. I'd tell him Ginny were the best thing that'd ever happened to me. It were like a bulb'd gone on in my head. I felt like what I did —ing counted and I couldn't go through life not caring 'cause what kind of a life were that?

Floyd said Providence must've got in my brain, making me think soppy —ing thoughts like that. He said, 'You know she's jeering you. She's out there right now with that uppity sister of hers saying what a —ing gull you are for thinking someone like her wants to be friends with someone like you. You're best off sticking with me, Jim, I'm the only one you can trust.' He were always saying things like that. But I trusted Kip as well. Floyd said, 'Kip's washed his hands of you. Why'd he carry on getting jailed if he gave a — about you?' I told him shove off. He said they weren't my real family. I said Kip's my brother. Half-brother, he said. And I thought if he didn't stop talking right —ing then I'd rip the —ing gizzards out of him. The train were coming and the air were shaking, like I were shaking. Floyd were kneeling with his hand on the rails. 'Wanna jump it?' he said. I said no. He said, 'Why not? Your dad would've. Not the substitute one. The *real* one.'

It were our game. Leap off the tracks last-minute, pretend we were sling-shotted over the hills and far away. Our great escape, to America, to Isaac the Pilot. The engine were out the tunnel and round the bend, a chuffing shadow filling up the world, wheezing and clumping and spitting. I thought it hit me but it were Floyd that hit me. We fell on the soil as the train dashed past. 'Dossy —ing bastard,' he said. 'I saved your life.'

15 May

A life is for ever. I've turned that phrase over so long in my mind. To take another's, to be handed a life-stretch. To be stuck in your own. Does he ever think about her? Out there living his, does she ever trouble him? Not her death. Her life. When we went to meet her that last night and she were playing piano in the rain. The porch roof had a leak and water came down on the piano. 'Knock Turn in E Flat Major'. A life is for ever.

2 June

Providence said we gave the dog a new start. The coins weren't enough, it turned out, but the veterinarian knew her family; Mrs D cleaned his castle and the sister were friends with his son so he fixed her anyway for free. I got more time with Ginny than I would've otherwise if the Mister'd been about. I s'pose I should be grateful for that. I dunno, do I? All over, nowhere, I didn't —ing care. All I cared for were I weren't getting beaten.

Mother Maeve found her first. She gave me a hiding. Told me I were a stupid boy, I must have my brains in my boots, I must've been born —ing yesterday, and I were crying, not 'cause of that but 'cause I were scared she'd run the dog out the house. She sat for ages at the kitchen table staring at —ing nothing and telling me —ing nothing then she said, 'You'll have to get rid of it by the time he gets back.' And I said, 'I can't, where'll she go?' but we both knew the Mister'd never have it. Providence said she'd talk to her sister. She said, 'Birdie'll know what to do.' I didn't like the thought of them pitying me, Mrs D and the sister. I already imagined they pitied me. It made me feel like Providence being my friend were a —ing favour, like it were with the vicar, like I were a —ing charity case. I said Floyd could have her but I knew the idea were potty and Providence's face told me the same. She didn't like Floyd as much as he didn't like her. Whenever I said his name she came over funny, sort of nervous like, and made up a reason to leave. I wished my brothers were around to help me but the older ones were gone and Ron weren't back five minutes before he were getting hauled in again by the Law. Petty larceny, cop-baiting, nothing that wound him up with more than a slap on the wrist and a warning to Mother Maeve, as if she could've —ing stopped it. Most days I didn't see her and the days I did she were boozed, sobbing for pardon like I were Jesus —ing Christ. I thought what she wanted it for weren't even the beating and the drink and that but how any of it'd come to pass in the first place, the fact I didn't know my true father and she'd lied to me all along.

I didn't have no choice. I still had that feeling, that fading away. Now they'd give me pills to cure it only it wouldn't —ing cure it, would it? Maybe it would in my head but not in real life, and I didn't feel like I were part of real life and that were the problem. Floyd said, 'Don't be soft, Jim, I can see you quite all right.' But even though he saw me I weren't really here. I were never a whole person the way other people were. I got to telling myself he were right: the only person I could trust to stick with me were him.

But even Floyd couldn't choke off the Mister. The old man came back one night wearing a sheepskin coat and a fistful of —ing knuckle-dusters like an evil rich king. Him and Ron pissed off to the Wagon and came home singing 'Raglan Road' at the tops of their voices. I assumed Ronnie told him then. Next day I woke to shouting. Ginny were gone from the end of my bed. The Mister had her by the scruff downstairs, shouting that he'd take her to the pound, and Mother Maeve said but she ain't no trouble, we can keep her, can't we? She wouldn't get under his feet. Ginny were trembling but it were the old Mum who got hit. The knuckle-duster knocked her out cold. She fell down the wall like a sack of —ing coal. I swore to the Mister I'd find a place for the dog by nightfall.

I went to Providence's house. My face were a mess and I guess the Mister'd bashed me 'cause I'd blood in my mouth. She said when I got there, 'Is Floyd with you?' I said no but honestly I didn't —ing know, I didn't —ing mind, all I minded for were getting a home for Ginny so she'd someone to look after her. Providence were kind to me. Took me inside. Mrs D were there. She patched my face with cotton. I didn't talk 'cause I knew I'd start blubbing again with the kindness and whatnot, I weren't used to it.

The sister, Birdie, she were just as decent. She made me a drink and sat down with me. She said, 'Providence told us the situation. It's OK, the Fairfaxes will have her.'

I didn't know who that was. Providence reminded me: 'The animal doctor,' she said. Then the sister explained how Maurice, the doctor's son, had always wanted a dog. Providence sat there smiling at me and I should've been smiling too, it were a good thing, I knew it were a —ing good thing, but for some —ing reason, now that it'd been said, I couldn't —ing stand it. I hated the —ing idea. I didn't know why I hated it so much but I did. That dog were the first thing I ever loved. Now the Fairfaxes' rich boy, who'd had everything given him on a —ing silver plate, were taking my Ginny away from me and there weren't a —ing thing I could do about it. All 'cause he were him and I were me.

Providence said, 'She'll go to a good home.' There were no point arguing. When the day came to hand her over, Ron came with me to the green. He were well-tubbed for once, said Birdie were a crumpet and he'd some making up to do. Ginny went by my heel. It were like going to a —ing funeral. Providence and Birdie and the Fairfaxes stood on one side of the path, me and Ron and Floyd on the other. I couldn't think of a single —ing thing to say to them that touched on the tiniest bit of pain I had in my —ing disappointed heart. I handed over the lead and went off and didn't look back. Floyd said it'd worked out good in the end. We were on our own again and that's how it should be.

But it weren't like that for me. I'd a feeling I'd no more feeling. That dog were all that'd made me real. She were a rescue dog but it weren't like that, it were the other way round, it were her that rescued me. There's a picture of us on the wall by my bed. Providence took it in the field one day with her sister's Kodak, soon after we'd had the paw mended. The sun's running away but I caught him. My arm's round her. A golden boy and his dog. I'm smiling. The happiest I ever saw myself is in a picture long gone.

∾

Dear Donna. I went to smash up a bloke today. Some big mad basterd in for slortering his bird pinched my smoking papers. I said dont you know what they did me for matey? Aint you heard about me? Im your worst —ing nightmare you sneaktheef —ing —, Im bigger and madder than you. Said Id smash his —ing skull on the khazi and when he were bleeding good and proper put his leery —ing face in a sheet of —ing glass, thatd teach him for taking whats mine. The officers carted me off to solitry, said to calm down so I bashed the —ing walls and there aint no getting out of here cause it aint here thats the problem its me, there aint no getting out of me. [Unsent.]

10

They drove on long enough that it grew dark. His stomach rumbled with hunger. He craved sea-pie and plum pudding, warm honest grub then dreamless, innocent sleep, the likes of which he'd not known in years, maybe ever – but Ron was out there waiting for him, and some things past could never be put right while others still had a chance.

'Come off,' he said. She did. They stopped in a siding.

'What's wrong?' she asked. He couldn't see her well in the gloom. When another vehicle went by, its headlights shone her up before she was scrubbed out again.

'I'll walk the rest of the way,' he said.

'Are you crazy?' Donna turned off the radio. A lorry sped past; she lit up then went out. 'He's another five miles from here. It's practically pitch black.'

He opened the glovebox, rooting for a torch. 'You should go back,' he said.

'Where?'

'Town. Your mother's. Wherever you came from.'

She was hurt. 'I'm coming with you,' she said.

'No.'

'I brought you here, I got the car. Now you're ditching me?'

'I never —ing asked you to come.'

'So you keep saying. How'd you have got here otherwise?'

'I'd have found a way,' he said.

She folded her arms. 'I'm not leaving.'

'Ron's dangerous.'

'And you're not?' She turned off the engine. They sat in silence. 'Sorry.'

'Don't be.'

'I said you shouldn't see him. I said it's a bad idea.'

'I don't care. I've got to talk to him.'

'Then this is the condition,' she said. 'I stick with you.'

Angrily, he got out of the car. Donna did as well. They glared at each other across the roof. Her eyes were unfeasibly liquid in the gloom, like thick daubs of paint.

'I decide,' he said. Then added, somewhat weakly, 'I'm the parent.'

She laughed. 'Sure.'

'What's that s'posed to mean?'

'Jesus Christ, Dad. You can't pick me up and put me down when you feel like it. Mum said this would happen. She said if I'm going, I'm going, I'm an adult now, she can't stop me. But he's not in it for you, Donna, she said. He's in it for himself. Always has been. He'll get what he wants then he'll drop you like a stone. Is that what this is?'

'I'm trying to protect you.'

'Don't bother. I don't need your protection. I haven't had it my whole life, why'd I start needing it now?'

'You think you know everything.'

'No, I don't. I don't know —ing anything, since you never told me.'

He thumped the roof. She said, 'Don't do that, bloody hell. It's a hire car.'

'So?'

'Someone has to pay for it if it's all bashed up.'

'What, the whole —ing car?'

'The damaged bits. Stop damaging it.'

He kicked the wheel and turned away, squaring up to a bin stuffed with rubbish. The wind-up thing switched in him now, tight as clockwork, faster, faster, he couldn't slow it down. Images arrived of the Ron he'd known, his shaved head, his fists, of them cowering in a cupboard from the Mister. He heard Donna open the driver's side. Then his own door opened and her voice called across the seat, 'Well? Are you coming or not?'

She started the ignition. A plastic bag blew across the tarmac, white and billowing. He booted the bin then got back in. 'It's late anyway,' she said. 'We're not staying long. We'll see him, you get whatever it is said then we leave. That's the other condition. OK?'

He didn't answer. He felt that if he looked at her he would hit her, so he carried on looking out of the window. If he hit her once he might not be able to stop.

'OK, Dad?'

'Stop calling me that.'

'What should I call you then?'

'Nothing,' he said. 'Don't call me nothing.'

Orange lamp posts framed a sloping car park fringed by waste containers. The concrete was empty save for two squat motors similar to theirs and a knackered Dodge camper van, the likes of which the Mister had obtained one winter and kept by a ditch near the rec field for reasons his brothers had guessed at. '*It's where Mother Maeve gets off to,*' Ron had said, picking his teeth. '*Where she takes 'er fellas. They're running a bisniss, 'im and 'er.*'

Donna pressed the buzzer. The door opened. A voice reached them from above:

'Lift's bust. Yer'll 'ave t' take the stairs.'

He took her hand. She looked so shocked when he touched it that he let it go.

Ron was hanging over the banister three floors up, peering down like a vulture off a branch. He had a foot wedged between the railings and his chin resting on his fists, the dull boy he'd always been, lounging at the school gates on the rare days he bothered to go, smoking his brothers' snout, waiting for Alf to turn up. 'What yer doin' standin' there? Yer comin' up or ain't yer?'

Donna went ahead of him, too purposeful to forestall. A cockroach skittered across the half-landing. When they reached him, Ron said, as though no time had passed, 'All right, Jimmo?' His brother's voice had a crack in it. He smelt of old carpets and lighter fluid. His hair was grown now, down past his sticky-out ears, and shiny with brilliantine. He opened his arms then dropped them. 'Yer look like shit if yer dun mind me saying.'

'You look like shit and all.'

Ron snorted. 'And I 'aven't 'ad ten years banged up ser what's my excuse?'

'It were eighteen.'

'Eh?'

'Eighteen years, Ron. Don't you remember?'

'Not much these days. My 'pologies for that. Memory ain't what it were.'

Ron turned to Donna, showing them teeth worse than Smiley's. ''Ere she is,' he said. 'Bloody 'ell, Jim, she's perfick. Come 'ere, darlin', say 'ello to yer Uncle Ronnie.'

'Hello,' said Donna.

'About bleedin' time too. Yer dad's misdemeanours took a lot from me.'

'You could have seen her,' he said.

'With that bird o' yers in the way?'

'You never tried.'

Ron gave him a thin smile. 'Let bygones be bygones, eh, Jimmo?'

They went into the flat. It was dim and stank of puff. Cardboard crates were piled high on the floor — *You get a lovely lot of Quavers in a bag! 36-PACK BUMPER BOX. Salt 'em & Shake 'em!* — and stuffed with table lamps and newsrags, dirty plates and scratchums, a bottle of tomato ketchup lolling on its side, blood-flecked from within. The window had no curtains. Through it he saw a flickering street light, mists of rain driving through the beam. 'Sit down,' said Ron, wiping his hands on his trousers. 'Make yerselves at 'ome.'

The settee was covered in a fine layer of hair. 'You got a dog?' he asked.

Ron was in the kitchenette, messing about with the kettle, snapping the switch on and off his long back stooped like a question mark. There was a dank yellow stain on his shirt like he'd sat against a wall fresh-painted with Colman's mustard. 'What?' he said.

'You got a pet, I said.'

'Nah.' Ron swore and yanked the plug out, chucking the appliance into one of the boxes. 'Kettle's on the fritz. I got booze. Vodka? Beer. Think I got beer. Yer hungry?'

'We already ate,' said Donna.

He reached across the table for Ron's carton of Embassy. Underneath it was a dog-eared photograph of Mother Maeve holding a baby. She was young, standing in someone's yard, not theirs, and the sun was shining. She looked almost hopeful. The baby might've been Kip. Donna saw him looking. He struck a match and turned the picture over.

Various bags of crisps landed on the hairy sofa. ''Elp yerselves,' said Ron, kicking a path through the junk and sitting opposite them. He opened a pack and started eating.

'French Fries.' Ron held them out. 'Want one?'

'They French?' he said.

Ron looked at them. 'Beats me. Me mate gets 'em. 'E's in the delivery bisniss. I've got all me food groups. Bacon's meat. Cheese's dairy. There's Scampi Fries for fish.'

'What about greens?' said Donna.

'Mm. Spuds are veg, ain't they?'

He watched Ronnie eat. Slow eyes, wet mouth.

'Yer watch telly?' said Ron, crumpling the bag and chucking it on the floor.

'Huh?'

'Dun s'pose yer know much about modern TV.' Ron reached

behind him for a magazine and opened it in the middle and showed them the evening's listings, with assorted programmes circled in pen. 'There's *Eagle Bruce*, yer'd like 'im. 'E's on at eight. 'E's a detective sort, out t' solve crimes. Only 'e's got' – Ron rubbed his fingers together in a way that reminded him of Drumsticks rolling shag tobacco – *'problems of a personal nature'*. He said that last bit in a stupid voice. 'First 'is bird's 'aving it off behind 'is back. Then 'e's got issues with the drink – 'is old man were bent, see, that's where it comes from. Sounds about right, don't it, Jim?' He sat back with one foot resting on the other knee; a toe like a new potato protruded from his sock. ''Is brain takes to working in mysterious ways. 'E thinks 'e knows what crimes are *about to 'appen before they 'appen*; 'e gets visions of what's gunna go on only 'e's never in time t' stop it. And all this builds up in 'is head, the bird and the booze and all this worry, an' the worse it gets the worse it gets so 'e comes t' thinking, well shit on me, what if *I'm* the one doing it? The crimes. What if 'e's dreaming up stuff 'e 'asn't done yet? 'E ain't a bad bloke, 'e's a good bloke. Just 'is brain's switched on t' certain things. Bit like yers. That's what they said, weren't it, Jim?'

'I don't recall.'

'Course yer recall. *Failure to understand the nature of yer conduct*. Weren't that it?' There was that stupid voice again. He could kill him, he thought. Slam his —ing head in the wall then smash out his shit-for-brains with one of his —ing poxy table lamps.

'We knew what yer did,' said Ron. 'Yer denied it out-an'-out, but everyone knew.'

Not everyone. Kip hadn't known. Kip had had his back. And he could have run it on a loop, endlessly, as he had at Wandsworth when the lights went out and the shouts died down and there was nothing left for him then but his thoughts, of Providence, of Floyd, of that end-of-nights and what came after, hearing it played back to him, every detail struck to heart from the sheen on the typist's desk to the pulse that beat in Kip's neck when he'd stood in the dock and tried to take the blame for him. *'Why'd you do that?'* he'd asked him after. Kip said, *'You're my little brother. If I don't look after you, no one will.'*

'You dunno nothing, you —ing lunatic.'

'Me a —ing lunatic?' said Ron. 'Pull the other one.'

'You act spotless. You've always been the bad seed.'

Ron leant across the boxes. 'Funny yer should call me that, Jim. After all, it ain't my fault Kip met 'is maker. Once yer got sent down 'e were never the same again. What yer did broke 'im in two. It weren't a year before 'is poor soft 'eart gave in. Bleedin' sap.'

'One more word and I'll —ing choke you.'

'Least that's something yer know how t' do.'

He lunged for him. Donna said, 'Don't—!'

'Not in front of yer daughter, mate.'

Ronnie's breath hit him in a sour gust. At Bedford once, he'd seen a man stab another man in the gullet with a tin knife over filched tobacco, a red pool leaking round the dying body like a cape, and he'd thought how easy it was if you dared; you just needed the will, you didn't have to be strong. Why shouldn't it be harder to take a life? The screws hadn't minded. *'Clear up that mess, yew litter of swines. Animals, the bleedin' lot of yew.'*

His hand closed round his brother's throat, a snug fit, his thumb wedged under the right earlobe and his middle finger under the left, with a hectic throb leaping about beneath his palm like a moth in a jar. 'Yer come to kill me?' spluttered Ron. 'That it?'

'No. I came to hear you say it.'

'Say what?'

'What you did to Birdie. When I were living with them. I know it were you.'

'Dunno what yer mean,' his brother gasped, gripping his wrists, pop-eyed.

'Yeh, you do. You know exactly.'

'Please—' Donna dragged him back. He threw her off harder than he'd meant to and he thought good, now she'll scarper, she'll see what I'm made of and she'll go.

'Go on, Jim, do me in, why not. Prove 'em right.'

'You think I won't.'

'I think yer will,' Ron wheezed. 'Yer've always bin —ed in the head.'

He dropped his brother. The screws stood over him. '*Yew're a savage, Maguire, are yew listening to me, boy? No self-control, that's your problem. Whatever yew touch in life yew'll destroy, whatever's good yew'll turn bad. That's written through yew like a stick of rock, isn't it?*'

'Yer reckon it were easy for me?' grunted Ron, scouring his neck. A purple rash was spreading there. 'Well do yer? My kid brother gettin' accused of those perverted misbehaviours. Folk thinking 'e's a —ing nonce. I'm a decent upright fella, ain't I? Always 'ave bin. How'd yer think that made me look?'

'How can you lie like that?' he said.

Ron laughed. 'Takes one t' know one.'

'You wrecked it,' he said. 'I could've stayed with them. Gone straight.'

'Yer blaming me for Providence now too, are yer? Putting that on me?'

'Don't you dare say her name.'

'Floyd ain't enough? Come on, Jim. They told me yer'd got with the programme. Di'n't that Grendon place sort yer out? Took yer bleedin' time getting there, eh.'

He would've gone at him again. 'Make it right while you can,' he said instead.

'Yer came all this way to act the —ing chaplain? Do me a favour, mate.'

'I ain't your mate. You've still got a chance to say sorry.'

'Who to?'

'The person you did it to. You can find her. It ain't too late.'

Ron lit a fag. 'I dun owe nothin' to no one. Yer might, but I —ing don't.'

He turned from his brother. Through the window, in the queasy radiance of the orange lamp, he saw a woman standing on the far side of the car park. Her shape was perfectly still, just as it had been when he'd seen her at the motorway service station. She wore a long, straight coat and looked directly up at where he stood.

'What is it?' said Donna, next to him. She hadn't left after all. He looked again: the woman was gone.

'Yer know she's alive, dun't yer?' said Ron.

He turned round. 'What?'

Ron stumped the fag and picked up the photograph of Mother Maeve.

'Yeh,' he said, 'thought that'd sort you out. She knows yer free, Jim. She's living down 'ere now. In Cornwall. 'As done for years, she's out by the coast. Not that I'd know much, she's never made no effort to see me, s'pose she cut us all off. This year's the first year I got a Christmas card. *To Ron. From Ma.* No love nor nothin'.'

A weight sank in him. 'They told me she'd died,' he said.

'Unless they got pen and paper in 'ell they're mistaken.'

'She never . . .' he began. ''Cause I didn't; she didn't ever . . . I thought she'd died.'

Ron dug out the card and gave it to him. It had angels on it in the snow. The letters were tiny and the lines were slanting.

To ron. tell james come now Ive got something for him its important. From ma.

He looked to the carpet. The TV rag lay open, *Eagle Bruce* ringed in red.

Ron wore the smile of the guilty free. 'Dun ask me what,' he said. 'But seeing as yer so bent on fixing history, Jimmo, I s'pose yer'll 'ave to go there and find out.'

III

11

I bought one of those rainproof capes from a kiosk and evaluated the Queen Victoria Hostel from under my hood. A couple passed by with bags held over their heads; they stopped and the man kissed the woman on the mouth, romantically, in the rain, like in the films, but she stumbled and almost fell over, then hit him on the arm and the moment was ruined. Tom came into my mind, and Philippa and Joe – a flat we'd rented in the Lake District hills when Joe was a baby, the children splashing in a kidney-shaped bath, clouds of white lather like meringues on the end of my daughter's nose – then I let them go again. I couldn't think about my family. They belonged with the mother and wife who burned the toast and packed the school bags and helped with the homework – the woman I sometimes looked at in the mirror and thought, for a second, *am I you?*

I had tried to consolidate myself. Replace myself. Erase myself. In building a new life, I had tried to trade in the old one and with it the other, stricken versions of me – sister, granddaughter, seventeen-year-old lying in bed until morning came. But those second selves never let me go. The more I rejected them the harder they came back, and always with the reminder that Philippa could one day be prey to the same, as would countless other women like her, numbed in heart and head by a boy like a Maguire.

I crossed the road and went inside. 'Good afternoon,' I said to the man at the desk, too cheerfully, as if I were selling something. I put down the poncho hood; perhaps he thought I was selling those. 'I'm looking for James Maguire. I'm a relative.'

The man's skin was fissured like a walnut. I could not think of a single life he had not lived. He leafed through a few sheets of paper but I could tell it was placatory.

'No visitors,' he said.

'But is he here?' I hadn't a doubt in my mind that he was. Providence had brought me back to him. I had lost my way and she had restored me. Ever since the day of his sentencing when a seed had been planted inside me, watered and warmed by my fury; ever since I had settled on my course of action, impossible to anyone but not to me, for I believed my sister would be with me and I wouldn't be doing it alone; ever since I had emptied my bank account of every penny Gamma had left me in order to procure a gun that had been smuggled across borders; ever since Catriona told me his parole had been granted – through it all I had trusted Providence. No matter the diversions in my path, she would deliver me to James Maguire and when I met him again I would kill him.

'I'm not at liberty to say,' said the man.

Quite why Maguire should elicit such consideration when he had shown none of his own was beyond me. A panel on the wall promised forgiveness in exchange for confession. But Maguire had never confessed. He could have done the decent thing after all his indecency, the last act that might have proved he had humanity, to say, I'm guilty, it was me, I did it and I am sorry. Cowardice ran in his family. God might accept a late admission, but I wouldn't.

Of everything, his denial was in a way the most intolerable. His continued claim that my sister had died not by his hands but another's was the final, loathsome insult.

'It's important that I see him,' I said.

'And who're you?'

'His sister-in-law.' I thought there had to be at least one.

He folded chunky arms and sat back and appraised me. He knew my type. I had the feeling he knew every type of person that ever there was. I had a wild moment of imagining drawing the gun from Gamma's bag and directing it at him, his hands flown up in surrender, his jaw slack with surprise, but even in that make-believe scenario it felt more likely he would close his palm around the barrel and tell me what he was telling me now, calmly, as he paused, unyielding, on the other side of the invisible divide between those who had been there and those who hadn't. 'Sorry, lady,' he said. 'I can't help you.'

∽

I waited on the street till it grew dark. The girl came out around eight. She stopped beneath Victoria's head, glanced both ways then set off in a westerly direction.

I tailed her to the end of the road, over the zebra crossing and through a tidy patch of green. She looked small against the trees, the park lonely save for a sad pile of clothes on a bench with two shoes poking out the end of it. What did Maguire want with her? What did he have planned? I had to warn her. I couldn't. When we emerged on the street she turned left so spontaneously I thought she'd seen me, but then she entered a brightly lit shop with WHEELS 4 HIRE blinking in the window. I paused then went in after her.

We stood side by side at a pair of booths. On the wall behind a plastic screen were a Greek flag and a blue-and-white evil eye hanging from a coarse twine. A thickset man with carpeted arms asked what the girl wanted. 'You wait, OK?' he told me.

She looked over. Whitesnake was playing on the radio. 'Go ahead if you like,' she said. She had a Home Counties accent, quite smart. It hadn't registered with me on the bus. 'I can wait.'

'No, no.' I smiled at her. 'You were here first.'

She gave me a quick, nervous smile back and resumed with the dealer. I picked up a leaflet and feigned interest in the price gap between an Escort and a Fiesta for a week – *fantastic value, satisfaction guaranteed!* – while trying to listen to what she was saying.

'Could I borrow that pen?' she asked me.

It was attached to its base by a cord, meaning she had to come over. I moved aside, guiding Gamma's bag along with my foot, but only slightly, not far, so I could see the purple stud in her ear and the way the sleeve of her lumberjack shirt rode up to reveal a tender slice of inner wrist, flecked with old cuts. Very neatly she wrote her name, *Donna Eddiston*, big rings clinking, and her date of birth, though I could only make out the year, 1971. How did she know him? He'd been in prison her whole life. She said thank you for the pen, and I felt emboldened, so I asked, 'Are you going anywhere nice?' as if we were in an airline queue waiting to check in our luggage. She hesitated then replied,

'I'm going on a trip with my dad.'

'Oh.' My expression replaced itself. 'That's nice.'

'Yeah. Get out of London for a bit . . .'

'You must be close.' I worried I'd overstepped the mark, so I added, 'I'm sorry. I don't mean to pry. I didn't ever know my father – so it's nice to hear things like that.'

Donna faltered. 'Yeah. It's not that we're close exactly. More of. You know. Haven't seen him in a while.' She put the pen back in its cradle. She looked wistful, a little uneasy, though whether about me or the prospect of the trip I couldn't tell. The man delivered her a price; she took an envelope from the pocket of her shirt and out of it a wad of notes, which she handed to him. He called out, 'Panda!' and a teenager emerged from the back and unhooked a key from the many on the board. It took me a second to realize it was the model of the car, not the name of the boy. Donna went after him. She turned at the door and waved to me, half-heartedly, a girlish, guileless gesture, like Philippa would do.

'Bye,' I told her. The door swung shut. I said to no one, 'Take care now.'

∾

The red Panda was outside the hostel when I got back. I drew my own car in a few spaces behind and removed the key from the ignition. The buildings were in darkness, the streets deserted. My hand shook as I unclipped my seat belt. I felt drunk, light-headed, the world unreliable and slender. I hadn't eaten since breakfast, at home with Tom and my children on that alien, snow-covered planet, and forced down a wedge of cake I'd bought at a news-stand but had no craving for; it was spongy and tasteless like loft insulation.

So there it was. He had a child. I should have recognized the name. The Eddistons had been a well-to-do family; I remembered a darling daughter driven out for paid-for education near Barnstaple, had seen her getting off the bus a few times in her knee-high socks and swinging grey skirt, a few years younger than me. She'd have had the baby after his trial, I worked out. Raised it alone. She'd have had to, wouldn't she? I flashed on the father's neat tie, his glossy sedan, the blooming hydrangeas on their polite front lawn.

James Maguire was a parent. A man like him had been given a baby. People could talk to me of justice and fairness all they liked, but there was no justice or fairness in that.

Did he ever glimpse Providence in her?

Did he ever imagine a stranger doing to his loved one what he had done to mine?

I was cold in my bones and would have kept the heater going but I didn't want to draw attention to myself by running the engine, so I hugged Gamma's bag on my lap and rolled the plastic cape into a bolster that would do as a pillow. I had to sleep but was afraid to, in case the moment I turned my back on my thoughts they prodded me awake, a dry finger tapping in the cold spent dawn, and for an instant my sister would be with me, still here, never gone, her lovely smile and her forever eyes, and my heart would soar, reach altitude, prick and burst.

One would imagine there were only so many times a heart could burst, but no, it just went on, it just went on, because although the heart saved more than was kind – her finding my face with her fingers when she was a baby, her lips on my eyelids kissing me night-night, 'Round and Round the Garden' and her soft little naked ticklish armpit; then later, when we were older, pretending to be film stars, Marilyn and Grace, in party frocks Gamma had found us at the jumble sale, hers too big so she kept tripping over the hem and insisting, *'It'll fit me tomorrow!'*, carried swooning by imaginary boyfriends across the sun-flooded fields of our home – sometimes it forgot, and this felt so cruel as to be surely deliberate, a forgetting whose sole purpose was to prompt the bittersweet pain of remembrance. I understood then, with hatred it felt scarcely plausible to possess, that at the point Maguire had killed her he had kept not only his own life but set in motion the birth of another.

I stayed as still as I could. It was a trick I had learnt, to see how still I could make myself. As still as a dead person, as still as Providence in the ground. I saw flowers on a wooden box, covered in loamy black soil. The *click slide thunk* of the shovel and earth.

A taxi pulled up to the kerb in front of me. A man stepped out; he swayed for a moment, taking money out of his wallet. I opened Gamma's bag and extracted the gun and pointed it at him, through the windscreen, my finger on the trigger. The man paid the cabbie then he walked away down the street and the taxi's orange light came on. I lowered the pistol. There were tears on my cheeks.

I rested on the pillow and yawned. My mind turned over,

turned strange. Portions of the hostel dissolved and regrouped. I heard 'Nocturne' playing on a back porch in summer, against the fallen sun, side by side with Providence, my head on her shoulder. *Don't go*, I thought. A sound came from the woods beyond the path. Dark shapes moved in the trees. *Can't you hear that?* But she carried on playing. I felt him coming for us – not just him but all of them, their hearts thumping yellow in their chests. I opened my eyes.

The hostel's windows were blank, glass reflecting the street light so that even if he'd been standing in one I wouldn't have known. Providence hadn't known, hadn't heard, hadn't heeded. Maguire was a man who liked to dwell in hidden places, unseen, and leap out on women passing who had an instant to meet his fiery eye and think, So this is what it comes to, the equation of my life, beauty plus terror plus hope equals this, the full stop, the final egregious waste of it, before the world pinched to black like a wick between damp fingers and they never had another thought in their pretty heads again.

∾

Banging woke me. I thought the car was tumbling down a mountain; I forgot where I was and my body ached and there was a muddy taste in my mouth.

A woman's face appeared in the glass. 'Open up, miss. Open the window, please.'

My neck throbbed. Gamma's bag was slumped on the gear stick and for a horrid instant I presumed the gun had slid out of it, the gloves too, sitting on the passenger seat for all to see. But no, the buckles were fastened and the seat was bare. I corrected the bag and crossed its handles and wound down the window. 'Is there a problem, officer?'

'You're not allowed to park here, ma'am,' she said. She'd got a better look at me and *miss* was a thing of the past. 'We'll need you to move on, I'm afraid.'

The sky was dull. Against it, the constable appeared unnaturally vivid, her carrot-coloured hair parted strictly in the middle. It took me a second to appreciate what she meant and that she wasn't here for him but for me. A pulse started in my temple; I felt it galloping there like a tiny horse. Further down the road, the red car was still parked.

'Sorry.' I put on my glasses. 'I locked myself out of the house. I was, er – waiting for someone to . . . Well, anyway,' I said. 'I must have nodded off.'

'Can I help you with that?' she asked.

I glanced again at the red car, the door to the Victoria. What time was it?

'With what?' I said.

'Getting into your house.'

'Oh, no. Thank you. My husband's there now.'

The officer looked surprised. She had freckles on her nose like ground cinnamon.

'It's nine,' I said, checking my watch; 'I'm late for work. If you don't mind—'

She put a hand on the glass as I tried to wind it back up.

'Is everything all right?'

'Everything's fine.' I tidied my hair and hoped she would

notice the make of the watch and conclude I was too well-to-do to make a habit of sleeping overnight in cars.

'Where do you live?' she said.

'Hm? Not far. It's no problem though. All's well, really. All's well now.'

She frowned. It made a careful pucker in a face that was otherwise so placid it could have been the back of a wooden spoon. She squatted on the pavement and rested her arm along the edge of the window. A thin magenta string was tied around her wrist. The shade was incongruous in comparison with the blunt black and whites of her uniform.

'Would you like me to speak to him?' she asked.

I thought she meant Maguire. Of course she didn't mean Maguire.

'Excuse me?'

'Your husband.' She tapped a finger on the frame. 'Check everything's – friendly.'

'Oh, everything's friendly.' I looked towards the Panda. The hostel. 'I really should get to work,' I said, as evenly as I could. 'Thank you, though.' I put Gamma's case on the seat next to me, steadily.

The officer glanced at it. I smiled at her.

'Business trip, is it?' she said.

'Sorry? Ah.' I patted the bag. 'I've been visiting my sister. Hence the problem with the keys. Jimmy's always saying I should get another set cut – that or a better memory!'

She looked between me and the bag. The bag and me. Out of the corner of my eye I saw two figures in the road, one in a green jacket and one in a checked shirt. I heard doors opening.

I saw myself hurtling off, the officer recording my number plate on her notepad, saying to her colleagues later, *There was something off about that woman*, but she rose in the instant the Panda indicated to pull out and seemed to make up her mind.

'Well,' she said. 'I won't keep you any longer. Look after yourself, OK?'

※

Crossing London was straightforward, the traffic sluggish and the Panda easy to shadow, but once we hit the motorway she hared off unnecessarily into the fast lane, catching and undercutting what few cars there were on the road, making it difficult for me to keep up with without being seen. We passed Reading and Swindon and Bath: I thought of Tom and wondered how yesterday's meeting had gone. At Bristol, we joined the M5. With every south-westerly mile, the suspicion gained on me that I knew where we were going. Dread rose blackly from my ankles. He wouldn't – would he? But we didn't come off where I thought we would; instead, we reached Exeter service station at lunchtime. It was too dicey to go in after them, so I changed clothes on the back seat then went to the loo in a copse behind some picnic tables. I bought a pasty and chewed it monotonously while scrutinizing the entrance.

Donna came out first. She stood against the car flicking through a magazine with Michael Hutchence on the cover. Several times she scanned for Maguire. I wondered if he'd done a runner. He'd have people ready to scoop him up; get his poor unsuspecting girl to drive him to a drop-off point then bolt without a backward glance because he didn't care about her, how could he? I felt affection for her, and pity. I hoped she had something else to put on than that bulky old shirt. Did she even want to be here? Had he forced her to drive him? I worried she had been trying to get a message to me in Wheels 4 Hire but I hadn't noticed. What if he had her at knifepoint in the car? She didn't look like someone being held at knifepoint. Where was her mother? Did her mother know where she was?

Finally, Maguire appeared. He dallied a bit then went into a BT phone booth. I walked behind the cars to get a better view of him. The phone was twisted up to his ear, his green jacket bouncing shards off the cubicle like the Palace of Oz. But it had been careless doing that, for he came out suddenly, and before I knew it had crossed to the car and Donna's face changed in pleased surprise and they got back in and sped off.

I had to sprint. They linked with the carriageway a minute ahead so I was forced to floor the accelerator to catch back up to them, which I managed to a junction on.

The remainder of the journey was punishing. I thought we would circle back on ourselves, resume the route I'd assumed we were taking, back to the village in Devon where we had grown up, but we didn't, we carried on, joining the A-road over Dartmoor. I couldn't think where we were going. They stopped again at a roadside shop: she went in for a bottle of water while Maguire smoked by the car and I watched, concealed, from behind a jet wash; they appeared to be in no hurry. On we went, south past Launceston, further into Cornwall. What light the day had left drained quickly. It grew harder to decipher my target. Headlamps passed in a blur. I was thankful when they peeled off, threading through hamlets, but then she surprised me by pulling snappishly onto a verge, forcing me to bypass and crunch to a stop in a private drive. I tilted my mirror. Her hazards were flashing. The doors were open. I thought, I've been had. They've seen me. But minutes later the doors slammed again and they passed by my offside and crossed a roundabout. My car convulsed back onto the road. I got stuck behind a bread lorry – AS WHOLESOME AS WHOLEMEAL GETS! – before overtaking perilously on a blind turn and catching sight of them just as they drew onto the forecourt of a block of flats.

They got out, first him then her, and went into the building. I parked on the road.

An hour passed. They didn't emerge. Mizzling rain doused the windscreen. It was bitterly cold. Exhaustion lured me: I walked up and down the street trying to shake it off, trying to get warm, wondering where Maguire had disappeared to, anxious that I no longer had eyes on him. Drowsiness and hunger muddled my reasoning; I questioned whether he would ever come out again – what the chances were that he'd clocked me, at the Victoria or at the garage or at any time in between, and this was their plan B, their emergency stroke to escape my radar, smuggled out of the back of wherever this was by whoever lived here, a vehicle at the ready. Possibilities crowded my mind, each one worse than the last. Recklessly, I ventured into the car park and stood in plain sight next to a camper van the colour of Tupperware, searching the windows for him. Who was inside? Who had he come to see?

They still had the Panda. They would come back for that,

surely? Donna, at least, was sensible. The thought calmed me. For the first time, I had an appetite. I'd not had a hot meal since home. Opposite the flats, further down the street, I'd seen a diner with a line of pink seats in the window like a Shearings coach holiday. It was risky in case they came out, but if they stayed then the night was long. From the front, I'd still have a good view.

I walked back down the road. There was no one around, the only sound my footsteps on the wet pavement. A pale moon hovered between the clouds like a fingerprint.

The restaurant, when I reached it, might have been a spaceship, so incompatible was it with its surroundings. I went up to the door and pushed; an old-fashioned bell rang.

Inside, it was warm. A waitress poured coffee behind a bar. A man in a suit sat on a stool with his back to me, his head dipped to a newspaper. I stood next to him and ordered the first thing I saw on the board, a burger deal with bottomless Coke, but something about the man threw me off and when I fumbled to pay I dropped my car keys.

I stooped to pick them up, and saw, and stilled. Between where his trousers ended and his shoes began were his socks, bright yellow, true yellow, like sunshine in July.

'Hello,' said a voice from above. 'What are you doing here?'

12

I loved Providence from the moment I met her. From the night we came home from the Fairfaxes' to find her waiting on our doorstep, swaddled in blankets, her blue eyes gazing up at me in recognition – for despite that unlikelihood, we *did* recognize each other, I felt sure of it – I knew I would love her all the days of my life. She was my sister (half-sister, Gamma supposed, and took pains to repeat – but we'd have no way of knowing until Mary showed up) and I repeated this fact to myself in joyful wonder. Providence was part of me. She had come from the place I had come from, and that meant I was no longer alone.

I devoted myself to taking care of her. It was all I wanted to do. Providence cried a lot, as Gamma said babies did, so I threw myself into a single pursuit: making her happy. When she was upset, I bounced her on my shoulder or rocked her in the cane pram Mrs Lovell had given us, singing her lullabies and reading her books; I gave her Celeste to play with; I walked her up- and downstairs talking to her about the faces in the pictures on the walls, of her dear family departed, Great-Uncle Clarence and the Maiden Aunts and Great-Grandpa Benjamin, or pointed out the sparrows in the trees through the window or showed her my ladybug-house made out of a jam jar – anything to make her smile or warble or reach for my face with her fat seashell hands and forget her troubles for a while.

I found I had a knack for it. 'You've always had that way about you, Birdie,' said Gamma, as though this were no surprise to her. But since I'd every day of my life been on the receiving end of Gamma's care, I'd never considered myself able to take on that role. 'See the way she looks at you,' said my – our! – grandmother; 'she thinks the absolute world of you.' As I did, her. I loved to play mother, wheeling Providence around the village's cobbled streets in her pram, her face a plum in her bonnet, her hair a curl of butter, stopping occasionally to fuss her blankets or put my head in close so I could smell her fresh, watery smell, of caves, of rain, of all and nothing. As she grew from a chirruping baby to a plump-legged toddler, our bond grew stronger. I took her to the playground and pushed her on the swings; I introduced her to the goats at the Brewsters' farm; we went on Tuesdays to the village hall where the wooden toolsets and dollies and silver tops came out, and she would laugh delightedly at the thumping hammers and the way the sunlight sheened off the spinning metal. From an early age I could tell her good nature: children poked her or pulled her hair or snatched her toy, but she never showed she minded, she just regarded them patiently, indulgently, as the vicar sometimes regarded us from his pulpit.

Providence looked special, too. Of course I thought so: I thought everything about her was special. But she did. She looked as though she had been drawn and only half coloured in. She looked like a glass of lemon Quosh that had been too much watered down. She looked like if you set a match to her she'd melt like candle wax. Her skin had a goldish sheen that reminded me of the flat-faced angels we hung on the tree at Christmas. Her hair was so pale it was nearly white, so that sometimes, when I found her playing on the living-room rug, flooded in heavenly sunlight, I had the sense that she had come from somewhere I had never been and knew things I would never know. I thought of her as set apart from other people. I couldn't express this notion to Gamma and besides I knew it was fanciful. Who didn't deem their loved ones special? Instead I guarded it privately, my secret. Providence was my gift. She was meant for me and I for her.

A year after she had sailed to our shores in her basket, Providence said her first word. We were coming back from church when a note rose from her pushchair: 'Bird.'

I clapped my hands. 'Yes!' I said, thinking of the sparrows. 'Where? Where is it?'

Gamma touched my arm. She smiled at me. 'I think she means you,' she said.

∽

I found the courage to ask Gamma the question that had been on my mind. It was a windy day and we were pegging out nappies in the yard. I had to stand on an upturned bucket to reach the washing line, which whipped and snapped between its ties. My sister was shaking her rattle on the grass, her hair gusting, her newfound chatter filling the air with notes. Music was how her voice sounded to me, tuneful and comforting and somehow distant, like an instrument being played behind a closed door in a grand house.

'Do you think she'll come back for her?' I said. I didn't ask about me. I had long since given up asking about me.

Gamma fumbled with a peg. 'Who?' she said, but she knew.

'Mary. Will she come back for Providence?'

A nappy flew off the line. I reached to pick it up. 'I don't know,' said Gamma.

Panic hit me like a stubbed toe. 'What if she does? What will we do?'

'Nothing. There's nothing we can do.'

I twisted the nappy in my fists until it burned. 'But she can't just change her mind,' I said. 'Providence is ours now. This is her home.'

'A child's home is its mother,' said Gamma.

I fought the urge to throw it down. 'But Mary's not her mother,' I said, my voice deep with bitterness. 'Not properly.'

Gamma put her arm round me. 'Now, little bird.'

I cast her off. 'Does that mean I'm homeless?'

'I beg your pardon?'

'If a mother's a home, then I don't have one. Do I?'

Gamma was injured. 'That's not what I meant . . .'

'What, then?' I tacked the nappy back on the line but my eyes were so full of tears I could hardly see.

Gamma gave me a peg. 'We have to trust,' she said. 'It's all in God's plan.'

'Is it?' I said. 'What if God had nothing to do with it?'

'God's to do with everything.'

I couldn't accept it. 'Even mothers who don't want their children?'

Gamma reached the end of the line. She stooped to pick up the laundry basket.

'I suppose she's not here to tell us, is she?' I said, getting off the bucket, helplessness sitting in me like a brick, the depth of my anger impossible to express.

Gamma folded the peg bag. 'Mary's . . . a troubled soul.'

'Then so am I,' I shot back. 'And so is Providence. All because of her!'

I wiped my eyes. I felt furious and scared. Furious with Mary for having me and having Providence and wanting neither of us. Scared because it turned out she could come back any day and take my sister away from me, when she didn't care about her like I did, she wouldn't protect her like I would. It wasn't fair that Gamma had to do it all, nor was it fair that I was taking it out on her now, when she'd done nothing wrong and everything right, and her patience and compassion were virtues I was trying to live up to but couldn't.

'Don't you resent her?' I said. 'Don't you feel cross with her for what she's done?'

But Gamma didn't say. I wished she would say. She never voiced hurt over Mary or said a bad word against her; it was just our duty to sweep up the mess she had made.

Providence started crying. I scooped her up and we went inside.

∽

In the spring of '58, we took to visiting the canal path. I would set off in time for Providence's nap, with sandwiches for lunch and a favourite book, *The Little White Horse* or a *Clever Polly*. Daffodils swayed fatly in the grass, their trumpets heralding the new warmth. The canal was bottle brown, unbroken but for a mallard skirting the reeds and shedding arrows across the water. I was reading on the low wall one day when I heard a whistling sound coming from further down the walkway. The air was so hazy that I didn't detect him at first, he must have been standing very still, about thirty yards away, then his shape hardened and I saw him coming towards me. I touched the pushchair, the wispy top of my sister's head. He had one hand in his pocket and in the other was a paper bag, held out ahead of him, to me. When he entered the tunnel under the bridge, the light stopped behind him and he filled with shadow. All I could see were the sharp yellow points of his teeth.

'What've you got there?' His voice bounced off the brickwork. *There, there . . .*

I heard myself swallow. 'My grandmother knows where I am.' *Am, am.*

'Do you want to come home with me?' he said.

'No.'

Oh, oh.

'I've got kitties at my house.'

I shook my head.

'You can feed them if you want. Kitties like to be fed.'

Providence stirred in her sleep. 'We've got to go home now,' I said. 'Our grandmother's waiting for us.' His eyes were black. I saw them shining in the dark.

'Here, kitty-kitty,' he said, tilting the bag to Providence. 'Here, kitty-kitty-kitty.'

I grabbed the pushchair and ran all the way home. Providence bounced about like a jack-in-the-box but she didn't cry, she didn't peep, she just stayed quiet as I ran for us both and kept on running, not daring to look back until I had turned onto the avenue and reached our door and closed it behind me, breathless, sure that if I did I would see yellow woods, a yellow sky, a grinful of teeth and the whole of that man climbing after me.

∽

Time passed and Mary didn't come. I lived in fear of it happening, every knock at the door a jolt. I remembered her turning up out of the blue that day we'd gone to the park and felt uneasy whenever Providence was out of my sight. But each day my sister came in from the street where she'd been playing with her friends, and we made sugar buns for tea then she went to bed with *Little Grey Rabbit*. All I could think about was keeping her safe.

I turned twelve. We were in the kitchen one afternoon making beef pies for the Maguire family. The vicar had organized a doorstep collection for them because Maeve had lost her job and there were four sons to feed and a husband who was never at home. '*There's scarcely any of them there but the littlest!*' Betty had complained. '*She'll not be grateful, you mark my words.*'

Maurice wasn't any better. He'd come over for help with his homework; we'd spent the morning doing arithmetic in the bedroom I shared with Providence – or, rather, I'd done arithmetic while Maurice had stared sulkily at the posters I had on the walls of Ricky Nelson and James Dean. 'Don't know what you see in them,' he'd mumbled, scratching the page with pencil scribbles of Supermarine Spitfires instead of the workings-out he was meant to have done. 'They're girly boys. Look – they've got make-up on like my mother wears!' I didn't feel much about the pin-ups one way or the other: Jenny at number 14 had given them to me for my birthday and I thought they made my half of the room look more grown-up. Providence, five then, still scattered hers with soft toys.

'They don't deserve it,' said Maurice now, crossing his arms as I weighed out flour.

'Everyone deserves a helping hand,' said Gamma.

'Not them,' said Maurice, stubbornly passing me a sieve. 'They're rotten, the gang of them. All that time I've had off school—' He turned to me, justifying himself. 'That's why I can't do arithmetic. It's the Maguires' fault, not mine.'

'I understand,' said Gamma. 'If that'd happened to Birdie—'

'You'd change your tune then—'

'I expect I would. But I'd *like* to try seeing the ins and outs of the situation.'

'What ins and outs?'

She tapped flour into a bowl. 'There are reasons,' she said. 'What goes on behind the scenes. It's never just . . . *badness*. People aren't born bad.'

Maurice huffed. 'Some are.'

Gamma wiped lard around a dish as the smell of frying beef filled the kitchen. She knew she wasn't winning. I felt torn between her argument and his. Gamma's line was always that we'd no right to judge, we couldn't possibly know a stranger's circumstances, but while I wanted to believe this, and to some extent I did, I was by then coming to suspect that she was too trusting, hopeful of other people's fundamental goodness to the point of naivety, and that Mary had given her no choice but to invest in this philosophy and stick to it. For an unpleasant moment I thought I wasn't so unlike a Maguire boy after all: both of us born of parents who couldn't care less. Part of me wanted to act like them, run wild, get arrested, show how full of frustration I was. Instead, I held it inside.

'Well,' I said, sassing her, 'if it's in God's plan, He'll look after them. Won't He?'

Gamma didn't think that was funny. 'Don't help if you don't want to,' she said.

I felt bad for upsetting her; I hadn't meant it, I'd been showing off. But Maurice said, 'OK then. Come on, Birdie, let's find something else to do.'

He went outside. I saw him through the window helping Providence untangle her skipping rope. I thought how out of place he seemed against our humble surroundings.

Gamma rolled out pastry. She watched me for a moment. 'You don't have to listen to other people,' she said. 'Whoever they are. Listen to *your* mind, know what *you* think, that's what's important – never mind anyone else. Do you see what I'm saying, Birdie?'

I thought that I did.

∽

I met the Maguire brothers for the first time when I was thirteen years old. It was the same day that Bill Mackey delivered us the piano. He'd saved it from the scrapyard on Seaton Hump. Bill knew 'Blue Moon' and hitched up his shirtsleeves and played it for us with lots of mistakes. The piano was a humble upright. It was knocked about and out of tune and some of the flats and sharps were jammed, but Providence didn't mind. I lifted her onto the stool and arranged her hands on the keys. She pressed them and got a happy fright. We laughed. She pressed them again. We showed her the very high notes and the very low notes, and she stomped her fists up and down the octaves to hear every one.

She spent all morning with it. Indiscriminate banging gave way to more organized arrangements – Bill showed her the major chords and after that she was away, the beginnings of melodies breaking through the din like plant shoots pushing at soil. Gamma and I were astounded at how quickly she took to it, and how proficiently. There had been signs early on if we'd thought to pay attention – how my sister's face lit up when we sang to her at bedtime, or when the jingle of the ice-cream van came past, or when, up at Maurice's house, Mrs Fairfax put on an Elvis Presley record, 'Are You Lonesome Tonight?', and she stopped what she was doing and listened, riveted, with an expression of fondness and remembering, as if she had stumbled across someone who had long ago broken her heart.

After lunch, Gamma said, 'That's enough now, it's a beautiful day, go outside for some fresh air; it'll still be waiting for you when you get back.' I'm not sure Providence believed that, imagining that the piano might disappear as swiftly as it had arrived, but I managed to persuade her with the promise of a bag of lemon sherbets I'd found in my skirt pocket. 'You're in charge now, Birdie,' said Gamma. 'Look after each other.'

It was the height of summer. The day was searing, the fierce sun blazing in a taut blue sky. Providence wanted to run. I said it was too hot for that. She said, 'Only because you can't catch me!' and dashed off down the avenue. I ran after her. By the time I turned the corner she was already halfway along the terraces so I made a big show of getting out the sherbets, saying how sweet and refreshing they were, before she let me reach her and grudgingly took one off me and unwrapped it. We ate the rest of the packet, sharing the last so it was even, passing it back and forth between us until it was a tiny, gluey filament.

Out of the village we went, Providence skipping while I walked alongside, past the church and towards the railway yard. 'Come and see,' she said excitedly when we got there; 'I want to show you something.' In the wall by the signal box was a small, deep alcove. My sister's voice was a whisper: 'I found them last week, with Mrs Lovell.'

Tucked inside the alcove was an intricately woven birds' nest.

'Fledglings?' I said.

'Shh! They're babies, they might be sleeping.' But they must have been sleeping very soundly for there was no movement at all coming from the nest. Providence touched it gently. 'Oh,' she said, biting her lip. 'They've gone. Where've they gone?'

I thought a cat had got them. 'I expect they flew away,' I said.

'Mrs Lovell said the foxes might have them.'

'I'm sure they didn't,' I fibbed.

A fine white feather, as long as my hand, blew out of the hole and landed at her feet. She picked it up. 'It's so soft,' she said, running it across her lip. 'Is it the mother's?'

I frowned. 'It looks like a dove's.' But that seemed unlikely.

'Maybe the dove tried to look after them,' said Providence. 'From the foxes.'

'Maybe she taught them to fly.'

Providence stroked the feather. 'You have it,' she said, handing it to me. I said I didn't want it. 'Then we can't put it back in there,' she said. 'Or on the ground. Feathers should be free.' She climbed the hill and put the feather on her palm and blew as hard as she could. It lifted, caught by a ribbon of breeze, which sent it up over the trees and away.

∽

She was in a strange mood after that, tired, I expected, from the piano and the heat, so we made for home. Providence hummed a tune she'd learnt as we went. We took a shortcut down Nail's Lane past the Brewsters' field, hurrying because I never liked to linger there: I could feel the wooden scarecrow's eyes on me, his flat face and crooked grin, something of that man buried in the thick yellow crop of my childhood, known and dreaded to me.

A shaven-headed boy was perched on the stile. He'd pushed the arms of his T-shirt up to reveal the small, hard apples of his biceps. I took Providence's hand.

'Oi,' said Ron Maguire. 'Where d'you think yer going?'

I should have carried on. Instead, I thought about what Gamma would do.

'Home,' I said, turning round. 'You should too.'

'What, to yer house?' He grinned. 'Can if yer invite me.'

I walked back to him. Providence's hand felt clammy in mine.

'You don't have to do this,' I said.

'Do what?'

'You could make better of your life.'

He laughed, it seemed with sincere amusement. 'Shut up, bitch.'

'You don't have to be a bully,' I said. 'You don't have to be a criminal.'

Ron drew on his cigarette. He scratched his bare knee and looked at me for a long time. 'Piss off,' he said.

'I'm trying to help,' I said. I didn't want to give up. 'Not everyone's against you.'

'What makes yer think I want 'elp? I dun need no one's 'elp. I'm fine as I am.'

Next to me, Providence squeezed my hand. She said, 'Birdie. They're coming.'

More boys were walking towards us. The oldest Maguire, Christopher, the 'grave felon', as Bill always called him, and the youngest, James, whom I'd only ever heard referred to as the 'littlest' and the 'baby', so it disconcerted me to see him close up as a rumpled ten-year-old, worldly in the face, his features pinched and indignant, his fair hair scruffy.

'What're you doing?' James asked Ron, with the swagger of a child looking to impress his brothers: his confidence was put on, I saw, so determined to convince that it bordered on hostility. He unnerved me in a way I couldn't quite define – more than the others, whose boldness was more straightforward somehow.

Ron answered, '— off.'

Providence hugged my side. I said to Ron, 'It's not too late.'

He climbed down off the stile. There was a knife in his hand, sunlight glittering off the blade. Providence started crying. I saw Maurice shaking in a darkened room, his bruised eye, his trembling voice: '*A proper one. With a leather hilt.*' I stepped in front of my sister, determined not to be afraid, but my heart was pumping so fast I thought it would burst through my chest.

'I'm gunna stick 'er,' he said. 'Stick 'em both. Make 'em bleed!' I tried to speak but my tongue didn't work. I couldn't move at all, not a single part of my body; I was rooted to the spot. Ron pushed me, not hard, for sport not for kill, a yellow-toothed sneer across his face. James said, 'Let's go,' or 'Let go,' but Christopher moved, or was it Ron who moved first? In a split second, Ron was thrown to the ground. Christopher pounded him in the ribs and he took as much as he got, the brothers brawling like savages, grunting and gasping, choking each other, their brutishness unlike anything I'd seen before; I was transfixed by the wildness of it, the animal ferocity, how they thumped and seized and hit and wounded each other, blood spreading on their clenched fists, their shirts hauled up over their backs. The knife was freed and thrown onto the road. I thought Christopher would come at us then too, but he didn't. He turned to me and said, 'Go.'

I didn't need to be told twice. I grabbed Providence and we ran down Nail's Lane. A police car was coming, its bells clanging; it stopped next to us and one of the windows came down. 'Miss – have you seen the Maguire boys? We've had a report of loitering.'

I told them everything. I pointed back the way we'd come and watched as their faces set in a determined grimace and they sped away. My sister was crying again. I held her and told her it would be all right. The setting sun flickered accusingly through the trees. A sad and sorry feeling gathered in my heart.

∞

My encounter with the Maguires stuck like flypaper in my mind. I didn't tell Maurice about it. I didn't want to admit that part of me had enjoyed the drama of our confrontation and that I thought of it more often than I should – of Ron on the stile, mean but simple; of the flint-eyed young one, James; and of Christopher, the victor, the one they called Kip, well, my memory of him wasn't to look at as much as to feel. I tried to recall the detail in his face, but couldn't.

Neither did I want to admit to a sense of disappointment, not in the brothers but in myself. Chance had been my meeting with the policemen and chance, in turn, my informing: if we hadn't run into them, I didn't think I'd have mentioned the episode to anyone but Gamma. What had it come to, after all? A brag, a threat, a shove; grandstanding words. The violence had been entirely between them – I hadn't been hurt. I was annoyed at myself for letting fear get the better of me, which, now I was safely on the other side, seemed spineless and unfounded: Ron would never have hurt me, he wouldn't have dared; it was all a big show-off, a weak boy playing at being a strong man. But the fact that I had done to the Maguires precisely what they'd expected me to do exposed the flaws in me. I had pleaded with Ron to make a change, yet I'd been willing to throw him to the wolves at the first opportunity. Gamma said, 'Don't trouble yourself, Birdie. They frightened you. It was wrong. Anyone else would have done the same.' But I didn't want to be anyone else. I wanted to be like her. Just as charitable, just as kind. I wished I had done things differently.

In the weeks and months after, Providence started to pull away from me. At home, she played piano nearly all the time: Gamma bought her some sheet music, the tunes taking her somewhere in her head I couldn't follow, and when she wasn't playing she was humming the melodies she'd learnt, a distant, dreaming look on her face. Then she started to spend longer away from the house. Often she would go out riding her bicycle until late, disappearing after meals for hours at a time. I said she was too young to be doing that, going out alone, but Gamma considered my sister to have been touched by God, the bestower of her musical gift and thus divinely protected by Him, and duly gave her more liberties than she had ever given me. The separation hurt. Gamma said not to fuss; Providence was adventurous, she loved the outdoors, our community would watch her. But I missed being the centre of her world. I wished for the days when she had relied on me, when it had just been her and me: a time when I'd been able to mother her and all she knew of life was through me.

As time passed, I began to suspect that she wasn't, in fact, alone, but was meeting someone. I grew worried about who that was. One day, I decided to follow her. I did so at a distance, watching her teeter on her bicycle to the Brewsters' field, where to my surprise she climbed the stile and disappeared in the crop. I hid in the trees, watching.

James Maguire was waiting for her beneath the wooden scarecrow. Next to him was a large black dog. Instinctively, I fretted. He was four years older than her. From a *'bad family'* (was that my voice I heard, or Betty Mackey's?). He was luring her away from me, sharing times with her I had no stake in. But even as these reasons passed through my head, I saw the faults in them, not reasons at all but excuses, showing me to be as weak-willed as I'd been with the constables. That he unnerved me was no grounds for dislike. My aversion came from his situation, his volatile brothers, the father everyone reviled, from anxiety I'd inherited from Maurice – and my challenge, therefore, was to appreciate, as Gamma did, that he was his own person, distinct from them.

Still, I said to Providence when she came home, 'Are you friends with James Maguire now?'

'Yes,' she said, washing her hands in the sink.

'Be careful.'

She turned off the tap. 'Why?'

I didn't know how to answer her. 'I'm just trying to protect you,' I said.

∾

That Christmas, our mother came back. I hadn't seen her in eight years. It was late in the day and Gamma and I were washing up. The house had been full all afternoon, our living room a mishmash of put-up tables strewn with crackers and tissue-paper hats. My stomach hurt. The bleeding had come on after the Queen's Speech, and while the adults played charades I'd kept absconding to the bathroom to try and stem the flow with a bag of cotton wool I'd found in a tub under the basin. I'd heard girls at school discussing their monthlies so I'd known it was coming, but it was more painful than I had expected and I didn't know what I would do when I ran out of wool or what Gamma would say when she found it all gone. I was thinking how to tell her when there came a knock at the door.

When I went to answer it, Mary wasn't standing right there but partway down the street, searching the dark fronts of houses. Her high heels sounded like spitting gunfire. 'There you are,' she said, turning when she heard me. 'Have you moved?'

She came towards me and was illuminated. I could tell she'd been drinking. Her eyes were glassy. She had a softer appearance than in my memory; I was as tall as her.

'I thought I'd the wrong—' she started. 'Number fourteen. Was it fourteen?'

'Sixteen.'

'It looks different.' She held a bag to her chest. It was the same one she'd had the day we'd gone to feed the ducks. 'Just like you, Bridget. How old are you now?'

Over the rooftops, carollers sang 'Silent Night'. There was a sob in my throat.

'Come in if you want,' I said.

The living room was warm and smelt of clementines. A fire burned in the grate, making the pink glass bells on the fir tree twinkle and glaze, lighting up the splashy foils in an open tin of Quality Street. Gamma was there. She had on a housecoat, the one with the buttons missing down the front, and for an illogical moment I thought she was leaving. Then I saw she still had a tea towel in her hands and was only wearing it because she was cold.

'Hello, Mum,' said Mary. 'Are you pleased I came? It's Christmas.'

Mary put her bag by her feet. Her face was damp from arriving or crying.

'Can I stay the night?' she said. 'Just one night, I promise.'

Gamma nodded. She said to the tea towel, 'Would you like to see her?'

We went upstairs to Providence's and my bedroom. My sister had gone to sleep early, worn out by the day. Moonlight streamed in through the window. Her complexion was luminous, like Mrs Fairfax's tarnished silver coming up with Goddard's polish.

'Is she healthy?' whispered Mary. 'Is she happy?'

Gamma said, 'Yes.' I thought, no thanks to you. Nothing has ever been thanks to you.

Next morning, Providence was courteous, even charming, answering our mother's questions as she might a teacher's, well-mannered but offering no expansion. She performed a new piece for her on the piano, stiffly, as if it had been requested of her by an examining board. Mary exclaimed over it afterwards, clapping and swooning – 'But this is exceptional! What grade are you now?' – and Providence smiled graciously and said she wasn't taking grades, she just played because she liked it, so Mary told me off for not encouraging her more and making 'the most of her remarkable talent'. I tried to keep my temper, not wanting to upset Providence, but she seemed, on the surface at least, unperturbed by the arrival of a stranger in our lives. 'I've got you, Birdie,' she said, when I ventured to ask if she was troubled by it; 'why would I need anything else?'

As the new year began, the four of us fumbled through our new reality. I felt as if I were treading a tightrope, terrified that at any moment Mary would leave and take my sister with her. But she showed no signs of going; instead she settled in as if she had every right to. She asked how our lives had been with the polite incuriousness of someone uninterested in cars being told that theirs had been fixed: I understood then that she'd no concern for the years we had spent raising Providence – the years I'd spent raising myself – and the toll it had taken on Gamma managing the things her daughter didn't want.

∾

A night turned into ten months. It was the longest time I had ever spent with my mother. She took pains to repeat how much of herself she saw in Providence ('I called her Catherine, but you weren't to know that'), which every time seemed a slight towards me, as my sister and I looked nothing alike. There was competition between us, certainly – to fry Providence's bread in the morning, to pack her lunch or praise her piano-playing, which grew more extraordinary by the day. The Fairfaxes bought us a phonograph; Providence listened to a piece of music, found the starting note and imitated it. 'She takes after me,' said Mary, closing her eyes, which when shut were round and slightly protuberant, with a reddish sheen like cracked tomatoes, as she drifted in reverie to 'Waltz in A Minor'. 'I've always had a musical affinity. Peter In London says I'm a born creative.' Peter In London came up a lot, as did a list of other names, mostly men's: Richard and Oscar and Anthony, Gregory and Mick, as if we should have known them because they were important enough, surely, to be known by everyone. Peter In London planned to stage an art exhibition for her, she said, once she travelled back. I had thought of her all these years as living by the sea and it had been easy to picture her there, a quiet, self-castigating life, lonely and spiked by longing for us, so to learn this felt like a cheat.

Mary showed us her art, the smaller, postcard-sized pieces, which she'd brought in her bag. They were exercises in brown and green – toad colours, I decided, with that same pimply, amphibious texture, slapped with gelatinous oils then covered in mosaics of what appeared to be debris recovered from the ground: bottle-tops, tufts of grass, slips of paper with words written on in childish script – *Meaning. Apple core. Juliet.* Gamma thought them striking but I couldn't understand them at all. I thought they were ugly.

At first, she made attempts to be motherly, but as time went on the cracks started to show. Mary rejected the room she shared with Gamma, preferring to sleep alone. So we put her cot downstairs in place of the piano and moved the piano onto the porch, which made a more romantic sound of it in a way, reaching us as it did from afar. But still she wasn't happy. She drank bottles of gin and left rattling carcasses around the house. She slept all day. She shouted at Providence when she played her pieces loudly or at inconvenient times. She drifted between rooms, bursting spontaneously into tears.

Then Providence came to me one morning.

'You've got to help me, Birdie,' she said.

I thought it was about Mary. 'What is it?' I said, putting down my book.

'It's Jimmy.'

I felt alarm, but she went on, 'It's his dog. When his dad gets back, he says he'll have to give her up! He'll have to send her to the pound. Oh, Birdie, please – help us!'

'Of course I will,' I said, putting my arms round her and soothing her tears. I was glad that she had come to me. Here was my chance to do right by the youngest Maguire, to make things better for him and in the same stroke be invited into their friendship.

I made a decision. Later that day, I went to see Maurice at his house. Straight away he misread my purpose: 'Steal something off a Maguire? I'm game.' But Dr Fairfax had tended the dog before at his practice and I knew he'd have good intentions. After a short discussion with Mrs Fairfax, in which it was decided the acquisition of a dog would benefit Maurice, and goodness knew they had the space for it, he agreed the pet would be better off living with them.

When I got home, Providence hugged me. 'Thank you,' she said. 'Just wait till we tell Jimmy! I knew you'd fix it for us, Birdie.'

I felt that I had. As I went to bed that night, I imagined my good deed travelling over the houses to where James slept, falling across his dreaming face like sunlight.

Shortly before my sister's eighth birthday, without warning, Mary left. We woke up one morning and she was gone, her bed made, the sheets folded. On the pile was one of her postcards: *Calling. Towers. A bear.* 'You keep it,' said Gamma. 'I don't want it,' I said.

We didn't move anything after she'd gone. We kept thinking she might turn up again but of course she didn't. In years to come, it became hard not to blame her for what happened. If it weren't for Mary, we'd never have had that empty bed. We wouldn't have thought to accommodate another person, and I wouldn't have seen the idea arrive with Gamma like the first snowflake of winter settling at her feet. But there it was, and is, and ever will be. Gamma suggested to me one wet autumn night in 1962 that that Maguire boy – I knew the one – needed a place to call home, and God had asked her to let him stay.

13

The suited man's features were familiar, but altered, like a close relative of someone I knew well. It was as if I had drawn him years ago then changed my mind, and wiped clean that attempt and begun another. His attention when he looked at me was complete.

I asked him, 'Do I know you?'

There was a delay, like the time lapse on a long-distance phone call. When he spoke it was languorous, a beat behind where it should have been: 'I've mistaken you for somebody else,' he said.

The waitress took my money. A vase-sized Coke appeared on the counter. I'd never been a Coke drinker; I couldn't remember why I had ordered it.

'Who?' I said.

He returned to his newspaper, a grainy picture of Nigel Lawson outside number 11, Downing Street. 'A friend of my wife's,' he said. 'You have the same coat.'

'Where is she?'

'The friend?'

'Your wife.'

He shut the paper. 'In Australia. She's saving the Uluhua bird from extinction.'

'I've never heard of it.'

'Neither have I. Fast on its feet, apparently. Flightless. I think she made it up.'

The TV screen in the corner flashed with red and blue lights, *ring-ting-ting!*, the person on the gameshow had won a hatchback. A car rotated on a glittering dais while the winner put her hands over her face and sobbed; the presenter's grin was Colgate-white.

The waitress refilled his coffee cup. The liquid was thin and had no steam coming off it. My companion dropped in four sugar cubes, one after the other, and stirred. His top lip was bigger than his lower one. He'd lost his scar or else I'd rubbed it out. I'd given him hair – yellow, like the socks, which was at odds with his age. He was younger than he should have been, but still old enough to be my father. I took my glasses off and put them on again. The lenses were smudged and hard to see through.

'They win holidays too,' he said, setting down the spoon. 'One got a trip to Egypt. I don't think I'd go if I won. It's thousands of pounds but I don't think I'd go. It's too far and I don't like flying.' He patted his suit pockets. 'Flightless bird.'

'Do you want this here?' the waitress asked, setting down a tray. The burger was sweating through its paper wrapper and the funnel of chips had spilt across the plastic.

'I'll sit in the window,' I said, Maguire and Donna appearing in my mind: for a moment I'd forgotten to remember them. I carried the tray to a view of the flats and put Gamma's bag on the bench opposite. I took the hat off the burger. The patty was greasy and there was a limp sheet of lettuce across the top, which came off like peeled skin.

The man went back to reading his paper. The TV chunnered on. I ate a mouthful of meat, which had texture but no taste. I checked the car park and saw the Panda still next to the camper van. I had the sensation of falling asleep then being woken, unsure of where the noise that had roused me had come from. Yellow light sparkled off the tarmac.

'A Wiltshire woman has been reported missing since yesterday morning,' the television was saying. Slowly, I tuned into it. They weren't referring to me, surely: a Wiltshire woman sounded so . . . comely, busty maybe, and irreverent, like the Wife of Bath. But no, suddenly there was a photograph of me onscreen – and it was an awful one, taken at Tom's cousin's wedding years ago after one of the miscarriages, which I knew straight away because I was holding a glass of champagne and I never drank in those days since I was always trying to be pregnant, so the only time I did was when I definitely wasn't. I worried the man had seen, but he was still with his paper.

'Forty-one-year-old Bridget Keller was last seen driving away from her mother-in-law's home at Drove Close, Bickleford' – and there was Wilma's house, and Wilma standing outside it, self-consciously delicate, wrapped in a ginger wool cardigan that made her look like one of her Sunday-perfect brandy snaps: 'Bridget? If you're out there, come back. It's not too late.' Then the camera snapped to Tom at our kitchen table, a framed picture of the children behind him, the salt and pepper shakers on the worktop, our fridge covered in Joe's latest attempts with the letter magnets: DOG MAD C R BOG. The whole scene was so bizarre and unexpected I almost started laughing. Tom had a heavy jumper on that I hadn't seen in a while and liked; I'd picked it out for him in the closing-down sale of a boutique in town. 'We're concerned,' he said. 'We don't know if she's safe.'

I was confused. Hadn't Tom seen my note? He must have. I'd left it by the bed, he couldn't have missed it. He and I had spoken many times about how Maguire's release would affect us: I'd always said that I would need space to come to terms with it, so here I was, taking space. I had never given him reason to suspect I'd do anything drastic. Then, as he carried on talking, I realized the circus in the kitchen was *because* he had seen the note, and presumably the police had too, and they'd put two and two together and spoken to Catriona and worked out my intentions, and now I was a loaded weapon, so to speak.

'My wife's in a vulnerable state,' he said. 'Our children miss her.' The person he was with, off camera (sitting in the chair I sat in, at the crumb-strewn tablecloth next to Joe's Mumm-Ra action figurine), asked, 'If Bridget were here, what would you tell her?'

Now Tom looked directly down the lens. I saw he hadn't been sleeping. His hair was unruly. I remembered the night I had met him, at a colleague's party when we were twenty-five, perched on the back of her corduroy sofa, smoking a roll-up out of a cracked window and laughing with his friends. His smile had opened his face like an umbrella.

'*That's a relief*,' he'd said to me when we'd sat down for the meal. I'd thought he meant he was hungry. I'd been too busy puzzling over the cutlery on the table and how many courses it indicated, and whether I'd have to stay for them all. Providence had been dead for a year by then and it was the first time I had gone anywhere. I wasn't used to socializing. It seemed pointless – worse than that, *insulting*, the frippery of it, the kitsch, the shiny baubles of idiotic small talk while my pain grinned horribly beneath. I didn't have anything to say for myself that wasn't Providence. I couldn't talk on the outskirts of things, act as if my life were normal when there was a huge hole blown through the middle of it that everyone pretended not to see; at the same time I couldn't speak about her either. I hadn't spoken about her with anyone. I could hardly say her name out loud.

'*Just I was hoping I'd get put next to you,*' Tom had said, smiling, filling up my wine glass then his. '*Sandra must have known. I'll thank her later. She says you work together?*'

I'd been a secretary in an insurance firm at the time. '*Yes,*' I said, drinking the wine. '*Actually, I've not been in much lately.*' And there it was, my dark little float, ready, always, to bob to the surface. '*Oh?*' he'd enquired, so I'd told him before the pasta arrived. I'd expected him to make a polite getaway – he struck me as polite, and there had been opportunity after the main course when the table disbanded to smoke and dance; instead we'd left together and sat by the river sharing the bottle of paint-stripper vodka he bought from the off-licence. It was the first night I'd fallen asleep thinking about someone other than her.

I loved Tom and I loved my children. It wasn't so easy as to say, if I loved them then I wouldn't be doing this. There had been times when I'd wondered if the adoptions would overturn my plan; whether Philippa and Joe would fill a void in me that made everything all right, giving me perspective and purpose I'd been lacking before and which diminished the looming presence of the Maguire brothers in my mind. But it turned out love could run seamlessly alongside its opposite: my devotion to my children and my hatred of those men were separate. There was no eclipse, rather a reluctant brand of coexistence, and as I watched Philippa grow towards the age I had been then – and before that, the age Providence had been when she'd died – it became harder to know where one ended and the other began.

'Bridget,' my husband implored me now. 'We want to help you. Please, come home. For the sake of our family.' And I saw in his expression, his bloodshot eyes and unshaven jaw, that Tom had never taken me seriously. All those times I had raged against Maguire, all my tears, all my diatribes, he'd read them not as intention but the stray threads of unprocessed anger, the aftertaste of grief. Finally, he realized what I meant to do. That it wasn't enough for me to lament Maguire's living – I had to stop it.

The news moved on. I forced down the rest of the burger while keeping an eye on Donna's red car. They came out a minute before ten. I got up to leave. Music was playing; I couldn't tell where from. It was a piano piece Providence had liked, speeded up from its original arrangement, sampled in a dance song. The suited man pressed the TV remote and the screen faded. One of his shoes had fallen off and lay sole-up inside the legs of his stool; the foot of the sock was duller than the cuff and there was a frayed hole in the heel.

'They're not leaving tonight,' he said. 'You can sit down again.'

I saw Maguire and Donna get into the car. One door closed then the other.

The car didn't move. Neither did I.

'He'll sleep there,' he said. 'He's not going until morning. Do you like this tune?'

I turned to him. 'I don't know it.'

'Yes, you do.'

'It's different,' I said.

'But the same.'

The song ended. I thought another would follow but the only sound was the steady hum of the refrigerators. He groped about under the stool for his shoe and when he found it he stood; the stool scraped harshly as he pushed it back. On his feet he looked thinner and frailer than I'd had him in my memory. His shoes were ruined and had no laces; they fringed the bones of his ankles like bad gums. There were sparse patches in his hair.

'See?' he said, signalling through the glass. 'They're safer in the car.'

'Than what?'

'Than in the building.'

I watched the Panda, waiting for it to move. It had always amazed me that James Maguire could sleep. That the world still gave him reprieve, that he could be cradled in blissful unconsciousness when he should have been alert to his act every hour without relief. I hoped Providence haunted him. I hoped she never left him, even in dreams.

THE SUNSHINE MAN

The suited man sat facing me, next to Gamma's bag, and set his hands on the table, palms down, with a patient, assured energy. Close to, he appeared artificially lit, as though he were sitting under stage lights. The table, too, had a synthetic quality, the grain too uniform to be natural, its surface unblemished. The cruet set was unfilled.

'What are you doing?' he said. 'Here, late at night. There, wherever you're going.'

'Excuse me?'

'I know who you are.'

I blinked. 'You saw the television.'

'Yes.'

'Will you tell them?'

'No.' He picked up a chip, examined it, replaced it in its cardboard fan and moved the tray away. I stood. 'Sit down,' he said. I checked the car. Its lights had gone off. I sat.

He turned the empty salt. 'You've never done it before. Have you?'

'What?'

'Killed someone.'

I heard the ocean in my ears. 'Of course not.'

'You've wanted to,' he said. 'So much anger with nowhere to go.'

He was caressing the handles of Gamma's bag with his clean, elegant fingers.

'Could you please not touch that,' I said.

'It isn't how you imagine. You've imagined it many times, haven't you, Bridget? Many ways. But it isn't like that. Have you seen the cat's eyes yet?'

'The cat's eyes,' I repeated.

'Have you seen them?'

'I don't understand. How do you know my name?'

'All these years you've dwelt on what happened to her,' he said. 'It's made you feel heroic. But you've been running. If you run to her, you won't have to look behind.'

The flood was rising. 'Who are you?' I said.

'He got away, didn't he?'

Water filled my throat and ears. 'I'm leaving.' I reached for Gamma's bag.

He caught my hand. He pulled me under. I was closer to his face than I'd ever been. I saw his small teeth. I saw his eyes that never blinked, shark-grey with a glowing yellow corona surrounding the pupil. For a long moment he was silent, we were silent, bound together in this soundless underwater world. I heard a voice from the sky:

'Are you a door or a window?'

I struggled to break the surface. 'You came in through a window.'

'Then a door. But you didn't ask me what kind.'

'What kind?'

'A revolving door.'

Daylight vanished to a point. 'Not that.'

'Why not?'

'It doesn't go anywhere. It just goes on for ever in the same place.'

He released me. I broke into the glare. The room was drowning gold.

'You lied,' said the man. 'You have taken a life. Why didn't you admit it?'

Salt stung my eyes. 'I don't . . .'

'You had no choice.'

'They were half of . . .'

'It was them or you.'

He was too bright to look at. It hurt to look at him. 'If I could have—'

'But you couldn't.'

'I'd have ended up like Mary,' I said, covering my mouth, as if my mother had got inside me down there in the deep, as if she had always been swimming in me and was yet to detach, slipping up and out of my throat like a fish— 'I couldn't end up like her.'

He leant towards me across the table with his forearms set parallel, like a sphinx. For a long time he observed me, seeming to make a series of rapid internal calculations.

'We had to harden our hearts,' he said eventually, 'in the place where we came from. Do you see now?' He studied my abdomen; he was trying to read my watch upside down. 'Life catches.' He nodded; the moment repeated itself. 'It multiplies and replaces and erases its host. It doesn't mind how it's come to be; it *simply wants to be.*'

Abruptly, he rose from the bench, a movement so exact it was surgical, and dusted his suit lapels. 'I've seen you for years,' he said. 'You've seen me too. Haven't you?'

'Yes.'

'You thought I was watching, but you were watching me back.'

I turned my wet face to the window. The rain had stopped. Everything was still and quiet and the small red car remained.

When I looked back, the suited man was gone. A yellow coin sat in the space there had been between us, like a perfect, miniature sun.

14

In January 1963, James Maguire moved into our house and took the bed downstairs. He was shy to begin with, never meeting my eye and choosing to spend all his time with Providence. Naturally that meant she wasn't spending time with me, but I told myself not to be petty – 'It was us or the children's home,' said Gamma, and more than anything I felt glad that we'd spared him that, for which my pinch of jealousy was a token to pay.

As time went on, his guardedness fell away. It began with a few words uttered, all perfectly respectful, which surprised me and I chided myself for that surprise, pleases and thank yous when Gamma served him his tea or gave him a pile of freshly washed clothes. Both seemed genuinely to take him aback: I wondered if he had ever been cooked a hot meal or ever worn a clean shirt. He followed Gamma's instruction and went to school every day. He completed his homework without being asked. He grew in confidence and held himself straight when he walked; he started to smile when Gamma spoke to him. He asked what he could do to help around the house. Gamma, who had always believed in the power of having something useful to do, set him to work washing plates, clearing the coal fire, fixing the washing line where it had unhooked from the privy. We acquired a television; Gamma liked to watch westerns in the evenings in black and white, and when it broke James spent all weekend mending it; once it was working again he brought in cups of cocoa so thick it could have held our spoons upright and a tray of odd hard buns I suspected had been lifted from the back of the Sweet Cakes factory, but I didn't say so.

'Isn't it wonderful?' said Gamma. 'The vicar's so pleased. He knows how fond James is of Providence. He says the friendship's the best thing to have happened to him.'

My sister clearly thought so, too. I saw how Providence idolized James, trailing round after him as he did his chores, drawing him pictures that she used to draw for me, giving him an extra ginger nut when she set out our tea. Her adulation unsettled me, but I suppressed my misgivings, deciding they were relics from our encounter on Nail's Lane.

As the months passed, however, my uncertainty turned to agitation: I began to wonder if it weren't her worship of him that troubled me but James himself. Something about him made me uneasy. I couldn't put my finger on it, nor could I shake it off. It was many things and at the same time nothing. How he made such an effort with Providence and Gamma but never with me: he only spoke to me when I asked him a question and even then the response was curt and addressed to the floor; often I caught him watching me with a cold, hard expression he never showed to the others, but when I returned his stare he glanced away. How he seemed to provoke – more than that, *savour* – rivalry between us for my sister's attention: I'd seen his smirk when she elected to walk to school with him instead of me, which admittedly was most days. I broached the subject with Gamma but I didn't know what I meant to say and however I expressed it, it came out wrong.

'You're defensive of her, Birdie,' said Gamma, 'it's to be expected. You're fifteen now.' She smiled at me. 'Nearly a woman, and women always feel responsible for others. You were the same when Mary was here.' I conceded I had been, and came to consider that my distrust of the youngest Maguire was more revealing of my problems than his. 'It's an adjustment for us all,' Gamma reassured me, returning to her sewing. 'Him, more than anyone.'

And it was an adjustment. Life *was* different now. The home I had known and cherished for years had catapulted away from me towards new, unfamiliar ground. I decided to go after it, ignoring the worm of disquiet that tunnelled its way into my heart.

Providence was happy. So was Gamma, so was James. We were a family.

∾

Occasionally, I heard him talking to himself. I came back from Jenny's house late one afternoon, knowing Providence and Gamma were at the market, to find a conversation was happening in the kitchen. At first I was pleased – I thought James had a school friend here, a visitor I could meet who might shed light on one of his dark corners – but when I went in I found him on his own, crouching by the sink and scratching a scuff on the wall.

'What are you doing?' I asked.

He looked up. 'Nothin'.'

'Who are you talking to?'

'No one.'

'Then what are you doing down there?'

'There's a leak,' he replied, in his usual drab tone. 'She said I should check it.'

But the cupboard with the pipes in wasn't open, and anyway I didn't like the careless way he referred to Gamma.

'Do you want to help me with tea?' I said, dropping my bag on the table.

'Nah.' He got up and left the room.

It was out before I could swallow it: 'Why don't you like me?'

He stopped. For a long moment he didn't react. Then he turned to me, and when he did the light played across his face in a complicated way, making him appear more experienced than he was, trickier, unsolvable. I took a step back.

'Course I like you, Birdie,' he said. 'What'd you ever do to me?'

∽

The question lingered with me that day and many after. Fleetingly, I thought about putting it to Christopher, the eldest Maguire, who had started by then delivering the post. The vicar had recommended him for the role: all these boys needed was a chance to prove their strengths, he maintained, but Kip's strength had been clear to me since his intervention by the Brewsters' field. I had tried to push my feelings for him away but this only made them come back stronger, and soon I was too tongue-tied in front of him to say my name, let alone ask why his brother might have taken against me. In any case, did I want Kip to know? I preferred him to think well of me, even if I couldn't be sure that he thought of me at all.

Kip was twenty-three. He had melancholy brown eyes and a thick flop of hair that he kept flicking back from his forehead with his fingers. I held him in my mind all the time, replaying our brief interactions and dialogues until I had squeezed every possible meaning from them and introduced some of my own. '*Hullo, Birdie*,' he'd say each day on the doorstep, '*and how're you this fine morning?*' He'd say the same thing every day, even if it was bucketing it down, always with a smile more attractive and intriguing than any I'd seen, even on the film stars in the posters on my walls. I started to think it was a private joke between us, and if it were then that meant he was fond of me, didn't it? I couldn't tell. I had no knowledge of boys. I told Jenny about my feelings, making light of them so I didn't make a fool of myself. 'Well, watch out,' she advised. 'The Maguires are crooked. Dad says so. He's probably only being nice to you because you took in his brother.' I thought that explanation more likely than my own, infinitely more desired one. What would Kip want with a lanky teenager with a flat chest and a gap between her front teeth? Still, it didn't stop my hopeful daydreams. One morning he saw Providence's bike in the hall with its chain hanging off and came in and righted it. In return she played him 'Nocturne in E Flat Major' on the piano; Kip sat in Gamma's chair on the porch and, with a smile on his handsome face, said there were many more good things in the world than he had realized.

∽

I decided to be practical and arranged for James to visit his old dog up at the Fairfaxes'.

'Why'd he have to come here?' said Maurice sullenly when I asked him.

'Ginny can come to our house then,' I said. 'It'll just be for an hour or two.'

But Maurice wasn't having that. He thought James would run off with her.

'Fine,' he agreed, grudgingly. 'But only for you, Birdie. I'm only doing it for you.'

I wasn't sure what reaction I had expected from James – excitement at seeing the dog again, gratitude to me for enabling it? – but it wasn't the one I got. He seemed not at all pleased to be bidden to the Fairfaxes': 'Up in their fancy —ing castle?' he said to Providence – ignoring me, the one who'd delivered the invitation. Gamma told him not to swear, but she was far more lenient than she would have been if I'd been the one effing and blinding aged twelve. I remembered when I had first visited Maurice's house and the permanent and profound impression it had made on me. But all the way up there James scuffed his feet, his head bowed, his shoulders hunched, like a man on his way to the gallows.

When we arrived, he refused to go inside and kept glowering

at the ground. Maurice came out to meet us, the dog on a smart leather lead. Providence called, 'Ginny!'

'That's not her name any more,' said Maurice stiffly. 'She's Soot.'

James grumbled, 'That's a screwy name.'

Soot bounded and jumped around him; Maurice looked like a water-skier trying to keep hold of her. 'Get off me, stupid mutt,' said James, shoving the animal away. She was undeterred; she leapt affectionately at him again. 'I said — off, why don't you? Get off! I don't —ing want you!' He hit her snout, hard. She whimpered and returned to Maurice.

We all stood in silence. Then Providence said, tearfully, 'I knew it was a bad idea coming here. Why did you have to rub it in, Birdie? You knew he'd be upset!'

I was shocked. 'Rub what in?'

'Making him see her again. You know how much he loved Ginny.'

I tried to defend myself. 'I didn't mean—'

'He *said* he didn't want to come. You forced him, and now look!'

'I didn't force him,' I replied, flustered and embarrassed, both the boys staring at me. 'I thought it'd be nice, Gamma did too. We thought he'd want to be with Ginny—'

'Soot,' interrupted Maurice.

'—see how well she's doing—'

'Now she ain't mine,' said James.

My cheeks burned. I was angry.

'I was doing you a favour. Why are you blaming me?'

'There's no pleasing some people,' said Maurice, although he for one looked pleased.

'Let's go, Jimmy,' said Providence.

'You *asked* me to help,' I said, the sob in my throat made worse when I saw James's sneer as he turned after her. 'Before. You asked me. You *thanked* me!'

'That's all you want, ain't it?' he threw back. 'You always want —ing thanking. I ain't a —ing sob story, *Bridget*. I don't need your —ing hand-outs.'

It was the most he had ever said to me. Stunned, I watched as he and my sister walked together down the lawn, through the Fairfaxes' gate and out of sight. Next to me, Maurice took my hand.

'Come on,' he said, squeezing it in solidarity. 'I know what'll cheer you up.'

We went down the track to pick blackberries. Normally he'd have been right, it would have cheered me up – I loved helping Mrs Fairfax make her September jam, the annual stir-up where we mashed hillocks of sugar into saucepans heaped with clumps of seeping fruit, blending it with a spoon then testing the wrinkled surface once it cooked and cooled – but today I couldn't shake my misery. I was hurt and furious and afraid – for my world that was too rapidly changing; for Providence, whose allegiances had shifted; and for what lay ahead now the worm in my heart had fattened and I could no longer deny it was there.

Maurice said, 'Do you want to come and live with me?' He was clutching the picking bowl to his chest, the blackberries a glistening mound sprinkled with dandelion hairs. 'I can ask

Mother,' he offered, self-consciously, looking at the bowl instead of at me. 'Just for a while. We've got all this room. It's such a big house, and only us in it.'

I didn't know what to say. 'That's so kind of you. But I can't.'

'Why not?'

'I'd never leave Providence. Or Gamma.'

'But *him?*'

Maurice wore a look of such contempt, such hatred, I couldn't bring myself to be like him, eaten up over the years by that emotion. I thought of Gamma. I thought of Kip.

'It'll get better,' I said, but I only half believed it now.

Maurice rolled a stone back and forth under his shoe before shunting it into a pot-hole. 'I thought you'd say that. You could at least be honest. It's clear what's going on.'

I didn't know what he meant. He kicked the stone up into the grass.

'That brother of his,' he said. 'The one that hangs around your house.'

'Kip?' I felt that just saying his name gave me away. 'He brings the post.'

'And the rest . . .'

'What's that supposed to mean?'

'How can you like him, Birdie?' he blurted. 'Providence is fooled by them and you're just as bad. You're a damned fool too. He's a *Maguire*. They're cut from the same cloth. When will you realize? Didn't you realize it just now? Hitting Soot like that? How he spoke to you? Where d'you think he learnt it from? Your precious mailman!'

'Kip isn't anyone to me,' I lied. 'I hardly know him.'
'You'd like to.'
'That's gibberish.'
Maurice spoke softly. 'I've tried to tell you so many times, Birdie.' He blushed. 'How I feel about you.'

I didn't want to look at him. I knew what I would see if I did: the same expression I no doubt wore around Kip, part adulation, part inhibition, but in Maurice it went further, spilling over into possessiveness, jealousy and, most of all, upset that for once he could not have what he wanted. His bottom lip jutted out like a peevish child. His and my summers since childhood had been spent in happy union, ghost-hunting in the attic, making go-carts out of old pram wheels and pushing them down the slopes of the ha-has, keeping written records of the tadpoles in the pond as we chronicled their sprouting legs and shortening tails until *pop*, one day they hopped out onto land and were gone. He had been moody recently, but I'd put that down to us getting older, the sense that we'd soon have to put away these games, which were already turning and readying to drop. But it seemed the terms of our friendship had permanently changed.

'You promised,' he said quietly. 'Now you'd rather be with someone else.'

'Don't be absurd,' I said. 'You're a being a baby.'

He threw his bowl down. Blackberries scattered everywhere.

'What did you do that for?'

'I hate you,' he said.

I stood among the bloody fruits in the wreckage of the day. 'Grow up, Maurice.'

'Like you have? You think you're so clever. You've fallen hook, line and sinker!'

'I'm going,' I said. I put my bowl down and left him before I cried.

Maurice shouted at my back: 'They'll do you in, Birdie. You know that, don't you? Now you've let them in. Whatever happens next, it'll be your fault.'

∽

I left school at sixteen, after my GCEs, in the same summer I discovered the Beatles. I listened to their LPs while fantasizing about John Lennon and writing poems to him in my diary. Providence learnt a bouncy rendition of 'Love Me Do', which she played for me on my birthday, while Gamma bought me the first edition of *The Beatles Book* and my sister and I swooned over their lives. The journal was published each month; I went to the newsagent's every first Tuesday to wait for the delivery and hoped I'd get talking to Kip. Frequently we spoke about music; there was a band he'd heard of called the Rolling Stones, they'd done a great cover of 'Route 66' apparently; I should hear it sometime.

Since our falling-out in the autumn, Providence and I had handled each other like china, aware the slightest strain on the fault that ran through our sistership could cause us to shatter. She was nearly ten by then and we had moved beyond the roles of carer and child, but our age gap was sufficient to mean we had little common ground – but we did have music. Our adulation of John and Ringo was something James was excluded from and so I guarded it with all my might, treasuring the precious hours she spent with me.

There was small overlap as far as James's and my lives were concerned. At Marlborough Avenue, we interacted hardly at all – I felt that I had made enough effort over the last year and a half for scant return and I'd never forget how he'd spoken to me at the Fairfaxes'. I begrudged that Providence could, but no one wanted to revive that day and I couldn't risk damaging our fragile conciliation. In any case, I was seldom at home. Sarah and Veronica were my friends, and Jenny Eldon at number 14. We spent our Saturdays putting tanners in the jukebox and trying cigarettes pilfered from Vee's mother's supply; I got a job at the fairground taking money on the Loop-O-Planes and during breaks swigged Babycham behind the circus tent with Artie the Amazing Acrobat, whose real name was Bernard. I tried not to think about Maurice, though from time to time he crossed my mind. I didn't know if I missed him or missed what he stood for: my youth that was now gone, and the simple, safe, loving home that no longer felt like mine. Was that James's doing, or an inevitable casualty of the passing of time? I felt I was on the edge of a significant crossing: the ending of one phase and the entering of another, my girlhood in the past and my teenage in the present, with all its romantic confusion.

Kip worked at the fairground too, driving the transport trucks. He'd started styling his hair with Brylcreem and to me he looked like Bobby Rydell. I was leaving the tents late one night when I saw him sitting alone on the step of his van, smoking a cigarette.

'Hey – Birdie,' he called.

I pretended I'd just noticed him. 'Hi,' I said.

He flicked the butt to the ground and twisted it out with his shoe. 'Just wanted to say . . . and look, I already said it to your gran but I never said it to you, just – thanks for having Jimmy.' I heard the feeling in his voice and was relieved we couldn't see each other well in the dark. 'That's all,' he said. 'Just – I appreciate it. I wanted you to know.'

'It's OK.'

'It'll help 'im,' said Kip. 'Having somewhere like that. A bit of care, a bit of encouragement. Someone making sure he gets to school. It'd've helped all of us.'

I didn't know what to say. The lights of the fair died behind him one by one.

'I get to thinking sometimes.' He ran a hand across the back of his neck. His eyes shone in the dimness. 'D'you ever reckon how it ain't fair, is it? What luck life gives you.'

'No,' I said. 'It's not.'

'Some days I s'pose I can get ahead. You know? Be a new man, stop getting roped. Push out and take Jimmy with me. I could be part of society, how society wants me to be – keep a job, make a living. Then others it seems like my whole future's fixed out for me and there's nothin' I can do about it. Jimmy's still got a chance. That's thanks to you.'

'It's Gamma really.'

'Still.'

'Anyway,' he said. 'That's what I'm trying to say.'

He started another cigarette. It took seconds to catch because the lighter kept failing; his face flared orange with sparks, lit then dark, lit then dark, like a city being bombed at night. 'How about you, Birdie?' He blew smoke. 'Where d'you come from?'

I said, 'I don't know really.' His silence compelled me to go on, but I didn't really want to. 'I never knew my father,' I admitted. 'I've no idea who he is.'

'That's a lucky break.'

I picked my nail until it hurt. 'Yeah.'

'I'd rather not know mine,' said Kip. 'Then 'e could be anyone. There'd still be a chance 'e was – I dunno . . . all right. An all-right man.'

'I've never considered who mine is,' I said. 'He just . . . isn't important to me. He hasn't been around for me, ever. Gamma's been around. That's it really.'

'Your old man never tried to see you?'

'Don't think so.'

'Your ma never said?'

'She never talked about him. I don't know who Providence's dad is either. Even if she told us about him – about them – I couldn't believe what she said was true.'

Another man called him from the back of the van; I heard doors closing. Kip got up. 'Well,' he said. 'Then Jim's luckier still. Having you. You've got things in common.'

I thought of James's split-level eyes, his remoteness, his animosity, how I couldn't relate to him at all. '*I ain't a —ing sob story. I don't need your —ing hand-outs.*'

'Jimmy's all right,' said Kip, before they drove off. 'He's full of it, but he's good. Down deep, he's good. Will you remember that, Birdie? Will you remember that for me?'

∽

A week later, after breakfast, Jenny's father knocked angrily at our door. Gamma went to answer it. I'd been packing Providence's satchel and went to see who it was. He was on the doorstep, cheeks flaming, eyes bulging, no longer the hapless wolf of our games.

'That boy you've got living with you's been spying on my girl!'

Gamma was affronted. 'What?'

'Been loitering in the tree by her window, he has, filthy beggar – getting his dirty kicks. She saw him; the little pervert was there last night. I'll kill him, Vi, you see if I don't!'

Providence came into the hall in her school uniform. 'What is it?' she said.

'Nothing,' I told her. 'Go upstairs. Brush your teeth. I'll be up in a minute.'

'Why?'

'Just go.'

'He's been watching her getting dressed,' Mr Eldon went on, as my sister trailed off to listen from the top of the stairs. 'We warned you, Vi – we said they were sinners!'

Gamma said, 'Now hang on a minute—'

'One more time and I'll call the police. Is that clear?' And he charged off down the avenue in his flapping greatcoat. Gamma went immediately into the living room.

James was sitting up in his bed, his knees tucked under his chin, his school socks pulled over his shins. 'Well?' she demanded. 'Is it true? Did you do that to Jenny?'

The eyes peering over the knees contained, for once, some emotion. 'No!' he said. 'It weren't me, I swear. Swear to God,

Mrs D, I ain't *never* gone over there. I don't know what tree he's even on about. I were 'ere all night last night. Weren't I? Ask Providence!'

'Mr Eldon's threatening the police,' said Gamma.

'She got it wrong. She must've seen 'im wrong. On my life, I swear it weren't me!'

We called Providence down. She confirmed his alibi, though I noticed with some degree of caution: I knew her too well to miss it, a trace, but unmistakable – of what? Fear? Compliance? Had I not believed James myself, I'd have suspected her of supporting him not because it was the truth but because she was afraid of what he'd do if she didn't.

I took her to school, leaving Gamma arguing with James about whether or not he was going in. 'Are you nervous of him?' I asked on the way.

'No.' But her reaction was too fast. 'Course not.'

'You can tell me if you are. I'll always look after you.'

'Well, I'm not. So you can stop worrying.'

After I'd dropped her, I went straight round to see Jenny.

'Oh, it wasn't James,' she told me, lounging on her sofa, flicking through a copy of *Mirabelle*. 'It was Ron. For starters, his head was all shaved. I don't mind really. He's quite cute, don't you think, in a delinquent sort of way?'

I was aghast. 'Ron?'

'Yeah.'

'You should mind,' I said. 'It's horrible. It's horrible if he did that.'

She turned the pages of her magazine. 'I suppose if he's bored . . .'

'Why did you say it was James?'

'For you, silly,' said Jenny. 'He's been dreadful to you ever since he moved in, you said so yourself. Consider it a favour. Daddy will ring the police and that'll be that.'

I sat at her feet, sick to my stomach. 'You shouldn't have done that,' I said.

'A thank-you would do!'

'You know their reputation. He'll go to prison. The police are waiting to stick him for something, it won't take much. This'll be it and then—'

'Exactly,' said Jenny. 'Then you won't have to see him again and you can have Providence all to yourself and life will go back to normal. Isn't that what you wanted?'

Her cat wound between my legs, as soft as an ear of summer barley. I reached down to stroke it, which it tolerated for a minute before twisting and swiping my arm.

'No,' I said, sucking dry the sharp pink scratch it had given me. 'We're not doing that. Put it on Ron or no one. James shouldn't have to answer for someone else's mistakes.'

∽

The day was 16 June 1965 and I was a month shy of turning seventeen. Providence and I had spent the afternoon polishing Bill Mackey's car in exchange for three and six. It was a pear-green Vauxhall Viva with a toffee-coloured interior, Bill's pride and joy, and I rinsed the metal while she scrubbed around the wheel rims with an old toothbrush, getting all the brake dust off. As we worked, we sang 'I Only Want to Be with You' and

'Hippy Hippy Shake', and it seemed impossible that we had ever fallen out or drifted apart. Over the last few months, Providence had come back into my life. Slowly but surely, she'd turned away from James. She travelled to and from school on her own (while James left on weekday mornings wearing his shirt and tie, I didn't for a moment expect he was attending); she became more involved with her classmates and claimed not to have time for him; and on the many occasions we couldn't find him and I asked her where he was, she grew evasive, saying, 'Oh, I expect he's off with a friend.'

'What friend?' I asked.

'You don't know him,' she said, and quickly changed the subject. James's role in the house had diminished too: Providence was no longer glued to his side and Gamma engaged him less. Though time had passed, I imagined his denial over Jenny lingered in their minds. I didn't correct their misgivings. Though the Eldons' allegation hadn't been followed up on, I let it hang over James's head. Ron's name wasn't mentioned. I could easily have mentioned it. But I was content with how things were, with Providence restored to the sister I knew, and if the occasion didn't repeat itself, I saw no reason why I would.

For supper we ate fish and chips. Once in bed, I fell instantly asleep and dreamed sticky, intense dreams about being lost in sun-drowned fields, pushing a route through stalks that never ended, a gathering sense of a figure behind me, coming closer and closer—

I woke into the thick dark. A sickly yellow glow was seeping across the walls. Something pressed firm and flat against my mouth. I tasted salt. I thought I was still dreaming and underwater in that dream, but no, those were tears in my eyes, and it wasn't water against my lips but a heavy human hand. I thought for a second it was Providence, but the smell was not hers, it was stale and carnivorous. I tried to speak. I tried to bite. I tried to stick my tongue out against the hot slab of skin and I gagged, my heart pumping and my legs shaking and a sudden wash of alarming cold thrown over me like a bucket of water. I realized with terror that I couldn't move. I couldn't breathe. He had his knee wedged between my knees and his elbows were pinned over my chest. I thought of Jesus Christ nailed to the cross. I thought He wouldn't have let this happen if I had been better at my prayers, if I hadn't doubted Him. When I gazed across at Providence's bed I saw to my relief that she was still in it, soundly sleeping, her face turned to the wall.

I could see nothing but a yellow slice of his cheek. The outline of his head was familiar – a shaved, pockmarked skull – and his gullet threw out a sound like water being dragged down a plughole. I felt hardness jabbing into the skin by my knickers. He had my nightdress up over my waist, fastening it across my stomach with his other knee. His fingers were between my thighs. I heard him say, 'Shut up. Just shut up and it'll be over.'

I knew his voice. It was ripe and needing. His thing pressed against me – I thought of Vee reading from her mother's romance novel and all of us rolling around laughing: *With his yellow chest and manly hair he resembled a lion or a god; he thrust his spear into her with a roar!* – and then with a rash of pain he pushed it hard inside me. I felt the hurt right the way up to my ribs, and warm liquid flowing into me and going out of me.

'That's it,' he said wetly into the pillow. 'Quiet now, that's a good girl.'

I smelt alcohol and swimming-pool chlorine. I squeezed my eyes shut, willing that when I opened them again I would be tucked safe in my sheets and it would all have been a nightmare, but then his steps were padding away and he was gone and I was alone.

After a while I got up and went to the bathroom, my lower half trembling. I wet a flannel and put it between my legs and wiped away blood. My fingers were darkly stained. It reminded me of Maurice and the blackberry-picking. When I looked in the mirror I did not know whom I was seeing. She was a woman now. I went back to bed and held Celeste to my heart until the weak white sun came dripping in through the window.

∽

In the morning, I stayed in bed. I told Gamma I was ill.

'What's the matter?' she said, putting her head round the door. 'You look like death warmed up.' She came in and sat on the mattress and felt my forehead for a temperature.

I moved away, pulling the blankets up to my chin. My eyes filled with tears. I didn't want anyone to touch me. I never again wanted anyone to touch me.

'You'll be late for the chemist's,' said Gamma gently. 'Mr Peet will be wondering where you are, he only just gave you the job. What's wrong, little bird? Look at me.'

But I couldn't. I couldn't or I would cry and never be able to stop.

'I'm not going,' I said.

'Come now,' she chided. 'It's your first week! You'll lose your wage.'

'I'm not well.' I rolled over. 'I can't go in.'

Later, I went downstairs and found James in the kitchen. He should have been at school. Instead, he was flicking through a comic and eating last night's fish and chips from a newspaper. I felt sick at the smell.

I waited for him to notice me. Then I asked, 'Did you let him in?'

James paused, a flake of fish halfway up to his mouth. At fourteen, he was every inch the sullen teenager. His expression was blank. How was it possible to wear no feelings on one's face whatsoever?

'Floyd?' he said.

I didn't know who that was.

'No,' I said. 'Ron. He was here last night. In my bedroom.' The words were knots in my throat, dragged up one by one on a coarse, wet rope. 'He couldn't have got in unless someone let him . . .' I stopped, my ears ringing. 'Unless you let him in.'

James ate the fish, unworried. 'I didn't let no one in,' he said. 'I were sleeping.'

'I don't believe you.'

He went back to reading. 'Suit yourself.'

I snatched the comic off the table and threw it on the floor. I saw the name *Bennett* printed on the cover in bold, looping type.

'Look at me when I'm talking to you, dammit!'

His dead eyes travelled down my body. I read amusement beneath the surface.

'Ron attacked me,' I said, and when I said it out loud it solidified into a terrible, immutable form, never to come apart all the days of my life. 'It was him,' I stammered, 'I saw him, he—' But the rope snapped and fell back down and I knew I could never speak about that shameful thing to anyone.

In the silence that followed, I didn't need to. James understood exactly what had happened to me.

'Guess you should've said before about Jenny Eldon,' he said, crumpling the fish paper into a tight, greasy ball. 'He'd have been carted off already then, wouldn't he?'

In a chilling instant, I realized he was right.

'Admit it,' I said.

'I didn't do nothin'.'

'Yes, you did.' My sob burst out of me, a rushing wave that swept away any last remnant of consideration I held for James Maguire. 'You knew what Ron had planned. You helped him. You sleep down here, for God's sake, it was easy!' I could picture it so clearly, his aiding and abetting, and it felt so obvious and inevitable I could have screamed. 'Lift the latch then back to bed, no one any the wiser, safe knowing you've finally got me because it's always been about that, hasn't it, James?' I wanted to hit him. I wanted to wipe that callous look off his face. I wanted to kill him. 'You meant to hurt me right from the start. You never liked me. You had to punish me.'

'For what?'

'You tell me!' I cried. 'Having Providence, having Gamma, having this house – security, love, bloody prospects, I don't bloody know, I've given up trying to find out and I've given up caring!' Every part of me was on fire, anger tearing through my head and hands. 'Why should I mind what you think about me? All I've done is try and help you, speak up for you when no one else did and this is how you repay me—'

He laughed. He *laughed*. I had never seen it. I had hardly seen him smile.

'Ain't you been sainted yet? St Birdie, saviour of the —ing feckless.'

'*What?*'

'It's you that had it in for me,' he retaliated. 'Looking down your —ing nose at me – I saw it, don't think I didn't. Thinking you're superior, St Birdie coming down on her cloud to tend those dirty —ing criminal Maguires. I were never good enough for your sister, were I? It were written all over your —ing face, still is, it's there right now. All what you've got and I've got nothing. All I've got's her and you didn't even want me having that.'

He narrowed his eyes at me, vapid and cruel and just like his brother's.

'Then you took Ginny,' he said. 'And it weren't enough to nick her – then you had to make me go see her when I said I didn't want to, make me see her all happy-ever-after with Little Lord —ing Fauntleroy, just to show me what I ain't got? Laughing with your rich —ing friends.'

'No. You're wrong.'

'Course I'm —ing wrong.' He pushed his chair back with a scrape, so hard it toppled over. 'I'm always wrong. I'm stupid, I'm thick, I'm gone in the —ing head—' He jabbed his temple with his finger. 'Why'd I be right about —ing anything? No one believes me. It ain't my fault you're frigid, you probably invited Ron to do it!'

Humiliation soaked me. I couldn't move or speak. I was back in the night with Ron's meaty hand across my mouth, his sour odour, the stinging pain.

'I'd never split on him anyway,' James said evenly. 'I ain't no —ing grass.'

'What's going on here?' Gamma appeared in the doorway, a bunch of flowers in her arms. 'James, what's this shouting? Why aren't you at school? And why is there furniture all over the floor?'

I didn't take my eyes off him.

'He's confessed,' I told her, and the voice that came out of me was, for the first time, measured, the voice of the righteous, the voice of a liar. 'He's admitted to what he did to Jenny, Gamma. He's been doing it to me too. He tried to attack me last night. I pushed him off before he could, but look—' I showed her the bruise Ron had left me. I was numb. I felt nothing. My heart folded in half and away. 'James Maguire is dangerous,' I said. 'You'd better call the police.'

15

The day took a long time to throw off the covers of the night. I woke in the back of the car with a dream still in my head. A feeble sun glowed through a colourless sky.

I touched my head, which felt as if I'd fallen on it. My breath came out in clots of steam and my reflection in the rear-view mirror was remote and disapproving.

The Panda left the flats at eight. It stopped again soon after, in a market square, and Donna stepped out and wandered the empty streets, checking the closed shop fronts. I parked on a side road and kept her in my sights. She went back and opened the car and said something to Maguire before getting in and staying there. We waited. A lone street sweeper trimmed the kerb. A truck pulled up outside a bakery. I turned on the radio and heard a Kylie Minogue song Philippa liked; I turned it off again. Piece by piece, the square awakened, lights coming on, doors opening. At half past nine, Maguire and Donna emerged and crossed the road and went into an olde worlde tea room with bunting draped across the window. I remained in the car and kept my eye on the door.

It was eleven by the time we moved. I went after them at a distance because there were few other cars on the road. The carriageway dropped and lifted towards Bodmin. Where were we going? Wherever it was, we were heading there fast. Donna drove over the limit, straddling the lanes then accelerating when they merged. The land on either side became wide and flat, the spectral towers of pylons mounting through the mist like alien tripods; then those, too, disappeared, the last marks of civilization before the barren moor rolled vast and eerie in the fog, studded with hulks of stone and weird, shimmering ponds of petrified muck.

My petrol light came on. I was busy consoling myself with thoughts of reserve gallons when, ahead of me, Donna's indicator flashed and she diverted into an Esso garage forecourt. There was one bay free, which she took, while I hovered with the engine running, my brain in pieces trying to work out what to do: wait for her to fill it then drive after them with a near-empty tank, or fill up myself and risk being seen? I was weighing my options when Maguire climbed out, his jacket stark in the monotone like a wedge of lime in a cloudy glass of water. Their cap was on the wrong side so he had to haul the hose over the back of the car. As he did that, a van drove off from the adjacent bay. Without thinking, I took it. I put up my hood and got out, my back to him, my hand shaking so vigorously that squirts of unleaded slopped out before I finally got the pump in the hole.

Presently, I heard him replace the nozzle. I made myself count to ten – a short eternity – before putting back my own, then strode head down to the payment booth, praying that Donna wouldn't recognize my coat and wishing that instead I'd brought Tom's anonymous TrustTax black anorak that he'd been given at an awayday last year.

'*It's a bit bloody boring,*' I'd said when Tom had got home that evening. We'd warmed up last night's lasagne and drunk wine on the sofa while he'd gone through the bag of freebies, saying as he tended to every six months or so that really he wanted to be doing something else, he was sick of phrases like *thunderbolt thinking* and *close of play* and besides he'd done his time for the firm, the work was soul-destroying. Then we'd laughed over the array of key rings and the cutesy accountancy teddy that inexplicably wore a mortar board. '*That's the point,*' he'd said. '*Plain and boring and utterly unmemorable.*'

I hid behind a raft of KP Snacks while Maguire paid at the desk. I heard him say, 'Cheers, mate,' to the cashier with such galling ease it took all my resolve not to shove him into the bottle counter. The sliding door beeped as he went back out. Quickly, I paid, but walking out I was in plain sight so I had to spend an agonizing half-minute by the buckets of newspapers, pretending to read the headlines and willing them not to look my way.

I saw the Panda move. While they were waiting to pull out, I dashed back to my car, returned Gamma's bag to the passenger seat and switched on the ignition.

Nothing happened. I turned it again.

Tick-tick-tick-tick.

I thumped the wheel, as if that would help, and depressed the clutch and thumped the wheel again. *Tick-tick-tick.*

The engine clicked and did nothing and died. I rattled the wheel and begged it, 'Come on!'

Tick-tick-tick-tick.

The Panda had gone. I took out the key and put it in again

and twisted and twisted, desperate. 'Come *on*!' *Tick-tick-tick-tick*. 'COME ON!' I pictured the turns they were taking, the miles they were covering. 'No. No! *Please*. Please, please, please, please—'

With a roar, the car came alive. I plunged the accelerator, laughing hysterically at the same time as thinking I might vomit. The engine throbbed heartily. I shoved it into first gear and with tyres squealing slewed hectically back onto the road, not checking if anything was coming; a lorry charged past, blaring its horn, massive tyres spraying my windscreen with grit. I undertook it and sped to ninety, searching the road for a flash of red, but I knew they had got away from me. How long was their start? Two minutes, three? Going at the limit – she was far exceeding that – they were a mile, possibly a mile and a half ahead: even with my foot to the floor it was too far to catch up.

Stay on this road, I told myself. Keep going on this road and you'll reach them, you will, have faith, you're with Providence. *Providence is with you.* Then a sign passed for an imminent junction and I knew it was over: I had no way of determining if they had come off here or not, and if I made the wrong choice I would carry on building the miles between us, travelling these bleak brown moors for ever and ever getting nowhere, until the end of the earth came and I went sailing over the edge of it with a gun in my bag and a wish in my heart and I would never see my children again. And as I was telling myself this, I saw him – at the last countdown marker before the slip road, a shadow of a man, incongruous but unmistakable, standing half-hidden in the hedge. The sight of him there on the verge was so odd I thought he was an illusion, and indeed when I drove past and checked my mirrors I could no longer see him. I put on my indicator and followed.

∾

Further on I saw them in a lay-by with their hazard lights blinking. I touched the brake then abruptly Donna sped out, her exhaust smoking; there was a second car parked behind them and a figure standing by it in an Iron Maiden T-shirt, hollering after them.

The road passed the airfield and continued towards Bedruthan. The sky was clearing, silvery blue scattered with wispy clouds like pinches off a slab of cotton wool, and attaining that expanded, stretched-out quality it did when near to the sea. I lowered my window. The air was fresh and invigorating. I found a tube of Fruit Gums in my bag and ate them two at a time, working for minutes after to get the gel out of my teeth.

We reached the hem of the land, the Atlantic beyond it a taut grey sheet. Donna skirted up the coast for a few miles before turning down a sharp hill between the back yards of houses, stuffed with wheelie bins and bicycles in various states of usability. Seagulls pecked the rubbish bags. The shortcut brought us out by the water, sage-coloured with riffles of white picked out and darkening to gunmetal as it neared the horizon. Walkers trailed their dogs along the esplanade. Salt spray washed over rusty green railings.

The Panda entered the car park for a B & B, the Waveside Boarding House. I drew in further up the road. I took Gamma's bag and locked the car and entered the building. The foyer was filled with knick-knacks for sale, lighthouse ornaments wrapped in decking rope and decorated with out-of-proportion seashells, driftwood signs proclaiming GONE SURFIN'! and a ship's wheel refashioned into a lazy Susan. The man behind the desk had the golden hair of a Californian bodybuilder and a nose with a neat snub, like someone had made him out of plasticine then pressed its end before he'd properly dried.

'I'd like a room for the night,' I said. 'Please.'

He referred to a clipboard. 'Business or pleasure?'

'Both.'

'Let's have a look.' He whistled through his teeth. I tried to read the grid upside-down but couldn't spot a Maguire, was there an Eddiston? Yes, there she was. Room 21.

'Do you have number twenty free?' I asked, seeing that he did. 'It's just – and look I know this sounds silly, but, well, I've recently lost my husband, a year ago in fact, and gosh I can't believe it's been quite that long – but, and I'm sorry to be telling you this, but it was his favourite number, number twenty, so yes, I always try if I can. It's only—'

'Say no more,' he said, smiling at me sympathetically. 'It's yours.'

I gave him a fake name and paid up front in cash. Room 20 was very pale blue with peeling window frames and damp patches on the walls. A seam of water glistened through the glass, and far off in the distance the squat shape of a cargo ship inched along the skyline. I fell gratefully on the hospitality tray, filling the kettle at an angle in the bathroom and unwrapping the packet of custard creams, which I ate in one go while sitting on the closed loo seat. The tea was hot and sweet. I ran the shower to piping and stayed in it until the heat grew too much to bear, then I dried myself and lay on the bed.

Exhaustion covered me. I fantasized about climbing into sheets as crisp as spring and burying myself beneath downy quilts of the kind they had kept at the Fairfaxes' house, and the sharp grab of sleep the instant the light turned out, a tug from beneath so quick as to almost be death. I forced myself to wake up, sit up, and reached for Gamma's bag. It felt like home. I wanted to go home. I wanted to see Tom and my children, and hold them and kiss them and tell them I'd never leave them again. I could see it now. A warm bath. Madonna songs playing in Philippa's room. The sound of Joe in the hallway with his toys. I'd have a day, maybe two. When Maguire's murder hit the news, Tom might glance at me over the tops of the children's heads, leaving the spaghetti to overboil; he might even venture to say it one night when we were getting ready for bed, me in the bathroom putting on moisturizer and he calling in, in an affectedly nonchalant voice, *It's odd, isn't it, you being away when that happened?* And he'd stand at the door, toothbrush in hand, and I'd turn to him and say, *Sorry, darling, but I don't know what you mean.*

I didn't want to wait any longer. I wanted it over with. Tonight.

For my idea to work, I needed the cover of darkness. My first job would be to get rid of Donna. I planned to climb out of the window and sneak round the back of the building to her car. I needed to set off the alarm. A rock to the window would do it. Snub-Nose in reception would hear and check his records, see the vehicle was hers and call her down to the car park. By that time I'd be back on the landing. I'd knock on the door of room 21 and Maguire would assume it was she, cursing whoever did it, biting her nails over the payout to Wheels 4 Hire – but it wouldn't be Donna, it would be me. I'd raise the gun and say, *At last, I've found you.*

I was relying on several factors to go my way, but I trusted that Providence would sustain me. I had no choice but to have faith in that. On the act itself, I knew what I was doing. I'd had two decades to make sure of that. I'd researched blood-spatter patterns and the steps I'd need to take to make it look like suicide. God only knew he had enough reasons to do that. When the police came, they would find the gun with Maguire, his prints the only ones covering it. Snub-Nose wouldn't have a name or number plate for me, just a faintly retained face and the story about a dead husband. How much would they care anyway? I'd read statistics about cons running themselves through after release, unable to live in the outside world or overcome by hopelessness. James Maguire was one of society's rejects. When there were decent people suffering, how much time, really, would the authorities give him?

I didn't expect to be caught, and yet of course there was a possibility I would be. I wasn't so set on my path that I couldn't see that. At least the children would be looked after, I thought. At least Tom would be able to explain to them, in time, my motivation for doing it. At least there would be one less predator contaminating their world. And at least they could say I wasn't their real mother. They could always find solace in that.

Often I had wondered about their real mothers – where these

women were, what they were doing – and even years after both adoptions I expected they might turn up one morning while I was loading the dishwasher and demand their children back. Though Philippa and Joe were legally mine, I believed in some dark, unexplored part of myself, a part that had existed since the summer I turned seventeen, that they would be better off where they came from. How could I imagine I deserved them? I didn't deserve them.

The day Tom and I married, I had known. When we had tried for babies and none of them stayed, I had known. Friends around me had fallen pregnant, one after the other as easily as nipping out to Tesco for a pint of milk, and flourished, and birthed their pink-skinned, feathery-haired infants while I gazed on, faltering in the baby section at John Lewis, touching the Baby-gros, and choosing the toy lamb I might have chosen for my own.

After the fourth, I told Tom I couldn't do it again.

'*I know,*' he'd said.

'*Do you?*'

'*Yes. I've been there too.*'

But he hadn't. It wasn't the same. No matter how kind my husband was, no matter how many tears he wiped or hot-water bottles he filled or cups of tea he brought to my bed, it wasn't the same. We both felt the losses in our hearts and minds. I alone felt them in the blood-soaked sanitary pads and tears shed on the loo, my knickers bunched around my ankles and my knees trembling with pain. I alone felt the death inside me of a life that hadn't even got started, tormenting myself with at what point, precisely, that fledgling heartbeat had stopped

– the moment between something and nothing, what was it, *why* was it? – just as that pulse had launched itself weeks before, astonishingly, from nowhere. I had visions of a tiny beloved cluster of cells falling through the night sky of my womb with no one there to catch it. I feared that they had been lonely, these tiny flames lit then snuffed, lit then snuffed, trying, trying, which was idiotic because they were inside me, and besides they had no consciousness; the sadness was mine, not theirs, for they had no feelings and they were not they. Somehow, though, I conveyed hostility. These longed-for visitors sensed that I would expel them; that I didn't want them just as I hadn't wanted the first. That I was never meant to be a mother.

A friend had said to me not long ago, meaning to be a comfort, that miscarriages were souls waiting to receive the right outfit for their journey. She said the lost ones came back and back until they found the right fit, and then, at last, by miracle of the mother having endured and remained and thus been justified in having her reward, there was a baby. And it was a comfort: those dozens of might-have-beens were coats thrown off; I didn't need to dwell on them. When her son was born, my friend said her first thought on meeting him had been, '*Obviously it's you, it was always going to be you. How could it have been anyone else?*' But I didn't know what I believed about that, about souls, about whether there was anything more to it than the arrangement of flesh and bone and nervous systems which, when right, resulted in life, and which, when wrong, did not. I didn't know what I believed about when a person became a person. All I knew was that I blamed myself.

Tom made appointments for us to discover what was the matter; he thought that was what I wanted. But I couldn't bear the examinations, the cold apparatus and probing, gloved fingers: the violation brought me straight back to the Maguires – my aggressor and Providence's – and I didn't expect anyway that they would find anything.

I was right. Mine was a moral punishment, issued by a divinity whose expectations I had failed to meet. I did not merit children, and no amount of poking or prodding, or number of doctors nodding across their desks alongside photographs of their smiling families, would change that. It had been decided on a cool autumn day twenty-three years ago.

The horror of that time had never left me: the tender, terrible weeks after my assault branded by fear, sorrow, powerlessness, by knowing that whichever way I turned, I was trapped. How pitilessly those weeks had turned into months. Then one morning it had struck me that I hadn't had a period in a while. I'd combed back through my diary and seen it: the tiny crescent moon I drew on the date I began, tucked into the margin like an impish, knowing smile. The last had been May. Dread had paralyzed me. How had I not noticed? I'd been queasy, but had put that down to the shock of my attack. I'd been more tired than usual, but I hadn't been sleeping, tormented by feelings of revulsion and guilt and the carousel of images that turned in my mind – of Ron hiding under my bed, waiting to creep out at the instant the sun went down; and of James, who'd been ordered to a youth detention centre following my charge of attempted rape.

Through it all, I had never considered that part of myself; I hadn't wanted to because it had made me feel shamed and spent and like the names I'd heard Betty throw at Maeve Maguire. But there was no running away from it now. I'd thought of the seed inside me, Ron's seed, growing against my will, and how it would continue to grow, and grow, and grow, until it consumed me entirely.

I couldn't have told Providence. She was ten; I refused to do it to her.

Later, after I'd lost her, I thought if I had, I might have saved her. She'd have sworn off the Maguires then for life – for *her* life – and she'd still be here. But I didn't.

For days, I hadn't been able to eat or rest; I'd barely spoken a word; I couldn't look at Gamma or my sister and I withdrew from my friends. '*Little bird, don't blame yourself,*' Gamma had said, sorry for me, sorry all over, attributing my distress to James and his betrayal of us, but little did she know and nothing did I tell her. My nights were endless and anguished. I'd lie awake until the small hours, willing my baby away, silently urging this fledgling life that the world was not worth coming into and it was not wanted besides, it would not be welcome, only to meet oblivion for a twinkling before waking in a flare, a giant wooden scarecrow rising at the end of my bed, his suit, his socks, his smiling teeth – but his face was the face of my assailant.

Time marched on. I'd swung between denial and dismay. I'd worn loose clothes to conceal my waist. At the chemist's, I'd hunted for bottles that could cure my condition; I'd spent hours at the library scouring books about herbs and hot water, sage, liverwort, nepeta. Nothing worked. The blood did not come.

Eventually, I'd gone up to Maurice's house. I hadn't known what else to do. When Mrs Fairfax had opened the door, surprised to see me after so long, I'd burst into tears.

'*I need your help,*' I'd said. '*Please – will you help me?*'

Dr Fairfax had known someone who could. A colleague who had a sideline in '*that sort of thing*'. I'd begged them not to tell the authorities. I'd begged them not to tell Gamma. So Mrs Fairfax had agreed to vouch for me when I'd informed my grandmother I would be staying with them for a few days to help look after the dog while Maurice completed his exams. Gamma had been pleased about it: '*A change of scene will do you good,*' she'd said, kissing me.

When the time came, it was done in a private clinic in Wellington. They never told me what they did with it after. Years later I'd heard about medical incinerators and thought that might have been what they did. On the day it left me, I sobbed and thought I would never stop. But I'd been glad of my agony; I wouldn't have swapped it for anything, it was mine, so I'd nursed it and held it, curled up in a ball on Mrs Fairfax's bedsheets, part of me numbed for ever.

I took the gun from Gamma's bag and held its cold, dead weight, directing its muzzle to the wall. From next door came the hum of Maguire and Donna's conversation. The hum grew louder. Donna was shouting – in fury or fear I couldn't tell.

I cleaned the weapon and put on my gloves.

Would he hurt her? His own daughter?

Yes. The Maguires destroyed everything. They destroyed women.

I opened the window. The frame lifted easily; a current of cool air came in.

The sky was darkening. I tucked the gun into the belt of my skirt and climbed out.

IV

16

It did him in to be shouted at, the angry person coming at him with their crazy eyes and their face twisted, like the officers with their billysticks, '*I'll regulate yew, yew wrong 'un, yew brute!*' or the Mister yelling drunk with his face on fire, calling him a whore's bastard, a shithouse son-of-a-bitch, kicking and clobbering him when he went to protect himself.

'Couldn't you have left it?' Donna was saying, pacing between the bed and the door in a way that set him on edge: all he wanted was a burn and to go to sleep and for her to stop shouting. 'One thing's all it'll take and you're back inside. Don't you get it?'

He didn't answer.

'Don't you worry about you?' she said, her gaze raking over him with mad urgency, searching for something she couldn't find. 'Don't you worry about *me*?'

'Yeh. I worry about you.'

'Then picking a fight with some bloke on the road's not the greatest idea.' She slumped on a chair. The blinds behind her were thin and peppered with holes. 'Urgh,' she said, drawing her knees up and resting her head on them so he couldn't see her face. 'I don't know what I'm doing,' came her muffled voice. 'I don't even know why I'm here.'

'Do you want to go home?' he said.

'No.'

'That bloke were making signs at you.'

'I don't care what he was doing. I couldn't care less what some stranger thinks.'

'It were disrespectful,' he said.

She raised her head. 'So was shouting out the window that you'd smash him!'

'Well.'

'He bloody well ran us off the bloody road.'

So they'd got out, he and this chap wearing a fegging poxy T-shirt in the middle of winter, and gone at each other like a couple of fighting dogs, and he'd heard Drumsticks in his mind – '*Box clever, Jimbob, you show 'im what for!*' – and he would've as well, given half the chance. But Iron Maiden didn't have the metal in him after all, and saw he'd cornered the wrong bloke and backed down like a chokey merchant after six days on number-one.

'You scared me,' Donna said. 'I thought you were going to kill him.'

'I would've if he hadn't said sorry.'

'Then where would that have got us?'

He dug out his smokes and struck a match.

'Don't think you can do that in here,' said Donna.

'What's he gunna do?'

'There's detectors.'

'Huh.'

'Smoke detectors.' She pointed to the ceiling. 'See?'

It looked like a little camera. 'Is it watching?' he said.

'No. It just tells if you're smoking and an alarm goes off.'
'Jesus.'

She opened her mouth to speak but thought better of it, then shuffled on the seat and looked over at him. He was getting to know her ways now and he liked that, it made him feel happy. 'I found the address,' she said eventually. 'Ladyfield Nursing Home.'

He snorted. 'Lady.'

'It's only a mile away,' she said. 'We can walk tomorrow, if you like.'

He put the fags back and got out his clothes and began the process of folding them, spread, tuck and pleat. Porter said that just because you were living on the farmyard didn't have to make you the pigs: *Take pride in yourselves, lads, shipshape and Bristol fashion!*

'I've changed my mind,' he said.

'Why?'

'Just have. I don't want to. Stick to the plan – Kip, then the other place, then back.'

'But she's practically down the road,' said Donna, not understanding. 'You might as well now we're here. We can see Kip and her in the same day. Ron said—'

'I don't care what Ron —ing said. He's —ing Looney Tunes.'

There was that searching expression again. He didn't like it.

'I think you're afraid,' said Donna.

He grunted. 'Right.'

'Of seeing her again. Of what she's got to tell you.'

'What's that then?' he said. 'Some big —ing secret, is it?' He finished with the shirts but now he didn't know what to do with them. '—ed if I want to know.'

'She said it was important.'

'More important than visiting her youngest when he's banged up all those years?'

'She might have—'

'She didn't. No writing, no phoning, no —ing nothing. Not even when Kip died. D'you know what they said to me at Grendon? *"Still no letters, Maguire? Sure she's still with us, are you?"* S'pose they felt —ing sorry for me, thought they were doing the decent thing. So I thought that'll be it then, won't it, that's got to be it, it's the only explanation. Now she wants to see me? Act like it don't matter? Nah. She can get —ed.'

'I'll be with you.'

'What difference will that make?'

She was stumped for a retort.

He said, 'We're not going. That's it.'

But Donna was right. It was enough to wrap his head around the fact that Maeve was still living, but her note – *I've got something for him its important* – had weighed heavy on him all last night, stoking a flame he'd long ago fought to put out, her words repeating as he'd hunkered in the passenger seat of the car, his shoulders numb, his feet frozen, memories rising in his delirious brain like developing photographs – of Maeve in her booze-stained dressing gown and her Shoulihan shoes (Ron's voice telling him, '*She worked for him all right, di'n't she? She worked those blokes good an' proper*'), smoking her fags and necking her grog, her tear-blotched cheeks and her reproachful eyes haunted by every wrong deed that had been done against her. What, then, did she have to give him now? What was the big emergency? He told himself it couldn't be that — not *that* — he was done with daydreaming, he was beyond it, he wasn't a child any more, making things up.

Yet the question picked at him, nagging his resolve. The second he'd seen Mother Maeve's writing on that card, it returned to him:

What if he wasn't your father?

For all the years that had passed, for all he'd learnt of himself and other people, for all that he'd talked himself — literally, at Grendon — out of thinking it, for all the reasons there were why it couldn't be true, he realized he had never, really, lost hope. Hope that the Mister was not his; hope that he had come from another, better man of whom he could feel proud: the one, as a boy, he'd thought of as Isaac the Pilot, a good, decent fellow like the officers at Grendon, someone to call him 'son' and 'lad', to care for him and see he was well. '*Isaac's a happy fantasy,*' the psychologists had urged him to see; '*he's not real. You know the difference now, don't you, Jim, between what's real and what's not?*'

But part of him had held on. Not to Isaac but to the promise of a stranger: that this person existed in the world, out there somewhere, wondering, just as he, Jimmy, wondered, waiting for a phone call or a knock at the door that would bring them back together. His real father was the last chance he had to discover he was nothing to do with the Mister, only half to do with Ron, and that he still had a decent drop of blood in him. Mother Maeve alone knew the truth. When she'd died, or he'd thought she'd died, she had taken the promise with her. Now, the promise was back.

He should go to the Ladyfield and find out. Donna was dead-centre. But he was scared. He thought he would rather keep that promise than have it taken away.

He punched the pile of shirts. It made a fist-shaped depression all the way down.

'Then why did you say we'd go?' said Donna.

'I dunno.' He sat on the bed. 'You seemed keen.'

She was disbelieving. 'You think all this is for me?'

'Ain't it?'

'No. For God's sake, Dad.'

She disappeared into the bathroom and slammed the door. He expected her to come right out again but she didn't. He'd no idea what women got up to in bathrooms: they went about it with a privacy he'd forgotten existed. He was starting to think she had sneaked out of the window, finished with him at last, when out she came in her pyjamas – they had blue and pink bears over them with rainbows and sunbeams on their stomachs – and took something from her pocket and put it in the bin.

'I don't need your pity,' he said.

'It's not pity.' Her eyes were brimming. 'I want to be here.'

She appeared small to him then, as she had on visiting days, sitting across from him on a plastic chair next to Rita. He hadn't been allowed to touch her, the screws pecking out their telling-offs: '*No contact! Keep your distance!*' But he could touch her now. He could hold her in her bear pyjamas and kiss her hair and tell her that he loved her. He'd never read to her at bedtime. He'd never been read to either, as a child, apart from

Tom's Midnight Garden once with Alf's judy. He hoped that Donna knew how he'd wanted to.

'I dunno why,' he mumbled, picking the quilt.

'Because I care about you,' she said. 'I care what happens to you.'

'That'd make you the first.'

'And so what if I want to see her? I'm her granddaughter, I've never met her.'

'Then you're lucky. She never did nothing for us.'

'She must have,' said Donna.

'If you count hooking blokes and shooting up and getting boozed then yeh.'

'But Mum said . . .' she started. 'She said your mother wasn't—'

'No,' he said, cutting her off. 'She weren't. She weren't nothing to us and that's the problem. She weren't nowhere. She weren't no one.'

He couldn't be bothered to explain. Years banged up taught you which people were worth debating with and which weren't, which would get over it and which would come give you a plunging in the middle of the night. Donna didn't know Maeve, she didn't know any of them. Thought she could waltz in playing happy —ing families and they'd all come back together and cry and hug each other or whatever they did on *EastEnders*.

'To hell with this,' he said, repacking the clothes. 'I'm going back to London.'

'I'm not driving you.'

'I'll drive myself.'

'You can't.'

'How hard can it be? Smiley had a —ing licence, it can't be that —ing hard.'

'Just stop a minute,' she said. 'Please. Let's talk about this?'

But he didn't want to talk. He was done with talking. What use was being here? What use did he have left in him or had he ever had, *yew worthless scrape of shit, yew scourge on the earth, yew reptile!* and the wind-up thing was rushing on him now, uncontrollably – his rage – blotting out the light, casting him in shadow until all he could see was Donna and if she didn't act now, if she didn't run—

An alarm went off in the distance. 'I'm not smoking,' he said, automatically.

She got up and opened the sash. 'What is that?'

The telephone rang. She picked it up. 'Yes?' She waited. 'Oh. Right. OK.'

She put the phone down. 'It's the car. That was him downstairs.'

'What about it?'

'Someone's broke into it. Shit! It'll cost me a fortune.'

'I'll go.'

She gave him the car key. He went downstairs and stepped outside and turned his collar up against the cold. The air smelt of salt, wonderful and ancient. Waves rinsed over rocks he couldn't see, silver froth surging and dispersing. He took out his fags and lit one; it took a while because the wind kept blowing it out, and once lit he had to suck hard a few times to get the end nice and burning. Somewhere in the night, the siren stopped its shrill.

He went around the back to the Waveside car park. Some

mainliner putting a brick through the glass; he'd been one of them once, sneaking for drug money, drink money, any money. They'd probably meant to nick it but hadn't known how to do wires.

It was eerie-quiet with no one around. He didn't like the silence. Nights should've been broken by bangings and thumps; he was nostalgic for the rally of conversations in the dark, the comfort of nearby voices, standing on his table to look out of the window and meet a courtyard of blokes all doing the same, five tiers of them, their faces pressed up against the grate. He'd imagined the constellations – Andromeda, Cassiopeia, Perseus – their stars wiped out by the glare of prison lights, but if he was lucky he'd clap eyes on the moon, hovering there as crisp and round as a disc of cream in the neck of a milk bottle. He'd liked space. Did still. The massiveness of it. He'd taken to borrowing a library book a week, rationed each one so he didn't run out of pages, and mainly liked novels, Hardy and Dickens and that one that wrote *Jekyll and Hyde*, but sometimes he'd picked out books about the universe, dying nebulae and exploding supernovas, galaxies infinite and filled with stars. Reading had been his one good thing. '*Can you find your one good thing?*' the psychs had asked him at Grendon. He hadn't known what they'd meant. '*Something you've been told you're good at. It could be anything, from however long ago.*'

Well, he hadn't been able to think of a single thing. He'd spent a week brooding on it then at the next meeting told the group about Miss Broderick, his one-time English teacher, how she'd taken him aside one day and told him he had a knack with words – a lovely one, that, *knack* – and gave him books she thought he might enjoy, and even visited Mother Maeve at the house to ask if he might be interested in tutoring? He'd sat shy on the stairs as his mother slammed the door and locked it.

'*I think that's it,*' he'd said to the group. Since then he'd read everything he could find. *The Catcher in the Rye, To Kill a Mockingbird, A Passage to India.* The stories took him away from the empty days and the loneliness of his own company; at Wandsworth they carried him far from the iron stairways, the high-mesh security fences, the swampy, toneless wall of noise through which no one sound cut through, the constant claustrophobia. They helped fill his mind with images other than Providence sitting cross-legged in the field, asking him to hold his hand flat so she could put a chain of daisies onto it. The sound of her laughter ringing through him like bells.

He'd wished then, as now, that he had never met her. Far better for her to be alive, and nothing and no one to him, than for him to have known her and she to have died.

A noise came from behind him. He turned. There was nobody there.

Funny, this feeling of being watched. He told himself it was a hangover from the clink's constant surveillance. It didn't seem right, probably never would, that he could walk out of a door, out of a building, as easy as that, and no one told him he couldn't.

The car, when he reached it, still had its lights going. The fair-haired bloke was circling it warily. He went over and touched the jagged glass left in the driver's side. Whoever did it hadn't known what they were doing.

'You got a brush?' he said.

'What for?'

'What d'you bloody think?'

The bloke appeared nervous in the flashing light. 'Do I know you?' he asked.

'No.' He threw down the fag-end.

'I'm sure I do. I recognize your face. Have you stayed with us before?'

'Nope.'

'You've been on telly then.'

He reached onto the seat for the shards of glass. 'Not that I'm aware.'

The man looked closely at him. Closer.

'We don't get many break-ins round here,' the man said. 'Not from the locals, at any rate. There must be bad blood blown in.'

He cut himself, swore and sucked the pad of his finger. 'Must be.'

The man backed off. 'Shall I telephone the police?'

'No.' He turned back to the job. 'Don't bother.'

It didn't take long to sweep up the glass. He found a plastic sheet in the dumpster and shut it in the door to keep it set. Kip had shown him the basics of driving; he considered the car key Donna had given him, how easy it would be to slot it into the ignition and leave her here.

He put it back in his pocket, retraced his steps to the sea and found a bench by the water. The expanse glittered before him. He glanced behind him, up to the Waveside. A light shone in their room. Was Donna still awake? No, he realized, it was the room next door. For a second he saw a woman standing at the glass, facing him, repeated in some way like déjà vu, but as fast as he'd seen her she was gone. He thought it'd been a long time since he'd had a proper stretch of sleep; he crossed the road and went back inside.

17

HM Prison Grendon
Group therapy meeting, 1979

4 February
It weren't my fault, he were —ing asking for it. Yeah I thrashed that —'s paintings. Ripped them off the —ing wall and tore them up, see how he —ing liked that. He deserved it, —ing nonce. What'd he expect? He started it, telling me mine were *loopy*, giving me his critiques like he knows —, telling me what I could and couldn't paint. It ain't none of his —ing business what I paint, ain't that the —ing point?

One more time and I'm for the super. 'Keep your temper, Jim, or you'll be out on the ghost train.' Well I ain't risking that, I ain't going back to the hell-holes, no —ing chance. I've seen it happen. Blokes shipped out in dead of night, here one day, gone the next, bed made like he never —ing slept in it. That ain't gunna be me, no siree. 'Then talk about it at therapy,' they said; 'bring it to the group.' What're you lot gunna tell me? You gunna tell me I'm batty, like he did? *Emotionally* —ing *disturbed*? All I did were paint Floyd. What's he —ing know about Floyd? He dunno —ing nothing.

The paints are —ed anyway. Be better if they set up a book

group. Now that'd be worth going for. I read three last month but I've got to make them last. It's nice when I get a big one 'cause I know it'll last me ages but they're not always the best, some of the best ones are short. I started writing my own. Bits and pieces, stuff I remember about Floyd. Thought if I were doing those letters I might as well do that too. I try and get hold of him in my mind and he's gone. Things we did then I try and get a picture of it only I can't, so I think maybe it didn't happen after all like I think it did. Writing it down helps me make sense of things. In how some of what's inside me feels to be in such a mess but when I get the word for it, it feels more manageable then. It's like sticking. I get a word, I stick that feeling down. Then I can look at it and work it out better. See it for what it is.

19 February
Floyd made me mad with how he used to go on about Providence. He went on about her all the ⸻ing time, he were ⸻ing obsessed with her. They said I were the one obsessed but I weren't, it were him. It were what I told you – about how she didn't really want to be my friend. That were his favourite 'cause he saw how it gave me the spike. He said she'd get tired of me soon, then I'd be sorry I'd turned on him. But I hadn't turned on him, that were just how he saw it. He were jealous of anything I had that weren't him.

When I said I were moving in with her, he lost the ⸻ing plot. I said it weren't my decision, but it were in a way 'cause the vicar'd offered too but I didn't tell him that. He looked like a man who'd just got mugged. I s'pose he had in a way. He said why can't I come and I said you've got a home of your own. But actually — and that's the thing — I never went to Floyd's house. It hit me the other week that I never went there. So I think maybe his place were worse than mine, if it were so bad he couldn't have me see it.

It got arranged fast. Up to then I'd been out to the foster lot when Maeve weren't up to it. Going away were always sort of a relief. There were no Mister for a start, no shindies late at night; no waking up to him shouting at the old Mum that she were a —ing tart then that wail of hers trickling upstairs like air leaking out of a balloon. People in suits turned up when I were a kid, asking me questions: 'Where's the safest place you can think of, James? How easy is it for you to fall asleep? Do you ever get headaches?' What the — kinds of questions are those? I kept thinking they'd get round to asking me why I weren't a real person. 'Cause I didn't feel real, I felt pretend. Like I were another boy wearing a Maguire boy's skin.

They said it were important I *belonged*. Fat —ing chance; belonging ain't bricks and mortar, is it? I thought there were only two people on earth I belonged with and that were Kip and Providence, and since Kip were banged up, that left only one.

Reason for it were I'd got done for smashing coins. Floyd were in it too, a fiddle off some cigarette machines, but he didn't get caught and there were no point both of us taking the flak. So it were enter the judicial or go to someone willing to take me.

Providence were glad — least at the start she were. Mrs D too. Birdie, the sister, were a different story. I thought she'd liked me before, she were always fine to me, then the closer I got to Providence it seemed the more she changed her attitude towards me. She were always keeping her beady eye out. I felt her even when she weren't —ing there, like she were my —ing conscience bearing down on me. She always had a side with me too. Always grilling me, she were bad as a —ing copper; all, 'Where've you been? Who've you seen? What've you done?' She didn't never say nothing direct – she were far too —ing worried about upsetting her sister for that – but I could —ing tell. She didn't think I were good enough for Providence or the house or none of it. And it were worse, her being phoney, than if she'd come right out and said it. Like how she were about Ginny, it were like she'd done me a —ing favour but the favour were for her and I knew it and she knew it, for how it'd make her look. For Providence to think she were crackerjack. It were always about that with Birdie. Having Providence like her more than me. I dunno why she had to start that between us, I never —ing started it. I s'pose as far as she were concerned, me going to live with them were the worst thing that could've happened. Until what happened later, obviously … But. Yeh. Hang on— Where was I?

Birdie weren't the only one who were pissed. Mother Maeve were too. She were mad about the situation all over, folk thinking she couldn't look after her brood and what's more I were an ungrateful sod, buggering off leaving her in her old age drinking Squires London Dry. She were only in her forties then, I don't think she knew how —ing old she were. When I left she stuck on me at the door, clinging on not letting go even though she'd never hugged me no time before. I felt like saying it's too —ing late, mate, but instead I got free and walked on my own to Mrs D's and didn't look back.

There were always homely smells coming out the house on Marlborough Avenue. Mrs D were a fine cook. She were fine altogether. I knew with her I'd been given a second chance – first chance, depends how you see it – and I gave myself a talking-to every day; I said, 'All right, Jim, now's the time to get it together, this is your ticket out.' And I did see it like that. Being there could put me on the straight and move me on to better times; it'd fill me back in so I didn't turn into a cut-out like my brothers and I wouldn't fade to nothing.

It were a good home. Warm and bright; even when it rained there were sunshine pouring through it. Everything were looked after. Stuff were kept that meant something – Providence's toys from when she were a baby, scraps of paper smeared in cake mix with recipes jotted on. I said to Mrs D, 'Why'd you keep all this?' 'cause the old Mum never kept —ing nothing, and she said, 'Little bits from a little life,' which I thought were a nice way of putting it. The house were always tidy, not in a strict way just in how it were cared for, and it were happy – it had a feeling of happiness inside it. Providence filled it with music. Beautiful songs, they were. I used to listen where I thought she couldn't see me, hiding out by the porch 'cause that's when the music were best, when she thought she were on her own. Then she'd stop in the middle of it and say, smiling all in her voice, 'Is that you, golden boy?'

I did everything I could to fit in with them. I tried and I tried. But whatever I did for Mrs D or Providence, Birdie were still off with me. I reckon the most part of it were that she saw some similarity of herself with me. Both of us were orphans in a way. Both of us scrapped by our parents. Providence were the same but she'd had Birdie so it were different for her. Seeing me made Birdie see herself and she didn't like it, she didn't want to be like me.

So she could've hardly expected me to grass on my brother when she wanted me to, could she? Just 'cause she needed me all of a sudden. I still dwell on that. What Ron did to her.

But I never let him in the house that night, I never did nothing.

What she did to me, though. Number of times I've heard I ought to be praying for —ing absolution. I ain't —ing praying. She's the one that should be praying to me.

∾

Dear Donna. Thankyou for your letter. It made me happy to get it. Your teacher must be teaching you good your lines are neat. I liked hearing about your birthday party. Ive never done bowling. Maybe when Im out you could show me how to do it? Therell be alot of things you can show me how to do. Your nine now. Thats a magic number. Thats the age I met Floyd so it has to be magic.

∾

2 March

He used to come in the back when the others were out. I preferred it that way 'cause then they didn't see him. I s'pose I thought he didn't reflect too well on me. Floyd'd been smart when I'd met him but he were scabby by then, thin like a scarecrow with his clothes hanging all off him. He'd shaved his head to look like Ron but he'd made a hash of it and it just looked mangy. Birdie nearly came across him one time in the kitchen but luckily I made him scarce. I knew if she saw him he'd scare her.

I didn't want them thinking he were the kind of company I kept 'cause that meant Providence were keeping his company too. Thing is, they hardly ever did. Keep company, I mean. Floyd were always on at me about hanging about just him and me, jumping trains or fishing for sticklebacks, whatever she were left out of. It were awkward pleasing them both. Providence said let's go to the field, then he were up in my ear getting narky about it, he never —ing left it, it were all I could do to get him —ing off me. I tried saying it to her but she wouldn't hear, she just closed off and said, 'I don't like him.' It were worst when he sneaked up on us unexpected, she really didn't go for that. I had to get cross with him when he did that. Then he were offended. I thought he'd — off but he didn't, he just tagged on wherever we were going, every —ing time, lagging behind so I had to say, 'Hurry up, you're slowing us down,' and Providence looked at me sort of hurt and upset so I did my best to ignore him after that.

I told her we'd get away one day, the two of us, without him.

'Just us,' I said. I swore it to her. 'We will.'

I s'pose Floyd were what caused it. Her cooling off towards me. It were subtle at first, then it got obvious the longer I lived with them. She knew then how much Floyd were about. How even if she didn't like him he were still my friend, he were still a part of me, and even if I'd wanted rid of him it weren't that —ing easy. Soon she stopped calling me her golden boy. I started to feel not so much like I had the sun in me no more. I kept trying to catch up with the sun, in the field, on my own, without her, but I never reached him.

6 March

Strange I can remember her face like it were yesterday. Her skin sort of lit from inside. Providence were the only clean person I knew. She weren't chewed up and spat out like the rest of us. She weren't angry or hitting, or sobbing and sad. It weren't like I thought about her in a lovey-dovey way. She weren't a sister to me neither. I dunno what she were. A friend, but special. More. Yeh. Someone that saw me in a way no one else did. She understood me and made me feel like there were a way out, some new road I could go on that I hadn't gone on before. When the borstal lot talked about their judys they said, 'How about you, you got anyone, Jim?' but I never told them about Providence. She were younger than me so it felt sort of wrong to put her like that.

When they sent me down for killing her, they said my mind were abnormal. They asked me why I drank and smashed stuff up, they called me deranged; they said Floyd were the problem, the fact he never left me. I couldn't get across how it felt. Like I were on a flimsy spinning boat in a storm at sea and Providence were my only direction.

I'm trying to get a picture of Floyd in my head . . . That's why I painted him. Why I'm writing him. So I can see him straight and you can too. Only it ain't easy, it's been such a long time since I met him. He's flitting in and out of my memory.

Is it lunchtime yet? Nearly. My brain's not working I guess 'cause I'm hungry.

20 March
I were fifteen when I did borstal. Only time I got banged up before Providence died but it were enough to give me a record and that's why they decided it were me who did her, not Floyd. All 'cause of Birdie. *Threatening behaviour. Intimidation. Attempted rape.* It weren't me, it were never —ing me. Ron were the one doing his Peeping Tom act. He were the one that broke in Birdie's room and had her. You'd think the pigs'd put two and two together, wouldn't you, say hang on, maybe it ain't that young 'un after all, maybe it's the one that's showing all signs of being a —ing nonce, ain't that more —ing likely? Ron'd been getting into all kinds of trouble, looking up girls' skirts in the picture house, garage —ing break-ins – Kip always said it were the sex cases that went in for nicking motors – and he'd already served as a YP. So why didn't they sit up and take notice? 'Cause they'd wanted me for ages, hadn't they? It were bingo to them, a full —ing house.

Attempted. Birdie didn't say I'd actually done it. Nah, she didn't have the —ing brass for that. But it got her what she wanted. Rid of me. That friend of hers backed her, that one that lived next door. Then the whole village were in on it, they had a —ing field day. And that weren't the worst part. The worst part were Providence. The look on her face when they carted me off, I took it with me and I thought on it every single night, still do. I told her the truth but she didn't believe me. She sided with Birdie, said next I'd be blaming Floyd, and Mrs D didn't count on me neither, why would they? It were Birdie's word against mine. I'd never win. It were her payback on me and the thing is – the —ing crazy thing is, and I've gone in circles on this, if she hadn't done that then I wouldn't have gone to borstal and I wouldn't have gone down this track so far and ... I dunno, I'm just saying, —ing maybe, Floyd wouldn't have got so mad and killed her.

24 March

I were frightened of going. All I knew of the lock-ups were what Kip'd told me. I were picturing high walls and stinking cells and boys built like shithouses ready to rough me up. 'You'll get through,' said Kip. He told me Severn Camp were a softer one, it weren't like Portland or Sherwood. I thought he were lying just to make me feel better. I weren't the same as Kip; I didn't have what he had inside him. I dunno – that quality of getting on no matter the problem. Finding a way round it. Seeing what good might come of it or be waiting on the other side. I didn't have that.

Turned out he didn't neither, in the end.

I couldn't have stuck it at a harsher nick. I could hardly stick it at Bedford when I were twenty-one so not when I were fifteen. I missed Providence. I missed having a home. I were a kid. We were all kids. Take away the swagger and what've you got? A bunch of lost boys looking for someone to tell them what the — to do next.

Kip weren't fibbing though. Severn Camp were an all-right place. It weren't like prison, it were more like here, with freedoms up for grabs so long as you toed the line with the screws and didn't try and scarper. Best thing about it were it overlooked Bristol Channel. I hadn't seen the sea before and I liked that, how huge and grey and sort of uncaring it were. Like it didn't mind what I'd done, it stayed the same for all of us no matter what'd gone on. I liked how different moods passed across it depending on the weather. In sun it got scattered with a million lights and in rain it got churning and messy. My mood were the same as the sea's sometimes and I felt then like I had company and I weren't on my own. I liked being by it all day, flat and shiny like a great big mirror.

I were lucky getting put on the gardening lot. The field work were good, being out in the open. Practical graft that had some purpose to it. The screws ran us about like sergeant majors – 'One onto yew, mister! One orf, sir! Enough of your bickchit, Maguire, what do yew think this is, one of Billy Butlin's?' I didn't mind that. I were just thankful I weren't on the building site 'cause the blokes there sent the jeebies up me, tough old HMP sweats in for a three- or four-stretch. The daddy were a geezer called Staines. He had a wheeze going where whatever lackey were on fag-butt duty were obliged to pass the ends back to him for selling on – flush 'em down the bog then wait for the float, dry 'em out after on the windowsill and Bob's your uncle, good enough to twist the tobacco out. There were a lad on the garden lot, a redhead Jock with a Bad Borstal crop; he told me if you ever tried sifting, you paid the price. One bloke had and next time they saw him it were like he'd been through a —ing meat mincer.

Staines weren't as tough as he looked. None of them were.

All big lumps of lads taller than me with their tales just as tall about their lives outside. Girls and money, fancy watches, motors, stuff I believed in till I realized if tricks were that good out there they wouldn't keep —ing it up and getting sent down, now would they?

Staines liked me 'cause I had what he called a *photographic memory*. I'd never heard that before. It came to my advantage 'cause I were able to think things up that weren't in real life and people seemed to get a bit out of it. Like when we got shook about the Feltham Terror. It were a tale going round when I were there, about a lag in that pen who called himself that. He'd lopped off some bloke's arm for clinching with his judy. Some said the bloke'd been saved; others said the ghost of the axed man roamed the camps at night, his stump dripping blood down the hallways, calling for the Terror, vowing revenge. Every noise had us jumping out our skins. What were that sound? Were it the wind in the bricks or the cry of the One-Armed Valentine? All of us quaking in our beds then Staines'd say, 'Tell us a picture, Jim,' so I'd tell a film I knew, *Spartacus* or *The Magnificent Seven*, one I'd watched on Mrs D's box, seeing the scenes played out in my mind then describing them as best I could so the others could see them too. Everyone lay listening, passing their rake-ups from bed to bed and I can see it now, chimneys of smoke shooting into the dark like the skyline over a hundred factories. I dunno if the Terror story were real or not. I don't s'pose it matters if it were or it weren't.

One good thing about borstal were that Floyd weren't with me. 'S not to say he weren't in my head, he were always in there, but in the days at least I didn't think on him. Working the soil with Redhead, hatching plots, sharing contacts in the yard or over grub; I learnt every useful thing I know about crime at Severn Camp. It's bone-headed in my view shoving us all together with time to gab and tip off, a —ing criminal fraternity up- and down-country getting sorted right under the screws' noses. I thought they were just as responsible for whatever we went on to do next as we were.

It were only in the dark that Floyd came back. Nights he got down by my bunk, he said, 'I'm waiting for you, Jim, I'll always be waiting' – and Redhead heard a noise and were yelling, 'It's him!', well, I weren't so —ing afraid of the One-Armed Valentine as I were of Floyd. I knew he couldn't've got in. Or could he? He got in —ing everywhere.

Each one of us had our thoughts to reckon with. Of our past lives, our old lives. Mine were of Providence. I thought of her every second I were there. I wondered what she were doing, if she were OK; if I concentrated I could hear her piano, that song I used to love, 'Knock Turn', and her down-a-tunnel sort of calling voice. It made Floyd go away. She were light and he were dark and if I put one across the other the light always won. I fell asleep with her light behind my eyes, and Floyd disappeared with the morning.

7 April
I wrote to her. Letters and letters, I dunno how many. I thought if she hadn't taken my word when I said it in person then maybe that'd work. She'd used to say I were golden good. No golden good person did what Ron did to Birdie. Why didn't she see that?

I took to drinking. I'd always drunk with Floyd, for his kicks more than mine, but there were more booze in borstal than in all the barrels at the Wagon. In Silent Hour we shared flasks that a couple of the screws'd rustled in, little scrawny blokes that wanted to keep Staines and the building lads happy so they didn't cause them no trouble. It's a —ing riot, that, ain't it – them saying we're the corrupt ones, they're —ing corrupt, the whole system's corrupt from top to bottom. Brandy and Hooch, we got to calling them, after what they brought in, thinking it made them the big men and we'd do what they told us then. Like — we did, but we took what they offered, me and Redhead getting pissed as newts while we penned our notes and took turns keeping the nick from the other officers. Porter were an honourable officer. He knew about the grog. He said to me, 'You don't have to respect what other people do, Maguire. You just have to respect yourself.'

Porter asked who I were writing to so I told him. I said she'd never reply, she'd likely never —ing read them, I didn't know why I were —ing bothering. He said if I'd written my plea down one time then that were enough, I should leave it now. He said words put to paper had the special quality of being spoken as many times as they were read. 'Leave her to think on it,' were his advice. 'She'll come back, son, when she's ready.' And if she didn't, he said, my going on wouldn't help. So, I didn't send no more.

Porter were a decent screw. Before I met him I didn't reckon that decent screws existed. But Porter were decent. He were a round, friendly bloke that made fun of us but in a way that showed us he were fond of us. He were sympathetic and he never made us feel like failures. He told us off for smoking but it were tongue-in-cheek 'cause he himself smoked like a top. If we hadn't no snout of our own he passed round his, a cigarette apiece: 'Have to shut you mouthy bastards up some way, haven't I?' I could tell he thought we were better than what we'd done and it were rare to be thought of like that.

13 April
I went into borstal a boy but I came out a man. I were seventeen when I got let out. First place I went were Marlborough Avenue. Mrs D answered the door. She'd turned into an old woman while I'd been off. I saw straight up in her eyes that I'd been cut. It were the same look Providence had given me when I left, like I weren't nothing to do with them no more. I part expected her to say it'd all been a mistake, she'd read my letters even if no one else had, and welcome me back saying, 'Jimmy, we've missed you, come in,' but course she didn't say none of that, she just said, 'I always thought the very best of you, James, and see how you've let us down.' Then she said I'd better get moving before Birdie came home.

I didn't think Birdie were still living there. Later I found out she'd stayed to look after Mrs D; she'd turned down a job, even a marriage proposal – who'd want to marry that sly —ing —? – 'cause the pain of my crime, *my —ing crime,* 'd made her gran sick. I begged Mrs D to tell me where Providence was. She said keep off or she'd have in the police. I said, 'Did she get my letters?' but I could tell by her face before she shut the door that the letters'd never seen the light of day. It were the vicar that let me know Providence had started at a music school in

London. She were thirteen then. Some fancy place for gifted people. It might as well've been the —ing moon for all it meant to me.

24 April
Months went by. Floyd came back to me again. He looked worse than he had before I left. I didn't think he were eating much 'cause he were thin as a rake and he kept getting himself beat up and his head had these weird —ing scratches all over it. I said, 'What're those?' but he never let me touch them. He said he'd get better from now on, now I were back, he'd get stronger. I knew he were getting back into himself when he picked up saying stuff I didn't want him to say, such as how Providence had done what he'd said all along she'd do, — off and leave. Such as why didn't I have a girlfriend, what were wrong with me, I weren't far off eighteen, everyone else did at my age so why didn't I?

A girl called Rita Eddiston started following me round. She spoke posh and her folks were rich. I couldn't think what the bleedin' hell she wanted to do with me. Floyd said she must like slumming it, why worry if it meant getting my end away? Rita were pretty. She were tall, with brown hair that she always wore in plaits. She had good, square knees. We used to have sex in a den in the rec then she went home to her fancy house with the gold lion knocker on the door. One night the Mister smashed my ear with a tyre iron and when Rita saw it she got a kick out of it – I dunno, sort of excited by it, I s'pose – and said it were time to introduce me to her folks. I said, 'Are you —ing joking me, looking like this?' But she thought it were a fine idea, said it didn't matter about that, they'd still dig me. Floyd said, 'She's the one digging it, Jim.'

Meeting them the first time were as bad as I thought. I didn't want to be there, I wanted to be with Providence. It weren't my world: only she were that. Rita's old man were a teacher at a boys' school where the moneyed —s went. I didn't know what cutlery were what sitting round their fancy —ing dining table with the silver forks and napkins in rings. My ear were swollen from where the Mister'd bashed it. Mr Eddiston offered me booze so I drank on top of what I'd already drunk then he said, 'So, tell me, James, what line of business is your father in?' The mother looked like she were sucking a —ing lemon. Rita were smiling, all smug with herself. I said sorry, I feel sick, I have to go.

I wandered about for a bit and ended up back at Marlborough Avenue. I knew that were where I were going even if I didn't tell it to myself. I didn't try the front door this time. I went round the back to the porch. Providence's piano were still there. I stayed there for hours on the step just thinking about her and hearing her music. It felt like she were with me. It started to rain but I didn't go nowhere, I didn't know where I would go. I didn't care if they found me, Birdie and Mrs D. I didn't care if I got nicked. I thought about doing something to get myself nicked so I could go back to Redhead and Porter.

Floyd were calling at me from the trees. The woods were thick and pitch-dark; I heard the rain smacking the earth and the coolness coming off it, that iron smell I've forgotten these years, it's so long since I've known it. He kept saying my name, from over there then over there, I couldn't tell where it were coming from. I tried to see him but I couldn't see him. Bit like now, when I'm telling you about him, when I'm writing him down, I'm trying to see him and I can't, he ain't there.

∽

Dear Donna. Do you ever get scared of the dark? I do. Things hide in it. Theyre stareing. Eyes in the dark stareing at me. ive seen them. I look in the mirror and all I see is dark and the dark sees me. I see the edge of a man but there aint nothing inside, he's made of dark Its all he is. [Unsent.]

18

He woke before it was light. Donna was snoring on her back with one arm up and out and the other across her chest, like she was ballroom-dancing with someone in her sleep. He dressed in the bathroom in the gloom (the bulb string made a noisy clank when pulled) then left, closing the door quietly behind him. Partway down the hall he turned back, reopened the door, scribbled a note on the pad by the telephone in letters that looked to have been written by a seven-year-old: *Gone to Kip. Back later.* There had used to be so many miles and days in between him writing to her and her getting it that it felt odd now to put down something instant and normal. He left it on her pillow. Then, thinking she might roll onto it or that it would get lost under the covers, he stuck it on top of her bag.

The dawn was frosty. A bleached sun inched above the sea. He walked up to the road and along a bit, where on the way in he'd seen a bus stop. It took a few minutes to work out the timetable and that the next towards Wadebridge was half an hour's wait.

A van in the pull-off was selling baps and jars of tea. He envied the bloke serving, done up like a Soviet tank commander in a furry hat and mitts like bear paws: 'All right, mate, what can I do you for?' The tea when it came was smashing and warm, beads of condensation clinging to the inside of the cup, and the bacon was fatty and salty. He'd spent so long on a diet of grey matter in its various forms that he couldn't get used to the grub out here, the variety of it, and that he could hand over money and receive something hot and good in return.

The bus came. He got on. It was dank and fusty with bodies inside. People read newspapers or looked at the floor: nobody looked at each other. He checked the address and asked the woman across the aisle from him if she knew how he could get there. She glanced at his paper then at him in a way that reminded him of Rita's mother at the dining table, like a bad sewage smell was passing under her nose: prison was a stink you could never get off. 'Thanks,' he said, when she told him, turning to look out of the window.

Houses and hills rolled by. The bus filled up then emptied out. The woman got off, dragging a small hairy dog after her. They came to the end of the line. He walked ten minutes and crossed a bridge and waited on a bench for another bus in the freezing cold.

Drumsticks' jacket was a thin match against the weather. Even so, there was some kind of warmth in it. '*Go on, Jim, you take it,*' Drumsticks had said four years ago, on the day his friend had gone out from Wandsworth; '*somethin' to remember me by.*' The green had always struck him as special; against the grey lock-ups it had been like a tropical bird in a wood of winter trees, a bit like Drumsticks in a way. Colour when there should have been none.

He recalled the first time he had seen Drumsticks – heard him, actually – lining up in the queue for showers, humming an upbeat tune he'd got from the radio, saying how the screws could take away his liberties but they couldn't take away that one. He, Jimmy, had just come over from Grendon, brain blown in, knuckles raw, the shock of his ghost train and what had led up to it squeezing his head like a boa constrictor. He hadn't thought he could cut it. Back in a tough nick, back in the stinking, rotten, useless system, he'd been too long away, too long in his mind; he couldn't, not Wandsworth. They'd done it to make an example of him. '*No violence at Grendon,*' the super had told him, quite gently, as he'd stood cuffed and sorry and stooped in his office; '*you know that, Jimmy, you were told on day one – the minute you're violent, you're out.*' The minute you're violent *against an officer*, he'd left off saying. For that was what had done for him. The bloke had been in the wrong place at the wrong time, it could have been anyone, it didn't matter who it was, he'd had to destroy something, make it cry, make it bleed, make it so the person he was doing it to felt pain that was worse than his but that was no good, it would never be worse than his. The wind-up thing had caught him. Fresh out the group meeting where, for the first time, he'd seen Floyd for what he was, seen his crime laid out before him, there the officer had been and he hadn't been able to stop.

He could have been transferred to Maidstone or Norwich, but no, they'd twisted the knife, making it Wandsworth to show him a lesson.

Days after his arrival there, he'd admired the jacket. Drumsticks had cheered him up, told him how he'd been wearing it the first night he'd got nicked, aged sixteen, for knocking off a truckful of beer, only it turned out not to be beer after all but crates of Drumsticks chewy lollies: by the time he'd realized it he already had the driver on a blade. He'd got too big for the jacket anyway, he said when he left; '*It fits you better, I want you to 'ave it, Jim, for old times' sake.*'

He had thought about those old times since. Puffing away in their cell, sharing stories of their pasts, the crackle of the rolling paper as it burned: '*I'm getting out, Jim, and when I'm out I'll go straight . . .*' When Drum had tried to do just that, scouring under their window bars with a plastic knife, replacing the mortar with chewed lumps of bread and the screws only noticed when they found a line of them on his cabinet like a string of mint imperials. How he'd used to call the WC the '*Double You Scuse Me*'. When he'd told Drum about Floyd and Drum had said, '*You're an easy touch, Jim, you should never've let him get away with it,*' and he'd had to say, actually, no, you don't understand, it weren't like that.

Drumsticks had still been his friend, after. His only friend since her.

The second bus arrived and he got on. Its driver had arms like butcher's hams and a tattoo of the Hanged Man stretched elbow to wrist. They passed signs for the adventure park, went past pitches and churches and schools and on beyond the town. The motion of the wheels put him to sleep. In his dreams he saw Providence on the last night he'd seen her, at the piano, her blue eyes surprised when she'd turned to meet him – then that scene was replaced by another, a rushing red sky over the Brewsters' crop, bloodshot clouds, the Yellowfields Sunshine Man grinning from his weathered board—

''Ere we are, pal.'

He woke. The bus had stopped. The driver was staring at him.

'You getting off or what?'

He stepped out onto the street. The paper in his hand was thin and crumpled, and slightly translucent, like an old chewing-gum wrapper. Rain smudged the ink, making it run. It wasn't like he needed the address anyway; he'd memorized the words, the puzzle they'd posed having troubled him since being locked up at Exeter. He remembered the Governor there telling him the news, a hoity fellow who'd sat behind his desk with his shiny golf trophies and itsy-bitsy cup of steaming Earl Grey tea and said, in between taking sips of it, that they'd hauled a body out of the river and identified him as one Christopher Maguire. '*Sorry about that,*' the Governor had said, as if it were no more significant than Rita crying off.

He'd thought, Not my Christopher Maguire. Another one. Not mine.

Of course, his.

When he'd asked the Gov how Kip had died, the Gov had answered, '*Drowned.*' Not, 'He drowned'. Just 'Drowned'. And he hadn't wished to ask how that had come about.

The location had perplexed him. Why Kip had been laid to rest there, in Cornwall, of all places. Now, he knew it to be Maeve. He had memory of an aunt, a sister of hers he'd never met, in Newquay. Maeve must have come south after he, Jimmy, was jailed, and never left.

Kip hadn't either.

Rain stung his face. Drumsticks' jacket was drenched. A girl bumped into him, carrying a baby. 'Excuse *me*,' she said, but he couldn't work out if she was sorry or wanted him to say sorry and anyway she'd gone. He stood in the bit outside Boots. A homeless man was sheltering next to a wiry dog; a slice of cardboard in front of them read COLD + HUNGRY PLEASE HELP. He bought a drink and a sandwich from a shop down the road and went back and handed them to him. 'Ta,' the man said, warily. He tore the roll in two, his fingers sooty like a chimney sweep's, and passed the bigger half to the dog.

'D'you know where this is?' He showed the sweep the location.

The man considered it. 'Yeah,' he said, wiping his mouth, ''s out that way.' He nodded back the way the bus had come. 'Past the social, past the park. First left.'

'Thanks.'

'What's your name?'

'Jim.'

'Well, Jim. You're a good bloke.'

No, he wasn't. *'You're wicked,'* he heard the screws say, *'you're nothing but a wicked, useless aberration!'*

He went down the street, leaning into the rain like a figurehead on a ship. The directions took him to the cemetery. He passed through the gate and walked among the buried in the cool dark paradise of the dead. The rain fell harder. Fat drops spat on the waxy shells of leaves. Everything was evergreen, ivy, fir and yew, creeping round the half-hidden gravestones. On plinths and pedestals, angels motioned to the sky in arcs of awe and apology, their arms cut at the wrists, wings crumbled, feet missing, fingers powdered, their stone limbs flecked by moss. The statues filled him with uneasy wonder – their burden, their piety, their blinded eyes yearning for something that could not now be seen.

At the back was a garden for ashes. He saw Kip's name right away on the last row. A small wooden cross with a tablet: *Christopher 'Kip' Maguire. 1939–1972.*

Mother Maeve had marked it, at least. He could visit it. Tell it sorry. But of course he would never tell it sorry, be one of those on his knees repenting; he could hear Kip's voice chiding him, *'Don't be soft,'* but in that affectionate way he'd had, where he'd known, even if it was never said, that he, Jimmy, had a heart that was easily squeezed and broken.

At first, anyway, there had been nothing to be sorry for. He wasn't guilty of killing Providence. He'd watched another man do it and now he was taking the heat: it made him a martyr, a hero of sorts. *Don't be a grass*; he was doing what Kip had always told him to do. So why had Kip been upset? His crime had been in befriending Floyd – if it weren't for Floyd then she would still be alive – and for that he was sorry, sincerely, and told Kip so, but Kip had turned to him before he was sent down with an expression of despair and hopelessness, of confusion and loss, the expression of a man who was searching for something he knew no matter how far he went he would never find, and had put his hands over his face and said into them, so quietly he could hardly be heard, *'I never meant for this to happen to you, Jimmo. If I could make you better, I would.'* The words and expression had stayed with him, haunting him, for months after – until the day, in fact, when the Governor had summoned him and shared his bad tidings – and only then had he been able to remove them from his mind, for they no longer existed in the world and therefore could not root him out and make him hear and see them again, and give him the same eerie, chilling impression that there was something serious he was missing in all this.

Over the years, he had imagined doing damage to Floyd. Sometimes Floyd was a man, and he took a bat to Floyd's door (what door, where?) and tied him by his wrists in the way the Mister had shown him. Other times Floyd was a boy and fixed before the harm was done – on that first day they had walked to school together, getting him that lunchbreak in the boys' privy, his slit, slumped body found hours later by poor Miss Broderick.

Back then, Floyd had been as clear as glass. A subtle companion who journeyed with him, his ally, the one he couldn't shake off. It had been Floyd who had pushed him in everything, given him his bottle, urged him as he had the night Providence died – *'Are you gunna let her walk away, Jim? Talk to you like that, eh, then let her walk away?'*

But as time went on, the more he had tried to imagine Floyd the more Floyd slipped away from him, like a bar of soap in the bath. The events of that night rearranged themselves into new, insistent forms, mounting in his unconscious and waking him with a shout – his or hers? – and a sudden sinking sensation, like missing the bottom stair in the dark. He'd tried to suppress these interlopers but all he saw in his troubled mind's eye was a man of nineteen stumbling down Nail's Lane to the police station, his T-shirt streaked in blood and snot, his bare feet blistered, and when he reached it he told them Floyd was the one who had done it but that he'd been there too, he'd been *part of it*, and they were sorry, truly they were both sorry, he didn't know how it had happened – one minute Providence was with them and the next he didn't know, *he didn't know* – something had come out of him, something bad. '*Take us*,' he'd begged. He didn't want to go to prison but was sure he needed banging up. The coppers had cuffed him and pushed his face to the floor: '*You want to come with us now.*'

Now had turned into eighteen years. *Voluntary manslaughter with intent to kill*. He was '*mentally disturbed*', according to the Judge; an '*uncontrollable character*' and '*a risk to public safety*'. They'd taken into account his being a teenager and there being enough to meet what they'd kept calling '*the threshold of diminished responsibility*' – but that summing-up would be etched on to him the rest of his days: '*You committed an evil crime, Mr Maguire, a frenzied attack on a defenceless girl who trusted you, and for that you shall be punished under the full power of the Law. You have shown no remorse throughout the course of this trial. You have failed to understand the nature of your conduct and the impact it has had on others. You have made no attempt to spare your victim's family by admitting guilt. Your Counsel argues mitigations of childhood trauma precipitating disordered personality and abnormality of mind; however it is the view of this Court that you have no emotional feeling. In light of that I have no option but to conclude that you pose a significant danger to society and should thus be detained.*'

Detained he had been – a year at Exeter, six at Bedford, a transferral to experimental Grendon with its talking treatments and rooms not cells, before a last-straw attack on an officer saw him ejected to serve the remainder of his tariff at Wandsworth.

At Grendon, he'd got used to being treated like a person. A human being. No security wall, no fences, no cell blocks, the kind of place (but there was only one) where they'd asked if he took sugar in his tea and gave him clothes that fit him so he didn't feel like a waster, like a wanderer, so he could get some respect for himself. Then just like that they'd sent him back out to the zoo. What had they expected would happen, putting him in those group sessions, making him talk, making him listen, going over and over and over it again, making him discuss it with the others till the fact was whittled out of him like a shining, pristine diamond? You couldn't give a man a mirror if you didn't want him to see himself. And through it all, the Judge's words had turned over in his mind with the dull, repetitive clunk of a belt in the washing machine – '*You have no emotional feeling, you have no emotional feeling . . .*' What kind of person did that make him, then? If he had feelings, for he thought he did, what were they if not emotions? Sham, like the rest of him, a wind-up boy turned into a wind-up man, the ghost of a man, of Isaac the Pilot, his rage tucked deep inside him, his hot-headedness – what was that if not *emotional feeling*? It was a feeling of no feeling, of being set apart from a world that had never wanted him in the first place; that hadn't helped him make things right so he could be included, just shunted him this way and that in hopes of an answer that somebody else would provide, then when that didn't work boxed him off like an animal. What was he but an animal if he was *lacking emotional feeling*? A snake, cold-blooded and dead to the touch. Drumsticks had said, '*Prisons kill all the feelings in you.*' What if there had been none in the first place?

The rain stopped. Clouds heaped in the west, feathery white, shot through with brown strings. He touched his brother's name and thought of saying something, but no words came. He left the cemetery. The jacket stuck to his skin. He put his hand in his pocket and felt the slip of paper, thin and disintegrating, and back on the street stopped by a bin so he could fish it out and chuck it away. When it was gone, he sat on a swing in the park. The frame was rotten and rusted. Two children argued at the top of a slide. Their mother wiped rain off the chute with her sleeve and kept glancing over at him.

Dear Donna. Do you like the playground? I don't know that about you.

Do you like apples? I don't know.

Do you like Rupert Bear? Do you like time machines?

I don't know, I don't know.

A helpless feeling came over him. It hit him like a wave. The people he had lost, let go, let down, never had. He closed his eyes and saw Providence looking at him as she had in the kitchen that time with Ginny. She had died for knowing him. He'd hurt her, though he'd loved her. He could never take that back. He could never unpick it or change it or make it any other way than it was. But he was here – unlike Drumsticks, unlike Kip – and he could try, for the sake of his daughter.

The mother and children left the park. He waited until they were out of sight so she didn't have to worry he was after them, then got to his feet and returned the way he'd come. Across the road, he saw a pub. He went to it and pushed the door. Inside it was warm, dark chairs, dark tables, a glowing hearth. A man was wiping glasses and hanging them upside down above the bar. He ordered a pint and sat by the fire. He didn't drink it but stared at it. Bubbles rose to the surface. He put his hand round it, then took it off, then put it back again. He picked it up and smelt it. Drumsticks had used to warn him about blokes outside who wanted him dead – '*You wait, Jim, just you wait and see*' – and who knew, maybe that was how Drum had gone in the end, the gas fire a decoy, and no one would look closely at a person like that because no one ever did – and he thought what a relief it would be if a stranger came to him now, just walked in and saw him sitting here with his undrunk pint and his jacket so wet it looked like it'd been painted straight on.

The door opened. He turned, surprised, deciding he must have conjured her up, this woman with her bag in her hand, for here she stood opposite him, out of place, out of time, not here for the establishment but for him, that much was clear by the way she lingered, scanning, unsure, before her eyes settled on him and her body breathed out.

'At last,' she said. 'I've found you.'

19

HM Prison Grendon
Group therapy meeting, 1980

17 November
Liars need good memories. Floyd told me that. Or did I read it somewhere? It stuck with me anyway. I've been called a liar so long it almost makes me believe it. All this writing I'm doing, I look at it after and I dunno what's real of it and what ain't. Some of it's stories, some of it's true, I get lost working out which is what. They want me to read it out here one day. Say it'll help me make sense of things. I can't do that though.

There's this dream I keep having. First time I had it's a month ago. It keeps coming back. Where I am's always different. Sometimes I'm with Providence in the field, other times I'm with Kip. Other times I'm with Floyd. The time of day stays the same. It's evening and the sun's gone down. I feel all right. Everything's safe. Then whoever's with me leans right close in my ear and says, *Look in the mirror*, and I wake up.

I dunno what it means. I dunno nothing these days. I knew where I were before I came here. Now all this talking's got my head in a spin. They said the point of Grendon's to face up to yourself. Well it ain't —ing worked, I don't think, 'cause now everything's knotted. Everything's mixed up and I just want it to go back to how it were.

22 November
They've put me on watch in case I get any ideas. This bloke on my landing at Bedford hanged himself with bedsheets; when the screws came they said, 'One orf, sir!', all pissing themselves laughing like it were some grand joke, like his life amounted to — and that's how it were to them. I've thought about doing it. Course I have. If I've the nerve. Then I remember Donna. Or I want a burn. Or some decent-smelling scoff comes by. And I think if I can just focus on the minute I'm in and just that, no time else but now, I can maybe find a way to carry on. Trouble is in prison you dunno what you're carrying on for. When I'm out, then what? What do I do then? I know how it is going back, nothing's the same as you left it. The world's gone on without you and you either jump on a moving train or stay where you are and get levelled. It ain't freedom out there. Freedom's in here – up here, and in here – and it don't matter if you're banged up or on a beach in Barbados, that's your ticket out and if you don't have it, you're —ed.

Everything'd changed when I came back from borstal. Providence were gone. Mrs D were an old lady. All that fell apart the second my back were turned, like I'd taken my eye off it for a minute and it went. When I'd lived at Marlborough Avenue, I'd got thought better of. People gave me the time of day. They'd reckoned they had the measure of me before but I'd made them think twice, I'd made them wonder if it weren't cut and dried, if there were a good bit in me that could've come to some use. Then they found out they were right after all. I'd done what they expected. Life made sense to them again.

More than a year I were back at home. Mother Maeve were hardly around and when she were she were high or half-cut. It'd have been better if Kip or Alf'd been about but Kip were banged up and Alf had hightailed north; last I'd heard he'd got hitched to a girl up there.

Ron were in and out of police cells. Theft, ABH, blowing safes; I didn't see him. He wouldn't've had the nerve to speak to me even if I had. He knew what I'd done for him. I could've thrown it on him with the Beak but I didn't. To this day I dunno if that were my principles or if I knew it wouldn't make the blindest bit of —ing difference. Keeping quiet about it got me in trouble so I told myself I wouldn't do that again. I'd stand up for myself next time. And I did, with Floyd. But still no one believed me.

26 November
Floyd got me spying on the house. We hid in the woods on our fronts like commandos. Shadows moved in the windows. Floyd whistled the tune to 'I Only Have Eyes For You' and put his fingers together, like this, and aimed them at Birdie's head, *Boom.*

He said she deserved what she got. But I could never've done that to Providence. Floyd said why d'you give a — about her? She's ditched you. I knew he were right, but still I waited for her. I thought if I could see her and she'd see me she'd be able to tell I were innocent. I didn't know when that would be though, if she were ever coming back. I went to the vicar's house like I'd used to and he took pity on me and sat me on his flowery sofa, same place I'd sat when I were ten years old, and told me Providence were happy at the music school, sitting exams, playing concerts, she were a star pupil, he said. 'Destined for greater things,' were how he put it. I thought, greater than what? Me, were what he meant. He told me it were just as well she weren't at home to see how Mrs D were getting worse, it'd only upset her. He said Birdie were a devoted child, tending to her, and in turn the Lord would tend them both. I thought, course He —ing would. Then he started on about the saving graces of God and how the Lord had the power to absolve our sins and the sins that had been done to us, well, all the time he were talking I were thinking how the good Lord never did no such thing for me. He'd never need to protect a man like the vicar – properly protect him, I mean – 'cause the vicar had finer people in his world than I did in mine so it never got put to the test. I've read a lot about faith. Tried to get into it. It'd make my time here a — of a lot easier if I thought there were pearly gates shining for me at the end of it. The conclusion I've reached is, it's easy to believe when belief makes your life better but never has to save it. God didn't care that Birdie did me wrong and stitched me up and made me fail. From the bottom to the top it's the same old tale, ain't it? You ain't never getting up the ladder 'cause for every rung you climb there's another one added to the top. You're just climbing and climbing going —ing nowhere.

3 December
I carried on with Rita. My heart weren't in it though. She finished school and started a college course. Her parents would've rathered she'd done teaching like her old man and moved in the house on Groveley Wick they had their eye on and married the lad they fancied for her, some posh cricket bat called Montgomery. Floyd kept teasing me I were her bit of rough. I weren't dumb enough to think it were anything other than her doing it to stick it to her folks. I drank to forget Providence. It were the only way I could, and when I started to remember her I drank more. Floyd kept plying me. We went to the rail yard and boxed each other till we bled. I thought she might come one day but she didn't.

One night the Eddistons had a party. Rita made me go. She said they were sorry for how they'd been with me last time; this time would be better, she promised. She reckoned Monty'd ask her to marry him. She said, 'Are you jealous?'

I said, 'I dunno. Up to you, ain't it.' She said Monty were all over her and I weren't and that's why she liked me. I liked her good square knees but that were it, which sounds harsh to say now but she weren't Providence.

No one were.

I kept thinking I saw her, thinking I heard her. But she were gone.

I did my best to scrub up. Combed my hair neat and nicked a shirt off the Mister which stank of Aqua Velva. Floyd were on the drive when I got there. I didn't think he knew where they lived. He said he were coming in; I said, 'No, you —ing ain't, why'd you have to follow me, why can't I do a single —ing thing on my own?' Rita came out and said who were I talking to? I'm trying to get Floyd for you now, I'm trying, he's *there* – red shorts, bare feet – but he keeps escaping me. Maybe he weren't there, at the party. Maybe he didn't come after all. I can't remember.

Rita and me had sex in her bedroom with the door open. She liked to do it in places she thought we'd be caught. She liked to do it full stop, 'cause that's all there were to it. Rita's easy to get clear, dancing round in her bra to Tyrannosaurus Rex. They were my favourite band since I'd heard 'King of the Rumbling Spires' in a pub and she bought me the record after, in the market, which I found weird 'cause it were like she were doing me favours. I can see her lying next to me, sucking her braid till the end of it went stiff like a paintbrush. She turned on me, she said, 'C'mon, let's give them something to talk about.'

The Eddistons' living room looked fake. They'd a two-bit Johnny Cash in a white suit and a bad wig, more like Elvis I thought. Rita's old man's face when he saw me were a picture. I thought I saw Floyd standing behind him through the window but when I looked again it were only my reflection. Her ma made a big —ing show of greeting me. She told everyone I were called James Mills. —ed if I know who that were. Then some prim — said, 'I'm afraid you're mistaken, Caroline, but that's a Maguire boy,' and it were only the bleedin' copper who'd had us that day with Ron's knife. I'd the idea of running off. Rita grabbed me before I could. She were dragging me round, showing me to people, deciding it were all good fun, but the fun were at my expense. I were ready to walk out when a bloke came over to me and said, 'Gordon tells me you know your way round an engine.'

So I said, 'Yeh, I've done a bit, what of it?' He said his Jag were parked out on the road, she were a fine runner but lately she'd been giving him gyp; could I look at her for him? There were a job in it if I could.

Then he told me, real soft, 'I know these people. I'm not one of them, Maguire. I came from nothing, like you. Grateful for a few leg-ups on the way and now I'm offering you one. I've got the garage down on Shipley, d'you know it? Prove yourself and the work's yours.'

Course I jumped at the chance. I went outside and turned up and down the street but I couldn't see no Jag. I reckoned I must've heard him wrong though so I went back to the house but the door were shut and when I knocked no one came.

After a minute the window came up and there were people laughing. Mr Edditson said through the gap, 'You can use that to unlock your prospects, son.' I didn't get what the — he meant. Then I realized it weren't a car key that bloke'd given me but a Yale. There were a shed out by the fence; the key went in fine and it opened on a grimy, shit-stained privy. I heard the first twangs of Johnny's 'Don't Take Your Guns to Town' before the window slammed shut.

∾

Dear Donna. Your mums a good person. Whatever went on between me and her she told me about you when she didnt have to. She kept on visitting me she never said I werent your dad.

∾

10 December
I'm not —ing answering that. What the —'re you asking me that for? I told you, I —ing told you a hundred —ing times, same as I told the Judge, same as I told the jury, stop —ing asking me when I already told you. That's this place's doing, making me think and think till I can't —ing think no more and they'll say I'm mad 'cause it makes me mad.

It's Floyd that's got to live with it. Him. *He's* the one that knows what went on in that field. *He's* the one that's got to reckon with having killed her. *He's* the one that's got to go over every —ing second of what he did so many —ing times they don't make —ing sense to him no more and it's like watching a stranger, it's like watching a stranger's life. *He's* the one that's got to live with *me* getting sent down for the felony he committed and never confessed to, not during the trial or before it or after it or never. I get blamed for it. Blame on me all my —ing life long. You ain't heard a —ing word I've said, you dunno — about it, none of you. I'm guiltless now as I've ever —ing been and that ain't never —ing changing. So stop —ing asking me about Floyd or I'll — up every —ing last one of you. Ain't you learnt nothing by now? I've got the Devil in me.

15 December
It were a bitter cold winter. No money for the coal fire so I took to wrapping up in *Daily Record*s filched out the bin. Undressing for bed were the worst; I had to do it at a hell of a lick then dive under the covers before Floyd snatched them off me. He were sleeping in my bed then. Said he were homeless. I said show me your home and he said, 'My home's with you, Jim, don't you

know that?' He were stuck on me like glue, every —ing hour sure as the sun comes after the moon. I thought I'd die if I didn't get away from him. Out that house, out the village, as far as I could get myself. Kip wrote to me saying he were out the lock-up now; he were staying in a shelter up north, had got in with a taffy from Newport who were up for starting an auto-repair business. *See, Jim?* were what he wrote. *I did it.* He'd set us up a savings bank account, he said – not much but enough to get started. Floyd said it were made up: 'When're you gunna learn, Jim? It's me or no one. I'm the only one on your side.'

I had to try though. I had to get up there and see my brother.

There were just one thing I had to know first.

It were just me and Mother Maeve at home. The Mister came back now and again with his tail between his legs from whatever bust-up he'd had with the lady he were shacked up with at the time. He never went for me no more though, didn't —ing dare. I were too big then and he only picked on people smaller than him. I thought how'd I ever been frit by him? He were low-rent, a —ing thug. I wanted so badly not to be his.

Floyd said not to stir things up. But things'd been stirred all my life so I had to find out. He said I wouldn't know Isaac the Pilot even if I walked right by him. I thought if he were hot-headed, I might. But everyone I knew were hot-headed. Kip were. Ron were. The Mister were worst. Was I as bad? When that clock gets to winding and I can't see straight, all I want is blackout so I don't have to see or think or feel no more and I can't —ing trust myself. We're all the same, every last one of us, same as all you, same as every man in every wing at

Grendon, the thieves and the nonces and the —ing butchers, we're all running from one problem to the next with our heads on fire.

I found the old Mum in the kitchen. She had a Pall Mall burning in an ashtray with a windmill on it. The tablecloth were dirty with eggshells. I'd packed a bag, pathetic how little I owned.

I said, 'I'm going.'

She said, 'Don't. I'm sorry. Forgive me.' But I'd heard all that before, it didn't mean nothing to me. Part of me were sorry for her and part of me thought pull yourself together, no one —ing made you have me, no one made you have none of us, but you did, so be a mother for once. But it were too late by then to be my ma.

'Who's my father?' I said.

She didn't answer right away. So I said, 'It ain't him, Ma. Is it?' Then I said I've got to know who he is; I pleaded with her to tell me. There I am —ing pleading but it's her who should be pleading with me, then she started crying so I put my arms round her, I didn't know what else to do. She kept saying, 'I'm so sorry,' and it were a relief 'cause I knew then I were right, I were *right*, she were apologizing to me 'cause she'd lied and I'd *known it*.

But then she said, 'I wish 'e weren't, but he is.'

So I said, 'Isaac?' and she were confused like she'd never heard that name before.

'You're your dad's,' she said, like I were slow, like I weren't all there; 'you all belong to 'im.' Like we were nicked —ing loot in a cashbox.

Triple choice. Your mum ever hit you with a broom till it knocked you out? She ever let your dad force a quart of vodka down you when you were eight years old then watch him beat you black for passing out? She ever see him push your head in the —ing fire 'cause you lied about that dog and sit back and do —ing nothing but —ing sob and drink and say it ain't her fault, it ain't her fault, it's *yours*. Your ma ever do that to you?

That's why I didn't count on a bloody word she said.

I know I should buy it. It's what she said, so I have to. Only I don't. I keep going back to that conversation, I can't shake it off. Now I can see Floyd quite all right. He's sitting by her at the table, dabbing eggshell off the tablecloth with the pads of his fingers. He's smiling at me. Why didn't he help me? He never helped. All he ever did were watch.

∽

Dear Donna. Do you dream? I hope you dream of nice things. Sweet things. I dunno what little girls dream of. Unicorns. Sherbert. Ive been dreaming alot lately. Of this boy I used to know. In the dream hes chasing me through forests calling my name. Ive got to stop and see his face, I want to see his face but when I turn round he aint there, just air. Leaves blowing in the wind.

∽

23 December
It were near Christmas like now. Frozen black nights. Sun going down before he'd even got started. I walked out the

village past the windows with gold lights shining in them, golden good, and fires burning warm in homes that weren't mine. I went by Marlborough Avenue. I thought if I said goodbye to it then, it wouldn't follow me the rest of my days.

When I reached it, Birdie were there. She were in a coat and a hat, I nearly didn't know her, letting herself in the door. I were shocked when I saw her. She were different. Worn out. Her hair were grown and she were less like a boy and her skin were grey like the Bristol Channel, lit by the light from the hall. We stopped and looked at each other, not saying nothing, me with my pack on my back and she with her key in her hand.

There were things going on in my head to ask. About Providence and Mrs D. Then she said, 'You're leaving,' and closed the door in front of her like I might've made a run inside.

Those questions left my head. I said, 'Why'd you do it?'

She folded her arms like she had to hold the answer in. But she didn't have the guts to look at me straight. She said, 'Providence is safe from you now.'

I said, 'You knew it were Ron. You could've got him. Why didn't you?'

Her expression were shut like a cellar. 'It didn't matter who it was,' she said. I didn't get what she meant. Course it —ing mattered. 'It might've been any of you. You're all the same. I thought you weren't, Gamma thought so too. But you are.'

I expected to be angry, I were waiting to be angry but I weren't, I weren't nothing.

'We stood up for you,' Birdie carried on. 'Everyone told us not to. They said what you were like but we didn't listen, we wanted to be good. Gamma spent her life being good.' She were twisting the key round and round in her hands. She said, 'Now look what it's done to her. You wrecked her, all you Maguires. I couldn't let you wreck Providence too. My sister's gone now, she's safe. You can't hurt her any more.'

I said I never would've.

Birdie spoke softer. She looked sad. Sort of lost. I can pick it out, what she said next, word by word; she said, 'There's a world between Providence and you, James. Maybe it's not how things should be, but it's how things are. If you want to do right by us, walk away. Leave us alone. Don't ever come here again.'

I stopped her going. 'Wait,' I said. 'Didn't she read my letters?'

She said Providence hadn't wanted them. 'She's moved on. She's forgotten you.'

I should've walked away. I know I should've. But I felt the clock starting. It were like someone were speaking out my mouth only it weren't me. 'You're only bitter 'cause Kip didn't want you,' I said to her. 'He told me he didn't —ing like you and you were all —ing over him and it were —ing embarrassing. Still you were —ing mooning on him, traipsing round after him like a lost —ing puppy. He said you were ugly. Ugly and stupid and horrible. He wanted rid of you but he were too nice to say it. Now who's —ing *good*?' I didn't mean any of that. I said it 'cause I were steaming. Kip never told me nothing about it, but I said it to hurt her just like she'd hurt me. She didn't look hurt though. She just looked cold and hard.

'D'you think I care about your brother?' she said. 'Gamma's dying because of *you*. Because of you and them and everyone who's ever taken advantage of her. You made her lose her faith and when she lost that she had nothing.'

I said, 'You dunno about me,' but I thought that she did. I actually thought right then that Birdie Doyle might know me best of anyone and maybe she had all along.

But she hadn't finished with me yet. 'Providence is something and you're nothing,' she said. 'You'll *always* be nothing. I've got her now, I got her back from you. You'll *never* have her. She'll never be yours.'

Snow were falling, soft and white. She went inside.

I shouted, 'Come back!' But it were only the shut door I were talking to.

I just stood there in the snow and the snow fell out the sky like feathers. Floyd were next to me. The clock were turning, slow then fast, it were spinning away from me, up through my feet and chest and through my hands and over my head, and Floyd were laughing, I couldn't —ing stop him, he were just standing there laughing like a —ing maniac and all I heard were his laugh and what Birdie said and I shouted after her,

'I'll get you. I'll take what you love and I'll kill it.'

You see, I did tell her. I did warn her who I were.

20

Donna didn't talk to him the whole way back except when he asked how she'd found him and she said, which made him depressed, 'I knew where the cemetery was and I found the nearest pub.' He told her he hadn't touched it, his pint, but couldn't know if she accepted that or not. She drove slowly with the busted window, the makeshift cover-up shivering.

Back at the Waveside he slept long and deep, as he had when he'd first had his own cell. When he woke before Donna and looked at the clock, 5 a.m., he remembered his daughter – *his daughter* – standing in the door to the pub and taking his note from her bag. '*Course I worried,*' she'd said. '*All I do is worry about you, Dad. It's all I've ever done.*'

After breakfast, they walked the mile to the Ladyfield Nursing Home, and though he didn't want to go, he had to make it up to her. She walked ahead of him, hunched in her red-and-black shirt and a hat with a bobble on top of it the size of a small orange. It was cold, the sea steel-smooth and the hills silver with ice. His throat stung with keeping up, and a knot chewed in his gut when he thought about seeing his mother again. Maybe that was all it was, but several times he glanced behind him, fretful, convinced he heard footsteps that matched theirs.

'What is it?' said Donna, turning round.

He blinked at the pavement, which glistened with frost.

'Nothing,' he said. 'Only— Don't you . . . ?'

She was impatient, still annoyed with him. 'Don't I what?' she said.

'It feels like someone's there.'

'You're remembering the old days.'

But they didn't feel that old, those days.

'You know there isn't,' said Donna. 'There's no one else. Is there?'

He shook his head. He squinted back into the icy mist that thickened, blotting out the cars, the garden gates, the postbox at the end of the road.

Donna carried on walking. He pulled his jacket tight and went after her.

∽

The home was a high brick building with staring windows and creepers climbing up it, set in a car park holding an ambulance and a Ford Escort. A woman in a sage-coloured tunic met them at the door. There was a short delay while she managed the fact they hadn't made an appointment, and sighed while organizing the paperwork so they'd know it was an inconvenience. He suggested they come back later but Donna said it was fine, they were happy to wait. She skirted the foyer picking up leaflets (*The Carers' Choice*; *Coping with Dementia*) before replacing them in their plastic slots, then got drinks from an upside-down water tank that shot jets of water into paper-triangle cones.

Finally the woman showed them down a corridor that smelt like the inside of a week-old lunchbox. He didn't know when he'd ever had the chance to smell the inside of a lunchbox. Mother Maeve had never packed him one. At Grendon once he'd been taken out for the day, to London, to see a specialist mind doctor about the confusion in his head; he remembered a paper bag with brown bananas inside, corned beef, crusts, his cuffed wrists battling the clingfilm.

The nurse opened the door and called inside, 'Maeve, you've a visitor.'

Words came back. He couldn't decipher them. 'Your son,' said the sage lady.

She went in and left the door ajar. There followed a hushed conversation. He'd expected it to hit him worse, hearing her voice again. Like a fresh coat of paint on the last words she'd said to him — '*You all belong to 'im*' — it'd either run over the pain or make it shine harder, but now it was happening he felt unmoved. It crossed his mind that this wasn't the right Maeve; his Maeve had indeed died years ago, the Grendon screws had been on to something and Ron was mistaken. He'd been fairly comfortable with the idea that she'd died. He didn't feel guilty about that. There could have been a way back if she'd turned up for him at the trial, not to speak but to be there, to show he'd a mother, and if the jury could see he'd a mother then they might have been able to picture him as a boy, a child, a baby, someone's dearest. He had never been anyone's dearest.

'Memory comes and goes,' apologized the nurse, coming back out. 'Good days and bad days, I'm afraid.'

Donna said, 'Don't we all,' which made her sound twice her

age, and it crossed his mind that she'd always had to be that way, older than she was.

'Are you ready?' she asked him.

'Not really,' he said.

Maeve's room was a cube containing a single bed and a sliding tray that went over it, on which stood a beaker of cloudy fluid and a thimble of pills. To his surprise, it was still decorated for Christmas. A plastic tree sat in the window with branches drooping; tinsel draped off the curtain pole. It struck him as a dark joke, to have left them up so long: Maeve had never gone in for Christmas. Once they'd had a fruitcake brought over by the vicar but she'd declared it chewy as boots so Kip and Alf and him had shared it between them, having it every meal because it was so lovely and big, thick-sliced in sandwiches, grilled and topped with knobs of melting Stork. There'd been no angels, no singing, no pillowcases. At Grendon, they'd done a Nativity scene, made papier mâché donkey heads and had a loaf of Hovis in swaddling clothes for the Holy Baby Jesus. Even at Wandsworth, there'd been effort. A card from the Sally Army, fried eggs for breakfast, listening with Drumsticks to *Carols from King's*.

She was sitting in a chair by the window, looking out on the frozen lawn. The chair had such a straight, high back that he couldn't see over the top of it until he went close, and there was the familiar shape of her head, slightly flat on top like an iron had kissed it, so unchanged by the years that it felt like a trick. He wondered how it could be that then and now should come back together so easily, if that was how time worked, for the passing of time seemed to him now a fake dismantling of events that otherwise had a natural, clinging urge towards one another, like two fingertips wetted with glue.

Donna hung back. He had a mad idea of his position between these two women.

'Who're you?' said Maeve, turning to him, her eyes watery and red-rimmed.

'It's Jimmy, Ma.'

'Who's Jimmy?'

'Your boy.'

'James?'

'That's right.'

She peered closer. 'You ain't James,' she said. 'That ain't your name.'

He heard the nurses in the corridor, the sound of a tea trolley coming past.

'This is my daughter,' he said. 'Donna. We've come to see you.'

'What're you selling, hm? I said I don't want no sales people.'

He held his hands out. 'It's just me.'

She stared at him intently and seemed about to speak, but the words became coughing. Donna offered the cloudy glass but Maeve shook her head, pressing a handkerchief to her mouth. The spasms stopped. There were tears on her cheeks but he thought that was the coughing. 'I'm waiting for Frankie,' she said. ''E promised me 'e'd come. 'E's all I've got. They said I shouldn't keep taking 'im back but I di'n't 'ave no one else. Did you see 'im?'

'No.'

He prepared to tell her that Frank was dead. Then he thought what was the point, and anyway maybe he wasn't dead, maybe he was still out there somewhere beating up women or other children he'd had, robbing stores, nicking motors, flogging drugs and jewellery. Maybe he'd been banged up, but even then Frank Maguire would find a way past it, over it, get the best out of it; he'd be daddy of the wing, set up his kingdom and sit on the throne getting full on the fat of the land because that was the way of the Mister.

'Who'd you say you were again?' she said.

He repeated it. An idea washed over her expression. She took his hand. Hers was like holding a swift; small and fragile, heart throbbing.

'I knew a boy who looked like you once. 'E was nice. Not like Frank's boys.'

I ain't Frank's, he wanted to say. He waited for her to say it. Willed her. *Say it.*

'Ron were Frank's boy,' he said. 'Weren't he?'

'You know Ronnie,' said Maeve. 'Worst of the lot. Dirty, lying fiend.'

'I saw him, Ma. He showed me a card you sent. For Christmas.'

'It's Christmas?'

He crouched so he was next to her. 'It was,' he said. 'You wrote to Ron. You said you had something for . . . a man called James. That's me. I'm James.'

She dropped his fingers. 'You ain't James. You're Floyd.'

He blinked. 'Ma.'

'You're that nice boy. I just said.'

'I think I know what you want to tell me,' he said. 'It's OK. I already know.'

'You do?'

'Yes.'

He waited. A minute passed. Then she said, "E was a boy in a magazine.'

'Who were?'

Maeve put the handkerchief in her lap. A robin hopped across the grass, head tilted to look in at them, its eyes gleaming before it flew into the brittle trees. The only birds he'd seen these winters were the grunting fat pigeons on the sills of his peter.

'See,' she said. 'Over 'ere.' She tried to stand by pushing off the arms of the chair.

He stood to help her. 'Can you manage?' asked Donna. The question wasn't for Maeve but for him. He could say he wanted to go now, and they'd go.

Maeve sat on the bed. Her nightdress was old and dotted with flowers. She could have been on another mattress in another house, two decades ago, with her shoes from Shoulihan arranged in rows on the floor. 'I should've gone to the police,' she said.

He stayed where he was. In the distance, in another room, a piano was playing.

'Why should you, Ma?'

She pushed the tray aside. 'So I could tell 'em it weren't Jimmy's fault.' She spoke so quietly it was almost a whisper. 'That 'e really believed it. It'd 'ave made 'em think kindlier on 'im. I could've said where Floyd came from. *Shown* 'em . . . They might've understood better then. That 'e weren't just in Jimmy's head, if they could see 'im too . . .' Her eyes travelled over him; he saw pain in them. 'A child's imagination – how can that be a crime? Only I couldn't do it. I di'n't want 'em watching me. Judging me. The bigwigs, the police, all that again, I couldn't—'

'Ma.' He touched her shoulder. 'It's OK.'

'D'you know Jimmy?'

She was hopeful, regretful, as she'd been on the day he'd walked out.

'Yeh,' he said. 'I do.'

'What d'you think then? Does 'e want Floyd back?'

The piano music stopped. 'Floyd's gone,' he said.

She reached down to open the cabinet by the bed, and took out a large brown envelope tied with a frayed length of string. She passed it to him.

'There're hundreds,' she said. 'Found 'em under Jimmy's bed when the 'ouse got took. There weren't much else to bring. Just I wanted to keep 'em. Thought 'e might want 'em back one day.'

The envelope was heavy. He untied it and opened the seal.

'Floyd Bennett,' said Maeve. 'Blond 'air, blue eyes. Like Jim. All those colourful covers – there they are – with 'is name big and loopy at the top. Always smiling, 'e were. Always 'appy. No wonder Jimmy liked 'im so much. Going on all those adventures, running over beaches digging 'oles in the sand. Trains, rockets, aeroplanes.'

He fingered the comics. There were hundreds, stained and ragged round their edges, stippled with age. FLOYD BENNETT – WILD BOY WONDER! FLOYD BENNETT & THE CURSE OF THE CAVES. FLOYD BENNETT & THE SECRET OF THE STONES.

The boy on the cover was his friend. Red shorts, bare feet.

'*Come on, Jim, let's go!*'

'Never 'ad no shoes on neither,' said Maeve, smiling for the first time, as if the memory was of somebody she'd loved. 'Frank's boys weren't like that. Never like Floyd. No surprise there. Bennett 'ad an airman for a father. Damn sight better than the one they 'ad. And see—' She leafed through the pile and took out one near the end. 'There were another with 'im in it. *The father.* That's what started it. This one were about 'im.'

He saw a handsome pilot in a flying cap, a hero of the Great War.

'Now what was 'is name?' said Maeve.

He opened his mouth. The pilot flew away.

Donna was by the door, examining her hands. Loosely he recalled a scene from his childhood, so misty and far away it could have been made up – but it arrived, bizarrely, with an afterglow of gladness. The Mister coming in late, in a fine mood for once; a box he'd pilfered from God-knew-where; the gentle thump of one of them scrolled up and batted on his head: ''*Ere you go, Jimmy, son.*' He'd have been seven or eight. Just about able to read. He saw a drawing of a boy in tatty shorts, a game grin and grubby feet. In one strip Floyd was hurtling over sand dunes, dragging a kite in his wake. In the next he leapt into a go-cart, waving to Jimmy to come with him: '*Oh, boy – let's see what we can find!*'

He saw the Mister at his bedroom door, backlit by a naked, swinging bulb. He saw Isaac the Pilot saluting him from the cockpit of a Tiger Moth, his goggles and uniform so accurate he couldn't think where he'd seen them to know them so well.

He saw the cruel PO at Bedford, an ex-Navy man with a head like a snooker ball, ordering them to strip so he could pat them down personally, checking all the intimate places a man might hide what he didn't wish to be found: '*You'll be all right, laddie, you'll be all right soon . . .*' He saw the tough old sweats at Wandsworth, *yes-Guv no-Guv*, and the jugging one of them got over an unpaid debt; then a voice behind them as they'd gathered round, dumbfounded, clutching their own marriage prospects in horror: '*Show's over, lads, let's get some help now.*' It had been Porter. Old, kind Porter from borstal. He hadn't clapped eyes on the good screw since Severn Camp, but there he was, at Wandsworth, with him, as gentle-mannered as before. Porter had asked him his name. '*Maguire*,' he'd said. '*No, lad, your first name.*' He realized he'd never told him it. '*Well, I'm Robert*,' said the screw. '*But you can call me Bobby.*'

A screw was a screw till he wasn't. He saw his own pathetic, grateful face when Porter had given him a spit in the yard. '*Put down for an 'aircut, Jimmy*,' he'd said in his West Country brogue. '*And tie your shoes and all.*' It'd struck him then what had been missing in prison – no, not in prison but the whole way along, the whole bloody show right from the start of his life – it was this feeling of mattering to someone, of being remembered by someone, of someone knowing his name and bothering to keep it in his mind, of caring about who he was and what he could be and what made him distinct from the next man along, of giving him identity that wasn't a number or a statistic or a reason why he'd failed, of reminding him he was human, or had started off as human, and had things been better for him he might have stayed that way, of having a soul and a heart and other things poets talked of, because why shouldn't he, if he'd had people to lift him up?

'*When I get out of here—*' he'd stammered when the smoke was through.

Porter had waited for him to finish. He'd imagined what the officer's life was like at home. There was a wife and two daughters, he knew. The wife was a nurse, the daughters were grown; one was a teacher and the other one studied the sea. He'd pictured getting out and being invited to their house, which would be cosy and welcoming, warmed by a burning fire, with dogs and blankets and a lovely meal cooking, just like there'd been when he'd lived with Providence. There would be talk round the table when they sat down, all five of them, everyone talking so fast they ran over each other; then a hand on his shoulder, affectionate, while Mrs Porter – Nancy – offered him spuds, and the children – adults now – smiled supportively, waiting for him to speak because they'd done enough of the talking, but it didn't matter what he said, he didn't need to say anything. They were all so pleased with him. Proud of him. He was part of them, a child of theirs, a son, a brother, a member of their family.

'*I were thinking,*' he'd ventured, putting out the butt with his shoe. '*When I'm out of here—*' He was nervous. '*I know it's a way off, but. Well. Mebbe I could come and visit you . . . ?*'

He saw Porter's pitying, sorrowful expression, worse than any he'd been given by the Judge, worse than Birdie or Miss Broderick, worse even than Mrs Edditson across the dining table. He heard the amiable screw's words as if he were here now, in Mother Maeve's room with the Christmas cards and the pea-soup smell, and it was clear.

'I'm not your father, son.'

Maeve lay on the pillow and pulled her shawl across her like a shell.

'Take 'em,' she said. 'I don't want 'em no more.'

He held the comics. Floyd smiled up at him.

'I forgive you,' he said.

She closed her eyes. 'I never met you. So I dunno why you'd say that to me.'

V

21

They stayed in the nursing home till after eleven then came out together and walked away down the road, back the way we'd come, she in her customary fashion a step or two in front of him and Maguire with a large, rectangular envelope wedged under one arm and his hands shoved deep in his pockets. Confident we were returning to the Waveside, I slowed my pace and afforded them some distance. It had been risky trailing them on foot to Ladyfield; Maguire had stopped several times, sensing me there, and I knew I was keeping too close to him but I couldn't risk a repeat of the previous morning.

Yesterday I'd woken later than I'd meant to. I'd left my room to find theirs, next door, being cleaned. I'd panicked. '*Have they gone?*' I'd accosted Snub-Nose at reception, who'd said he hadn't known we were a party. '*But have they checked out?*'

He'd consulted his records. '*No,*' he'd answered, disturbed by my demeanour, '*not yet. I expect they've gone out for the day. I'll tell them you're looking for them?*'

I realized my mistake. '*No,*' I'd made light of it, backtracking; '*it's a surprise. They don't know I'm here . . . It's a birthday thing.*'

I was too frantic to care that he didn't believe me. Long hours passed. I convinced myself they'd got wind of me and bolted. All I could do was wait. I spent all day powerless at the window, fretting like a mother on the eve of war, until at four o'clock the Panda finally, miraculously, returned, turning off the road towards their space. As I heard them settling back into their room, I could hardly move with relief. But with it came the crashing realization that I was completely out of my depth. Today had been my fault.

I'd overslept because of the night before. I'd lain awake until first light, wondering how I could have been so stupid as to risk everything. The car-alarm plan had started well enough, the glass shattering beautifully, but Maguire had scuppered it, surprising me last-minute by being the one who came down and not her. I'd almost run into him, forced to flatten myself against an outside wall while he passed in a green streak, close enough to smell, a mulchy, not altogether unpleasant scent of damp tree bark. I'd made the snap decision not to quit then but to follow him down to the car park, deciding anyway this was better than the hotel room, a clean shot in open air then my vehicle on the road for a getaway.

What had I been thinking?

Snub-Nose had already been there — of course he had, why had I assumed he wouldn't? — ineffectually circling the flashing car like someone sizing up a convertible on a forecourt. I'd had to abandon my course but was terrified I would be seen. I'd taken cover down an alley at the back of the inn, where I'd peeled off my gloves and, for want of a better idea, tucked them inside my top, under my bra strap. The alley was packed with sticks and thistles and layers of rubbish, crumpled plastic, sodden lengths of kitchen roll; I picked my way across the mire, stumbling on my bare hands; a sharp edge cut me. I'd heard the men talking, then

Snub-Nose coming by on the other side of the brick. In the yellow blaze of a street lamp, I'd seen blood on my palms, and two eyes beyond, glinting at me from the shadows. At first, I'd thought they belonged to a cat. Then, I'd thought they couldn't. The gaze was too still, too flat, to be living. I put my hands out. The eyes became starlight and vanished.

By the time I'd made it back inside the hotel, I expected Snub-Nose to be at the desk. But the lobby was empty. I'd taken the stairs two at a time, the gun digging into my back; it was all I could do to operate my room key, my fingers slippery, dropping it on the carpet then grappling to pick it up again, as I slid through the door with seconds to spare. Snub-Nose battered on 21. Then Donna's voice came: '*Who is it?*' I'd met my reflection in the bathroom mirror, hair dishevelled, coat streaked with muck, chest inflating and collapsing with adrenaline, with imprecision, with the stupidity of what I had done.

How could I have been so careless? But I knew. I'd wanted it finished so I could go home. I'd been impatient, driven by wild physical instinct that felt close to kamikaze.

That wasn't right. It had never been right.

Providence had brought me this far. She had steered me when he'd got away; she had helped me when they'd left me behind; she had protected me by keeping me hidden – and she had returned them to me now. My sister was with me. I wasn't alone. She would show me when the time was right, and until then I had only to trust.

I couldn't do it on my own. I needed her. I always had, from the moment I'd held her in her God's Providence blankets in the candlelit kitchen at Marlborough Avenue all those years ago; I'd needed her more than she'd ever needed me. I wasn't cut out for revenge. I had no abilities; I wasn't special. I had no reason to succeed but for love.

When my sister turned two, Gamma had knitted her a cardigan. It was the most intricate thing I had ever laid eyes on, a tapestry of blue and purple wools, every shade of those colours I could think of. I'd thought, then, but it's for a baby; Providence was too young to appreciate it, it made no odds to her if she was wearing that or the boys' clothes in the cupboard. Seeing that cardigan, though, I understood for the first time what love was. It didn't care for approval or gratitude. It was love for love's sake, colour for colour's sake, trying for the sake of knowing you had tried. My sister had beamed when she was given it; she'd treasured it into her teenage years and finally put it on Celeste, for the simple reason that she wanted always to be able to see it. I thought of the many things she would now never see. The orange-black pelt of a tiger. A clear sky with a kite flying in it. My face, her own.

His, before I killed him.

We reached the Waveside, where I had already put my belongings in the car, ready to move the instant they were. I got in behind the wheel. Maguire and Donna went inside and came out again soon after, he carrying their bags and the bulky brown envelope, all of which he tossed onto the Panda's back seat. They got in. The driver's glass had been replaced by a plastic sheet, attached around the rim with duct tape. I let them turn out onto the road before I started my engine and went after them. Once in the traffic, I locked on to their red car ahead, clots of smoke chugging from its exhaust.

THE SUNSHINE MAN

They turned inland, going north. Immediately, I knew where we were heading. Providence was always ready to take us there. She knew how our journey ended.

We were going back.

22

It was freezing in the blown-out Panda. Donna wore a pair of fingerless gloves, khaki and threadbare, stiff on the wheel; her rings made sharp little ridges in the wool.

'Did you call her?' he asked, as the road climbed away from the sea.

'Yes.'

'Like I said?'

She went down a gear. 'Yes.'

'When?'

'Last night,' she said. 'After you'd fallen asleep. Don't you believe me?'

He kept his eyes on her. 'What'd she say?'

Donna stopped at some roadworks and blew on her hands.

'Just she was glad I'm OK. Said she'd been worried.'

'What,' he said, 'that I'd done something to you?'

'No. That I wasn't coming home. That I wouldn't want to.'

'Why?'

Donna shrugged. 'We've been fighting a lot lately.'

'She's still your mother.'

'Yep.' She glanced briefly behind them, at the envelope on the back seat. 'She's still that.'

They got moving again, joining the A-road up country. In

the wing mirror, he noticed a cream hatchback, with them since Bedruthan, turning off in the same direction. He couldn't clearly see the woman at the wheel; she was obscured by the glare of the sun.

'What did you tell her about me?' he said.

'Not much.' She was cagey.

'Weren't she bothered?'

'She asked if you were treating me well. I said yes. That's all she wants to know really.' Donna's gaze flitted over him before returning to the road. 'You left her high and dry, you know. It'd be bad enough having a baby on your own these days. Let alone then. Granny and Grandpa disowned her for a while. When she said she was keeping it. Me.'

''S that right?'

'Then Granny gave in and took her home.'

He hesitated. But Donna was forthright. 'I thought she must've thought about getting rid of me,' she said. 'I mean it must've crossed her mind. She says it never did. But I think it must've. It would have crossed mine. She never said that to you?'

'I weren't around to say it to.'

'Guess not.'

There was a pause. Then she asked, 'How did you find out about me?'

Rita had written him a letter soon after he was sent down. *There's something you should know. I had a baby and she's yours.* Blokes in the nick said watch out, mate, she'll be pulling a fast one, but there was never any doubt in his mind that he was the father. Why else, for the rest of her life, would a girl like Rita choose to be tied to a man like him?

He'd had an inkling months before. Passing Mrs Eddiston on the way to Marlborough Avenue, the last time he'd gone back to the village: '*I hope you're happy*,' she'd said. '*Poor Rita. Our poor girl. You've ruined her!*' Later, he'd pushed the judgement away, came up with other reasons for it — that he'd called it off with Rita after the party, that he'd ignored her efforts to see him. Anyway, he'd had greater prospects on his mind.

He didn't tell Donna that. He said, 'She wrote me a note.'

And when that note came, he had understood. If Rita had told him, she must want him to be part of it, even if that part was locked up behind bars. Birthday cards, Christmas cards, visits, he'd vowed to do whatever he could. He didn't love Rita. He didn't expect for a minute that she loved him. But here was something to live for, to get good for, to get out for; a reason, a new start, something pure that he hadn't made any mistakes about.

'Why're you looking at me like that?' said Donna.

'Like what?'

She took a turn. At Launceston, they crossed the county line. As they went deeper into Devon, the landscape became recognizable. The fields, the treelines, the texture of soil and sky, they were sewn down hard within him.

'Did you come get me just to piss her off?' he said.

'Who, Mum? Yeah. A bit.'

'That the only reason?'

'And seeing as you don't have anyone else.'

He rubbed his nose. 'D'you feel sorry for me?'

'Course I do. You're my responsibility.'

'Then what about what I did?'

She waited. 'I know about that.'

'Then how —ing can you?'

She didn't answer straight away. He thought she would leave it, because what more was there to say than what he'd already said to himself, but after a while she spoke. She talked calmly, looking ahead through the windscreen and never at him.

'It was awful what you did,' she said quietly. 'There isn't a word. There's nothing big enough or horrible enough for what you did to Providence Doyle. I grew up in its shadow. It was all I was known for, being your daughter. The daughter of a killer, and I *hated* you. I wished every day that I wasn't yours. I'd rather have been anyone else's but yours. I hated coming to see you. Mum made me come and I never, ever wanted to. I was scared of you. I hated how you looked at me. I hated how you looked. Every time for weeks after I had nightmares. I was scared of you coming to our house in the middle of the night and doing to me what you did to her. I never wanted you to get out. Ever. I wished you were dead.'

She swallowed; he heard the click of her spit over the steady purr of the engine.

'Then I got older,' she said, 'and something changed. I don't know what. It was Mum, partly. She always said that doing a bad thing doesn't make you a bad person, but I think that's bullshit. Of course you're a bad person for doing that. You can't say, oh, I murdered on Monday but on Tuesday I'm with the homeless so that's all right, that evens it out. Like, I'm a *complicated person*, I'm a human being with *facets*. Give me a break. But I thought – I've only got one dad. There's only one, whether I like him or not, and I didn't know if I *did* like you because all I had was that shadow, and what people told me, I didn't have anything else. Then Mum showed me the letters. She'd saved them for me. She hadn't given them to me before, when I was little, because she thought they'd upset me and confuse me and I think she was right to do that. I'm glad she saved them though. I read them last year, in one big go, which wasn't what you meant them for but it helped me in a way. It took me days, there were so many. I read them lots of times. Mum told me not to expect very much. I didn't expect anything. I knew about Floyd and that you'd figured him out – that you'd been figuring him out all the time you were writing me those letters – and I felt' – she paused – 'defensive of you. There were so many versions I'd been given. From Mum to the Judge to the papers. I thought I should try figuring you out for myself. Make up my own mind for once. Decide what *I* think. I haven't made it up yet, by the way. But I'm trying.'

He didn't say anything for a bit. Then he said, 'Thank you.'

'What for?'

'I dunno,' he said. But he did know. 'For trying.'

∽

They drove on. Memories came to him. Of Providence playing piano in the rain, 'Knock Turn in E Flat Major', the notes diving between the folds of the night; of walking down Nail's Lane, rehearsing in his mind what he'd say and knowing he'd never get it right, he'd never be able to tell her how he felt; of the Brewsters' field glimpsed through the trees, bright with rapeseed, as high as his head and yellow as a pack of Anchor butter.

A sign passed for Crediton, their village a few miles on. It seemed unreal that the grounds of his youth still existed – that they hadn't been a figment of his imagination, as had so much else, the man who had no feeling, who'd invented a fiction, a whole life, to excuse his wicked offence. The psychologists had pressed him, when things grew clear:

'*Would you say you're a storyteller, Jimmy? Do you like to make things up?*'

Floyd was the one who'd made things up. Floyd had been the one who'd pushed him to the final frontier: '*Are you gunna let her walk away, Jim? Talk to you like that, eh, then let her walk away?*' And the psychs had answered, '*It wasn't Floyd saying that. Was it?*'

Bits of the town were familiar, the pub and the newsagent's, but there were new shops now and old ones missing. He saw the bank and asked Donna to stop.

'What for?' she asked.

Kip's account would have earned interest by now – enough to turn the page, enough to give Donna. '*This money's for both of us,*' Kip had said when he, Jimmy, had travelled north and found his brother in a shelter; '*I'm gunna put your name on it too. It's ours.*' The letter had been sincere, it turned out; Kip was done with the lowlife; he wanted to find work and a place to live and he thought he had; it was all lined up for them in Wales, to start new. Prison was a cycle, he said, and the only person who could break it was him. '*I'm gunna get it right this time, Jimmo, and I want you along with me. What d'you say, little brother?*'

He wished he'd said no.

He wished he'd walked away from Kip as he'd walked away from Mother Maeve, because then he wouldn't have made plans with his brother. He wouldn't have tried to include Providence in those plans. He wouldn't have thrown out Kip's counsel against doing that, stayed deaf to his brother's urging to leave her out of it. He wouldn't have gone back to the village to persuade her. He'd never have met Floyd again, and they'd never have found her on the porch at Marlborough Avenue, in the rain, playing her music, and he'd never have asked her, *'Do you want to go for a walk?'*

'What you were saying before,' he said to Donna.

She turned off the engine. 'What about it?'

He didn't look at her. 'I'm glad you told me,' he said.

'Me too.'

'And I'm glad you came.'

She turned her rings, beneath the gloves.

'We don't have to go back there,' she said.

'Yes, we do.'

'Why?'

'Without Floyd. Just me. I have to. I have to see it.'

'It won't change anything.'

He opened the door.

'Wait—' said Donna, but he didn't hear the rest of it; he was already crossing the street, thinking here was where he turned it for good, a new leaf, for his daughter, for them both. He didn't see the cream hatchback parked a few cars down, or the woman getting out of it in an ankle-length coat, a bag in her right hand as she followed him in.

23

The first thing I saw was myself. I was by the door, replicated on a pile of newspapers in a three-foot-high crate with *Southern Herald* printed across it, looking unsuitably relaxed beneath the headline: LOCAL WOMAN MISSING SINCE MONDAY. The photo had been taken two autumns ago in the garden at home. I was holding Joe. His half-face had been pixelated out but I could see his blond curls and recall I'd felt happy that day, orange leaves blowing, Tom inside lighting a fire, the apples from the tree knobbly underfoot because despite my best intentions each year I never got round to picking them in time.

I wished I'd worn something with a hood. Why hadn't I thought of that? Because it would have felt theatrical, like I was play-acting an assassin in a French *film noir*. Still, I pined for such a garment now, my collar drawn up to my ears in case someone recognized me. In case *he* did. There was only so long I could avoid detection.

The bank had an air of hygienic efficiency and an aroma of carpets and fresh ink. I saw Maguire straight away, his curved shoulders and uncaring stance, his hair different from how it'd been on the first day, the oil come out of it so it was soft and tufting, sticking up in startled bits at the back like the ears of a tawny owl. I joined the queue behind him, rummaging through Gamma's bag so I could keep my face hidden.

An elderly gentleman stood between us, patting his pockets for a pen. Maguire turned to him and said, 'There's biros on the desk; shall I get one for you?'

I hadn't seen his face this close since we were young. Since his parting words to me on the doorstep in the snow: '*I'll take what you love and I'll kill it.*' I had submitted those words in evidence; the prosecution had read them aloud in court and a light gasp had risen from the jury like a balloon. The eyes were clear beneath the heavy lids, his gaze at once lazy and severe. I froze. I waited for his attention to land on me – for that sheen of acknowledgement and for him to say my name; I could sense him about to say it – but the man thanked him and walked off to a counter and Maguire was called forward to the clerk. I stopped a few paces away, trying to hear what he was saying.

'Certainly, let me check that for you.' The clerk was as practised as an air steward in her waistcoat and neatly knotted tie; her fingers click-clacked on the keyboard.

'Oh—' she said after a moment, then leant towards the screen and lowered her voice, and he lowered his, and I couldn't catch anything they said after that.

The bank became busy. People's gazes lingered on me longer than was natural; I perceived hushed conferences, whispers with backs turned, a ripple of interest skimming in my direction. I couldn't imagine I looked much like the woman in the photo any more, my hair shorter and my greys established. I certainly didn't feel like her; I felt freed from the wondering of that period and at the same time tied to the implications of its conclusion. I resembled a woman on holiday, which I had been in a way, as recently as two years ago, occupying as I had the hinterland between my sister's death and the justice she deserved.

I left the queue so I could stand to one side of him, near where the old man was filling out an application form. The stares grew intense. Maybe it was an air I was giving off, of worry or anticipation, of fear or excitement; I had so many passions inside me it was hard to tell them apart. I ought to find out what the *Herald* was saying. More pleas from Tom. A character-dismantling from Wilma, too subtle and restrained to be cyanide – deathcap poisoning, perhaps – or a neighbour coming out of the woodwork who had always wondered about me, considered me closed-off and remote, unsociable (strange for a woman), not desiring for one reason or another (*'and she always kept her reasons to herself '*) to be part of the mothers' group – and, well, there was an explanation for that, with those children who weren't really hers . . .

I could withstand all that. What I couldn't were references to Philippa and Joe.

When I let myself, I touched on thoughts of my children like a burn. Philippa doing maths homework in the kitchen, her satchel dropped by the table with its exhausted band of Velcro and array of troll-doll key rings attached to the zip, her coat tossed over the back of the chair, her head tilted on one side as she chewed her lip in concentration, got frustrated, flipped the pencil to the rubber end and scrubbed out what she'd done. Tom in the background packing Joe's rucksack for Monday's trip to the aquarium (or was that Wilma, having moved in to cover my absence?), a water bottle, cheese sandwich, his waterproof overclothes in case of rain. Joe clutching his Glo Worm, asking where I was.

I had to take flight from these things. I couldn't put myself in the context of my children; I had to disconnect, as I'd learnt to do; I had to be the girl I'd been in 1970 – before then, in the summer I'd turned seventeen and a man had crept into my room while I was sleeping and ended the world as I knew it.

Maguire's face from the side was a hard, smooth trophy, as blank in expression as a marble bust in the cool underground chamber of a gallery. The sculptor had scored lines in the right places, the peeled-egg contour of the eye socket, the clean, plunging slope of the nose – but there was no life there, nothing beyond the materials that had been used.

He left the counter and walked back down the line.

I followed him. The crowd receded. A sign caught my eye by the door. It was a bright yellow square with a smiling sun and a pound sign on it.

SUNSHINE BANKING — GO A LITTLE FURTHER.

A little further.

I went after him, ignoring myself on the way out.

24

Donna was parked around the corner. He heard the radio before he saw her, tinny pop music that sounded like it'd been made by a computer not a person, and opened the door and got in. She turned it down. 'It's so cold,' she said. 'Did you get what you wanted?'

'Don't matter,' he said. 'Let's go.'

'Put your seat belt on, then.'

The strap got stuck coming out, which made him tug harder, violently. She tried to help but he pushed her off. 'I can —ing do it,' he said. 'I'm not a —ing baby.'

'What happened? You look pissed off.'

'I am pissed off. Just drive.'

She started the car. Houses streaked past. He thought about reaching behind him and tossing the envelope out on the road. He wished he had never been given it. He didn't want it. He wanted Floyd in the past, Mother Maeve in the past, the Mister and the whole damn picture in the past; he didn't want to think of them ever again. But he'd never move on if he didn't. Porter had agreed – '*Get it done, lad, get it finished*' – and had found a way, on the quiet, to help him make this trip. '*The system always says no,*' Porter had advised; '*but let me find a way round it, son.*' He didn't know how it had been done, just that he, Jimmy, needed to be back to meet his probation officer next week, and that Porter must have bent the rules for him, told probation one thing and arranged another. Why? Because Porter liked him. Because he believed in him. Because he understood that he, Jimmy, had to face the truth as the person he was now, one man, one history, one evil he had to accept. What he'd said to Donna was bang-on: he had to meet that place knowing what he'd known since Grendon. The field pulled him in like a planet.

Then again, what did moving on mean? What *was* the rest of his life? In the nick he'd had ideas about what that might be, who he might be if he'd the right to be anyone. He'd played out scenes in his mind of what the real world looked like, for real people – but these, he realized, were borrowed from books and stuff he'd heard on Drumsticks' radio, not real experiences because he hadn't any, and if you didn't have experience then you never got the part. He told himself he hadn't a right to his freedom – he'd given that up on the night she'd died; and there was no guarantee he had it in him to feel happiness or satisfaction or any of those emotions the Judge said were missing – but then other times it struck him that living in penance the rest of his days helped no one and was in its own way self-serving. And always, there was Donna. It wasn't about him, it was about her, and she already had a dad who was useless banged up so why make him useless now?

'*You've got something to offer, Jim,*' Porter had said. '*Everyone's got something to offer.*'

What had he got? A hot-headed temper and a cage to prove it. But Porter had made him sign on for the writing course and talked him into doing the tests, which he'd failed so he'd made him do them again until he got the certificate, the first of his life, a splodgy red badge stamped on it like the wax seals of olden days. Porter read his tales about Floyd and liked them; he wasn't sure if the screw knew the truth: '*He's a character all right, gor blimey.*' He made him write journals, articles for the prison rag, short stories. The stories took a long time to get down because his handwriting was poor and the words were spelt wrong and couldn't be understood. '*I reckon you're dyslexic,*' said Porter, and sent him for another test but this one was done on him. In the months before he came out, the kind officer told him he had qualifications now. There were charities that hired ex-offenders: if he could give an account of himself, he'd every chance at employment.

'*You could set yourself up,*' Porter said, '*if you had the means. You could teach courses, Jim. In prison, like the ones you've done.*' He hadn't thought much of it. The idea of him turning into one of those smart-booted clean-smelling educated types that came in once a week? Drumsticks always said the outside was against them. But he trusted Porter. He'd trusted Drumsticks too, in a different way. Two sides of himself, one in the cells and one in the library, in the lessons, with the growing suspicion that there was more to life than what there'd been so far, more to him too, as there was to every man, Smiley and Drumsticks and Staines and even the old Terror, you were never just the thing that you'd done. So he'd planned to enrol on the classes, as Porter had encouraged: '*I'll be calling you sir next time I see you.*' He'd needed a couple of hundred and he'd have paid it back to Alf.

When that hadn't worked, he'd remembered Kip's savings account.

'I went in to get my money,' he told Donna now. She turned to him. 'Kip set me up some funds. It'd have been earning interest. I thought it'd be enough to get me going.'

'With what?' she said.

'A job. Getting on my feet. For you and your mum. For me.'

'It's gone,' she guessed. 'The money.'

'Yeh.' His guts hurt.

'Where?'

'I dunno.' But he could reckon his bets. The account had still been in Kip's name. When he'd died, Mother Maeve would have closed it. He imagined Ron on a downer, Maeve herself, the Mister if he was still knocking about.

Did it matter? No. Never had.

'I'd have given you half,' he said. It came out childish, as if she was interested in that. 'That's what I decided. Half for you, half for me. I know it ain't much . . . after—'

'I don't need it,' said Donna.

'That ain't the point.'

'You don't have to look after me. I'm not a kid any more.'

'I know,' he said. 'But all that about me being your responsibility, that ain't right.'

She shook her head. 'It doesn't—'

'That ain't how it should be. You're *my* responsibility. You're my child.'

They were approaching the village now, travelling down country lanes bordered by ferns as brown as copper and the sky just one shade lighter. There it was: the park on his right, the canal and the rail yard, the church, the old vicarage, the one-time Wagon now advertising HAPPY HOUR 2 PINTS £1! on a poster on the door.

'D'you know what I'd like?' he said. 'To stay in one place. Stay in one place the rest of my days and be happy. Just a place that's mine that I made for myself and no one gave me and I don't owe no one for.'

The car slowed. 'We can still turn back,' said Donna.

'I ain't turning back.'

'And then what?'

He looked at her. 'Up to you.'

Daylight was fading. The sun was low and burning in the trees.

Is that you, golden boy?

'I'm sorry,' she said.

'What for?'

'Just am.'

'Don't you ever say sorry to me.' He turned to his daughter, his little girl, his grown girl, his brave, determined girl – but no, not his, her own, everything and nothing to do with him and all the same still willing to walk by his side. She had been good to him. Now he would be good to her. 'You hear?' he said. '*Never.* You never say that to me.'

They drew in on a verge by the Brewsters' field. An old part of him, a habit he'd never thrown off, thought Floyd would be waiting there. But there was no Floyd, now as there hadn't been then, on an early summer's night eighteen and a half years ago, when fallen rain lit up the earth and owls kewicked in the high trees, sounding like flutes.

25

When I was little, I used to ride my bicycle down the lane to the village, pushing hard on the pedals then freewheeling the rest of the way, spokes clicking with every rotation until the slope levelled out and I had to scuff my shoes on the tarmac to stop; I could hear that scuff now, dry and soft, and touch the grazed, worn texture of my leather shoes after months of the toes doubling as a brake. (*'For all that's good in the world, Birdie, will you please learn how to ride that bike properly?'*) There was the house that always had a wooden crate out front selling eggs for a florin, pink rods of rhubarb and jars of mint jelly; there was where the red phone box had stood, replaced now by a dull-grey one. I saw the turf where Maurice and I had built a den, packing it with handfuls of springy moss and planning to spend the night in it before the Fairfaxes and Gamma said no; and, further on, the path Providence and I had taken on the day the piano had been delivered, running with our sherbets, drenched in sun, when she'd gone to show me the fledglings.

It was a long time since I had driven this way. I'd had Mary in the car with me then; she'd never got a licence and Peter was too busy to take her, and she'd sat staring rigidly out of the window with her fists clenched in her lap, rosy with cold, like little beating hearts. I'd thought she was in shock, grief-stricken like me, and at last – at least – we had this thing in common, this unimaginable, foulest of things, and if there was a flicker of light to come of it then it might be that she would talk to me, that we would find a way to cross the gulf that had always separated us, but then we stopped by the green so she could be sick in the grass and when she got back into the car she said, '*You should have stopped it, Bridget. You should have looked after her better.*'

My impression coming back was that everything was less green than it had been in my childhood. Not just because of the season but that the place felt smaller now, contextualized by the outside world I'd been ignorant of when I was young. Could that be the same church I'd been brought to every Sunday? It had used to seem a cathedral. The school, too, was diminished, a short Victorian lodge with sheds attached. I remembered flying out of the gates – same gates – at the close of the day, racing back to see Providence as a baby, desperate to be with her and hold her and play with her, and smell her sweet honey smell that hid in the soft fat folds of her neck. Only the Fairfaxes' house on East Hill remained as grand as my memory had it. It had been turned into an artists' residence; the couple had since moved abroad. I wondered what Maurice made of the conversion. Last I'd seen him had been on my television at home, Professor of Archaeology at a top university, interviewed on *News at Ten* about a finding at Stonehenge. For some reason I hadn't mentioned the connection to Tom. We'd sat watching with our cups of tea and shared box of Roses as the tape flashed up his name, and I'd wondered if he was married now, if someone had kept their promise to him. I'd said nothing, and Tom had got up to let the cat out.

Ahead, the Panda slowed. Its brake lights shone. I hung back to let them pass Mrs Lovell's shop, now a Spar, and found myself at the top of Marlborough Avenue.

For a moment I stayed there, looking down the street. It was largely unchanged, a row of terraces in russet brick, but with many more cars parked outside them now, on both sides, each with two wheels hitched up on the kerb. A man and his dog walked down the road away from me, mist rising from their feet, the dog's tail gaily going.

I opened Gamma's bag and took out the gun. I wiped it clean and set it on the seat beside me, then I squeezed her bag into the footwell. Donna's car vanished from sight. I took the shortcut down the avenue – the walker stepped up on the pavement – and passed number 16, which had a holly wreath attached to the door and a reindeer of fairy lights at the gate. The curtains were partly drawn; I couldn't see well inside. A figure passed back and forth across the window, a woman, I thought, talking to someone in the wings, maybe talking on the phone. She'd have smart Laura Ashley wallpaper, I decided, instead of the stuff Providence and I had designed, our ham-handed drawings encouraged by Gamma because we couldn't afford the proper sheets. Was the fireplace still the same? Was the kitchen? Did they still have the leaky porch out back, filled now only with birdsong?

When last I'd left, I had sworn never to see the house again. Losing Providence and then Gamma months after, the only mercy was that my grandmother had been too ill by then to grasp what had happened. She'd been too poorly to attend the funeral, and when she'd asked every day where Providence was and when she was coming back, I'd said she was on her way, it'd be any time now. All the while, my grudge against Mary grew. The things I held against my mother piled up in delicate, teetering creations, like a nest of china in a dresser. When Gamma had fallen sick, I had tried to contact her, and after weeks of failed attempts discovered she'd moved to Spain, where she was making earthen pots in a villa in the mountains and had set up a yoga retreat with her boyfriend, a twenty-seven-year-old named Luis. '*You don't want me there, Bridget,*' she'd told me weepily over the phone. '*What good can I do? I'd only be in the way.*' She'd returned for Providence's burial but even that was fleeting – '*I'm too weak for this; my heart can't stand it*' – and hadn't bothered with Maguire's trial. The pain and anguish of that ordeal had been mine alone to bear, and for all my resentments against Mary, her vanity, her flakiness, her pride, her selfishness, the fact she had never told either of us our paternity and worse still didn't deem it to matter, this was the greatest. The Mackeys had come to court and so had the Eldons; the vicar had been on the first day and the Lovells on the last, who'd then insisted on me living with them before I left for London. I had hardly seen Mary in the years since, except when she came back when the pots failed, then Luis failed, then she had a fling with Anthony or Mick, pretending the reason for her resurfacing was to see me, but I knew better, then she caught scent of the next gamble and was off without a word until next time.

Maguire had more family at the trial than I had. I would

never forgive Mary for that. Though my community came, and for all I loved and was thankful for them, they weren't my family. I was forced to sit day after day watching Kip tell us his brother was innocent – innocent! Even as forensic photographs were shown, images from which I'd tried to avert my gaze but which I found myself horribly compelled to see: the mess he had made of my sister's body, the aggression he'd inflicted on it for no reason other than his pleasure. Kip had tried to take responsibility. I supposed he had thought it was noble; he was that sort of person, fancying himself a saviour but amounting to no more than a crook.

In any event, no one had fallen for it. James's fingerprints were all over the scene. All over her. I kept thinking of what Kip had told me at the fairground: '*Jimmy's all right. Down deep, he's good.*' Sitting in court, I didn't believe the brothers knew the difference. Bad or good meant nothing to them. They were just words, attached to neither meaning nor consequence. The Maguires had shattered every foundation I'd grown up on, every conviction I'd held dear. They had eclipsed the light Gamma had looked to find in everyone, and with it her own had dimmed. I'd thought when I was a teenager that Kip was distinct. I'd thought a lot of things when I was a teenager that didn't turn out to be true. For Kip was just as ready to discard the facts when it suited him; he didn't care a scrap for me or my mourning. To him, it was irrelevant who had done those terrible things to Providence – if it was James or Kip or the figment they called Floyd, what did it matter? My sister was already dead. But it did matter. I needed a confession. I needed someone to say, it was me and I must be punished.

I rounded the corner. They were turning off the green, travelling out of the village.

A white feather landed on my windscreen. I braked suddenly, reaching over to grab the gun before it was thrown into the footwell. I expected the wind to lift the feather away but there it remained, quivering, the length of my hand and as pure as driven snow. And I realized then that I had known all along we would return here. I had known it the instant Maguire had stepped out of prison. I had known it all the years in between. I had known it when the Judge had passed his sentence and Maguire was sent down and I'd seen the field then, in my mind's eye, a glowing sun beckoning, a crooked man, everything coloured yellow. Prison would never be enough for her murderer – and as for getting free, how could that be? Providence was bones in the ground, she would never be free, she would never know the sun on her face or the moon in the heavens and he didn't deserve it.

His life must end here, where hers had.

I drove on down Nail's Lane. Their car had pulled in opposite the stile. I reversed, stopping short of the bend, and killed the engine.

My breath was even. My head was clear. I did not think about Tom. I did not think about Philippa, or Joe. I thought only of Providence, of that day we'd come home to find her on our doorstep, her blue eyes casting over my face like a lighthouse beam thrown across the sea. The white feather flew away.

I put on my gloves. With the gun in my coat, I walked towards them.

26

'This is it,' he said. They stood looking over the gate. The earth was stubbly; a pair of crows took flight from the bristle in a clatter of wings. In the middle of the field, the Sunshine Man was a shabby outline, weathered by elements and age. Letters were missing from his banner: YELLOWF ELDS SE D OIL – A TAS E OF SU SHI E.

'I've never been here,' said Donna. 'Not *here*-here, I mean the village. Mum didn't want to. As far as I know, she never came back after Granny and Grandpa moved.'

'Let's not come back again,' he said. 'There's other places we can go.'

'Like where?'

'You choose.'

He felt her smile rather than saw it. 'I'll be waiting,' said Donna.

∾

He went in alone. The field was still. No breeze moved in the trees; no sound worried the silence. He walked before the wooden man and touched his flaking board; yellow paint came off with his fingernail. The man's gaze was locked on a point over his head, blind to the seasons that had passed, deaf to all he had heard, forever fixed between old and new.

How had it come to be? The last time he had been here.

He remembered it now. He saw it as it was.

Spring 1970. He'd been staying up north with Kip, drawing plans for Wales; he wanted every detail organized by the time he asked Providence, to show her he could be responsible, that she could depend on him despite what she thought. '*You'll never find her,*' Kip had said. But he'd already managed that; he'd telephoned the vicar and asked and been told – Providence was back in the village, seeing Mrs D through her final days. '*I'm going,*' he'd said to Kip; '*I have to try.*' His brother had urged against it. '*Don't,*' he'd said; '*those people won't change, they're bad for you. Go somewhere nobody knows you.*' But he wouldn't be turned from his plan. He had to see her again and convince her, make her understand that he'd had nothing to do with those things he'd been accused of, he wasn't the person Birdie had made him out to be, he could still be golden good.

There had been a dozen chances to change direction. To have listened to Kip. To have left for Wales and never troubled her again. But he had stayed his course, thinking it was the grown-up thing to do, not to be a quitter but to make good. How different life might have been for him if he hadn't. But he'd made those choices. Just him.

Once he'd settled on his goal, he'd felt as close to content as he reckoned it was in him to feel. Even Floyd was leaving him alone. Sometimes he caught his old friend out by the bins at the shelter, cowering, and on cold nights, but fewer, huddled in a corner, whimpering into his folded knees. But Floyd never spoke.

They'd hitched a ride south. When they'd reached Devon, Maeve was nowhere to be found. Rumour had it she was living at a relative's but no one moved to track her. The Mister had gone too. So had Ron. The house was abandoned. He and Kip had spent the night there on the stinking settee and the more hours that passed, the more Floyd came back, sliding under doors or between the blankets, creeping out from gaps in the walls.

'*Coward,*' Floyd whispered to him in the dark. '*You're scared she won't have you. Why'd she want you? You're nothing but a bastard. Nobody wants you.*'

He'd thought about not going through with it. '*Don't be sissy,*' hissed Floyd. '*Be a man, like your father. Your* real *one. The pilot.*'

He'd said, '*He ain't my father. I made him up.*'

'*Naw, you didn't. He's part of you. Like I am.*'

The month had been May. The countryside was liquid, like the watery paintings in the Eddistons' front room, colours runny-blue, grasses soft and wheatfields gold. He'd borrowed Kip's jacket and gone to Marlborough Avenue to meet her. Rita's mother had passed him on his way – '*Our poor girl, you've ruined her!*' – and he hadn't dwelt on that because he'd been intent on seeing Providence. On what had to be.

It had started to rain. The rain soaked his jacket. He'd got there and knocked on the door, sodden to the skin, so nervous he couldn't stand still. Then he'd remembered the move with Kip, a new country, a new day, the fresh air blowing him clean.

No one answered. He'd gone round to the back path, between the woods and the houses. Floyd had come with him; he'd heard his companion trampling the leaves, and the warm, sturdy beat of his footsteps. Piano music drifted through the rain, towards them. It was ages since he'd heard that song.

'*There she is,*' said Floyd.

Or had it been him who said that?

There'd been a leak in the porch roof. Droplets plink-plunked on the keys like a second pair of hands. Her hair was long and golden like a streak of fire on a dark hillside.

'*Is it you?*' she'd said, without looking up. Her voice was the same. Full of echoes and longing. But she was a young woman now, with a mystical poise about her he would never possess himself. The music ended. Her eyes were blue and she'd been crying.

'*Has it happened?*' he'd said.

'*Not yet.*'

'*I'm sorry.*'

She'd risen, moved towards him but hesitated on the step. '*So am I.*'

He hadn't thought they were talking about Mrs D any more.

The rain stopped. Light came through a crack in the clouds. Providence glowed in it. She'd worn a dress with white petals on, down to her ankles with a trailing belt round the middle. The hairs on her arms stood up in the cold. For a minute, neither spoke.

'*Do you want to go for a walk?*' he'd said.

27

As I'd anticipated, he crossed the boundary on his own. Donna didn't see me. She got back in the Panda while I edged along the trees. I knew the field well, the openings in its borders unchanged. After the shot was fired, I planned to escape through the tunnel on the west side. Providence would help get me there. I felt no fear. She would see to it that I would already have departed by the time Donna rushed to him. How would his daughter react to his death? Would she be distraught? Betrayed? Relieved? How shocked would she be? Maguire had given her no clue that he intended to take his life – but now that she thought about it, now it had happened, perhaps it made sense: if he was going to do it anywhere, he was doing to do it here.

But I had no time to think about that. I had no worry left to give that girl.

I climbed the stile and entered the field. I felt invincible, invisible, not in my skin.

Yellow, the place had been in my mind. It had been then, and before, and ever after, the colour of his violence and her death. Now, in winter, the ground was barren and brown, the terrain stumpy and awkward, sawn-off stalks with split, feathered endings like old pastry brushes. Against that extinguished palette, James Maguire was weakened and drained of light, stooped beneath the seed-oil man, where he'd done it, where her body had been found bruised and beaten, wetted by rain, her petal dress smeared with blood.

He was touching the dirt, facing away from me. He looked like a boy making sandcastles on a beach. In my hand, the gun beat out its cool, consistent rhythm. My pulse kept along with it, pumping fresh as a baby's, in clean, fast blips. I went closer, close enough that I could see the strip of skin between his hairline and the slippery green of his collar.

Above him, oblivious, the seed-oil man towered over me, his black eyes faded, his trousers cut short. Once, he'd been a fixture in the village. What had they called him? The Sunshine Man. He'd been put up around the time I was born. I recalled his likeness visiting me, at night, in dreams, when I was young, in the land between awake and asleep where I didn't know for sure; he would climb in the window with his teeth and his grin, a smell of daffodils, wearing the face of James or Ron or Kip Maguire, the face of my father, and put his hand on my mouth and I'd wake, sweating, into the terrified dark.

How much smaller, like everything else, the Sunshine Man seemed now. Still the size of a man, but a less important one. As a girl I'd thought of him often, but he hadn't crossed my mind since then. He was a man I'd followed, a man who'd found Jesus, a man at the canal, a man who'd attacked and killed. A man who'd worn a suit and said, *'I've seen you for years. You've seen me too.'*

I held the pistol steady, as I'd learnt, my left hand supporting my right, thumb over thumb, middle finger below the trigger guard. My focus was entire. Maguire sensed me there, and turned his head to meet the sound.

The field stood still, like a painting. We were all three of us frozen in time – Maguire, the Sunshine Man and me; there was no life moving, no wind turning the leaves or sounds drifting in from the village, no bird calls, no aeroplanes flying, no clue that we were anything more than a photograph taken years ago and now developed.

My children would be coming out of school.

She'll be home soon. There, there, don't cry. Mummy's not forgotten, she'll be home soon.

I lifted the gun and levelled it at his head.

28

He didn't know why he had taken her there. Just that it might have reminded her of him. He wanted her to see how yellow it was, startling and unreal, and remember how it had been when they were young, chasing the sun into evening, squeezing his last drop of light.

In the middle of the field stood the scarecrow. Providence had sat at his feet, tucking her dress over her knees. '*I never liked him,*' she'd said. '*I wish they'd tear him down.*'

He'd sat next to her. She hadn't moved away; she hadn't seemed to mind.

'Bet they don't,' he'd said. '*He'll still be here in twenty years.*'

She had gazed up at the sky, then back towards him. '*As long as I'm not.*'

And he'd thought it was now or never.

'*I'm leaving,*' he'd said. Before he could doubt it: '*I want you to come with me.*'

She'd smiled at him, surprised but not mad. '*What?*'

'*I'm going away.*' He'd felt encouraged. '*With Kip. Over the estuary. We've planned it all, we're ready to go. I've got money saved, there's a job in the works. It'll be—*'

'That's good, Jimmy,' she'd said, running the belt of her dress through her fingers.

'*So you'll come?*'

She'd shaken her head. '*No.*'

He'd said too much, too soon. '*Why not?*'

Her blue eyes had met his, fleetingly. '*I can't.*'

Of course she couldn't. Not yet. '*We can put it off till Mrs D—*'

'*It's not that. It's . . . everything. My school. London. I've got a life there.*'

'*You can study where we're going,*' he'd said, not hearing. '*I've already looked into it. There's places like the one you're at – good ones too. It'll take me a while but—*'

She'd interrupted. '*I've got a boyfriend.*'

He'd laughed, an unnatural sound that didn't seem to come from him. '*What?*'

'*A musician,*' she'd said. '*A . . . cellist. At the music school. He's French.*'

'*Does he want to marry you?*'

She'd blushed at his question. '*Well. I don't know. Maybe. It's not . . .*'

He hadn't believed her. '*Why're you lying?*'

She'd looked afraid. '*I'm not.*'

'*Yeh you are. There's no —ing boyfriend. You're just lying to fob me off.*'

'*I'm not,*' she'd said again.

'*You're a kid,*' he'd thrown at her, as everything disintegrated, every plan he'd built collapsed to rubble. '*You're just a little —ing kid!*'

'*I'm nearly sixteen.*' She'd crossed her arms. '*What're you anyway? You're not a man.*'

'*Yeh I am, I've been to prison.*'
'*Gamma said it was a children's home.*'
'*Same thing.*'
'*No, it isn't.*'

And he'd been shamed; there he'd been thinking he was a hard man when all he'd done was have a spell in a boys' home like a second-rate con, like a second-rate man, for that's what he was, second-rate all over. Course she didn't want him. Why would she?

'*Don't you know what I did to Jenny Eldon?*' he'd said, getting to his feet, chilled by his wet clothes and his idiot jacket and the day that had fallen apart. '*To your sister?*'

'*I don't think you did that,*' said Providence.

'*Nah? Well, I did.*'

'*You said in your letters you didn't.*'

'*I thought you didn't read them.*'

She'd got up too. Mimicked him: '*Well, I did.*'

'*Guess what then?*' He'd kicked the scarecrow's boot. '*I lied. It* was *me. All of it. I did it. I did everything they said I did and I don't —ing care.*'

'*Don't be a child.*'

'*Me?*' He'd searched her face but all he'd met was a wall; he couldn't get past it; he couldn't stop himself bashing it, saying things he didn't mean and the more he said the worse it got, the harder it was to come back from so he didn't come back, he kept going, over the edge and down and down: '*I ain't the one who —ing ditches her friends, you know that ain't very —ing mature. You think you're perfect, you're as much of a bitch as your sister—*'

'*I never ditched you.*'

'*Yeh you —ing did. Not just about the charge. Before. It were like one day you decided you didn't —ing want me no more and that were it. Sorry, Jim. Story of my —ing life.*'

She'd been fiddling with the belt again. It must have been very interesting to look at because she hadn't answered him. He'd wanted to rip up the scene and start again.

'*I didn't know what else to do,*' she'd said, choosing her words. '*It was Floyd.*'

He grabbed the lifeline. He could still rescue it.

'*I told you we'd get away,*' he'd said. '*Without him. Didn't I? Didn't I swear it? Here it is then, I've done it — I did what I said I'd do. Floyd ain't coming, we can leave him behind—*'

'*No,*' she'd said, taking a step back. '*Jimmy, you're not well.*' She'd spoken calmly, holding her hands out flat like she was confronting a wild animal. '*You need help.*'

'*Then come with me.*'

'*I tried to help you back then — I tried so many times but I didn't know how. I was young. We both were. Please, don't look like that. I thought, an imaginary friend, it was sweet in a way—*'

'*Shut up,*' he'd said. '*Just shut your big —ing mouth.*'

'*At first we were children. It was OK then. I didn't mind it so much. Then we got older and . . . it scared me. Because he was clearly so real to you. A real person. It wasn't pretend, I didn't like it any more. I thought . . .*' She'd bowed her head; her parting was a neat pale line. '*When you got sent to borstal, I thought maybe that was what you needed.*'

The field spun away from him, the Sunshine Man, the light sinking into the trees, all of it uprooted and carried on a whirlwind and with it every last hope he'd had.

He'd searched around him for Floyd, but all he'd seen was a buzzard tilting against the sun. All he'd heard were her words coming at him, again and again.

'*I was starting to be frightened of you,*' said Providence. '*I didn't want to be with you.*'

'*So you left me on my own?*'

'*That isn't what happened.*'

'*Yeh it —ing is. Now you've got out and you don't give a — about me, you've made your plans so — it. I thought you gave a —. But no, you dropped me like everyone else.*'

She'd walked away. '*I've had enough of this,*' she'd said. '*I'm going home.*'

'*What about me?*'

She'd challenged him. '*What about you?*'

'*I love you.*' He had never spoken that word before and no one had spoken it to him. It hadn't seemed a word he would ever say, but there it was, thrown between them, uncaught. The sun cast in at a steep angle. She'd appeared to him in its dying rays as a statue, someone he could never touch or possess, a lifeless form that felt nothing for him.

'*I don't want you,*' she'd said. '*I don't want to be friends. Leave me alone.*'

A high-pitched note, poker-hot, rang between his ears like a taut red string. Providence regarded him with a glazed, neutral expression, as if she'd been gripping his wrist off a precipice hundreds of feet in the air and had only just realized she couldn't hold on.

'*I know it was hard,*' she'd said. '*Your family, your father. Ron . . .*'

He'd felt himself shaking. The wind-up thing was in him, about to come out of him, thumping out of his chest and he'd never get it back—

'*I'm not like them,*' he'd said.

He'd read sympathy and sorrow in her face, and worst of all he'd read pity.

'*You've got to forget me, Jimmy,*' she'd said. '*Move on. You've got your plan with Kip, go and do that. Go and do something, I don't care what. Stop making excuses for yourself.*'

His heart had filled with tar, a stuck, black heart.

'*What did you say?*'

'*I said go and live your life. Stop acting like I'm the only one who can save it.*'

The red string snapped. Providence walked away but her words stayed with him. He'd known what she'd meant. *You're wrong, you're cracked, you're evil. One of your two friends in the world don't exist and the other one's standing here telling you you're nothing—*

Floyd had appeared beside him in his torn shorts. '*Oh, boy,*' he'd said. '*She's gone and done it now.*' And it had been his, Jimmy's, voice that called, '*Come back*' – but it was Floyd who'd been talking; it had been Floyd but it sounded like him. She didn't slow down. Floyd took up a rock in his hands, chunky and jagged, and chased her. Providence ran but his friend ran faster; Floyd had always been quick, flying his kite, racing along the beach, hurtling downhill in a cart. The wind-up sprung loose. He'd tried to hold on to Floyd but Floyd was stronger than him. There was nothing he could do. Floyd was the part of him he couldn't stop.

THE SUNSHINE MAN

He had knocked her face down in the dirt. He'd pinned her to the ground and he'd hit and he'd hit – '*Oh, boy, let's see what we can find!*' – the rock pitting and smashing the back of her head, and he'd watched as that thin-skinned fruit turned black, turned wet, the hard, blunt crack of split bone as blood sprayed up not in Floyd's eyes but his, and there was a biting stench like the one that came out of the abattoir on Pig Sundays and she'd never made a sound and he'd never looked away, just carried on watching, unable to move, half here and half there, as Floyd hunched over her, grinning as the world steeped red.

Afterwards, they ran.

29

The first spots of rain touched my glove. Gently they landed on the barrel of the gun, soft and sparing. At the instant Maguire faced me, I had the impression of disturbing a wolf after its kill; his manner was timid, defensive, bold and wary at the same time. The sickle-shaped jaw had some growth on it now, the eyes were wide and uncharacteristically alert; his hair was wet from the flurry with one strand pushed forward and stuck on his brow. The green jacket glimmered like a colour belonging a million miles from here – a tree frog in a rainforest; a shard of ice shooting through space a hundred light years away.

He rose to his feet in a whole, fluid movement of the body, like the twist of a corkscrew. Three metres away, he was a head taller than I; he stood with his fists by his sides, lightly clenched, shifting his weight from one foot to the other like a child who needed to be excused but was afraid to put up his hand. I wondered if he would lose control of himself. He was about to be slain, after all. In the few seconds I had left before I did it, I thought of the many notions that would be travelling through Maguire's head. Recognition of who I was, a basic impulse to begin with then latching itself on to logic, for of course this was me and the reason I was here, and why *we* were here, pitted against each other in the Brewsters' field. Fear, yes, I saw in him; but I also saw submission, verging on inclination; his fists uncurled and he stood square on to me with his fingers fanned in half-surrender, but he did not put them up; he did not ask for mercy.

Rain sliced diagonally between us. He was unmoved by it; he kept his eyes on mine and I realized he expected to be shot and had known it would happen — by inkling, by prophecy, by the strength of his self-loathing at knowing what he had done. For I saw in that moment that he *did* know. At some occasion during the years locked up, Maguire had come to accept what we had accepted all along: that he alone was responsible for my sister's murder; that there was nobody else at whose door the blame could be laid. This consequence was one he deserved and he invited me to deliver it, and already forgave me for it.

Providence's music carried through the trees. He heard it too, faint notes rising and falling in melodies we thought we remembered and no one else remembered but us; I saw him then as she had seen him, as all the ghosts of the past now appeared to me — slighter, lacking dominion — and although I had told myself over the years that he was nothing, worse than nothing, he was worthless and pathetic and undeserving of my consideration even in the moment I considered him, such mantras were reiterated with a kind of hate-filled obstinacy, descriptions that might just as easily have been ascribed to any offender with whose path my own had lamentably crossed.

Now I saw, truly and clear-sightedly, how insubstantial he was. He was not a man but a boy, eternally the nineteen-year-old who had killed my brilliant, one-of-a-kind, beautiful sister, stalled in his scant, insignificant life and he was insignificant now, he was insignificant to me. All the Maguires were. Those who had trespassed and sinned against us; they were gone, leached of their might. They had lost their capacity to hurt me.

I put my finger on the trigger. The rain paused and the clouds split and the field filled to the brim with radiance, wet light glistening off every surface in seams of dazzling white. The Sunshine Man was drenched so brightly I could hardly decipher his frame, a sparkling divinity, and next to him, somewhere, James Maguire, but I couldn't tell where.

I squinted and in my blindness saw my children, arms open, coming towards me. *Mine*. My children were mine. Loved by me and raised by me, with tears kissed dry by me and worries chased away by me; I was their mother, who had held them when they were sick and comforted them when they were sad, who had fretted over bumps and rashes, who'd kept sleepless vigils at their bedsides in case of fever, who'd sung 'Close to You' forty times through the bars of their cots until they had fallen asleep, who'd wiped noses and scabs and caught nosebleeds, who'd told them I loved them every day for the simple fact that I did. I remembered Philippa's smile with her gappy front teeth, Joe's pudgy arms clamped round my neck, his warm skin in bed next to me on nights he couldn't go off and Tom had to be consigned to the spare room. I had wrestled so long with the knowledge that there was no one on earth I shared blood with but Mary, who'd never wanted me in the first place, never felt pleased at being my mother; and my father, whomever he was. And if that were the case then what did that attachment come to, what did it mean, for my children were mine in every sense that mattered and had value and consequence in the world.

THE SUNSHINE MAN

I thought of the day I'd gone duck-feeding with Mary: '*Aren't you going to go home?*' I thought of following a stranger into a haunted yellow field. I thought of Maurice and the Fairfaxes and how kind they had been to me. I thought of finding Providence that cool autumn evening when bats swooped like plumes in the dark, waiting for us on the doorstep like a wrapped present. I thought of what I had done to James Maguire and the places where our lives had intersected, permanently and for ever, impossible now to tell apart or separate one from the other. I thought of the time since my sister had died; of meeting Tom, of marrying him and the challenges that came after. I thought of seeing Philippa on the first day the agency had brought her over, of letting her come to me, slowly but surely; of the years Tom and I had spent coaxing her out of her shell and discovering her courage, of helping her grow into the happy, wilful, self-assured child she was now. I thought of bringing Joe home to his new life with us, the vanilla-scented heft of him, his trusting eyes looking up to us for the answers. I thought of Gamma. '*The Lord doesn't always give us what we want. That's because He's planning to bring us something else.*'

A white feather landed on the ground between us.

I pulled the trigger. The bullet hit him right between the eyes.

30

South-Western Echo, *Saturday, 21 January 1989*

ANONYMOUS ASSASSIN STUNS LOCALS
Residents gathered in a field near the mid-Devon village of Newton Prior yesterday afternoon on hearing what witnesses described as 'a loud explosion'. The incident happened at 14:40 off the B7138 heading west towards Framlington. Mr Reyes, a shopkeeper, told the Echo, 'It sounded like a bomb had gone off. It was very loud. Some of us were afraid.' A second bystander added, 'It was gunfire if ever I've heard it.'

Panic turned to puzzlement when the community mascot known as the 'Sunshine Man', which had stood in the field since 1948, was found to have been vandalized. The long-standing effigy, an advertisement for Yellowfields Seed Oil, which used to be produced on the land, had been a much-loved hallmark of the village since after the war. Bizarrely, the wooden man had suffered a gunshot to the head and been felled, bringing down with him decades of local history. 'We don't know who would do such a thing,' said Richenda Rossi, chair of the parish council. 'What did he ever do to hurt anyone?'

Police combing the area for a discarded weapon have so far uncovered nothing.

'Our concern is if this individual, or individuals, is in possession of an unlicensed firearm,' said PC Ben Walton. 'At present we have no weapon and no suspect. We and the community remain thankful that no one – of flesh and blood, at least – was hurt.'

Newton Prior has endured infamy before, due to the murder in 1970 of fifteen-year-old Providence Doyle. Her killer James Maguire was freed from prison last Monday.

VI

31

The week I shot a man clean through the head began like any other. It ended in my living room, sitting opposite a young police officer with a doughy complexion, whose pen stayed poised over his notepad with naive uncertainty while the cup of tea I'd made him grew cold. Between us were a pile of newspapers: KELLER FOUND BUT NO KILLER. VIGILANTE VANDAL: 'OFF WITH HIS HEAD!' DID RUNAWAY MOTHER MISS HER TARGET?

'We're just pleased you're home and well,' said the officer, who had introduced himself as Tyler or Taylor; 'my apologies again, Mrs Keller – but we have to make sure.'

'I understand,' I said, offering him the plate of digestives. He put out a polite hand, fingers together, like a paddle. 'I feel silly about the whole thing, to be honest. It's quite embarrassing to have wasted people's time.' I turned to my husband and saw his flicker of consent. 'Maguire's release threw me, I admit. We'd quarrelled, Tom and I, and I – well, I suppose it was the last straw. Not wanting to go into detail, of course.'

'Of course,' said Tyler, clearing his throat. 'Every marriage . . .' He petered out.

'Are you married?'

'Engaged.'

'Ah.' There was an uncomfortable silence. Tom covered my hand with his.

'I'm afraid it was a case of getting ahead of ourselves,' he said. 'When Catriona phoned me, I went straight to thinking the worst. It was easier than imagining my wife had walked out on me. Regrettably, it seems Catriona got the wrong end of the stick.'

'You can see why,' I put in; 'I was very upset when I saw her.' I turned to Tyler. 'I'd spent years anticipating his freedom; I was shaken when I heard. So, yes, I told Catriona how I felt. But I never meant it like that. And naturally I didn't tell her about Tom and me arguing; if I had we could've avoided all this nonsense. But then I saw Tom's pleas in the papers. It was terrible, very difficult. I'd only meant to be gone a few days, I hadn't meant to worry anyone. Least of all the children. I feel awful about it.'

Tyler looked towards our clasped hands. I saw his young mind turning.

'I made a mistake,' I said. I let the silence sit for a minute, while whatever train of thought he'd been on seemed to derail. 'We've been racking our brains as to what could have happened. All I can tell you is that I was nowhere near James Maguire or Newton Prior on Friday. Why would I want to go back there? Why would I want to go within a mile of that man?' Tyler nodded gravely. The pen was still to make contact with the page.

'Do you know,' Tom added, 'there's a piece in one of those red-tops saying aliens did it?' He laughed. 'I mean, what next? Spacemen issuing a warning, apparently.'

'About what?' said the officer, disconcerted.

'Environmental apocalypse.'

'Oh.'

But among the wilder conspiracy theories were those that ran close to the truth. Reports had appeared over the weekend:

∾

Married mother-of-two Bridget Keller, of Bickleford, Wiltshire, returned home on Friday following four days missing, hours after a gunshot was fired through a billboard near Newton Prior in Devon. Keller is half-sister to murdered schoolgirl Providence Doyle, who was slain in the village in 1970 and whose killer James Maguire was freed from prison on the day Keller vanished. 'Bit of a coincidence, isn't it?' said one resident. 'It's got to have been her. Though why she shot the sign we can't think.' A spokesperson for North Devon Police said: 'We're in touch with Mrs Keller, whom we're pleased to confirm has been found.'

∾

'I think we'd better stop reading the papers,' I said. 'It's Philippa and Joe I worry about . . . Children can be so cruel. Parents, too. All this gossip.'

Tom said, 'I never should've gone to them.'

'It's not your fault. You thought it would help.'

Tyler sipped his tea. Tom let go of my hand. The skin he left behind felt cool and alone. I risked a glance at him while the sergeant was distracted: I didn't want any message that passed between us to be evident or surmised. '*I'm sorry,*' I had told him on Friday, late at night when I'd let myself in the front door. The house had been silent, the children in bed, his duvet on the sofa within easy reach of the telephone. I'd dropped Gamma's bag and stood at the threshold, brittle and wrecked, unsure of an invitation, and told Tom everything: about the journey to London, the release, about meeting Catriona; about the expedition south, the flats, the seafront hotel; about tracking Maguire to the Brewsters' field where I'd finally met his eye and known I could not do it.

'*What I've put you through,*' I'd said. '*And the children. Can you ever forgive me?*'

'*You'd better go and see them,*' he'd said. '*Now. No, Bridget, forget the coat. Now.*'

I'd climbed the stairs. Tom's voice had travelled with me: '*When Catriona rang, I thought of course that's what you'd done. All that hate. All that time. How did I miss it?*'

'*You didn't miss it,*' I'd said. '*It was right there in front of you.*'

'*But I never thought you'd . . .*'

'*I always meant to come home. You believe that, don't you?*'

'Well,' the sergeant said, clicking shut his unused pen. 'Thank you for your time. I'm sorry to have troubled you. These are enquiries it's in everyone's interests to make.'

'I appreciate that,' I said.

We got up. I smoothed my skirt. Next to me, Tom asked, 'Still no gun?'

Tyler put on his coat. 'Afraid not. And without that we've got no steer on who could have been at the scene. The field's so far out, no one saw anything.' He did up his buttons. 'Owning and firing an illegal weapon's no joke: you'd be looking at a seven-year sentence. Make light of this poor wooden chap all you like, but it's a serious crime.'

'Of course,' I said quickly.

The officer smiled his goodbye. Tom showed him out. The house settled down again, its familiar sounds returning: the radio playing in the kitchen, a wartime song Gamma had listened to; the remote buzz of a hedge trimmer in a garden down the road.

Tom came back in. 'Well then,' he said. 'Dare we hope it's over?'

I put my arms around him, my head on his chest. His jumper was scratchy and warm against my cheek. 'We can dare,' I said.

∽

Next morning, I woke at the usual time. It was still dark. I heard the sound of the heating coming on, a rattling chuckle in the pipes. I put on my dressing gown and went downstairs. Everything was quiet and still. On the mantelpiece, the children smiled in their school photographs; grey cardigans, navy tees, Philippa with a couple of her incisors missing. I opened the curtains. The windows were misted; frost covered the lawn.

I went out into the garden. Beneath my feet, the grass was stiff with ice. A sound startled me; the cat shot over the fence and dashed in a black streak into the shed.

I followed. Inside, it was gloomy and calm. I deciphered outlines: shelves of cans with chewy dried paint round the lids, the children's hanging sleds, some art projects of Philippa's that were too big to keep in the house, and Joe's old cot which I'd been meaning to sell in the village magazine but hadn't yet brought myself to part with. 'Come on,' I coaxed the cat, straining to see where he was. Nothing moved. Nothing sounded.

Gradually, I got used to the dimness. A tiny light in the corner caught my eye, a spark like the first star of evening.

It had been years since I'd touched it. I pulled the zip and the material split, and with it the quiet, up the height of the piano and over the top and down the other side.

The tarpaulin, cast off, swam around the instrument's base. I put my fingers under the lid. With a creak, it lifted. The keys gleamed, their ivories bright and glowing. I rested my hand on the middle octave. My fingers looked disembodied in the dark, like noblewomen's hands in caliginous paintings. I pressed a note; it whined a flat, hollow song. No one had played it since we'd put her belongings in storage. No one had played it since her. I hadn't been able to lose it so we'd brought it in here, to sit silent in its canvas mausoleum, never touched, never talked about. Philippa had started on violin, not piano.

The stool was tucked underneath. I pulled it out and sat down. When I closed my eyes, I could feel it: the warmth of my sister sitting next to me, her shoulder brushing mine, her soft hair; I could see her smile. A tune played softly from an open window, not ours, not next door, further down the street. It was one I knew, the distant music melody of twilight on a breeze, the pattering of rain in a metal bucket on a back porch in summer.

I heard her say my name. I was both the person she said I was and I was not that person. I was a child, running home to

Gamma from the canal bridge with Providence's pram, and I wanted to tell that child, stop running, it's all right, stand still where you are.

No one's coming.

I left the lid lifted, the piano uncovered, and I let her be – or, rather, she let me go, out towards the light, towards the dawn, back to my family, who were waiting for me; I saw them in the kitchen, through the glass, a living, moving portrait, one I could never have drawn but now it was before me I could not contemplate any other. Tom setting out bowls, the children arguing over cereal, the mess and marvel of a life I'd never expected.

Only Tom and Catriona knew what I had meant to do that day.

And James Maguire.

He knew.

My escape from the field returned to me in pieces, as it had since the moment I'd got home. A split picture, unreal and impossible, rearranged and reassembled as many times as it took me to understand how I had ever got there or ever got away. The shot, the dropping of the gun, then the sprint, feeling him fast behind me, chasing me as he'd chased her, certain he was catching me at last, the whole of him rushing after me, his smile and his teeth and his watching eyes— but when I reached the car I'd turned to find I was alone. The Panda's door was hanging open, Donna gone from inside. I'd heard their voices, or the voices of approaching people. Stunned, I'd floored the rental back to London, barely breathing, barely thinking, arriving hours later that felt like seconds; I'd parked outside the shop and put the keys in the box. I'd taken a taxi to the station, where I'd dropped the gloves in a waste bin by the terminal, and boarded, finally, a coach home.

The gun was clean, I'd promised myself. There wasn't a trace of me on it.

Then I'd remembered, as we'd left the city for the dark countryside, the feather on the windscreen, the sudden brake: my hand moving to catch it . . .

'*You mean you left it there?*' Tom had demanded, after I'd woken the children to kiss them and comfort them and an hour had passed before they'd fallen back to sleep. '*I didn't mean to,*' I'd told him. It had happened so fast; I'd been ready neither for the force of the blast nor the changed target at which it was directed. I should have stopped to retrieve it, but my flight response had been impossible to override: getting away was all I could do. '*I thought it was safe,*' I'd said. '*I cleaned it. It was meant to be safe.*'

It wasn't safe. My fingerprints were all over that gun. I could see it now, lying on the rain-drenched land.

Maguire had picked it up. I knew it as certainly as I knew my own name.

No one's coming.

Was I sure about that?

Now, he held my fate in his hands. Any day he would give me up. I fully expected him to. He hadn't yet.

32

One year later
The train flew north in the waning light, running close enough to the coast that he could pick out curls of seafoam, lifting and falling, and kittiwakes skimming low and fast across the water. A boat drifted far out on the horizon; a castle surged out of the waves like the knobbled hump of a sea monster. Land and brine were even and vast.

He disembarked at the end of the line. The town was peaceful and dark. A half-moon shone through the clouds. He walked to his hotel and telephoned Donna, as she'd asked him to. He slept well. Early morning, the sound of the sea woke him, waves lapping round the lighthouse; he had boiled eggs for breakfast, then packed his notebook and a sandwich for lunch and waited for the bus in the cold. Donna had bought him a coat for Christmas. It was thick corduroy, military green, and was the warmest thing he owned.

The bus was empty, like the streets, like the pavements, this stiff time of year that was neither here nor there, past the end and before the beginning, like walking out of the nick three hundred and fifty-seven days ago. It had taken him time to get here, to be willing – not fixed but willing, content inside the man he was now, understanding of the fact that a person could change, for bad and for good, and that he was trying, and that was enough.

Midmorning he arrived at the nearest stop. He walked the rest of the way. The sun came out, pouring silver on the sea and illuminating islands that trailed like stepping-stones out to the deep. The institution came into view, a long low arch like an aircraft hangar, surrounded by white-block crosses. He didn't think any of his lot had been here – every other young offenders' bang-up in the land, but not this one – and he reflected how things never really changed; his lot or another lot, his brother or another's brother, the years kept passing and the sea kept rolling to shore, the earth kept turning, the boys kept coming and coming back and when they left they left room for others, and after this place was a second, a third, a fourth, being pushed around the country like a billiard ball, and as long as they were out of sight and out of mind, it was someone else's problem.

He stopped at the gates and took the postcard from his bag. It had landed at the flat a month ago. Donna had been over that day, inviting him to spend Christmas with them, and brought up the pile she'd collected from the hall. The card had stood out immediately – it showed an old, gritty photograph of a man in a spacesuit, turned towards a splendid night sky. *Commander Rick Daly in the Mare Tranquillitatis*, it read at the bottom, and on the back was a first-class stamp and his address written in tidy block capitals.

He held it now, for contact more than a need to remind himself of its sentiment – that her hand had also touched it, had chosen it and penned it, had put it in a postbox near her house, down the road, her children with her, on their way to do something else.

Now, she'd have thought, when it had gone. *It's finished.*

He'd read about her after, in the papers. For weeks they had printed her picture, articles debating her state of mind and the youngsters she had left behind in order to pursue her mission. No proof had come of it, just speculation. No proof, but the piece he'd had.

There they had been, together. And there he had been, after, standing over the gun in the field where she'd dropped it, the scarecrow felled at his heels like the longest shadow. The weapon had glinted before him on the soil. He hadn't gone near it; he hadn't touched it.

Wait and the police would come.

Not for him this time, for her.

He'd heard Kip's voice: *You know what to do, Jim.*

And he had. *Act above board. Start as you mean to go on. Walk the straight and narrow.*

It was either in you or it wasn't.

Donna had been running towards him. She'd held him when she'd reached him, patting him for injuries, and he'd backed off, saying he was fine: he didn't want her to detect, between them, hidden in the folds of Drumsticks' jacket, the cold chunk of metal he had just picked up, of which she'd stayed ignorant all the drive back to London and the time beyond and even to this day, saying as she had then, and sometimes did now, that that woman must have been insane; they should have reported her, she could've killed him, why couldn't they go to the police?

'That ain't who I am,' he'd told her. *'That ain't what I were brought up to do.'*

For a fortnight, he had kept the gun under the floorboards in his accommodation. He'd known it was stupid, the stupidest thing he'd ever done, and when his probation person visited he'd been convinced the guilt was written all over his face, plain to hear in his stumbling words, to see in his skittish gaze and refusal to meet her eye; but she'd seemed untroubled, bored by the process, the monotony of her workload, and she'd been doing it long enough now to know how twitchy cons got when they were let out. He'd been ready to face the storm, every night waiting for a knock on the door and a voice to come through it – whose? The village constable, the Bedford screws, Mr Eddiston, despite the fact he knew that man to be long dead: *We know what you've got in there, Maguire.* Every night he'd seen Providence in his mind – but she, or someone, for once, had been looking out for him, had spared him, and one warm, dry day at the start of last February, he'd gone without issue to the Kent coast, a part of the country he had always wanted to visit, and boarded a ferry out to the North Sea.

Alone on deck, he'd dropped the gun over the rail and watched its small, exact entry into the water. Her evidence had drowned, absorbed by the forbearing deep.

Unlike his own, which would sail alongside him always.

He looked down now at his thumbs, either side of the postcard. Neat, clean, square-trimmed nails. The same thumbs as had stolen the breath from a young woman's throat in 1970 – not belonging to the boy he'd called Floyd, but his, him, for ever.

THE SUNSHINE MAN

He turned the card over. The blank side bore the message: *Forgive, and you will be forgiven.*

He put her words in his pocket but didn't let them go.

An officer came out of the gate. 'Mr Maguire,' he said, putting out his hand. 'You've brought the sunshine with you.' The man smiled. 'How does it feel to be free?'

Author's Note

HM Prison Grendon was established in the 1960s as an experimental psychiatric prison, today a therapeutic community prison, that sought to treat mentally ill prisoners instead of simply shutting them away. It was devised as an alternative to the traditional prison system and promoted communication, trust and building self-awareness so that an inmate might come to understand why he committed his crime, and therefore stand a better chance of not committing it again. The keystone of Grendon's approach was group therapy, where prisoners would meet regularly to discuss their offences and the offences of others: the men were encouraged to offer their perspectives and thus begin to consider and contextualize their own situation.

I have taken some artistic licence in allowing Jimmy to engage in psychotherapy when he is, for most of the book, in denial about his wrongdoing. Grendon would not have accepted him had this been the case, but in order for his story to unfold in the way I wanted it to, I've had to bend the principle slightly. I hope that devotees to Grendon's progressive, broad-minded and compassionate philosophy, of which I am one, will grant me this privilege.

Acknowledgements

[to come]

Emma Stonex was born in 1983 and grew up in Northamptonshire. After working in publishing for several years, she quit to pursue her dream of writing fiction. *The Lamplighters* was a *Sunday Times* bestseller. She lives in Bristol with her husband and two young daughters.